Encircling 2

ORIGINS

BOOK TWO OF *THE ENCIRCLING TRILOGY*

Also by Carl Frode Tiller,
available in English from Graywolf Press

Encircling

Carl F. Tiller (signature)

Encircling 2

ORIGINS

A Novel

Carl Frode Tiller

Translated from the Norwegian by
Barbara J. Haveland

Graywolf Press

First published in Norway in 2010 as *Innsirkling 2* by H. Aschehoug & Co.
(W. Nyggaard), Oslo. This English translation first published in 2017 by Sort
Of Books, London.

This publication is made possible, in part, by the voters of Minnesota
through a Minnesota State Arts Board Operating Support grant, thanks to a
legislative appropriation from the arts and cultural heritage fund, and a grant
from the Wells Fargo Foundation. Significant support has also been provided
by the National Endowment for the Arts, Target, the McKnight Foundation,
the Lannan Foundation, the Amazon Literary Partnership, and other generous
contributions from foundations, corporations, and individuals. To these
organizations and individuals we offer our heartfelt thanks.

Encircling 2 was published with the financial support of NORLA.

The author wishes to thank Marita, Oline, Othilie and Cornelia.

Published by Graywolf Press
250 Third Avenue North, Suite 600
Minneapolis, Minnesota 55401

www.graywolfpress.org

Published in the United States of America
Printed in Canada

ISBN 978-1-55597-801-3

2 4 6 8 9 7 5 3 1
First Graywolf Printing, 2018

Library of Congress Control Number: 2017937994

Cover design: Scott Sorenson

Cover photo: manicproject.com

Encircling 2

ORIGINS

Ole

Namsos, July 2nd, 2006. From the Bronx to Otterøya

It's so hot. I roll down the window and rest my elbow on the door, look at my watch, quarter to twelve, he should have been here fifteen minutes ago; well, he shouldn't be long now, nothing to do but wait. I raise my hands, yawn as I run them over my head and down to the back of my neck, lace my fingers together and shut my eyes, sit like that for a few moments, relaxing. It feels like Friday, that's for sure. It's Friday, I'm totally knackered. Thank God it's the weekend soon. A moment more, then I yawn again, open my eyes and there he is, over at the back of the shopping center, talking to a boy in a green and white Domus jacket. Is it Benjamin? Well, well, it *is* Benjamin, how about that, so Benjamin's got himself a summer job at the supermarket, has he? Well, that's good to see, Jørgen should've got himself a summer job, the days are far too long for him the way things are now, left it a bit late to find a job now, of course, but I suppose I could ask Torstein whether he's had any thoughts yet about painting the barn, be a fine job for Jørgen, that would, and if that doesn't work out, I might have something for him to do at the fish farm, need to get the vaccinations done soon and we could probably do with an extra pair of hands then. Ah well, we'll see.

I stick my head out of the open window and am just about to give him a shout, but I don't get that far, he's already spotted me. He raises his hand and gives Benjamin a kind of a wave, the sort of cool flick of the hand he's picked up from the rappers on TV or something, doesn't even look at Benjamin as he does it, keeps his eyes on the asphalt as he saunters over to me. I watch him slouching across the parking lot, taking in the big, baggy pants, the red cap he's wearing back to front and the skateboard under his arm. I smile to myself, can't help it, he's trying so hard to be hip it's funny. I place my left hand on the sun-baked steering wheel, turn the key in the ignition with the other, the engine coughs and splutters a bit, but then it starts. And then I remember the bag from the state wineshop that's lying on Daniel's carseat. I forgot to take in the stuff I bought there yesterday, so I turn around, grab my jacket and lay it over the bag, although I don't really know why I'm doing this, Jørgen doesn't get upset any more, he's seen me take a drink often enough to know I'm not going to turn out like his dad, so I don't need to go hiding the booze. I sit a moment, then I tug the jacket off the carseat, uncovering the bag again, how stupid can you get, I turn back round, see Jørgen stop and spit out a *snus* sachet, he cleans the inside of his upper lip with his tongue, spits again, then walks on. I lean over the passenger seat. There's an empty cola bottle and a crumpled, ketchup-smeared hot-dog paper lying on it, I brush them onto the floor, open the door and straighten up again, look at Jørgen and smile as he flops down into the seat.

"Hi," I say.

"Hi," he says, laying the skateboard across his thighs and slamming the door shut. He smells of aftershave and tobacco.

"Watch that skateboard doesn't get in the way of the gearstick," I tell him."It's a deck."

"Sorry," I say, "I always forget you're really a skateboarder from the Bronx. But in these parts it's still a skateboard."

"Moron," he mutters, saying it without looking at me, trying to look pissed off, but I can tell he thinks it's kind of funny, he sits there trying hard not to smile.

"Maybe you say skateboard out here on Otterøya, but in Namsos we call it a deck," he says, "or a ride, or a wood. And it's not *skateboarder*. Just *skater*."

"In the Namsos ghetto, maybe," I say. "But not in the rest of Namsos, surely?"

"Moron," he mutters again, trying to look even more pissed off and aggressive, but I can tell he thinks it's funny, he's sitting there biting the inside of his cheek to stop his lips from widening and softening his face.

"Yeah, yeah, fasten your seat belt, will you." He turns to me, pretending to look gobsmacked, as if to say real men don't wear seat belts, a look that seems to be asking: are you serious?

"Jørgen, just fasten your seat belt," I say, look at him and smile.

"Jeez," he says, gives a snorting little grin and a despairing shake of his head, then he turns to the side and grabs the seat belt. As he does so I catch sight of something in his jacket pocket, a bag with something shiny inside, pushed part-ways out of his pocket when he twists around.

"What's that?" I ask.

"Huh?" he says, looking at me as he draws the belt across his chest.

"That there," I say, nodding at his pocket. He glances down at it and it seems to dawn on him what I'm talking about, he looks up at me again, tries to appear unfazed, but he's rattled, I can tell.

"A chain," he says brightly, gives a little shrug and tries to look as though the question surprises him, but he's un-comfortable, I can see, tries to avoid my eye, all casual like. He looks down, pretends to be having trouble slotting the seat belt into the lock.

"Oh?" I say, "Can I see it?"

He glances up at me again, and suddenly he looks angry, turning belligerent from one second to the next.

"For Christ's sake," he says. "Relax, I've got the receipt."

"What's that supposed to mean?" I ask.

"That I didn't steal it," he says.

"I never said you stole it," I say.

"No, but that's what you think, I know it is," he says.

I look at him, saying nothing. I'm not sure whether he actually has stolen the chain, it could be that he stole some money and bought it with that, I don't know, but at any rate he's hiding something, that much I can tell. He stares straight at me and I see how he's working himself up, he probably thinks he'll seem more innocent if he gets himself all worked up, tries to kid me into believing that he's innocent by acting all angry and hurt.

"Here, see for yourself if you don't believe me," he yells

and he plants his feet on the floor of the car, lifts his butt slightly, sticks his hand in his back pocket and pulls out a slip of paper. "See," he says, holding out a receipt to me: Ofstad's Jewelers, 1,499 kroner, it says. I read it again then I look at him.

"Fifteen hundred kroner?" I say. "And where did you get fifteen hundred kroner? You didn't even have the price of the bus fare into town yesterday."

Silence for a moment, then:

"For fuck's sake! I borrowed it from Benjamin!" he snaps, spitting the words out, and then he sits there and looks at me, sits there with his mouth hanging open, shaking his head, trying to look as though there's no earthly reason to doubt his word. I don't say anything for a minute, just hold his eye. Don't know how much pressure I ought to put on him, either, I must be close to acting and sounding like I'm his father, and I know how he reacts if he thinks I'm trying to take over his dad's responsibilities, nothing gets his back up as much as that, so I have to be a bit careful. But still, I can't let him get away with it either, I'd be doing him no favors if I did.

"Okay," I say, placing my hand over the seat-belt buckle. "I don't like you owing somebody so much money. Come on, let's go see Benjamin, I'll pay him back for you." I nod towards the steps at the back of the shopping center.

I look at Jørgen and Jørgen looks at me for a second, then he seems to accept that he's been found out, he doesn't say anything, simply turns away and sits there looking sullen. I don't say anything right away either. I almost feel a little sorry for him, he's so desperate to be "streetwise" as he calls it, to come across as being so smart and hard to fool, and yet he's this easily found out. I run a hand over my head and sigh, sit for a second or two, then I press down the clutch, put the car into first gear and pull away, hear the faint rattle of the trailer as I run over the speed bumps in the parking lot.

"So—I take it you've been selling something you shouldn't have. Again. Am I right?" I say, with a resigned, almost weary note in my voice. I turn to look at him. He doesn't say anything, just sits there, sullen-faced, he doesn't deny it and I realize that I've guessed right, realize that he's been selling drugs for some of his older mates again.

"And what do you expect me to tell your mother now, eh?" I ask.

"I don't give a shit what you tell her," he snarls.

"Oh yeah?" I say. "Well, you can take it from me that she gives a shit about what I say."

"The fuck I care," he says.

"Humph," I mutter. "And you'd been doing so well lately. Don't you realize how disappointed she's going to be?"

"Well, don't tell her then," he says. I stop at the junction, shoot a glance at him before turning out onto Gullvikvegen, face the road again.

"Trying to shift the responsibility onto me now, are you?" I ask.

"Huh?"

"I might be the one who has to tell her what you've done, but it's *you* that's letting her down," I say.

He says nothing for a moment, only sits there glaring through the windshield. A gang of workers from the Highway Department is paving the road just before the roundabout at Vulken Maritime so I brake to a halt, there's a string of cars coming towards us so we'll just to wait a bit. I prop my head on my left hand and sit like that watching the road workers, it's so hot they've taken off their shirts; they're working stripped to the waist, shoveling and raking out the smoking black asphalt in just their orange work pants.

"Like it was any of your business, anyway," Jørgen mumbles.

"Jørgen, come on," I say, looking at him.

"You're not my dad," he says.

"I know that."

"So why d'you act like you were?"

"Jørgen, your mom and I are together, you live in my house, don't you think I have a right to set a few rules?"

"D'you think I'm gonna put up with all kinds of shit from you just 'cause you happen to own the house I live in?" he breaks in.

I shut my eyes for a fraction of a second, then open them again. I've heard all of this so many times that I practically know it by heart. I raise my eyebrows and sigh.

"No, I don't think that. And to be honest, I don't think I give you that much shit, anyway."

"Like I even want to live in your rotten house," he mutters.

"Jørgen, I know . . ."

"Like fuck you do," he breaks in. "You don't know what it's like, living way out in the sticks when all your friends are in town."

"There's nothing stopping you from making new friends on Otterøya, you know."

"Yeah, right."

"But there isn't."

"Jesus Christ, can you see me in one of those green overalls with 'Co-op' on the back?" he asks.

"Name me a single kid of your age on Otterøya that goes about in green overalls with 'Co-op' on the back," I say. I drive on, move into the left-hand lane and past the road workers. Their voices grow louder and I catch a whiff of fresh, hot asphalt as we go by.

"Well, maybe not," Jørgen says. "But they're all just a bunch of hicks out there, that's the point. Don't you get it?" he says, scowling.

"If you ever tried to get to know some of them I think you might find they're not as different from you as you imagine."

"Yeah, right!"

Silence for a few moments.

I shift from second to third and put my foot down as we drive out of the roundabout, shift from third to fourth and accelerate even more as we drive into the Vika tunnel.

"Everybody else moves from there into town, but Mom and I did the exact opposite," Jørgen goes on. "I wonder why," he says, feigning puzzlement in a way designed to make it quite clear that he already knows the answer to that question. "Could it have had anything to do with Mom wanting to keep me away from Dad, do you think?" he asks, then he pauses for a moment before turning towards me and making an attempt at a sneer. "You don't think Mom really loves you either," he goes on. "You know we only moved in with you because she wants to keep me away from Dad. And my friends, of course," he adds.

I don't say anything right away, should maybe be mad at him for being so out of order, but I'm not, it's so far over the top that I can't quite bring myself to get worked up about it, just feel a bit sick of the whole thing. We drive out of the tunnel and along the stretch past the Bråten

Ski Center, see the warm air shimmering above the gray asphalt up ahead.

"Not everything has to do with you, Jørgen," I say.

"No, but this does," he retorts.

I'm about to say that his mom and I actually decided to have Daniel after the two of them moved in with me, but I don't, I'm not going to be drawn into a stupid discussion about how much his mom and I love each other, you have to draw the line somewhere.

"I know you'd like me to get mad at you," I say. "But it's not going to work, so you might as well forget about it," I add.

"Why the fuck would I want to make you mad?"

"Maybe because you'd like to go on believing that I've got something against you," I say.

"What the fuck's that supposed to mean?"

I don't answer right away because I know what's going through his head. He feels he'll be letting his dad down if he likes me, so he needs to tell himself that we don't get along, that's why he always has to try to provoke me, do his best to make me mad. He tries to stir up trouble, start arguments, so he won't have to like me. I turn, about to say this to him, but I stop myself, best keep his dad out of all this, for Jørgen's sake if nothing else. I turn to face the road again.

"Playing the shrink now, are you?" he says.

"Playing what?"

"The psychologist."

"All I'm saying is that I've got nothing against you," I say. "In fact I really like you."

"As if you could say anything else, when you're living with my mother," he says.

"Jørgen, hey, I like you," I say again. "I like you so much that it scares me when you screw things up for yourself the way you do."

"Well, if you've nothing against me why d'you make fun of my style?"

"But I don't."

"Oh, no? So that comment about the Bronx was just my imagination, was it? And all that talk about how baggy my trousers are, and how you can see half my backside and all that—is that just my imagination too?"

"But I'm just pulling your leg, you know that, don't you?"

"Pulling my leg," he snorts. "You're making fun of me, and I'm fucking sick of it!"

I look at him, say nothing for a moment, he doesn't think I'm making fun of him, I know he doesn't, I realize he's only saying this because he has to get at me somehow for confronting him on the thieving and selling hash. I found him out and now he needs to pay me back, to go on the attack, so he grasps at a silly little thing like this.

"Okay," I say, "then we've misunderstood each other. I thought you knew I was kidding, but you didn't, so I'll stop it," I say, as good as admitting that I've spoken and acted out of turn too. It's probably best, that way he might not feel quite so humiliated. "Sorry," I add, look across at him, but he doesn't even glance at me, just sits there with a face like thunder. He's probably dreading what Helen's going to say when she hears he's screwed things up for himself again. There's silence. I drive past the Vemundvik junction, up, over and down the hill and out onto the Lokkar bridge, drive with one hand on the wheel and the other out the window, feel the wind rushing along my bare forearm and up inside my shirt sleeve. I smell the sea. I look out of the side window and across the sparkling blue fjord. It's a glorious day, the sun shining and the water like glass.

I shoot a glance at Jørgen as we drive across the bridge and onto the island.

"Want a smoke?" I ask, pulling the pack of tobacco out of my breast pocket and handing it to him. Don't really know why I do this, neither Helen nor his dad has anything against him smoking and I know he's inhaled a lot worse things, but even so, I'm not in the habit of offering him cigarettes.

"So now all of a sudden you want to be friends?"

"Aw, come on, Jørgen," I say, giving a little sigh.

"You can't get around me just by offering me a cig, if that's what you think."

"D'you want to roll yourself one or not?" I ask, eyes on the road as I say it, then I turn to look at Jørgen again. He sits for a moment more, still with a face like thunder, then he takes the tobacco pack from me. "Roll one for me as well, will you please?" is all I say. I can't be bothered arguing, there's no point. If I'm going to help Jørgen change his ways there's only one thing to do and that is to behave much as I'd like him to behave, to set a good example, it's the only way. If we just stay calm and speak nicely he'll gradually learn to do the same. I only hope Helen can stay calm when she hears that Jørgen has screwed up again, that she manages to talk to him instead of freaking out and threatening him with everything under the sun. There's no telling how she'll react, one day she can shrug off something that other people would call a disaster, the next she can throw a fit over the slightest thing, it depends on how she's feeling, mentally and physically. Whether she's been in a lot of pain or not.

There's a tractor right in front of us. I can't be bothered sitting behind it around all the twists and turns up ahead so I take the chance, pull out and overtake, zoom past it doing well over a sixty miles an hour and nip in just before the crest of the hill, feel the tickle in my stomach as we sail over the top. I breathe in, let out a quiet sigh, I don't really feel like saying anything to Helen about what's happened, although she has a right to know, of course, she is his mother, after all. But still, I'm worried that no good will come of it, worried she won't be able to handle hearing about it and that she'll do something that'll make matters worse than they need to be. And anyway, I've been working hard all week, I'm knackered and I don't want any trouble either.

"Here," Jørgen says, handing me the pack of tobacco and a freshly prepared roll-up.

"Thanks," I say, sticking the cigarette in my mouth and slipping the pack back into my breast pocket. "Got a light?" I ask, shooting another glance at him. He takes out a silver Zippo lighter I've never seen before, opens the lid with a neat flick of his thumb, shuts one eye and curls a hand round the roll-up as he lights it and inhales deeply, sucking in his cheeks: it's such a pose, trying to smoke like a Hollywood tough guy. He hands me the lighter without a word, doesn't so much as glance at me, just winds down the window, props his elbow on the sill and sits there trying to look cool. It's almost comical, he's like a little kid, telling clumsy lies and going into the huff like a little kid when I call him on it, and yet he likes to see himself as macho man. I light my cigarette and hand the lighter back to him, drive with one hand on the wheel and the roll-up in the corner of my mouth.

A moment passes. Then: "I won't say anything to your mom," I say, blow smoke out of my nose, glance at Jørgen then look at the road again. "On one condition, though. That if I offer you a summer job at the fish farm you'll take it." I glance at him again and he looks at me, doesn't answer right away, just sits there looking surprised.

"Okay," he says, trying to sound laid-back, but he's both relieved and pleased, I can tell by his voice that he is, he's so keen to give the impression that he doesn't care what his mother and I say or think, but when it comes right down to it he does care and now he's relieved.

"But Jørgen," I say, eyeing him sternly, I have to show him that I really mean it this time. "This time you're going to show yourself worthy of our trust, right?" I say. "You stop selling hash and all that other crap. And as far as the job is concerned—you turn up every morning and do whatever's asked of you," I say, then I pause. I'm just about to ask if that's understood, but I don't. I have to be careful not to dent his self-esteem, he's so touchy, his pride is so easily hurt and if he feels he's being treated like a child or ordered about I run the risk of ruining everything. I have to be sure to leave him with the feeling of having some sort of choice, it's the only way to get him to go along with it. "Okay?" I ask.

"Yeah, okay," he says, taking another drag on his roll-up.

We drive down the hill and past the church and suddenly I feel a bit more cheerful, feel pleased with the way I've handled this. I think this will be the best solution for all concerned. I've not only saved Helen from having to hear that Jørgen has screwed up again, I've actually fixed it so that Jørgen is going to start working as well, that's almost the best part, that should keep him out of trouble for a while.

Dear David,

Yesterday I took a walk up to the forest where we had our camp and where we used to run around with warpaint on our faces and bows and arrows in our hands. I'd never been up there as a grown man before, but when I saw the ad in the newspaper saying that you'd lost your memory and urging anybody who knows you or knew you to help you to recover it, I plucked up the courage to do so. And I found just as many traces of our childhood as I had thought I would: old arrows, spears and clubs, bits of the rope ladder we had hanging from our lookout post, rusty barbed wire from the stockades we used to put up, poles and stakes that once formed the framework of our brush shelters. I wandered around among all these ruins of our child-hood and just as I had expected they sparked off a landslide of memories inside me, a landslide that just goes on and on and that I'm going to try to share with you in this letter.

You may be wondering, though, why I should start by writing about our camp, why I should have gone there, of all places, in order to trigger this landslide of memories, and not to our old primary school or the football pitch; to one of our many fishing or swimming spots; to the moor where the ski carousel was run or to the community center where the Christmas parties were held, or why—possibly most obvious of all—I hadn't simply stayed here, on the farm that you and your mother moved to in the early 80s when she and my dad were together and where you and I shared so much. So why didn't I do that, why did I go up to our old camp?

I did it because that camp encapsulates, if you like, the whole of our childhood. Because the things that happened and the things that we got up to at that camp evoke the essence of what it was like to grow up on the island of Otterøya in the late 70s and early 80s, and because I assume that this in turn is as much a key to understanding how you became the person you are as it is to understanding how I became the person I am.

I don't really know when I became fully aware of this. Probably not until I started writing this letter to you. But something inside me has always known how important this part of my childhood was. Obviously, otherwise I wouldn't have been so sure that this was what I ought to write about first, and otherwise I wouldn't have thought back on it as much as I have. Because remarkably often, when I smell the scent of pine and juniper, when I hear the sound of a chattering thrush or dry twigs snapping underfoot as I push my way through a dense raspberry thicket, when I feel the soft tickle of ferns on my bare legs or spider webs clinging to my face as I accidentally blunder into them, I'm transported back to the time when I was ten or eleven years old, running around the camp with you and the other kids. Only rarely do these things remind me of all the walks in the woods that Dad and I took, of hunting for elk, deer and grouse, of felling trees and chopping wood or other things that might come just as readily to mind for anyone who has spent their whole life here on Otterøya.

But even though I've found myself thinking back remarkably

often on building the camp and playing there with you and the other kids, I've never felt the presence of that time as strongly as I did yesterday. Walking along the winding, pine-needle-covered path that leads up to the campsite, handling our old spears and clubs again, looking down on the housing estate from the particular angle you see it from when you stand at the top of what we called the grottoes—all of this caused the camp to rise up again before my eyes: the brush shelters, the totem pole with its intricately carved bark, the smoking campfire with the ring of stones around it, suddenly there it all was, and in it a bunch of small boys sitting, standing and walking around with quivers on their backs and bows slung across their chests.

I saw it so clearly: I had just tumbled off the lookout post and bashed my foot, and you and Per were standing over me, asking if I was okay, did it hurt? I didn't say anything, but the look on my face must have told them all they needed to know.

"Will I take the rest of your watch for you?" Per asked. He had two seagull feathers stuck in his hair and around his waist he wore a loincloth with fringed ends that his mother had made out of an old sheet.

I broke off a blade of grass, fixed my eyes on it and said nothing.

"Yeah, do that," you said to Per. "And be quick about it, you never know when they might attack."

"Who might attack?" I muttered crossly. But such questions were taboo, they could destroy our imaginary world and I regretted it as soon as I'd said it. "Apart from the Husvikings, of course," I added hastily.

"You can never underestimate the Husvikings," you said.

"No."

"They're armed to the teeth with fiberglass bows and they shoot first and ask questions later."

"Yeah."

Pause. "Feeling better?" you asked.

"Yeah."

"Good, then you can get back up there and take the watch yourself."

We had no enemy, so it was kind of hard to stay motivated, but an attack could come when you least expected it, so there was really nothing for it but to get up there and keep a lookout anyway.

But then.

"What are you lot up to?" a voice behind us asked.

"By Manitu!" you cried and spun around.

But it was only the girls. Eva and Karoline.

"What are you doing?" they asked again.

"Nothing," you said, eyeing them fiercely.

The girls came over to us. They looked at me. Oddly enough my foot had started to hurt again as soon as they appeared and I was no longer sure that I could get up unaided, the pain was so bad.

"Have you hurt yourself, Ole?" Eva asked.

I gave a little wince, to leave no one in any doubt that I had hurt myself. But I didn't cry.

"They got me too," you suddenly piped up, putting a hand to your cheek. "Stupid cowards. They had us outnumbered."

It took me a second to catch on. At first I just sat there staring at you, so no wonder the girls were suspicious.

"How about you, Per?" you asked quickly. And Per played along. Oh, he hadn't escaped unscathed either, he announced. But it was okay, it was just a graze.

"Have you been fighting?" Eva asked.

We barely glanced at her, said nothing. Simply went on tending our wounds.

"Well, have you?"

Still not a word to be heard, just soft moans.

"Oh, well, bye then!"

"Okay," you said. "If you promise not to ask any more questions, and if you promise not to tell anybody, then yeah, we've been fighting."

"You have? Who with?"

"No, we've said too much already."

The girls shrugged.

"Fair enough."

We looked at one another. We didn't really care what they said, but still.

"Do you know where we can find raspberries up here?" Eva asked, pointing at the pail she was carrying.

We look at one another again. Raspberries? Now they were going too far, this was no time to ask about raspberries.

"We've got other things to think about," you said.

"Okay," the girls said, shrugging again. And off they went. Suntanned legs swished through the grass. A minute or two passed. We yawned and chewed blades of grass and couldn't have cared less about where the girls had gone. But where exactly had they gone? A fuzzy bumblebee flew by and landed on a wild onion flower, all set to gorge itself on nectar and we fell to studying the bee and trying to take an interest in it, but it wasn't interesting, so in the end we sauntered after the girls anyway.

"Not there," Per called when we spotted them down by the stream. "There's loads of raspberries down below the camp."

"I thought you had other things to think about," Eva said.

I didn't hear that and neither did you or Per, so we didn't comment on it either. We found the path and immediately took it upon ourselves to escort the girls down the hill to the raspberry thicket, where there were sure to be snakes or other things that they needed us to protect them from. We were all suffering from minor injuries, bruised and battered after the battle we had just fought. There was no way we could hide this from the girls. We limped and hobbled along, but we assured them that we were fine, really. All things considered, that is. The girls said annoyingly little to this, but at least they listened to what we said and they didn't laugh.

"Shall we help you pick them?" you said when we reached the raspberry thicket.

"Are you sure you have time for that?" Karoline asked.

"Oh, yeah, they won't be back now anyway."

"What?" said Karoline, making it plain that she'd forgotten what we'd just been through. A look of annoyance flashed across your face but then you changed tactic and gave a big yawn instead.

"Huh?" you said, blinking lazily.

That did the trick.

"Well, who was it?" Karoline asked.

"The Husvikings," you said.

Karoline and Eva looked at you. So what had happened, they wanted to know.

You couldn't talk about it, you said, you had sworn an oath.

The girls turned to me, hoping that I would be more forthcoming. But they got nothing out of me.

"It's better that you don't know any more than you already know—for your own good," I said.

"Let's talk about something else," you said. "Let's pick raspberries."

Fine. So we picked raspberries. You and me and Per, Eva and Karoline, we plucked the nubbly red berries off their stalks, opened them up to check for worms then dropped them into the pail. The raspberry branches jagged and scratched our bare legs and when I looked down I saw that mine were criss-crossed with red streaks all the way up to my knees. They smarted, but it was no big deal, we'd been through a lot worse. Every now and again we sneaked a peek at the girls. Per had eyes only for Eva, while your eyes and mine were on Karoline, because we thought she was the prettier one. Like all the other girls she liked you better than me, I knew she did, but that could change, couldn't it? If I just did this instead of that, if I just spoke like this instead of like that, if I just tried hard enough, was daring enough? Oh, Karoline. With her brown eyes and shining black hair hanging halfway down her back, she looked so exotic. "Karoline looks like that gypsy singer, Raya," you'd said once. And she did actually. Although if she'd stuck a daisy in her hair she would have looked even more like her.

"You look like Raya," I blurted out as I was dropping a handful of berries into her pail.

I hadn't meant to stand so close to her. So close that I could smell the scent of raspberries on her breath.

"Raya?"

Her mouth was set in a straight line. Didn't she know who Raya was?

"That gypsy woman," I said.

Karoline shrugged, edged away and carried on picking. She looked almost offended, but . . . well, maybe she didn't know what a gypsy was either, maybe she thought I meant it as an insult. I didn't know what to do. I felt like saying that Raya looked nice, but I didn't dare, so I just stood there, gathering berries for the winter or something like that. Per and Eva had become more and more wrapped up in each other, they kind of drifted further down the slope and you and Karoline and I stood there in silence.

One minute.

Then: "But a duel, that they wouldn't hear of," you said, right out of the blue.

"Huh?"

Your eyebrows shot up and you clapped your hand over your mouth, letting everyone know that you'd been thinking out loud, that you'd said too much. Oh, well, since the girls had heard that much, they might as well hear the rest, you thought, and you launched into a detailed description of the battle between us and the gang from Husvika. Without any warning they had sent a rain of fiberglass arrows down on the camp, and if it hadn't been for the fact that we knew this forest like the back of our hand and knew, therefore, where to take cover, we wouldn't be standing here now, Karoline could be sure of that. When the Husvikings had run out of ammunition and the time had come for close combat, you had called out to them that both sides would be spared unnecessary suffering if we settled our differences instead by a duel between yourself and their chief. But like the yellow dog he was, their chief wouldn't agree to this and so it had ended in a terrible battle from which no one had escaped unhurt.

"That sounds really dangerous," Karoline said.

Well, it wasn't exactly a walk in the park, you had to admit.

But why didn't we just go and tell the grown-ups?

You didn't hear that question. The grown-ups and everything to do with the grown-up world could never be allowed to intrude into our fantasy world, because if they did it might instantly fall apart. But you had suddenly caught sight of something extraordinarily interesting on the ground. A really unusual insect, maybe. Or some sort of stone that you'd never seen before. It could have been so many things, you were bound to find something if you rooted around in the dirt a bit.

But Karoline wasn't to be put off.

"Hmm?" she said, and all of a sudden she had that lopsided grin on her face, the one that always made us seem so much smaller than her, even though we weren't.

She was really starting to piss you off, I could tell by your face. But then she did a complete about-turn and suddenly she was the Karoline we liked again. There was no way she would ever dare to pick raspberries here after hearing that, she told us, or at least not on her own.

Your face immediately lit up.

Oh well, it wasn't as if she'd be on her own up here very often anyway, because we were almost always here, we just didn't always let on that we were.

That was comforting to know, Karoline thought.

We were glad to hear her say that, you and I, and for a little while we just picked raspberries for her and life seemed sweet. But time passed and no matter how good life in the forest might be I still had to be home by five o'clock, because dinner would be on the table.

"I suppose I'd better be going," I said.

"Oh, no," Karoline said, tilting her head to one side. "Can't you help me to finish picking first?"

I wavered for a moment.

"Okay, bye, then," you said. You were keen to get me out of the way so that you could have Karoline all to yourself for a while, I knew that.

"Oh, please, Ole," Karoline said. "Just until the bucket's full."

I wavered a moment longer, this was so unexpected and so wonderful, to have her begging me like this, and even though I had a suspicion that she was only doing it to annoy you and make you jealous, I was already looking for excuses for not being home in time for dinner.

"Yeah, I think maybe I should be getting home as well," you

said, probably hoping that she'd beg you to stay too, and then you looked at your watch, to show Karoline that you didn't have all the time in the world.

But then Karoline did another about-turn and was suddenly cool and careless again.

"Oh, all right," she said with a shrug. "Bye, then," she said to us both, then she turned away and carried on picking.

Silence. Neither of us wanted to leave, so now we were in a fix. But you had the answer, because what was that: Shh! You shaded your eyes with your flattened hand, peered in the direction from which the sound had come.

"Did you hear that?" you whispered to me.

"Yes."

"What?" Karoline asked, she hadn't heard anything, because she wasn't used to be being constantly alert and on her guard like us, half-savage as we were.

"They're back," I said.

"Caramba, I left my spear in the tepee," you said softly. "We'll have to think quick."

"Is it the Husvik?" Karoline asked.

"Shh," you said, putting a finger to your lips. "This way, but hurry," you whispered, nodding towards the grottoes.

"But what is it?" Karoline asked. She didn't budge, but there was a faint glow in her eyes now, and this filled us with joy and awe.

"Yep, it's the Husvikings," I said.

"But we can't stand here talking, there's no time to waste," you hissed. "Come on!"

So we ran. You first, then Karoline, then me. Oh, this was how it was supposed to be, just like this. My heart pounded with delight and excitement as we ran, bent double, along the path. We were old hands at this, you and I, and we were at constant pains to share our knowledge with Karoline: on no account should she step on dry twigs, and she had to watch that no raspberries dropped out of the pail because if they found raspberries on the path they would follow the trail and then we were done for. This was it.

"In there," you said when we reached the top, pointing to an opening under the big rock, and we bent down and ducked inside. "We're safe here, they'll never find us here," you said. For a while there was total silence. But then I let out a fart and Karoline giggled. Neither farts nor fits of the giggles were appropriate at such a critical moment and I could see that you were annoyed at us both. You didn't say anything, but you kept a straight face and reminded us of the seriousness of the situation by getting up and scanning the path downhill. Silence again.

"So is this where you hide when the Husvikings come?" Karoline asked.

"Yeah, nobody knows about this place but us three," I said.

"Not any more."

"No, but you have to promise not to tell anybody else about it."

"What if I won't?" she said. She had that lopsided grin on her face again, that grin that made us feel smaller than her. I never knew what to do when she was like that, it confused me.

"You'll find out soon enough," you said, turning round and sitting down again.

But Karoline didn't look the slightest bit scared, she was still wearing that lopsided grin and she looked you straight in the eye, defiantly.

"Oh, is that so?" she said.

You glared at her. But then her mood changed again and she was back to being the Karoline we liked.

"Imagine if that rock were to fall in on top of us," she said, a fearful look coming into her eyes. She glanced up at the glistening, black, dripping rock above our heads. "Imagine if there was another landslide and a rock landed on top of that rock—we'd be squashed to death."

"That's a risk we'll have to take," I said. "We've got no choice."

But there was no great risk of that, you said. Landslides were pretty rare in the middle of summer. They were usually caused by water freezing in the cracks and crevices in the mountainside, because then it expanded, shattering and loosening the rock.

"How come you know things like that?" Karoline asked in amazement.

You shrugged and said oh, you really couldn't say.

"I don't know how you do it," Karoline said. "You know everything, so you do."

"Ha, ha, no, not everything, nobody can know everything," you said, you could no longer resist her flattery and your voice bubbled with pleasure.

"Well, you know more than anybody else in the class!"

Aw, you said, you weren't so sure about that, although there might be some truth in it, but . . .

"Oh, but you do!" said Karoline.

Silence again.

Then Karoline said: "Okay, I'd like to get out now,"

We told her it was better to wait a while, the danger wasn't over yet, but she wouldn't listen, she wanted to get back to the raspberry bushes. All right then, we said, but she wasn't to come running back to us saying we hadn't warned her. And we got up and crept back out of the cave.

"Hang on," you hissed. "I heard something—shh," sticking a rigid arm out behind you, signaling to Karoline and me to stay still. Then: a rustling in the bushes further down the path.

"I heard that too," Karoline said.

"Shh," you said again.

Oh, this, this was real, so real that I was almost trembling with excitement and suspense.

"Hand me one of those stones, Ole," you snapped, motioning with your head towards some pebbles lying around the mouth of the cave. Quick as a wink I picked some up and handed them to you. You took them, aimed and threw one of them far down into the bushes.

"Oh, God," Karoline whispered fearfully, "what if you hit one of them in the eye?"

This was only a diversion, you explained. You had thrown it way beyond them, to make them think we were down there and head off in that direction instead!

"Boy, you're so crafty."

We were in too tight a spot for you to bask in her adulation. Instead you put your finger to your lips again. We stood there, listening, all three of us. All we could hear was the chattering and squawking of the thrushes, the occasional distant sound of a dog barking and the steady drone of an excavator down on the building site.

"Either they fell for your trick or it was just a cat," Karoline said.

"A cat? No way that was a cat!"

And this time you were right.

"Is this where they are?" a voice said. And who should appear but Eva, Per and someone else who had been on a motoring holiday to Østersund in Sweden and must just have got back. It was Hauk.

"Oh, hi, Hauk!" Karoline said.

How was Østersund, we wanted to know and we began to wander down the hill while Hauk told us all about his vacation. Oh, yeah, the zoo had been great. Yeah, and they had all these different fizzy drinks that you didn't get in Norway and most of them were really good, loads better than orangeade or limeade anyway. And ice cream was called "glass" in Swedish, and Donald Duck was called "Kalle Anke," and say they wanted a slice of bread with chocolate spread, did we know what they asked for? "Gås." "Gås" like in "goose"? Uh-huh! We all had a good laugh at that. And Hauk had lots more to tell: about the Swedes at the campsite who swore all the time and went around in clogs and tracksuits, and how brilliant it was to have smoked bologna for breakfast, and about the minigolf course he had played on. He told us about Swedish guys with long yellow hair who drank beer from the can and made such a racket at night that the other campers couldn't sleep. He had brought a slice of a foreign country back to Norway and now he was bursting to share it with us. And everybody except you and I was laughing and happy and all ears, saying wow and oh my God every now and again, and since none of them had ever been to Sweden they were really interested in knowing what the Swedish was for this, that or the other. And oh, Per wanted to know, was it right that down there you could buy a quartz watch with a built-in stopwatch and an interval timer? Course you could. Was it cheaper to buy it there? Oh, yeah, everything was a lot cheaper in Sweden, Hauk said. And on and on he went: the road signs in Sweden were yellow and there were some roads where you could drive up to ninety miles an hour.

"Ninety," Karoline gasped.

"Yeah."

"The cheetah can run faster than that!" you butted in.

"Huh?"

"The cheetah can do a hundred and ten!"

Karoline rolled her eyes.

"Aw," she said. "Away you go and hunt for the Husvikings."

"Shut your trap," you said.

"The Husvikings?" Hauk asked.

"David and Ole and Per have been fighting the Husvikings, you see," Karoline said, smirking.

"Oh, yeah, I don't think!" Hauk said.

"Think what you like," you said, trying to look as if you didn't care whether they believed us or not, but you were furious, everybody could see that. Oh yes, you were in a dangerous mood now. Suddenly a grin flashed across your face. You sidled over to Karoline and then, as you passed her, you knocked the pail of raspberries out of her hands.

"Oops," you said, grinning.

At first Karoline was speechless. She stared at the berries lying scattered on the path like a scarlet rash. But then she turned to you.

"Fuck!" she screamed, "I'll get you for that."

"God, how can you be so childish," Eva said.

You laughed right in her face and then you turned to Hauk and eyed him coolly through half-shut eyes, looking alarmingly unafraid. You stood like that for a moment, but he didn't do or say anything, he didn't dare. Two seconds. Then you turned to Per and me.

"Come on," you said, making sure to tramp on the raspberries as you walked off.

Neither Per nor I did that. We shrugged and eyed Karoline and Eva apologetically, but we were loyal warriors who stuck with you through thick and thin and so we both wandered back to the camp with you.

Otterøya, July 2nd, 2006. A pink onesie

I turn onto the narrow dirt road leading down to the farm. Torstein's sheep are lying down by the old milk-churn stand and I slow right down, nudge the car through the flock, rev the engine to get them to move, but the sheep just go on lying there basking in the sunshine. They look at me, blink weary eyes and show no sign of moving. I rev the engine a bit harder several times, and this time they start to bleat, a bell tinkles faintly. I rev up again and suddenly they all jump up and trot off into the field. I sit and watch them for a moment or two, then I release the clutch and drive on, loose grit scrunching nicely under the wheels as I do so. I roll slowly over the little hilltop and down to the farm.

Oh, to see the farm lying there at the end of the pale-green birch avenue, freshly painted and well-kept, with the sparkling blue sea beyond, it does my heart good. To see the house and the cottage and the barn lying there bathed in sunlight, it makes me so happy. There's no place I'd rather live, this is where I belong, on the farm that my great-great-grandfather started. Like Knut Hamsun's Isak Sellanrå, he came here. With his own hands he felled the trees from which he cut timber, with his own hands he built up this farm and it's been handed down from my great-great-grandfather to my great-grandfather, from my great-grandfather to my grandfather and from my grandfather to my dad, and every one of them has prided himself on making sure that the farm would be in as good if not better shape when he passed it on than when he took it over. And that thought, the thought of how much hard work has been put into this farm over the years, fills me with respect and gratitude; it encourages me to work even harder and put up with that much more. Because now it's my turn to carry on the family tradition and make my mark on the farm, now it's my turn to develop the business and bring it up to date. Just as my great-grandfather invested in a reaper and later in a tractor, and just as my grandfather started breeding mink and foxes, I'd like to be remembered for switching to fish farming. And it won't end with me either, I'm glad to say, one day it'll be Daniel's turn, one day he'll take over and live here with his wife and children. Or, at least I hope he will, although obviously there's no guarantee, but as long as we make sure that he thrives and is happy here I can't see why he wouldn't. I mean, it's actually such a great gift, to be able to grow up on and spend your life on a farm like this, simply to grow up knowing that you're part of this line that doesn't stop with you. If you ask me that alone is worth every bit as much as the countryside, the fresh air and the peace and quiet, because being a part of such a line, it makes you feel sure of who you are and who you should be, it gives your life direction and if you ask me that's what Jørgen lacks and what he needs more than anything else, it's because he doesn't have all this that he's so restless and aimless, I'm certain of it.

I glance across at him and smile, but he doesn't look at me, just sits there doing his best to seem laid-back, so I look away again, drive with one hand on the wheel and the other dangling out of the window. The plumber's here already, I see. The white pickup truck is parked alongside the steps of Mom and Dad's house with the new washing machine in the back, well tied down and wrapped in plastic. I park next to the pickup, reach round behind me, grab the state wine store shopping bags and get out of the car, set the bags on the ground and stretch, then I pick up the bags and stroll across the yard to the house.

"Don't forget we've got a deal, Jørgen," I say. "It's work for you on Monday, right?"

"Yeah, yeah," he says, sounding a bit pissed off again, maybe he feels he's being dictated to after all, maybe I didn't quite manage to make him feel he had a choice. I stop on the steps and stand there watching him, he leans his skateboard up against the wall, kicks off his shoes and opens the door. "I'm goin' up to my room to lie down," he mutters.

"Now?" I say.

"I'm tired, for fuck's sake," he snaps.

"Hey, no problem, I wasn't getting at you," I say with a disconcerted little laugh.

"Yeah, right," he says. "Is this something new you've started?"

"What?"

"Everything you say to me sounds like an accusation," he says.

"Aw, Jørgen, come on," I say. I put my head on one side, look at him. "Now you're being unfair," I say.

"You see—now you're accusing me of being unfair," he

says, raising his voice. He stares at me, pauses for a moment. "I just don't know why you can't stop remarking on every single thing I say and do. I don't know why you can't just leave me alone. I don't need you keeping me right all the time. Show a little faith in me, for Christ's sake."

I raise my eyebrows, gaze at him in astonishment.

"But Jørgen, I just offered you a job. If that isn't showing a little faith in you I don't know what is."

"You haven't offered me any fucking job," he says. "You just blackmailed me into working at your goddamn fish farm, that's not the same thing at all."

"Jørgen," I say, running a hand over my head and sighing, "I made one condition, that's all . . ."

"You know what," he says, breaking me off. "When I'm at my dad's there's nobody trying to keep me right all the time, and you know what, when I'm there I behave pretty much the way you'd like me to behave. But here, here it's nothing but nagging and nitpicking and snide comments the whole fucking time, and then I certainly don't feel like behaving properly."

I look at him, and I'm just about to say that maybe Tom Roger doesn't interfere because he doesn't care as much as he should, but I bite my tongue—I might as well tell Jørgen that his father doesn't really love him, and that wouldn't be right of me. I scratch the back of my head, look at him, then drop my hand and sigh.

"But Jørgen," I say, lowering my voice so no one else will hear. "You know I have to react to the fact that you've been selling hash again, you know I can't stand idly by when you do something like that?"

"Yeah, but this isn't just about that, is it? It's about the way you always fucking treat me, the way you talk to me," he says. "And no, I don't see why you have to react to the fact that I've been selling hash either. I'm all in favor of free hash and you damn well know it," he says, and then he nods at my state wine store bags. "Hash does a lot less damage than what you've got in those bags and as long as that's legal I don't see why I shouldn't be able to buy and sell a few grams if I want."

I look at him, don't quite know what to say. I can't get into a discussion about free hash right now, I can't be bothered anyway, we've discussed this so many times that each of us knows exactly what the other is going to say. I shut my eyes and take a deep breath, hold it for a moment, then open my eyes and breathe a little sigh, making it plain to him that I'm not in the mood for this, that we have to let it go, both of us. I look at him and smile a rather weary smile, he stands there staring at me for a second, then he gives a snort, he doesn't show the slightest sign of meeting me halfway, he doesn't say a word, just turns on his heel and walks off into the house.

I stay where I am, gazing at the steps for a second or two. "Well, well," I mutter to myself, then I shake my head and follow him. I step into the hall and see Jørgen disappearing into his room. After a moment or two our bedroom door opens and Helen comes out. She's still in her nightie, her hair all mussed up. She comes towards me with Daniel on her hip, dear little Daniel, his face lights up the minute he sees me. He smiles, displaying his one tooth.

"Ba-pa," he says putting out his hands.

I look at him and smile. She's put him in a pink onesie, I notice, I don't like him wearing pink, know I shouldn't care about such things, but I can't teach myself not to, no matter how hard I try, I can't, but I don't mention it.

"Well, well, if it isn't little Daniel, if it isn't the best boy in the whole world," I say, keeping the smile on my face as I set the state wineshop bags on the floor. I put out my hands and take him, lay my cheek against his warm, soft one and rock from side to side, close my eyes and say, "Mmm." "Oh, it's so nice to see you," I say. I open my eyes and see that Helen is on her way back into the bedroom, she just turns and walks away, doesn't say a word, doesn't even say hello.

"What's the matter, Helen?"

She turns and looks at me. I take a step closer, catch the scent of her, the warm fug of sleep and cigarettes.

"What's the matter?" she says. "I'm in agony and I've hardly slept and Daniel's been crying and crying and he's just about driving me up the wall, I feel like throwing up."

I look at Daniel, look at his chubby hands and his lovely rolls of baby fat, dear little Daniel, it cuts me to the quick to hear her talk about him like that, I don't like her doing that, especially not when he's listening, I mean I know he doesn't understand what she's saying, but I still don't like it. I lay my cheek against his again, cuddling him while I look at Helen.

"Well, why don't you ask Mom to give you a hand?" I say.

"Your mother!" she says. "No fucking way, I wouldn't give her the satisfaction."

"What?"

"I know damn well there's nothing she'd like better than to have me asking her for help, but that's not the main reason she wants to help, no, no, she's out to prove that I'm not capable of looking after the house and the kids."

"Oh really, Helen," I say.

"You should've seen the look she gave me when I took

Daniel over there the day before yesterday," she says, putting her hands on her hips and nodding at me. "Oh, yes, and you'd no sooner gone this morning than she was over here working on the flowerbed," she says. "And of course she made a point of leaving the spade and the little rake on the porch so I'd see them when I went out for my morning smoke," she says, and she crosses her arms and smirks. "She does everything she damn well can to make me feel lazy and useless."

"Helen, come on, you shouldn't take everything the wrong way."

"I'm not, but I'm onto her, so I am," she says. "For God's sake, Ole, she's forever doing things like that. Only the other day she came in here and scrubbed all the pots while we were out."

"She just wants to help, Helen. And besides, she feels it's good to have something to do, she's not the type to sit twiddling her thumbs."

"Oh, kiss my ass!" she says. She shuts her eyes and shakes her head, then she opens her eyes and looks at me again. "What do you think she'd have said if I'd scrubbed all her pots while she and your dad were out, hmm?" she says. "Hmm? D'you think she'd have been pleased, or d'you think she might've been offended?" she asks. She stops, looks straight at me, and I look at her, don't really know what to say. "She'd have been offended," she says. "Of course she would, she'd have been furious, and she'd have had every right to be, because traipsing into some-body's house and cleaning it like that, it's as good as saying they don't keep it clean enough. It's a sneaky way of telling people they're no better than pigs, that's what it is."

"Or maybe she just wants to be useful," I say.

"Useful," Helen sniffs. "If that's what she wants why the hell doesn't she join a fucking aid agency or something. I'm sure they'd have a use for her and be happy to have her. In fact I'm sure she could run a whole aid agency single-handed, the way she's working at the moment, racing around the fucking farm like a fucking Duracell bunny. It's not normal."

"Helen, please," I say. "Don't make this into a problem."

"But it is a problem, for Christ's sake," she says.

"You don't think . . . isn't it more that you need a problem right now, something to vent your frustration and anger on?" I say. "So you fall back on the old cliché of the meddling mother-in-law. You're crediting Mom with opinions and motives she doesn't have, just so you'll have somebody to offload all your anger onto."

"Yeah right, because nobody could possibly be mad at your mother," she sneers.

"Hey, Helen," I say, and I lay my cheek against Daniel's again, cuddle him as I look at Helen and smile.

She looks at me and smirks.

"You know what, Ole," she says, "I really don't give a shit what your mother thinks of me, she can clean the whole house from top to bottom once a week if she likes, that's fine by me, but she still won't make me feel the way she wants me to feel," she says and she looks me straight in the eye, still with that smirk on her face. "And she can just carry on telling the neighbor's wives about how much she has to do in our house, because I don't give a fuck what they think of me either."

"Wow," I say. "I don't know what to say, when you . . . would you like me to speak to her?"

"Ole, aren't you listening to what I'm saying?" she says,

still smirking. "I don't give a shit what she thinks of me and I don't give a shit about all the rumors she spreads about me, so you can do exactly as you please."

I look at her. I'm about to say that I know she's not telling the truth now, but I don't, there's no point in pursuing this, not when she's in this mood, we should talk more about it some other time instead. "Right then," I say, giving her a faint smile. "I'd better be getting to work. I have to finish clearing that cottage plot up on the hill for the viewing next week," I say. "Should I ask Mom if she can look after Daniel for a few hours?"

"By all means," Helen says.

I stand there looking at her, feeling suddenly at a loss. If I take Daniel over to Mom she'll use that against me later, I know she will, even though she says it's okay, she will. But if I leave Daniel here with her she'll end up climbing the walls because she's so tired and she got so little sleep again last night, I can tell just by looking at her that she will. So I really don't know. I just stand here looking at her, hesitating.

"Okay," I say, looking at her and smiling. "You try and get some sleep."

"So I'll be in a better mood and easier to live with, you mean?"

"Humph," I sigh, turning a rather sad, weary face to hers. "I meant just what I said, Helen. No more than that."

"No, of course not."

"Helen, hey."

"Yes, yes," she says, shaking her head as she raises one hand and kind of waves me away. Then she turns around and heads for the bedroom. "Oh, by the way," she says, looking back at me, "have you seen my diary?"

"No," I say.

I look at her, I know she was writing in it in bed yesterday when she was feeding Daniel and it's on the tip of my tongue to ask her if she's looked there, or on the bedside table, but I don't have a chance. She simply turns away without a word, walks into the bedroom and shuts the door behind her. I stay where I am, eyes fixed on the door for two or three seconds, then I give a faint shake of my head and let out a small sigh, my heart always sinks a little when she's like this. Oh well, I would probably be just as cranky if I'd had as little sleep and was in as much pain as she is, so I'll have to try to be patient with her, she doesn't mean any harm by it, and anyway, she'll feel better once she's caught up on her sleep. And besides, I bought some wine and some whisky. I can soften her up with that, she usually loosens up once she's had a little drink, so it'll all sort itself out. I look at Daniel and smile.

"Now then, shall we go over and see Granny and Grandpa, you and I?" I say. "Hmm?" I say. I kiss his cheek, rub his little button nose with mine, then I turn and walk off, walk out of the house and out onto the steps. Two swallows swoop down to the barn and I turn Daniel around and point them out to him, but they dart under the roof ridge before he can see them. I walk down the steps and into the yard. And there are Mom and Dad, sitting on the cottage porch, having coffee and listening to the radio. Dad puts his hands on the wheels of his chair and rolls it slightly farther forward and only now do I see that he has the cat on his lap. He picks it up and lets it drop onto the step. The cat lands softly, pads down onto the grass, sits down and proceeds to lick one of its paws.

"Hello," Dad says, looking at me.

"Hello there," I say.

I pat Daniel's back as I stroll over to them. I look at Mom and smile. "Do you think you could mind Daniel for a few hours so Helen can get a rest?" I ask.

"Well, I had actually been planning to finish painting the window-frames," she says, nodding towards the two windows to the right of the door. One of them glistens with fresh white paint, the other is scraped and ready for painting, I see, the pot of paint sitting on the grass underneath it with the brush lying across the top, so she must have been just about to start. "But well . . . I'll have to put that off till later," she says.

I look at her, there she goes again, she always does this when I ask her a favor, she makes it sound like she's making a sacrifice for me. Even if I ask her to do something I know she really wants to do, she still has to give the impression that she's depriving herself of something. It's annoying, but not worth getting upset about. And maybe it's her funny way of showing that she loves us, an attempt to show that she would go out of her way to help us, I don't know.

"Great," I say, looking at Mom and smiling. She picks up a white rag and a bottle of turpentine from the porch rail, soaks the rag and wipes her hands with it. They glisten in the sunlight and the gnarled veins on their backs stand out even more clearly than usual. She looks at Daniel and smiles.

"Who's Granny's lovely boy?" she coos. "Eh? Has Granny's lovely boy come to see her? Are we going to keep each other company again today, you and me?" she says. She puts down the turpentine-soaked rag, pushes her glasses a bit farther up her nose and then she stretches out her arms and claps her hands at Daniel. "Come to Granny, pet," she says. "There now! But what on earth," she suddenly says in a slightly different voice. "What's that she's put on him—a *pink* onesie?" She stares at me open-mouthed and almost gleefully for a moment or two, then she shakes her head despairingly and turns to Daniel again. "Dear, oh dear," she says, cooing again, "come to Granny, my pet," she says, "we can't have you wearing a pink onesie, a sturdy little boy like you, no we can't," she says.

I look at her, saying nothing, but feeling a little annoyed with her for starting all this again. I don't like Daniel wearing pink either, but that's really neither here nor there because I did tell her that Daniel would be wearing clothes in all sorts of colors, and that she has to respect. And she talks as if it goes without saying that Helen must have dressed him—if anything, that's even more annoying: has she put a pink onesie on him she says, although she knows very well that I dress and change Daniel just as often as Helen, but she acts as if she doesn't know that, acts as if things are exactly the way she imagines they are and I'm supposed to feel that there's something wrong when they aren't. It's a kind of protest, I think.

"You've got diapers and formula, haven't you?" I ask and she looks at me and nods, then she buries her face in the hollow of Daniel's throat and rubs her nose back and forth.

"Mmm, yummy, yummy, you're good enough to eat," she says and then she looks up at me again, gives her glasses another nudge. "Yes, but Ole," she says putting on this kind of plaintive voice, "you shouldn't let her dress him in pink, you really shouldn't," she says, wrinkling her nose. "Hmm?" she says. "You have to talk to her about it, promise me you will."

"Oh, Mom," I say.

"No, but you have to," she says, and then she looks at me, pauses. "Well, I mean I can't talk to her," she says. "If I do she'll fly off the handle right away."

"Oh, Mom, now you're exaggerating, and besides . . ."

"Ole," she breaks in, twisting her lips into a smile that says in matters like this we both know she's always right. "Helen doesn't exactly dote on me," she says, "that's no secret."

"Oh, don't talk like that," I say. I put my head on one side and stand there looking a bit sad, and I feel a bit sad too. The idea that she thinks Helen doesn't like her, that she thinks Helen is out to get her and would like to be rid of her, that is kind of saddening. "Helen just feels sometimes that we live a bit too close for comfort," I say. "She finds it a bit hard to get used to us popping in and out of each other's houses whenever we feel like it and . . . well, you know . . . that's why she can seem a bit . . . standoffish at times," I say. "But that doesn't mean she doesn't like you."

The cat has wandered over to me, he weaves around my legs and I crouch down and stroke his head, he closes his eyes, tilts his head back slightly, purring blissfully. I glance up at Mom again, she's sitting there looking at me with a smile on her face that says she doesn't believe a word I've said.

"Yes, well," she says, closing her eyes then opening them again. "But still, a *pink* onesie," she says. "I doubt if your dad would have let me dress you in pink when you were a baby. Would you, Steinar?" she asks, turning to Dad.

"Nope," Dad says. He tips his wheelchair back slightly and swings it to the side, nudging the newspaper that's lying on the rail as he does so and knocking it into the flowerbed underneath. I get up and go round to pick it up; there are two brown coffee rings on the front page, just under the green lettering of the masthead: *Nationen*. I bend down, pick up the newspaper and put it back where it came from. "Not that it seems to have done this one much good, dressing him in blue," Dad adds and then he looks at me and smirks.

I look at Mom and pretend I didn't catch what he said.

"It was me that put that suit on him, Mom," I say, lying to her face, don't really know why, maybe to protect and defend Helen in some way, or maybe to make it clear to Mom that I really don't care what color Daniel's clothes are.

"There, you see, it didn't do the slightest bit of good, him wearing blue," Dad says with a faint grin, nodding at Mom then looking at me again. He picks up his coffee cup, leans forward and blows on his coffee while he waits for a reply. I eye him a little helplessly. I almost say that I feel secure enough in my own masculinity not to mind changing my kid's diapers, but I don't, I can't be bothered arguing with him about this.

"It's okay, Ole," he says. "I'm only joking." He always does this, he always says he's joking or pulling my leg when he gets in one of his little digs, but when he's with his friends he voices exactly the same thoughts without a trace of humor, so I know he means what he says. I look at him and smile, act as though I believe him when he says it's just a joke.

"So how long's Helen planning to sleep for this time," Mom asks. *This* time, she says, making it sound as if Helen does nothing but sleep. I look at her and smile, ignore the note of accusation in her voice.

"Just let her sleep," I say. "If you have to go out or if

you need anything you'd best call me on my mobile and I'll come," I add. "I'm only going up the hill to clear the last cottage plot, so I won't be far away." She doesn't say anything for a moment, just gives me a look that is both surprised and mildly exasperated, then she raises her eyebrows and shakes her head, making it quite clear what she thinks about leaving Daniel with me if she has to go out. I put my head on one side and give a rather strained little smile.

"Now Mom," I say. "Helen hardly slept at all last night and she's in so much pain that she scarcely knows what to do with herself sometimes."

"Oh, is she?" Mom says, in a voice designed to make it clear that she doesn't believe Helen gets as little sleep or is in as much pain as we make out. I look at her, saying nothing. To be honest I think she could put up a better front, I think she could make more effort to keep her doubts and suspicions to herself. I almost feel like lying and telling her that the doctors have actually found out what might be causing the pain Helen's having. It would be so good to present my mother with a diagnosis or something that would quash her suspicions. But I don't. I can't lie and I won't. I just stand there looking at her. She sets Daniel on her knee, takes his hands and jiggles him up and down as if he's on a horse, opening her eyes wide and saying "clippety-clop, clippety-clop."

"Oh, by the way," she says. "I saw they were looking for part-time help down at the Co-op. Why doesn't she apply for that?" she asks, looking straight at me and giving me a stiff smile. I don't answer right away. It doesn't matter how many times I tell her that Helen isn't fit to work, not the way she is at the moment, she will not drop it. She acts as if she takes it for granted that Helen is looking for work, hoping that this will make me see what she has apparently long since recognized: that Helen is more than well enough to work and that what she really needs is a good kick up the backside. I look at her, realize that I'm getting a bit tired of this, I think she could be a little more understanding, considering how low she was herself at one time, she ought at least to be able to show Helen a little more understanding than she does.

I look at her and force a smile.

"I'll let her know," I say. "But Mom," I say, and then I pause, look at her and smile again. "You mustn't go comparing everybody with yourself, you know. Not everybody is as much of a glutton for work as you are," I say, telling her what she wants to hear, it's the best way to stop her criticizing Helen. This might not even be about Helen, anyway. When Mom starts hinting that Helen's neglecting her duties it might be that what she really wants is for us to remember that she has never done that. This might be her way of saying she'd like us to show respect for how hard-working and conscientious she has been, how she soldiered on and how much she sacrificed after Dad was left paralyzed. She's been far too hard on herself at times, Mom, in fact if you ask me she's been just about running herself into the ground lately. I've told her so many times that she should take it a bit easier, but it does no good. I look at her. "And anyway," I say, "times have changed. Maybe people just aren't used to working as much or as hard as you and Dad did," I add, making sure to give him his share of the credit.

"Yes, well, that's as may be," Mom says. She likes this turn in the conversation, I can see, her face immediately brightens up. She tries to hide it by burying her nose in the hollow of Daniel's throat again, but I can tell that she's pleased. "Well, that just how things were in those days," she says. "I had to learn to work hard to keep things going, because there wasn't much help to be had," she goes on, adopting this very matter-of-fact tone, trying to make out that it was no big deal, but I can tell by her face and her voice that she's gratified and she shows no more sign of bitching about Helen, maybe she doesn't feel the need as long as she's being given credit for always being such a hard and conscientious worker.

"Yeah, yeah," Dad says, breaking in and grinning wryly as he picks up his coffee cup and takes a sip.

Mom turns and gives him a dirty look, she holds his eye for a moment or two, but doesn't say anything, simply gives a little sniff, then she turns away again.

No one says a word. The flies are buzzing around the flowerbed. "In the Summertime" is playing on the radio. I look at Dad, he puts his cup down on the rail, then he looks at me and grins and I don't really know what to say, I never really know what to say when he gets like this. It's hard to make any comment without referring to the fact that he's disabled, I mean it's because he's disabled that he plays up like this, I know it is, it really rankles him that Mom had to run the farm almost single-handed after his accident, and this is how he reacts, by being sarcastic in a kind of mean, spiteful way. Another moment or two passes and still no one says anything, and then I feel a surge of guilt, because I know that any mention of how hard-working Mom is only reminds him of his own inadequacy, it's been like that ever since the accident so that was a bit thoughtless of me.

"No, we're going to go in and put another outfit on you, so we are," Mom says, acting as if she isn't the least bit bothered by Dad. "Aren't we, Daniel?" she says. "Yes we are, we can't have you wearing a pink onesie, can we? Not when you're called after a big, tough lion killer," she adds, and she gets up off the step. "Talk to you later," she says, looking at me and smiling for a second, then she carries Daniel off into the house.

Neither Dad nor I say anything. On the radio someone is talking about the semi-finals of the World Cup being on television this evening and a bumblebee drones quietly past. It lands on one of the sunflowers growing up the side of the house and the flower bobs under its weight for a moment or two.

"Well, I'd better be getting on, as well," I say.

"Yes, indeed," Dad says. "If you're going to sell off your birthright then you'd better get on with it." He looks at me and smirks.

"Dad, come on," I say.

"Well, it's true, isn't it, there's a lot to get rid of," he says.

"Look, we've been through all this."

"Yes, and a whole lot of good it did, seeing as your mind was already made up," he says, still smirking.

I'm about to start explaining why it makes sense to sell this plot and the others I've cleared for summer cottages, but I don't, he's heard it so many times before and to be honest I think he does understand why it has to be this way, it's just that he cares so much about our land, that's why he acts the way he does. It may only be a matter of a few acres of rock, heather and blueberries that we can't use for anything, and it may well be that we need the money, but that doesn't mean it's any easier for me to sell it, I've never said it was, not when we're talking about land that's been in our family for generations. I run a hand over the top of my head and give a little sigh. I almost say that selling the land is as hard for me as it is for him, but I don't have the chance, because just then the plumbers appear, carrying the old washing machine. They come up the basement steps and along the hall. It's Svendsen himself and his apprentice, their backs are straining, they're a bit red in the face and their mouths are drawn so tight you can't see their lips.

"Oops, looks like we'd better get out of the way," I say, moving aside. The plumbers don't say a word, they just sidle past us, taking short, quick steps, edge down the wheelchair ramp and over to the van, then they dump the washing machine onto the gravel with a thud.

"Holy shit," the apprentice puffs. He takes off his cap and wipes his brow with the back of his hand.

"That's a beast of a machine," Svendsen says. He rests his elbow on the side of the pickup and lets out a loud "whew," stands for a second or two getting his breath back then he looks up at Dad. "Twenty-five years old, was that what you said?" he asks.

"Yep, twenty-five," Dad says.

"The machines they're making these days are a bit lighter, to put it mildly," Svendsen says, taking off his work glove and running a hand through his gray, almost white hair.

"Maybe so," Dad says, "but I don't really recall it being all that heavy," he says, trying to seem a little surprised. I can tell by his face and his voice, he's pretending to be surprised by how heavy they think the machine is, so we'll all think that he must have been a real he-man in his day. I can read him like a book, and I know that's what he's after. I look across at Svendsen and his apprentice, they're still struggling to get their breath back before heaving the washing machine onto the bed of the truck. "But of course I was a young man when I carried it down those stairs," Dad adds, then he picks up his cup and takes a sip of coffee.

"Aye, I'll bet you were," Svendsen mutters, shooting a glance at the apprentice and raising his eyebrows. The apprentice grins back at him. It hurts me to see this, I turn to look at Dad, but he doesn't seem to have noticed and I feel a little relieved, I know how that sort of thing can get to him, he's so touchy. I look at him, look at his skinny legs—thighs and calves so thin that even the narrowest trouser legs lie in folds around him on the wheelchair seat. I watch him for a moment and then I feel myself being overwhelmed by concern and fondness for him. I have the urge to say or do something that will make him happy, something that'll make him feel useful or whatever.

"You know that complaint I filed against the guy who built the new jetty," I say. "We've got an arbitration meeting with the Consumer Council coming up soon, you wouldn't consider coming with me and giving me a bit of support?" I ask, saying the first thing that pops into my head, but it wasn't such a stupid thing to say because I know such situations are right up Dad's street, he loves it when he has the chance to show that nobody can take him for a ride, and this arbitration meeting could easily provide him with just such a chance. "I'm completely hopeless at things like that," I add, just to emphasize that I really could do with his help, and it's true, I *could* do with his help at this meeting.

"You mean you need a grumpy old bastard like me, is that

it?" Dad says, grinning and speaking loud enough for the plumbers to hear us, calling himself a grumpy old bastard, but grinning all the while to let the plumbers know he's only joking, he wants them to think: here's a man who stands up for his rights, that's what he's after.

"Well, if you want to put it like that," I say and I glance at the plumbers and chuckle, like I'm in on the joke.

"Nah, you know what, Ole," Dad says. "You're nearly forty and if you ask me it's a bit ridiculous for you to come running to me every time things don't quite go your way."

I stand there staring at him. The plumbers glance at us, then they look at each other and grin again. I feel my cheeks start to burn, this'll make a great story for Svendsen to tell, it'll be all around the island in a couple of days, I'm sure. I look at Dad, feeling both embarrassed and annoyed, I mean, how often do I ask him for help? I don't know when I last asked him for anything and yet he goes and does this, making me look like a little boy who runs crying to his daddy every time things get difficult. Although I know why he says these things, of course, I know he's doing this to make himself look like the man he longs to be. He's the one who needs help, not me, but he talks as if it was the other way around, reinventing himself as a man whom I'm somehow supposed to be totally reliant on, that's what he's doing. I stand for a moment just staring at him, and now it's his turn to blush, he must realize that he's gone too far, making a fool of me like this, he must realize that I can contradict his statement, any time I want, make fun of it even. I've half a mind to do it too, I've half a mind to point to that wheelchair and ask who cries for whom when things get difficult, but I won't, I wouldn't sink that low. I shouldn't grudge him this fleeting sense of having some power in his life.

"Ah, well," he says with an attempt at a grin, he knows it'll put him in a bad light if I say what I'm thinking, so he's trying to laugh the whole thing off. I look at him and try to smile back, as if confirming his version of what's going on between us, as if acknowledging that he was only joking. "It'll be fine, I'm sure," he carries on. "Just you put me in the picture and I'll come with you."

"Great," I say, still smiling. I shoot a glance at the plumbers, but they're not looking our way, they're both hunched over the washing machine, trying to get a good grip on it, and I turn back to Dad. "Right, well, see you later," I say and raise a rather limp hand in a wave.

"See you," he says.

I turn and make my way across to the car and all at once I feel a little tired, a little heavy-headed after all that's been said and done this morning. It's been a bit much, all this, first that bother with Jørgen, then with Helen, and finally with Mom and Dad. Oh, well, it'll all work out okay in the end—this, too. I open the car door and heavily slump down onto the seat, look back at Dad as I start the car, he picks up his newspaper, gives his thumb a little lick before opening it. I feel a surge of pity for him. I know he doesn't want to be pitied, or at least that's what he's always saying, but I can't help it, no matter how many years it's been since the accident, sometimes I still feel pity for him. Not so much because he's in a wheelchair, but because he's never been able to reconcile himself to that fact. He won't admit it to himself, but everybody around him knows that he hasn't reconciled himself to it, not altogether, not properly. He still has this urge to help in ways in which he can't possibly help, and this bothers him more than he's prepared to acknowledge, maybe even more than he actually realizes, because I'm not sure he's aware that it's this urge that lies behind his constant need to call attention to himself and appear bigger and more important than he is. I don't think he is, I don't think he realizes that this craving for attention represents a vain attempt to free himself from his handicap. I drive out of the yard and up the slope, hear the rattle of the trailer as I turn onto the bumpy farm track running up to the top of the hill.

I'm almost a bit embarrassed by the kind of goody-goody, comic-book language I used the other day in my description of our life at the camp. I kind of feel as if it was written by someone trying to make fun of the kids being depicted or at best someone who sees only their cute, harmless sides and doesn't take them seriously. But that's not the case at all, believe me. Obviously we didn't talk exactly the way I've written, we may not have used expressions such as "armed to the teeth" and "yellow dogs" all that often. But if I'm to present a clear picture of the imaginary world we inhabited up there in the forest and of how we saw ourselves and each other when we were running about up there, then this is the language I have to use. It's much the same as me writing that we wore feathers in our hair and loincloths made from cut-up sheets. I seem to remember that one of us did show up in a get-up like that one summer's day in the late 70s or the early 80s, but it wasn't a regular thing. Most of us wore perfectly ordinary shorts or faded bell-bottom jeans, I think. But if I'm to show how we saw ourselves and each other and, not least, how we would have been viewed by outsiders, then it's more correct to kit us out with loincloths than with jeans. Because in our minds we were all Indians.

And this Wild West-inspired fantasy world was very much

your creation. It was you who decided what rules applied in the camp, what it was okay to do and what wasn't okay, how we should or shouldn't talk. The rest of us interpreted your rules in our own way, of course, and acted accordingly, and since most of us read the *Silver Arrow* comics, the *Deerfoot* books and various other key sources of inspiration, naturally we sometimes came up with our own suggestions or ideas about how to shape our fantasy world. But everything that was said or done still had to be approved by you before it could be incorporated into this part of our boyish society, if I can call it that. You made no comment, for example, if I called myself Swift Horse or Per wanted to be known as Strong Bear, but when one of the little kids said he wanted to be called Obi-Wan Kenobi, you got annoyed and told him to find himself a proper name at once. Nor did you like it if we said things like "I've got to get back for dinner" or "My mom and dad said I had to be home by six" because that brought elements from the real world into our imaginary universe and as you'll see from my last letter this could confuse and spoil things, jolting us out of the dream world we inhabited. But the worst sin anyone could commit was to remind us of what we all knew really: that we didn't actually have any enemy. Both the real-life camp and the imaginary universe that went with it were built, after all, around the idea that we had an enemy that we had to defend ourselves against. The fact that we kept watch, that we made weapons and built stockades around our brush shelters, that we practiced hand-to-hand fighting and laid all sorts of plans for attacking and retreating, all of this we did because we had to defend ourselves against an enemy. So to say out loud that this enemy didn't actually exist, to admit that the kids from Husvika were no threat to us and probably never would be, would be tantamount to destroying the whole foundation of everything we did, all the effort we had put into it would seem worthless without an enemy, all the pleasure we got from playing at the camp would be gone, our life up there in the forest would become meaningless.

And that was exactly why, as chief, you would take drastic action to keep alive the notion that we were under constant threat. Not only would you get angry and upset and attack the culprit both verbally and physically, the way you did with Karoline and Hauk, but in order to repair the damage I know for a fact that one night you actually sneaked out of the house and up to the forest and tore down everything we had built. Shelters, stockades, lookout post, you destroyed everything, and afterwards not only did you blame the Husvikings, you were even crafty enough to plant clues that confirmed that this had indeed been the work of the kids from Husvika. "Look!" Per cried, pointing to what we all recognized as a baseball cap belonging to one of the Husvikings. Only later did you admit that the Husviking concerned had left the cap lying in one of the goals at the football pitch and that you had taken it and left it next to the toppled totem pole, where Per found it.

And you achieved your aim, of course. "Revenge!" Per cried. "Death to the Husvikings!" I screamed. "No mercy!" you yelled, brandishing your spear above your head.

And as if that weren't enough, just after this, when we'd got over the shock and were busy rebuilding the camp, who should come strolling up the path but Hauk and the girls, each carrying a berry pail.

Well, we asked, now did they believe us, now did they see what sort of enemy we were up against?

The girls were stunned, they just stood there staring at the ruins.

So it was true after all, they mumbled. We hadn't been speaking with forked tongues when we told them about the Husvikings.

You frowned.

"Why on earth would we lie about a thing like that?"

No, the girls had no answer to that. But at least they no longer doubted us. And could they help us to rebuild the camp?

We shrugged and did a good job of hiding the fact that there was nothing in the world we would like more. Well, we said, they could always lend a hand.

"But weren't we going berry picking?" Hauk asked, looking at Eva and Karoline.

"Oh, honestly, Hauk," the girls burst out. They couldn't just shut their eyes and pretend that nothing had happened. They had to help, of course they did, they could pick berries any time.

"Okay, be like that," Hauk said.

"Oh, for heaven's sake, can't you help as well?" the girls asked.

"Nah," Hauk muttered, the look on his face saying he wasn't interested.

A sniff and a grunt.

"Jeez, how selfish can you get," Karoline said.

"I didn't think you were like that," Eva said.

And they tossed their heads, letting Hauk know that he had gone down drastically in their estimation.

Hauk, poor bastard, said not a word as he slunk off into the raspberry thicket, but it wasn't hard to see that he was hurt. I felt a twinge of guilt as I watched him go because he was a good friend and, like you, I knew that his mom and dad had forbidden him to take part in our activities at the camp, so he couldn't have helped us to rebuild it however much he might want to.

But we didn't say anything about that to the girls. No, no. We let them get themselves all worked up and indignant at the idea that anyone could be so selfish and, even though I did feel kind of guilty, that didn't stop me from feeling a little bit pleased too. There was no getting away from the fact that most girls thought Hauk was handsome, so it was good to have him out of the way for a while.

Then we got back to work.

Per mended the lookout post up in the birch tree and two of the littlest kids tried to dig a deeper hole for the totem pole to stand in. Meanwhile Karoline was wrestling with one of the stakes for the stockade. We hurried across as casually as we could, you and I. "Let me get that for you, Karoline," you said, beating me to it. I had thought, not to say hoped, that she might be a bit mad at you for knocking her berry pail out of her hands, but she didn't seem to be. Quite the opposite, in fact. Not only did she immediately let you relieve her of her burden, she even thanked you in the way you liked best of all:

"You don't find that at all heavy?" she asked when she noticed that you were only using one hand to carry the stake.

"Heavy?" you said. Your face was scarlet, your arm all but breaking in two, but you acted as though you had no idea what she was talking about.

Laughter from Karoline.

"What?" you said, looking more and more puzzled.

"Oh, nothing," Karoline laughed, not wanting to say it.

And you shook your head and sauntered on, chuckling, with the stake under your arm. "Women!" you muttered.

As well you might. Well, I for one didn't understand them. I mean, how could she be so keen on you so soon after you had tramped all over most of the raspberries she had picked? It was unbelievable. But I wasn't giving her up that easily. As soon as all of our joint projects were finished I started to give the girls some advice on how to build a good, solid brush shelter that wouldn't collapse at the first faint breeze to sweep through the forest. If Karoline and Eva were me they would, for example, borrow Per's tomahawk and use that to sharpen the ends of the poles, I told them, because then you could stick them more firmly in the ground and the shelter would be more stable.

The girls were impressed.

"I never thought of that," Eva said.

"You're so smart, Ole," Karoline said.

Oh, I didn't know about that, but I had built a few shelters in my time, that I couldn't deny. Well, I didn't have to tell them, Karoline informed me. I was thrilled to hear her talking to me like this and it was all I could do not to let it show.

"But it's not as easy as you might think to sharpen a pole if you've never done it before," I said, keeping my delight in check by becoming all matter-of-fact and technical: you had to do this and this, and for heaven's sake mind your fingers. But, well, I was right here, as she could see, so if they needed help all she had to do was ask and I'd be at her service—if I had the time and the possibility, that was.

Okay, so did I happen to have the time and the possibility right now?

"We—ell," I said, trying to play hard to get by dragging it out.

No, no, she could ask David instead.

So then I had a busy time convincing them that I wasn't all that busy. I scratched my chin and thought for a while. "No, actually I can leave that till later," I murmured to myself. Then I looked up at Karoline and nodded. Yes, of course I could give them a hand now, that shouldn't be any problem.

"Oh, great. Thanks a lot, Ole."

And then all I had to do was borrow Per's tomahawk and get to work. I sharpened the poles we had, went into the woods to cut down some more and once I'd sharpened those it was time to start building the framework for what was to be their tepee. My forehead glistened with sweat, but the girls didn't need to help me, I assured them, they would only be in the way, I'd be just as quick doing it alone. And I'd rustle up pine branches for the tepee covering while I was at it.

Wow. But wasn't I at least going to take a break? Karoline wondered.

A break? What for?

They both laughed, they just didn't know what I was made of.

Oh, it was so good to hear them say things like that.

Well, okay, they said. They might as well go and collect some bracken while I was working.

Bracken?

Yes, for the floor. So it would be nice and soft to sit on.

What? Well I never—the girls thought the ground was too hard to sit on comfortably? Okay, okay, I laughed, then they'd better go off into the forest and find their bracken, and in the meantime I'd finish making the tepee.

Oh, this was the life. Not only had we an enemy we could stand against shoulder to shoulder, now we also had women whom we could help and maybe even give our lives for if the situation demanded it.

Perfect, in other words. Your diversionary tactic had worked and everything was perfect in the camp again.

This just shows, by the way, why of all of us you were the brains behind our imaginary world. Because there was no one to touch you when it came to storytelling and yarn-spinning. In fact I've never known anyone like you. If, for example, I asked you what you'd done the day before, you might say that you'd been coley fishing with your grandfather, even though you hadn't been coley fishing at all, you'd actually gone blueberry picking. As if the fact that you'd been blueberry picking was something you wanted to hide, or as if you felt that there was something special about going coley fishing that made it worth boasting about. At other times you would launch, unasked, into descriptions of books you'd read or television programs you'd seen—books and television programs you couldn't possibly have read or seen, or that might even prove to be nonexistent. And if we happened to be talking about someone, whether it was a kid or a grown-up, you almost always had some story about them that nobody else knew and that would later turn out to be a pack of lies. And it didn't need to be anything dramatic, designed to spellbind us, your audience. Sometimes it was, but just as often all you would have to tell us was that this person or that had an uncle who was a welder, or that the person concerned was really good at drawing.

I've often wondered why you did things like this, why you lied without any thought of gaining some kind of benefit or advantage from it. I mean, you risked getting a name for being the sort of person the other kids couldn't trust and whom they wouldn't want anything to do with. I spoke to Eva about this when I ran into her down at the Co-op today. She works as a psychologist in Namsos and she cited your family situation as a possible explanation for why you were the way you were. Berit, your mother, wouldn't tell you or anyone else who your real father was, and since you and she had lived with your grandfather he had, to all intents and purposes served as a father figure for you. And, since he was such a domineering control freak, you had a particularly strong need to create for yourself a world in which you and only you called the shots, or so she thought. So from that point of view, all the lying, the yarn-spinning, the fantasizing, was actually a survival mechanism, she said. Your imaginary world was a place in which you had the power you didn't have in your normal everyday life.

This all sounds very neat and logical, but I'm not sure that it's correct. Unlike today, when the lives of most kids are totally regulated and supervised by adults, we were given plenty of scope and had more than enough time to ourselves. None of the kids on Otterøya went to nursery school, not as far as I can remember, because when we were at that age, our mothers were at home. Or if they went out to work they had grandparents or babysitters to look after their kids, and this meant that we were free to run around the farms and roam the forest and the seashore. And later, when we started school and more and more of our mothers started going out to work, there were no after-school clubs where we could be looked after. Hardly anyone on Otterøya ever locked their door, but the few that did gave their children their own doorkeys to hang on strings around their necks and when we came home from school, alone or with a friend, we could look forward to hours to ourselves without any adult interference. So I find it kind of hard to see how excessive control on Erik's part could have forced you to take refuge in an imaginary world in which you ruled the roost.

There was no doubt, though, that Erik could be controlling and domineering, not to say a bit of a tyrant. Years after your mom got together with Arvid and you moved from Otterøya to Namsos, I had a summer job at the sawmill where Erik worked for the last few years before he retired and there he behaved pretty much like a general among the rank and file.

"Johnsen, come here," he said to one man who had just been taken on.

"It's Johansen," the man corrected him.

"If I say your name's Johnsen then Johnsen it is," Erik retorted, and if he was trying to be funny then he hid it well, because he neither laughed or smiled, and to the guys at the sawmill that poor bastard was Johnsen until the day Erik retired. If anyone wasn't pulling their weight or made a mistake, especially if that mistake held us back or caused problems for the gang in some other way, Erik would usually punish the culprit by refusing to let him make up for it. His language could get pretty colorful at times, but usually he would simply dismiss the person concerned with a brusque wave of the hand and fix the fault himself, quickly, neatly and efficiently, leaving the sinner feeling useless. The only positive thing I can find to say about this side of Erik was that he was the same with everyone, high or low. He was as far from being a yes-man or an ass-kisser as you could get and he could be as rough on an odd-job man or the owner himself as he was on the other men at the sawmill.

The only reason he was able to act like this without it having greater, more serious consequences was, of course, that he was as big and as strong as he was. He was well over six feet tall, took a size twenty in a shoe and had an enormous pear-shaped face with two close-set black eyes. With a mug like that he could scare the wits out of just about anybody and if anyone was stupid enough not to be scared they soon would be, when he tore off his shirt, baring his chest—as he was quite liable to do when he was staggering around the community center, blind drunk and spoiling for a fight. As with all the local gatherings, everyone, from teenyboppers to pensioners, attended the parties in Årnes and Devika, and when I was a boy it wasn't unusual to see a half-naked Erik "rearranging" somebody's face, as he was wont to put it. But no sooner had Erik beaten the living daylights out of his opponent—and I never saw it turn out any other way—than he would do a complete about-turn and be as nice as could be, showering the other man with kindness and compassion. This was probably a sign that he was capable of remorse and possibly that he was afraid he might have gone too far, but such abrupt changes of mood, and the fact that remarkably often Erik and his fellow brawlers were the best of pals again as soon as they lowered their fists, also shows that there was seldom any serious or deep-rooted issue behind their battles. Brawling at a party was more a kind of ritual, it seemed, a good fight had a value and a function that did not primarily have anything to do with revenge or injustice, or a slight or insult of any sort. In fact insults tended rather to be welcomed and regarded as the perfect excuse for finally starting a fight. I think these brawls acted partly as a purge, allowing the combatant to give vent to his feelings and expend energy that he could not use or find outlet for in other ways, and partly as a way of proving to himself and everyone else that he was a real man, one who would never walk away from an honest-to-goodness fist-fight.

This last was important on Otterøya. The macho culture is still strong out here, but it was even stronger back then and each in their own way the island men all strove to live up to an ideal of manhood that most town and city dwellers would have considered hopelessly out of date. A true Otterøya man preferred home-brewed hooch to brand name booze from the state wine store; he smoked roll-ups, wore checked flannel shirts and when he wasn't out walking with that manly, slightly rolling gait that townies claimed we had and have, he was driving around in a car or a boat a little bigger than he could actually afford on the money he made at the herring oil factory in Vikan, the mink-feed processing plant at Fosslandsosen or wherever he happened to work—if he wasn't a fisherman or farmer and thus self-employed.

This is of course something of a caricature, but most caricatures have a grain of truth in them. Otterøya was a community in which men were men, as they say, and even my dad, who I knew had voted Socialist Left in more than one general election, hated fairies and laughed at women who tried their hand at traditional male jobs. He never ceased to be amazed, for example, by Hauk and Grim's mother and father when they moved from Oslo to Otterøya, because when they went anywhere in the car it was just as likely to be the wife that drove as the husband. I'm sure Dad was never aware of it himself, and he would probably have sworn it wasn't true if anyone had suggested it to him, but for him being in charge of the car seemed to be a metaphor for being in charge of the family and it went without saying that that was a man's job. The only valid reason for a woman to get behind the wheel when her husband was in the vehicle was if he'd been drinking and wasn't fit to drive, although even that wasn't always a good enough excuse. "I'd have to be pretty damn drunk to be as much of a danger on the road as the wife," as Dad always said.

All this can, of course, be seen as typical of the brash way middle-aged men have always behaved—convinced as they are that they and their ilk have been selected by nature to run society. But if you ask me the macho culture on Otterøya has made a lot of men far more full of themselves than normal. For instance, I've always tried as far as possible to avoid going shopping in Namsos with my dad, because he's never satisfied with the quality of the service or the merchandise, and if he spots an article with a little flaw in it you can bet your life that's the one he'll want, just so that when he reaches the checkout he can demand to get it for half-price. "No, I'm sorry, I can't let you have it for that," I remember the checkout girl at the hardware store saying once, when he demanded a discount on a toaster with an almost invisible scratch on the enamel. "Aw, c'mon now, of course you can," Dad said and he didn't look like he was joking. He seemed totally unconcerned by the line forming behind us, he simply stood there staring at the assistant, waiting to see what she would do and, young and unsure as she was, she didn't dare to do anything but agree to giving him a discount. Dad walked out of that shop afterwards having had confirmed yet again what he was always angling to have confirmed when he did this sort of thing: that he was a real man and that, like all other real men, he wasn't easily fooled, he knew his rights and he always stood his ground.

Likewise, he believed he had a perfect right to say exactly what he thought, no matter how little he knew about a subject, and not just a perfect right: he seemed to feel he had a duty to share his usually very strong opinions with other people. I don't think I've ever seen him get information from anywhere except the *Namdal Workers' Weekly*, the television news and *Nationen*, but even when talking to people he must have known to be better informed and more abreast of events than he was, like the headmaster at the school or the highly knowledgeable chairman of the local historical society, for example, he would lay down the law, telling the person concerned exactly "what was wrong with society today." He was a real man and real men "didn't mince their words," they "called a spade and spade" and "didn't beat about the bush," to quote three expressions he was fond of using of himself.

But still there was one thing that real men in general and my dad in particular did not talk about and that was, of course, feelings. Because feelings could knock a person off-balance and since a real man had to be ready at all times to make important decisions on behalf of himself and his family, he always had to be in control, he had be rational and "keep a cool head," as Dad used to say. The only time when an exception could be made to this rule was when he was drunk, or raging mad or both, because naturally real men had a *karsk* or two on a Saturday night and as I say they weren't easily fooled. If provoked it was quite permissible to "see red," "lose your temper," or "blow a gasket"—all of these also favorite expressions of Dad's.

I first became aware of this inability and reluctance to talk about one's feelings when it began to dawn on me that my mom was mentally ill. I was in early primary school at the time, Primary Two maybe, I don't really remember. But at any rate I noticed that she was beginning to neglect her personal hygiene, she stopped washing herself and her clothes and she started to smell. Both this and the fact that she spent less and less time on the housework and more and more lying on the sofa, doing absolutely nothing, made me feel more and more worried. She could be up one day, down the next, but during her worst spells she would lie in bed upstairs for days on end, just crying and smoking. She hardly spoke at all and if she did open her mouth it was mostly only to moan and complain and make unfair accusations, mostly aimed at herself, but also at Dad and me. Dad believed that hard work was the cure for all ills that weren't of a physical nature, and in an attempt to force her to get out of bed and get on with her chores on the farm I remember he tried refusing to tend to her and wait on her as long as she stayed in the bedroom. But then she went from skimping on her appearance and personal cleanliness to not washing or caring for herself at all, and from eating far too little to eating nothing. And as with all the other strategies he had tried he had to abandon this one too.

Even worse, though, were the times when Mom actually did try to pull herself together. After weeks at a time when simply turning over in bed appeared to take a massive effort, she would suddenly seem to find reserves of energy that only minutes before neither she nor Dad nor I would ever have imagined she possessed. She would hop out of bed, pull on her clothes and start tidying up, washing floors, mucking out the barn or going over all the homework I had had since the last time she had been up. It was as if she had a clear moment when she saw how bad things were and then she panicked and attempted to catch up on everything she'd left undone—and all in the course of the first day. She had to cut my hair, wash the windows and bake bread; she had to call on the woman next door, rearrange the furniture in the living room and darn Dad's socks and mine. Nothing could wait. Everything was done at breakneck speed, with no thought for anything else—until she ran out of steam or began to see how ridiculously she was behaving. Then she could throw a fit because she had missed a little bit of dust on a windowsill; she could freak out because she had forgotten to mail a letter that wasn't the slightest bit urgent, or dissolve into tears because I wouldn't eat the food she had just cooked— even though it was the second hot meal she had dished up that morning and even though I had already told her I was full and didn't want anything. I didn't like her cooking, she would sob, she was totally useless, she was a burden to everybody around her, she'd be better off dead. Slowly but surely all of her new-found energy would drain away until there was nothing for Dad to do but take her upstairs and put her back to bed.

But even though I stopped bringing friends home because I was afraid the other kids would notice that something was wrong with her; even though I took on more and more of my mom's household chores and even though there were times when I was so worried about her that I couldn't sleep properly at night or concentrate on my schoolwork during the day, Dad made no move to talk to me about what was going on, not to begin with anyway. Or at least, he may have made the odd hesitant, half-hearted attempt to do so, clapping me on the shoulder and asking how I was doing, but when—me being my father's son—I said I was okay he just left it at that and fooled himself into believing that I really was okay. I'm not sure, but I don't actually think he was capable of talking to me about it, I don't think he had the words for it. Dad preferred us to "find something to do together." We went camping at Salsnes and took a drive across the Swedish border to Østersund, and he made a start on several little projects on the farm that he tried to get me involved in. He meant well, I'm sure, and it was all fine as far as it went, but it didn't help one little bit, and these days I always look a bit doubtful when I hear someone talk about there being a more physical, manly way of dealing with emotional upsets. Don't get me wrong, I've tried taking refuge in work myself when things got tough, but that never solved anything.

Physical pain was a very different matter. Not that a true Otterøya man could ever say anything that made it sound as though he was moaning or complaining, but it was important to let everyone know if you were in pain, because there was a lot of prestige to be won from "gritting your teeth" and "taking it like a man." I don't know how many times I've heard the story of the time when Erik's brother Albert, who lived next door to you, had an accident with a cross-cut saw in which his right hand "was severed from the rest of my body," as he put it. At any rate, he picked up the hand, walked down to the road and stopped a passing tourist who was on his way from Aglen Campsite into town.

"Sorry about the limp handshake," Albert had said, smiling and holding out his severed hand.

How true this story was I don't know, but that's not really the point. The variety and popularity of such yarns shows that strength and toughness were valuable assets among the island men and that this was the image of the typical Otterøyan male most of them cherished. Those few who dared to openly undermine this image were usually vilified and ridiculed and jeered at when the other men were together. And in the case of particularly drastic, blatant rejections of the macho values—if someone came out as a homosexual, for instance—the individual concerned ran the risk of having the shit kicked out of him. Like most men on the island, Dad would never have done such a thing, but when one of the players on Otterøya's sixth division team came out of the closet and had all of his front teeth knocked out by a teammate who "couldn't bear the thought that he had taken so many showers alongside a butt pirate," my dad seemed to have more sympathy with the assailant than with the victim. "Maybe he went a bit too far, but what a fucking thought, eh? To have to stand there being drooled over by another man," as he put it when we were having dinner one day.

But it wasn't just fairies and women that the men of Otterøya tried to distance themselves from in their efforts to seem like "real men." City folk also came in for their fair share of abuse. Although it's true that bad-mouthing townies had as much to do with local pride and creating some sort of identity for oneself as an Otterøyan. It had to do with experiencing a sense of fellowship and solidarity by highlighting and preferably exaggerating how different one was from people elsewhere and—there's no getting away from it—for many it also had to do with concealing and living with a feeling of being inferior because they came from the provinces.

But the Otteroya man's attempt to distance himself from town and city dwellers was also an attempt to live up to the macho image of a real man. Whenever my dad and Erik were discussing townies the underlying assumption was that they were priggish, stuck-up, fussy and far too full of themselves. According to my dad it was hard to tell the women from the men when you walked down Havnegata in Namsos, and he was sure that the Oslo guy who had bought the cottage plot on the other side of the bay would sell it again as soon it came time to fertilize the fields. Well, did we think a man from Oslo would be able to take the smell of slurry mingling with his whisky and soda on the terrace of an evening?

The reception given to Hauk's and his big brother Grim's hippie family when they moved to Otterøya from Oslo in 1979 or 1980 was another sign of much the same attitude.

Lasse and Lene Albrigtsen, Hauk's parents, had no friends or relatives in Otterøya and when people asked them what had made them move from the capital to this of all places they would often start to talk, without a trace of irony, of how they had longed to experience the true, authentic life of the countryside. They would wax lyrical about the joys of growing your own herbs and vegetables and breathing clean, fresh air. But even though this was actually true, it wasn't the whole truth, because it didn't take long for word to get around that Lene was a drug addict and that Lasse had forced her to come with him to this remote corner of Norway in a desperate attempt to get her as far away from the drug scene as possible.

I can still remember how exciting we thought it was the first time we visited their house, and how intriguingly different it was from what we were used to. Our houses smelled of soft soap, tobacco smoke or boiled cod, but when we walked into the Albrigtsens' living room we were met by a sweetish scent that my dad insisted in his worldly wise fashion, when we described it to him, had to be marijuana, but which later turned out to be incense. The walls were hung with the Albrigtsens' own brightly colored works of art; from the attic, where Hauk's mom practiced what I later learned was yoga, came the sound of soft, Indian-inspired music and after we'd been there for a while—once we'd said yes to staying and having dinner with them and a barefoot Lasse Albrigtsen not only served up an emerald-green soup he had made from nettles he'd picked from the hedgerow outside, but also instructed us to sit on the floor with our legs crossed while we ate—we really felt we were doing something we had always dreamed of doing.

It's easy now to see that the Albrigtsens' lifestyle appealed to the Indian in us and that it was this that made us feel so much at home there, on that first day and all the days after that. Lasse Albrigtsen had long hair that he sometimes kept in place with a headband. He went around barefoot and often bare-chested, the time of year and weather permitting, and since he had been practicing meditation and yoga all of his adult life he was as lithe and supple as we imagined an Indian would be. I don't think it would have surprised us if he had said "Ugh" or greeted us by raising one hand and saying "How," he seemed so much like an Indian to us.

Years of drug-taking had left Lene with a coarse, husky voice and a rather worn, haggard face and this was not how the comic books and films had taught us that squaws should look. But she also had her own pottery workshop in the basement, where she made pots inspired by the art of the Pueblo Indians, and she often wore dresses trimmed with long fringes that would have looked good on any woman in *Silver Arrow*.

Obviously, though, it wasn't just the more superficial aspects that fired our American Indian fantasies when we were at the Albrigtsens' place. Both Lasse and Lene talked about self-sufficiency and living in tune with nature. In their garden they grew potatoes and cabbages, not to mention zucchini (which none of us had ever heard of) and they picked plants that grew all around us but that we had always thought of as weeds, or at best no more than animal fodder, and used them in weird vegetarian dishes or made tea from them or hung them from the kitchen ceiling to dry and used them as herbs. To us, this last was a sure sign that Lasse and Lene possessed the same secret skills as the medicine man of an Indian tribe and although we never said anything we were very impressed.

Mind you, I seem to remember that Hauk and Grim weren't as wild about those sides of Lasse and Lene that we admired, or not all of them, at any rate. Their parents would not have a television in the house, for example, because apparently television made you lethargic and apathetic and killed the art of conversation. And when, incredible though it seemed, they eventually did give in to pressure and buy a TV, they put it in a small, cold, unfurnished room that would be so uncomfortable to sit in that no one would think of doing so unless there was "something worth seeing" on, as Lasse said. And it was Lasse and Lene who decided what was worth seeing, because while they may have been more easy-going than our parents where most things were concerned, on this one matter they were anything but. Hauk and Grim weren't allowed, for example, to watch the Westerns that we loved more than anything else, because they were American, they glorified violence and were almost always racist in the way they portrayed Native Americans. Besides which, John Wayne was a fascist according to Lasse, and anyway he wasn't nearly as tough in real life as he was in his films: "Did you know he's actually terrified of horses?" he used to say to us and then he would laugh at how ridiculous he thought the man was—thus also letting us know how stupid he thought we were for idolizing him.

But as I may have hinted earlier, when I wrote about the Otterøyans and their efforts to present themselves in a certain light by distancing themselves from other people, after a while we began to see that the very things we found so fascinating and appealing about the Albrigtsens were more or less the same things that made them seem so suspect to my mom and dad and to Erik and Berit. At first, just after word got out that Lene had been a drug addict, they had quite naturally been afraid that the home of the hippie Albrigtsen family would become a "drug den in our safe little Otterøya," as Dad put it. But no one ever saw anything to suggest that Lasse and Lene used drugs. And anyway, everybody on the island knew that certain shadier local characters had already approached the Albrigtsens, hoping that by mixing with such liberated individuals they might have the chance to give rein to sides of themselves that the small village community did not normally allow them to express— "They're probably hoping they'll get to take part in orgies of sex and drugs," as your mother said. The fact that Lasse sent them all packing reassured the locals and led most of them to abandon their suspicions and speculations concerning Lasse and Lene and their possibly drug-fueled, debauched bohemian lifestyle.

There were other things about the Albrigtsens, though, that the Otterøyans still weren't too sure about. Okay, so Lasse did his sowing by the stars and the apple tree that Lene had brought with her from Oslo was planted on top of the placenta from Grim's birth. Such things were just seen as adding an eccentric dash of color to everyday life on Otterøya and were a source of much hilarity to the locals. But the Albrigtsen family's general behavior and lifestyle acted as a constant reminder that there were alternatives to the way in which the fairly homogeneous population of the island lived and this in turn was regarded by many as a threat. My dad, for example, could get extremely hot under the collar over the fact that Lasse and Lene went in for organic farming. Instead of showing an interest in it, keeping an open mind and possibly learning something from Lasse and Lene's farming methods, he took it as a criticism of the way he and all the other farmers on Otterøya farmed their land. Lasse and Lene's relaxed easy-going, take-things-as-they-come attitude to most things was automatically interpreted by your mother as laziness and sloppiness, and that they built their new shed out of logs and chose to give it a grass roof was in Erik's opinion one of many examples that they were only playing at farming and that they were going to "get a real smack in the face from reality some day," as he put it.

That Lasse and Lene dared to realize sides of themselves that the small village community did not allow the islanders to express and which were therefore left to smoulder inside them as suppressed urges and longings, this also did its part to fuel hostility to the Albrigtsens when they first moved in. Even though Lasse was in no way effeminate in his character or his gestures he was definitely a "new" man and the fact that he dared to have long hair and wear colorful clothes, and that he never made any effort to seem tough and strong and brave, all this felt like a serious provocation to many Otterøya men who struggled and strived every single day to follow all the rules and regulations imposed on them by the island's macho culture. So, not surprisingly, a rumor spread that Lasse was actually a "butt pirate" and, as if that weren't enough, one night after the family had been living on the island for about six months, Albert and a gang of younger men who believed that such scum had no place on the island paid them a visit and in a collective fit of rage tore up some of their vegetable crop, trampled flower-beds and painted "fucking fairy" on the wall of their house— obviously in an attempt to convince themselves, each other and everyone else that they were real macho men from Otterøya.

But I shouldn't exaggerate: there were also situations in which the men of Otterøya showed themselves in a more nuanced light and even undermined their image as macho men, of course they did. I remember, for example, one of the first occasions when your mother paid one of her secret visits to our house. Mom was over at her sister's in Levanger and I can still remember how Dad almost seemed to become a different person when Berit walked into the room. I'd never seen him light candles before, but he did that night and all of a sudden he no longer seemed to think that red wine tasted like "undiluted blackcurrant cordial," because he poured a glass for her and for himself, and in the long-stemmed blue crystal glasses at that, the ones that Mom had bought at the pottery in Grong and that Dad had sworn he would never drink from because it was pretentious crap and sheer madness to spend so much money on glasses when you could get ten times as many for half the price in an ordinary shop. And it didn't stop there, because he didn't drain his glass in two or three gulps, he didn't curse and swear and he didn't start pontificating on this subject or that. But what impressed me most of all was that he didn't just listen to Berit when she started coming out with what my dad would normally have dismissed as "rubbish" or "drivel," "sentimental claptrap" or "female tittle-tattle," he actually had a conversation with her and spoke frankly about himself and his affairs in a way I've never heard before or since.

I was nine or ten at the time. I sat up in my room, listening in on their conversation. At some point my dad had changed into a man I didn't recognize. Today it saddens me to think of that little incident. I realize of course that I was witnessing a scene in which a man was entering into a relationship with a woman and so it's not all that surprising that Dad turned himself into the sort of man he thought Berit would like. But it wasn't just an act, of that I'm sure, and so I can't rid myself of the thought that Dad showed some of his actual potential as a man and a human being that night. In fact this little incident makes me wonder what he might have been like if the Otterøyan macho culture hadn't set such clear limits for what a man could and could not be in everyday life. Maybe he would have been able to reveal those sides of himself a little more often, maybe he would have been a little less angry, less brusque and stern, a little gentler and easier to live with.

I may be rambling a bit here, but what I'm trying to say, what I'm getting at, is that we grew up with male role models who always did their best to seem like "real men." And here, perhaps, lies the answer to why you made up stories and lied as much as you did. Perhaps your lies and your tall tales—or many of them, at least—were attempts to present yourself in much the way you imagined Erik to be. I'm not sure, but I think the imaginary Wild West-inspired world that you dreamed up and became so absorbed in when we were playing up at the camp also had something to do with this. Because our Indian universe allowed you to play at being Erik. Everything we had read and heard about Indians—that they were brave, strong and proud, that they were wild and noble and could never be intimidated—these were all qualities we recognized from the way Erik and the other men around us tried to appear. So it wasn't only the Albrigtsens who had something in common with the culture of the North American Indians as we knew it. The ideals, values and norms depicted in the *Deerfoot* books and the *Silver Arrow* comics, in Captain Miki and Commander Mark, in *Centennial* and *How the West was Won,* were pretty much the same as the ideals, values and norms we knew from the macho culture on Otterøya, and when we thought we were being little Indians, in many ways we were being little Otterøya men.

Otterøya, July 2nd, 2006. An old acquaintance

I splash a little aftershave onto my palm and pat it lightly over my cheeks. The weekend at last. Oh, it's going to be good. It's been a hard week, I'm totally wasted, aching in just about every bone in my body. I lean over the sink till I'm almost touching the mirror, pluck a long black hair out of one nostril and straighten up again. "But now it's the weekend," I murmur, and I look at myself in the mirror and smile, hold it for a moment, smiling and trying to look bright and cheerful, and I feel this strategy starting to work: seeing yourself as brighter and more cheerful than you actually are really does make you feel brighter and more cheerful. I feel that weight starting to slip from my shoulders. I do up the last button on my shirt, straighten the collar, humming softly to myself—another way of fooling yourself into believing that you're in slightly more sparkling form than you actually are. Humming is associated with light-heartedness and when you hear yourself humming you tend to believe that you're feeling more light-hearted than you actually are. Even when you know very well it's a form of self-deception, you happily go along with it. "Or, you do anyway, Ole," I murmur.

I stand there smiling at myself for a moment longer,

then with a nod at my reflection I turn and and walk out of the bathroom. I'm looking forward to switching off now and doing absolutely nothing, except get mildly drunk with Helen and watch TV, maybe listen to some music or read a bit of *Growth of the Soil*, thought I'd remembered more of that book than I had, so I'd better finish reading it before the book circle meeting next Sunday. If there's one thing I hate it's turning up unprepared for the book circle, so I'll just have to keep going. I walk down the hall and into the kitchen. All's quiet in here, but Helen's sandals are outside the terrace door so she must have got back from wherever she's been. I wander into the living room and there she is, sitting hunched over her gossip mag and rolling a cigarette. I stop, smile at her.

"Hi," I say. She doesn't answer right away. "Hi," I say again.

"Hi," she mumbles, without looking up from her magazine.

A moment passes and still she doesn't look up at me. I stay where I am, looking at her. Have to watch what I say now, she's not in the best of moods it seems, the pain's probably bad again, maybe she didn't sleep too well either, it's hard to say.

"So, how's your day been, then?" I ask, regretting it as soon as I've said it. Now she's sure to make out that I know she's had a rotten day and that I ought to know better than to ask something like that. I'm getting to know her now, I know she takes just about everything in the worst possible way and on days like this she never misses a chance to take offense, maybe it's her way of justifying the fact that she's in a bad mood: shifting the blame for her misery onto me or something, I don't know. I look at her, feel myself preparing mentally for some sort of out-burst, an attack. But it doesn't come.

"Same as usual," is all she says, again speaking without looking up. She smooths the roll-up, raises it to her lips, moistens the wafer-thin paper with the tip of her tongue, turning the end from white to shiny gray. I smile and nod, relieved that she didn't seize the opportunity to take offence.

"It's going to be good to have a couple of days off now," I say. I make my voice sound brighter and more cheerful than usual, trying somehow to cheer her up along with me.

"Mm," she says, still not looking up from her magazine. She pops the cigarette into her mouth and gropes for the lighter that's lying on the table, finds it, lights up and inhales.

"Will I open a bottle of wine?" I ask, eyeing her and smil-ing. She glances up at me, juts out her upper lip and exhales downwards. The gray column of smoke breaks as it hits the tabletop and swirls slowly up to the ceiling.

"Not for my sake," she says, looking down at her maga-zine again.

"I bought that Australian one," I say.

"No, thanks," she says, taking a puff of her cigarette and flicking over a couple of pages.

"That one you really liked," I say.

"Yeah, but no thanks," she says, putting a hand to her mouth and picking off a shred of tobacco that's stuck to her lip.

"Fair enough," I say. It's kind of heavy going when she's like this, I mean I know she'd like to have a couple of glasses of wine with me. I don't know many people who enjoy a little drink as much as Helen, and I know she's forcing her-self to say and do the opposite of what she really wants to do right now. It's always the same when she's in this mood, maybe she wants to punish herself or something like that, I don't really know, it's not always easy to figure her out. Ah well, I'm not going to let her drag me down along with her, she often tries to do that when she's in this mood, so I have to watch my step. I just stand there for a moment or two, then I turn and stroll out of the living room. It's best to leave her alone for now, give her a little time and she'll come around, I'm sure she will. I can't see her staying sober on a Friday night, she'll help herself to some wine eventually, and whisky too. I go into the kitchen, take the whisky bottle out of the shopping bag and pour myself a shot, then I wander through to the computer room, pick *Growth of the Soil* off the desk and wander back through to the living room. I might as well grab the chance to do some reading since she's not in the mood to talk.

"Where's Daniel, by the way?" I ask. I raise my glass to my lips and take a sip as I sit down in the armchair. I feel everything in me gradually relax as the spirit burns its way down.

She looks at me, lowers her eyes again.

"Your mother asked if she could keep him till tomorrow," she says.

I feel a little ripple of pleasure run through me as she says this, feel like getting more than just mildly drunk tonight, I could do with it. Great to have a babysitter, it couldn't have worked out better.

"Oh, right," I say. I look at her and smile, but she doesn't glance up from her magazine so I open my book at the page I've turned down and start to read.

Silence. Then: "Ole, have you been reading my diary?" she asks.

I look up from my book, stare at her open-mouthed. What did she say? What did she just ask me? Does she really think I've been reading her diary. I keep my eyes fixed on her, but she just sits there smoking and gazing at her magazine.

"Oh, honestly, Helen. Do you really think I'm that bad?"

"I don't think anything at all," she says, still not looking up from the magazine. "All I know is that somebody's been reading my diary, or handling it at least. I left it on my bedside table after I'd been writing in it the other day, I'm quite sure I did. But that's not where I found it this morning. I thought maybe it had fallen down behind the table, but it was in the drawer," she says. "And that seems a bit odd to me."

And then she looks up from the magazine, fixes her eyes on mine and gives a hard little smile. She holds my gaze for a moment, then looks down at the magazine again. There's total silence. It's on the tip of my tongue to say that I haven't seen her diary and that I know nothing about it, but I don't, because it must have been Jørgen of course. Jørgen's been reading her diary to try to find out if I've told her about him selling hash. He knows that if I had told her Helen would be bound to write about it in her diary and he's fallen for the temptation to sneak a peek at it. He's scared, poor kid, of course, that has to be it. I can't tell her that, though, because if I do she'll know I went behind her back, and I don't want that, she'll just use that as an excuse to explode on me and I can't face that right now.

"Well, maybe it fell on the floor and I picked it up and put it in the drawer?" I say.

"Ah, and you just happened to remember that now?"

Silence.

"I haven't been reading your diary, Helen," I say, trying to sound as sincere as I can. "Christ, do you really think I'd do that?"

"I told you, I don't think anything at all," she says, slowly turning the pages of her magazine.

Long silence.

Then: "How about taking a run over to Sweden first thing tomorrow?" Helen says. I glance up from my book, she's looking at me with that hard little smile on her face. "We could pick up cigarettes, stock up the freezer a bit," she adds. I say nothing for a moment or two, just stare at her: she's out to torment me now, she knows I feel like getting drunk tonight and that I won't be fit to drive first thing tomorrow, that's exactly why she's suggesting this, suggesting it so as to make me feel guilty, make me despise myself, see myself as a bad husband, a bad father who'd rather get drunk than take his family on a trip to Sweden. She thinks I've been reading her diary and she wants to punish me for that, maybe she noticed that I looked pleased when she said Mom was going to keep Daniel for the night, she must have done, and this is her way of spoiling that pleasure. "Hmm?" she says, still with that smile on her face, making herself look happy to make it even harder for me to say no, I know that's why she's doing this, she hasn't the slightest notion of going to Sweden, she's just pretending she wants to so she can act even more disappointed and annoyed if I say no.

"We'll see," I mutter. I feel my good mood starting to melt away. After a moment I lift my book, act like I'm going to carry on reading. But she's not about to give in, she keeps goading me.

"Yeah, but don't you think it would be nice with a day

out?" she asks. "I'm sure Jørgen wouldn't mind a trip to Sweden either. To pick up some *snus* if nothing else. And I'm sure you're mother would be only be too happy to have Daniel to herself tomorrow as well," she adds, looking at me and smiling.

"We'll see," I say again. My voice is strained now, bordering on angry, and I don't want to give her the satisfaction of seeing me angry, because that's just what she wants, but there's nothing I can do about it. I fix my eyes on my book, try to read, but I can't concentrate and she can see right through me, I know she can, she knows exactly how I'm feeling right now. I don't take my eyes off the book, but I can tell that she's sitting there looking at me. I wait a couple of seconds and then I glance up at her as casually as I can. She holds my gaze for a moment or two then she snorts and gives a little sneer, looks down at her magazine again, as if to say: that's put you in your box, as if to say she's shown me up for what I am: a drunk, an irresponsible father who puts getting drunk before taking his family for a day out in the car. Or something along those lines. I'm not like that, I'm not like that at all, but she makes me feel as if I am when she carries on like this. Moments pass and then I feel my cheeks start to burn, feel my blood starting to boil. It never fails, she always has to bring me down when she's having one of her days, it's like she has to drag me down into the black hole along with her. I get so sick of it, I mean I know it's not easy being her, of course it isn't, she's been through so much in her life it's a wonder it hasn't left more of a mark on her than it has—neglected throughout her childhood, beaten half to death by Jørgen's father and on top of all that she's in pain and not getting enough sleep, so I can well understand if she has her bad moments but still, it's hard going being around her when she's like this. I have to be as supportive and sympathetic as I can, but God knows it's not always easy.

I pick up my whisky glass, drain it, feel like getting myself a refill, but decide against it. If I pour myself another drink now she'll only use that as an excuse to get even more uptight; she'll hold it up as proof that I really am the no-good drunk she's making me out to be and I can't take that, so I simply sit here, gazing at my book, but the words are just a blur and I find it impossible to read.

Silence.

Then Jørgen suddenly turns up the music in his room, I hear the thud of the bass and the voice of some rap singer blaring out up there again.

"Oh, for God's sake," Helen mutters.

I raise my eyes from my book and look at her, but she doesn't look at me, she sits there staring at the ceiling. I watch her for a moment or two, then carry on reading.

We sit for a couple of seconds. Then:

"Does he have to play it so fucking loud?" she mutters.

I glance up from my book again, she's still staring at the ceiling, her mouth is tight, her lips narrower than usual and she's breathing quickly through her nose, looks like she's getting herself worked up. The music's not that loud, in fact he's got the volume turned down lower than normal, so she's got no reason to get worked up about it, but she is, she's going to vent her anger and frustration on Jørgen. Either that or this is some sort of attempt to make it up with me, it could just as easily be that, yeah, that's probably it. If she'd really been mad at Jørgen she would be on her feet yelling at him to turn it down. Either that or she would have found something to bang on the ceiling with, but she just sits there, letting me know that she's mad at him, so this is probably more an attempt to make it up with me. She's complaining about him so we can find common ground in our irritation over the loudness of Jørgen's music. That's what she's trying to do. First she dragged me down, now she wants to build me up again, it's always the same when she's having one of her days, she does everything she can to put me in as foul a temper as herself and no sooner has she done that than she starts working to lighten the mood. I don't like it when she does this. I don't like it when she tries to control my mood like this, because that's what she's doing here, it's got nothing to do with her feeling sorry for being angry, at least I don't think it has, it's more like an attempt to gain control or something, an attempt to control me, something like that, yeah, unless it's the wine that's doing it, yeah, that could be it, she wants to have a drink every bit as much as I did and if she's to be able to have a drink without looking too foolish, she has to make it up with me first. What do I know. I look down at my book again, don't say a word, I don't feel like softening and meeting her halfway.

"You'd think he'd have a little consideration for the rest of us," she says.

I look at her again, hesitate, don't really feel like meeting her halfway but there's no point in getting all self-righteous about it either, can't face ruining our Friday evening just for that.

"Let him play his music," I say, looking at her and wagging my head, standing up for Jørgen a bit. That means even more to her than me getting upset along with her, I know it does. I suppose she sees it as proof of a sort that I like her son, that must be it.

"Yes, but listen to it," she says.

"I know, I know," I say, wagging my head again, still making light of Jørgen's loud music. "Why don't we put on some music ourselves," I say, with a nod towards the sound system. "It would save us having to listen to rap music at least," I add. I look at her, she doesn't say anything, but she gives a little shrug, letting me know that that's fine by her. I pick up my empty whisky glass and cross to the sound system, run a finger along the row of albums.

There's silence for a moment or two.

"Sure you won't have a glass of wine?" I ask, trying to sound offhand, keeping my eyes on the albums. I yawn and try to look as if I don't care one way or the other. I have to be careful not to smile and seem too upbeat now, mustn't rush it, because if I do I'll only disturb her rhythm, I know her well enough to know that. If I suddenly start sounding too bright and upbeat she's liable to lose the feeling that she's in control of the mood and then she could take it into her head to spoil everything again. "Hmm?" I say, glancing over at her. She screws up her nose and waggles her head, trying to look as if she can't decide but I know she's made up her mind to say yes.

"Oh, all right, maybe I will have a glass after all," she says.

"One second," I say. "I just have to find a record first."

"Just as long as you don't put on any of that Swedish golden oldies crap of yours," she says.

I look at her, give a little laugh, it's probably safe to laugh now.

"I don't know why you've got so much against old Swedish pop music," I say. "There's a lot of good Swedish pop music. Listen to this, for example." I pull out a record by Sven-Ingvars, teasing her a little by pretending I'm going to put on a golden oldie from the 1950s.

"Don't you dare," she cries, putting her head on one side and eyeing me darkly.

"Okay, okay," I say, laughing a little as I put the record back, I feel my spirits lifting, we're getting along fine now, we're starting to climb out of the black mood and into a brighter frame of mind and that's good. I pull out a Creedence Clearwater Revival album and slip it into the CD player. There aren't all that many records of mine that she likes, but she thinks Creedence is good, she's even been known to put on one of their records herself, I've noticed. I stand up, eye her questioningly as John Fogerty's gravelly voice issues from the speakers.

"Nice one," she says, nodding approvingly. I look at her and smile, step into the kitchen and pour myself a whisky, then I open one of the bottles of wine, get a glass out of the cupboard and go back to the living room. I set both glasses on the table and start to pour wine into the wine glass.

"Thanks," she says, smiling.

But I don't stop pouring, I'm deliberately slow to react, fill the glass almost to the brim.

"Whoa, whoa," she says.

And then I stop pouring. I look at her and smile innocently, but she's onto me, she smiles slyly back at me and I immediately feel a little ripple of happiness run through me. It's kind of like a sign that smile, a sign that we both want the same thing from this evening. We're going to get nicely drunk and chill out together.

"There you go," I say, putting the bottle down on the table.

"Thanks," she says.

I sit down on the sofa, pick up my whisky glass and take a little sip. It's good to be past that tricky patch. I feel a surge of happiness, feel my spirits lift, and I have the urge to say or do something to show this, but I'd best wait a while, I mustn't overdo it and seem too chirpy, otherwise Helen might find this brighter mood too good to be true and then she could take it into her head to destroy it all again, I know her. A moment passes, then I put a hand to my back and wince a little, I don't even have to think about it, I've resorted to this ploy so often that it's quite instinctive. I try to hide my happiness by pretending that my back hurts.

"Ow," I say, half-closing my eyes.

"What's the matter?" Helen asks. "Is your back hurting again?"

"No, no," I say, but my hand's still pressed to the small of my back, I'm still wincing. "It's okay," I say, trying to sound like I'm putting a brave face on it.

"Are you sure?" she asks. I look at her and nod, it feels good to have her show concern like this.

"Yeah, yeah," I say, taking my hand away from my back. "It comes and goes, I'm not sure what it is."

"Well, if it goes on like this you'll have to see the doctor," she says.

"Nah," I say.

"Yes, promise me you will," she says, putting on a worried expression, overdoing it a little, but it feels good nonetheless and I laugh and wag my head, like I'm playing down the pain in my back, letting her know that it hurts but that I can live with it.

"Men," she says, shaking her head despairingly.

I chuckle softly and take a little sip of my whisky. "Just

have to go to the bathroom," I say, and I go to the bathroom, pee and return to Helen. Her glass is already empty, she's sitting hunched over her magazine and doesn't look at me, so I seize the chance to pick up the bottle and fill her glass again. She looks up when she hears the faint glug-glug of the wine.

"Are you pouring me another glass?" she says, but she's only saying it for appearance's sake, I know her, she feels like getting drunk every bit as much as I do, but she likes to think that I'm leading her on.

"Huh?" I say, giving her a kind of puzzled look as I carry on pouring, act as if I'm not quite with her.

"Oh, well," she says. "One more glass can't hurt."

"No, I'm sure it can't," I say with a little laugh as I put down the bottle, a laugh designed to encourage her to drink with a clear conscience.

"Well, if I get drunk tonight, on your head be it," she says, and then she looks me straight in the eye and smiles that kittenish smile of hers.

"I'll take full responsibility," I say, with a little laugh. "But maybe we should go down to the beach and have our drinks there," I say. "Seeing as we've got a babysitter and all," I add.

"Oh, yes, let's do that," Helen says brightly, looking at me with wide, rather eager eyes. It feels good to see her like this. Okay, so she's overdoing it a bit, pretending to be slightly more enthusiastic and delighted by this idea than she actually is, but it makes me happy anyway. I smile at her, have the urge to pay her a compliment or something.

Moments pass and I'm just about to tell her that she has the loveliest eyes I've ever seen, but I don't get the chance, because suddenly there's a knock at the door.

"Yeah?" I call out.

I stay where I am on the sofa, my eye on the door and who should come in but Per, his massive body almost filling the doorway. He looks at me and grins, standing there in camouflage pants and a white T-shirt several sizes too small that's probably meant to show off his muscular chest and shoulders. I look at him. I'm not really in the mood for visitors right now, I'm a bit too tired to want any company but Helen's, but I return his grin and try to look pleased that he's dropped in, what else can I do?

"Well, hello there," I say. "It's yourself, is it?"

"Me and none other," he says, marching into the living room. After a moment Helen gets up and heads towards the kitchen. "You don't have to go on my account, you know," Per says with a look of mock surprise. He eyes Helen for a second, then he lets out that loud, bluff laugh of his. He looks at Helen, then at me and I chuckle and act as if to say: nice one, very funny.

"No, I just thought I might get you something to drink, that's all," Helen says.

"Oh, well in that case, don't let me fuckin' stop you," Per says with another laugh. "Right, well, I'd better sit down before I fall down, eh," he says, and he drops down onto the leather armchair, cups his hands round his knees and sits there looking at me. He's about to say something, but before he can get that far:

"D'you want whisky or wine, Per?" Helen calls from the kitchen.

"Whisky or wine?" Per repeats. "Only a townie would ask a question like that," he says, and he looks at me and grins, and I grin back, feel I kind of have to.

"What?" Helen shouts from the kitchen.

"Are you trying to insult me?" Per calls back. He slides forward to the edge of the seat, with a look on his face that says he's only joking, then he sits there with his eyes fixed on the floor and the corners of his mouth twitching with sly merriment. He moistens his lips and waits expectantly for Helen's reaction.

"What d'you mean by that, you stupid bastard?" Helen asks. There's not much she can't handle, she's neither upset nor shocked by Per's way of talking and Per likes that, I can tell. He looks at me and gives a little laugh, then he plants a hand on his knee again and turns towards the kitchen, smiles slyly and smacks his lips, as if to let me know that he's about to fire off another witty remark.

"Excuse me, did my wrist look limp to you when I walked in?" he calls. "Hmm?" he adds. There's silence for a moment, then I hear Helen laughing in the kitchen. "Fuck no," Per goes on. "You can keep your goddamn Ribena, gimme a whisky," he says, and then he turns to me and lets out a big, booming hohoho, and I look at him and laugh back, try to laugh as heartily as him, but I can't quite manage it, it comes out as a half-hearted chuckle and I quickly lift my glass to my lips so he won't notice, I take a sip and put my glass down again.

"Just bring the bottle, Helen," I say.

"See, now there speaks a real man," Per cries.

"Oh, yeah, you're such big men, you two," Helen says, coming into the living room with the whisky bottle and a glass for Per. "But maybe we should just go down to the beach now," she says, "while it's still warm and sunny?"

"Yeah, let's do that," I say.

"I just have to pack a few things," she says, putting the bottle and glass down on the table and disappearing back into the kitchen. I pour a drink for Per and fill up my own glass.

"Thanks," he says, wrapping his great mitt around his glass. "I'm half-cut already. I've just left Knut and his lady friend, you see, and they got out the gin," he adds before taking a little slug of whisky.

"Lady friend?" I say, looking at him in amazement.

Per smacks his lips, takes his time answering. He sets his glass down on the table and grins at me. He must be enjoying the feeling of having some news to tell and he's trying to prolong the pleasure by not giving it all away at once.

"Knut's got himself a lady friend?"

"Uh-huh, you mean you hadn't heard?"

"No."

"Ah, well," he says.

Two seconds.

"Aw, come on, out with it, man!" I say, raising my voice, letting him know that I'm as impatient to hear more as he wants me to be. He's enjoying this, I can tell, it's like the news he has to tell becomes bigger the more impatient I am to hear it, and he laughs happily.

"Well, you see," he says. "Three or four weeks ago Knut replied to one of those ads in the personal column. From this Russian woman. And now, fuck me if she hasn't gone and moved in with him."

I realize I'm sitting there gawking at him.

"Must've been love at first sight, eh?" It just comes out.

And Per laughs that big, booming laugh of his again. I stare at him for a moment, then I burst out laughing too. I feel a little twinge of guilt for laughing at Knut like this, but it was funny and I can't help it.

"Yep, must have been," Per says, coughing and spluttering a bit as his laughter dies away. "But for fuck's sake," he says, "I mean I know there aren't that many women to choose from here on the island, but to actually go and buy a Russian female," he says, and he looks at me and shakes his head sadly. I don't say anything for a moment, pick up my whisky and take a sip. He's probably trying to draw me into talking shit about Knut now; he's pretty desperate to have a wife and kids himself, Per, and he can't resist the chance to talk about how desperate other people are, I know. Maybe he's had this same thought, maybe he's considered getting himself a Russian female, and now he wants to check what I and other folk would think of that, testing the water to see whether we would laugh at him behind his back if he did. I wouldn't put it past him.

I put down my glass.

"And guess how old she is?" he says, nodding at me as he says it.

"No!"

"Twenty-three!"

He roars with laughter and points at me. "I know—that's exactly how I looked when I heard," he says.

"And he's what . . . forty-six, forty-seven?" I ask.

"Forty-six."

"Wow," I say.

"What the fuck do you have to talk about with an age difference like that," Per wonders.

"I don't think polite conversation is quite what Knut has in mind." And we both burst out laughing. I look at Per as he slaps his thigh and gives that big booming laugh of his, a laugh that fills the whole room, and I chuckle happily, pick up my whisky glass and take a sip. Maybe

I shouldn't have said that, I feel kind of bad for making fun of Knut for hooking up with a Russian female. I should really say something to let Per know that I don't see anything wrong with it, but I don't have the chance because just then Helen comes back into the living room carrying a blanket in one hand and a wicker basket in the other.

"You've no room to talk, you're eight years older than me, remember," she says with a nod to me. She takes the bottles from the table and pops them in the basket.

"Yeah, but I never said I was looking for polite conversation either, did I?" I retort. I turn to Per. He looks at me, then he slaps his thigh and roars with laughter again and I chuckle again.

Three seconds.

"Look at you, talking so big now that your friend's here," Helen says.

I turn to her, she looks me straight in the eye and suddenly that cold, hard smile is back on her face, an angry, almost menacing smile. I don't say anything for a moment, just feel the laughter fading on my lips.

"Nah, I'm only joking," I say, trying to keep my smile in place.

"Oh, is that what you're doing?" she says.

Silence.

I give her a look that says please don't, my eyes begging her not to grab this chance to fly off the handle, but she's not about to oblige me. She holds my gaze for a second or two then she picks up her wine glass, knocks back what's left in it and puts it in the basket too, then she blinks calmly, almost carelessly, turns and looks at Per.

"Well, shall we head down to the beach?" she says.

"Yeah!" Per cries. He doesn't seem to have caught any of this, he slaps his thighs and jumps up. I try to catch Helen's eye, but she's not having it, her glance kind of sweeps past me as she turns around and walks toward the terrace door. I sit where I am for another moment or two then I get up slowly from the sofa, watching Helen's back, tense and rigid as she marches off across the terrace. All it took was one rather tasteless little joke and she's a completely different person than she was only moments ago. She's slipped back down into that black hole, that hostile mood again, or at least she looks as though she has. I feel a flicker of unease as I walk out the door.

We cross the lawn. The terrace door of the cottage stands slightly open and the voices on the television can be heard all the way over here. Sounds like Dad's watching the football—World Cup semi-finals or whatever it is. We take the path down to the shore, no one says a word and the unease grows inside me, there's no telling what Helen might do when she's in this mood, she's liable to do anything, especially when the wine really starts to kick in. We stroll down the little hill, over the dry, yellow grass and across to the tables and benches on the beach, still without a word being said. An oystercatcher stands on a rock, piping away, and from across the water comes the low chug-chug of a fishing smack. Other than that all's quiet.

"Better get some wood for the fire," I say, making no move to start looking for it myself. It's a good way to get rid of Per for a while. I'd like to have a word with Helen without him around.

"I'm on it," Per says, just as I thought he would, playing the man of action he so wants to be. He wanders off whistling towards the little sandy beach that runs along the edge of the forest, he must have spotted some driftwood over there. I wait till he's out of earshot then I turn to Helen. She's set herself down on the bench, sits there with her eyes closed, letting the sun warm her face.

"Is something the matter?" I ask.

"No," she says, but she says it in a short, offhand sort of a way designed to let me know that this isn't true. She doesn't even open her eyes when she says it, just sits there, soaking up the sun. I don't say anything for a moment, just stand there watching her, and I'm about to say that I have the feeling she's annoyed at me, but I don't get that far because suddenly she opens her eyes and smiles at me, and it's as if all her anger is suddenly gone, it's like turning off a switch, and now she looks genuinely happy.

"What could possibly be the matter?" she asks, smiling and looking at me as if butter wouldn't melt in her mouth. I don't answer right away, I feel a bit confused, simply stand there staring at her. Moments pass.

"Oh, nothing," I say. My heart sinks a little at these abrupt changes in her mood, but I smile and give a little shake of my head as I bend down to the basket and take out the bottles. These sudden shifts, these mood swings, they confuse me, and maybe that's the whole idea, I wouldn't put it past her. I'm not sure if she's doing it deliberately, but she might feel that confusing me is a way of controlling me, like she doesn't want me to know where I have her, so she uses my insecurity to control me and make me the way she wants me to be. This is just one of many ploys she's learned to use earlier in her life, I suppose. When you get beaten and pushed around and have no say in anything whatsoever, obviously you're going to find other, more covert ways of gaining power, and this is no doubt one of them. I pour whisky for myself and Per and a glass of wine for Helen, pick up her glass and hand it to her.

"Thanks," she says, eyeing me.

And then Per appears. He didn't pick up the driftwood after all. Instead he's lugging an enormous tree root, he'd have done better to bring some of that driftwood, but Per is Per and he'll never change. He's like a little kid sometimes, and now he wants to show how strong he is.

"Wow," Helen says. "Isn't that heavy?"

"Heavy?" Per says, as if he doesn't know what she's talking about. He stands there with this enormous root in his hands, as if to let Helen know it weighs so little to him that he can't even be bothered to put it down while he's talking to her. He's so transparent that I'm almost embarrassed for him, but I can't help liking him for it as well, there's something sweet, something reassuring almost, about his rather simple way of behaving and I realize I kind of like it.

"Yes, heavy," Helen says, looking at him and laughing.

Per eyes her for a moment in mock bewilderment then he turns to me and shakes his head. He drops the root onto the ground with a crash and brushes off some bits of bark and dirt that have stuck to his T-shirt.

"Aw, that's nothing to a big strapping man like Per," I say, feeling this fondness for him and saying something I know he'll appreciate.

"Ah, I don't know. I used to be in pretty good shape, but my body's not what it was," he adds, as if it'll look better if he makes light of my words of praise, lend more credence to the compliment while at the same time making him seem like a man who doesn't like to blow his own trumpet. "But you don't really need to be that strong now," he goes on. "Twenty or thirty years ago a farmer needed to have a bit of muscle," he says, "but now . . . ," he looks at Helen, nods at her, ". . . with all the farm machinery we have nowadays, you could run the farm as well as I can, I'm sure." Then he turns to me and grins. "They soon won't need us men at all, Ole," he says, and he bends down, grasps one of the thickest branches on the root. "And then it won't matter so much if our bodies aren't what they used to be," he says, squeezing out a yawn as he snaps the branch in two.

"Oh, I think you're wearing pretty well," Helen says. She laughs and nods at the snapped branch, letting him see that she's impressed as well.

"Thanks," Per says. "I try to stay reasonably fit, obviously," he says, and then he turns to me. "Well I have to, you see, for the ladies. If there's one thing I've learned it's that women are lying when they say they don't like a bit of muscle, so from that point of view the old biceps do still come in handy," he says and then he turns to Helen again. "Isn't that right, that women are lying when they say they don't like muscles on a man?" he asks her, laughing, then he pauses, turns to me again with a taunting look in his eyes. He's like a little kid, making fun of me because I'm not as muscular as him.

"Are my muscles that puny?" I ask, pretending to sound a little surprised and looking down at my arms, then I look up at Helen and Per again. Neither of them says anything right away, but they exchange glances that say, "Yes, they are actually," and then they both burst out laughing, laughing at how puny my muscles are. I shouldn't let it bother me, I know—I mean, how childish can you get—but I feel it getting to me a bit all the same.

"Nah, your muscles are just the right size," Helen declares, sounding like a mother soothing a hurt child or something. She pauses, then she meets Per's eye and bursts out laughing again, and Per starts to laugh too, and it's getting to me more and more, I'm starting to get a little annoyed, but I don't let it show. Instead I act as though I despair of them, shake my head and try to look like someone who's pretending to be crestfallen.

"Okay, okay," I say. "Fortunately, though, there are other bits of me that are big enough for you." It just slips out and I'm feeling quite pleased with this remark, it gives my self-esteem a little boost, I can tell, firing off a retort like this. Okay, so it was a bit crude, but it was funny. I glance at Per, chuckling happily, and Per gives his big booming laugh again.

"Yes, well I know how upset it makes you if I don't say that," Helen says, tipping her head back and draining her glass in one gulp. Then she puts down her glass and looks me in the eye. And suddenly she's wearing that cold, hard smile again. It's like turning a switch off and on. I just don't get it.

"Ah, now it's all coming out," I mutter and I try to laugh, but don't quite manage it.

"Pour me some more wine, will you," Helen says, pushing her glass over to my side of the table.

"Please will you pour me some more wine, you mean," I reply, doing my best to keep it light and playful, and I look at her and smile.

"Are you going to start dictating how I should talk now too?" she asks, still smiling that cold, hard smile.

"No, I might as well try to dictate the wind and the weather," I say, still keeping it light and playful. I look at

Per and give a little laugh, then I turn to Helen again. She's just sitting there looking straight at me and smiling that hard smile of hers.

"So, do I get some more wine?" she asks, motioning towards her empty glass. "Or have you perhaps decided that I've had enough?"

"Well, it is nearly bedtime," I say, ignoring her aggressive tone and manner and still keeping my tone light and playful, possibly in an attempt to lure her into a different, less hostile frame of mind, I don't know. "Oh, well," I say, and I pick up the wine bottle and refill her glass. She's a bit drunk already, I can tell just by looking at her, it doesn't take much at all with those pills she's on. She's already in a very different place from me. I set down the bottle, shake my watch out of my shirtsleeve.

"Gosh, is it only ten o'clock?" I say.

"Yeah, yeah," Helen says. "I know, the night's still young."

"Huh?"

"Why can't you just be a man and ask me not too drink so fast?" she says, and she looks at me and grins as she picks up her glass and takes a big gulp. I don't say anything for a moment, don't exactly know what to say. I have every reason to ask her not to drink so fast, but that's not actually what I meant. A moment passes, then she puts down her glass and looks at Per. "Ole doesn't like it when I get drunk, you see, because then he's got no control over me," Helen says with a rippling little laugh. "But now," she suddenly announces in a bright, jaunty voice, "I'm going for a dip." She jumps up and starts taking off her clothes. She pulls her shirt over her head and tosses it onto the bench, then she reaches her hands behind her back, unfastens her

bra and slips it off. I just sit there staring at her, desperation tearing at my gut, and I can't get a word out. I try to
smile and look as if this isn't anything to get upset about,
but it's a pretty agonized smile. A moment passes, then
she bends down and pulls off her underpants as well. She
smiles at us, trying to look as if there's nothing the slightest bit shocking about this. "Anyone want to join me?"
she asks as she throws her underpants on top of her shirt.

Silence. "Hmm?" she says.

"I think I'll pass," I say.

"Me too," Per says, taking care not to look at her, he
must realize how embarrassing this is for me and I suppose he wants to spare me that much at least. He may
come across as loud-mouthed and uncouth, Per, he's not
always as tactful as he might be, but he can tell that I'm
not happy about this.

"Oh, well," Helen says in a kind of airy, girlish voice,
then she makes her way down to the water. I watch her
tiptoeing unsteadily over the wet, blue-black stones, we
don't say a thing, Per and I, the crackling of the fire and
the occasional cry of a gull are all that break the silence. I
glance at Per as I put my hand to my whisky glass, feel a
surge of warmth and affection for him. I really appreciate
the way he's dealing with this. He can be a bit too brash
and blunt, Per, but he's being tactful here, pretending there's
nothing wrong, behaving the way a good friend should, he
doesn't so much as glance at Helen.

"Oh, by the way, I ran into Eva in town this morning,"
Per says, looking at me and shaking his head. "Christ, she's
aged. I hardly recognized her."

"Oh?"

"Just the way she was dressed, like an old bag."

"I can't say I've noticed, although I see her almost every day at Daniel's nursery," I say. "It's just the same as with that guy I see in the mirror every morning," I add, shooting a quick glance at Helen and giving a little laugh, she's waist-deep in the water now, shivering and looking as though she's plucking up the courage to duck right under. I turn back to Per.

"Yeah, time flies," he says. He looks at me with his bleary, boozy eyes and gives a little laugh as well. "It's pretty scary," he adds.

"Yep," I say. I look at him and smile as I take a sip of my whisky, then I notice the grave look in his eyes. He holds my gaze, smiles a little uncertainly. He's looking at me the way people do when they want to say something, but aren't sure whether it's okay to do so. Maybe he wants me to say that I find it scary too, the thought of how quickly the time goes, not just reply flippantly the way I just did, but say it like I really mean it. He's scared and he wants to hear someone say that that's perfectly normal, maybe that's what he's angling for. I put down my glass and just then I hear Helen squeal. I shoot another glance in her direction, she's in up to her shoulders, gasping as she tries to acclimate herself to the freezing cold water.

"Aw, I think everybody our age has their moments," I say, turning to look at Per again. I have to try to humor him a little. "I mean, we're at that age when it starts to dawn on us that we're not going to live forever and that we're not going to achieve all the goals we once set for ourselves." I say. "It comes as a shock to a lot of people to realize this," I go on, trying to somehow make it easier for him by making out that it's perfectly normal to worry about such things, although I'm not entirely sure what it is that's worrying him, but I don't think I'm too far off the mark.

"Yeah, right," he says. There's a kind of a glow in his bleary, booze-soaked eyes, he gazes at me intently, waiting to hear what I'm going to say next, waiting maybe for me to tell him about something that came as a shock to me, something that will make it easier and less embarrassing for him to tell me what's worrying him.

The fire crackles and some glowing embers fly out from one side. I follow them with my eyes, watch how the wind catches them and carries them up and out across the water where they die and disappear.

"Yep," I say. "I have my black days too, you know."

He nods, but doesn't say anything, eyes me gravely, waiting for me to tell him more about these black days and what they involve. But I don't say anything, don't quite know what to say. It's a bit sudden all this and I'm feeling a little confused, it isn't like the Per I know at all, to talk so openly about things like this. I don't remember ever seeing him like this before and it knocks me a little off-balance, suddenly it's like I don't know where I have him.

"But you've done well for yourself, man," he says. "New baby son and all that."

"Yeah, I know," I say, then I stop. I don't really know what to say so I just sit there waggling my head. "I have, but . . . it's just that . . . everybody who has kids says it's the greatest thing that's ever happened to them. And it is, in a way . . . but sometimes I find myself thinking it's all a big lie, a lie that we need to believe in if we're to cope with all the challenges of being a parent," I say. "That it's something we tell ourselves to give us the strength to get through each day or something like that," I add, not exactly sure where all this is coming from, not exactly sure why I'm saying it either, maybe it's an instinctive attempt to comfort him by reminding him that it's not all sunshine and roses for me either, I don't know.

"But you love him, don't you?"

"I'd give my life for him without a second thought," I say like a shot. I look Per straight in the eye as I say it and I feel a little thrill run through me, because it was so spontaneous, which only goes to show that it must be true, and that makes me happy.

"There you are then," Per says. "Now me, I don't have anyone I'm willing to give my life for." He gives an anxious grin as he picks up his glass, keeps his eye fixed on mine as he drinks, watching carefully to see how I'll react to what he's saying. I look at the table, gaze at a white splatter of congealed bird shit. Just for a second, then I look up at him again, this really isn't the Per I know and I realize that I'm growing more and more uncertain, I don't really know what to say, so I just sit there, playing for time.

"But at the same time you have to remember that things don't necessarily get any easier just because you have a kid," I say, following the line I started with, trying to make his problem seem smaller by reminding him that life's not exactly a walk in the park for me either. "There are times when I feel like running from the whole deal," I say, "and there are times when I'm so shit-scared . . . that I've made the wrong choices or that I'm not up to it all, stuff like that . . ."

"There've been days when I didn't dare go out of the house," he says suddenly.

There's silence. He looks me straight in the eye, with that anxious grin on his face, like he's waiting to see how

I'll react. I don't say anything, don't know what to say, because this definitely isn't the Per I know, and I feel a surge of unease.

"Sometimes, when I'm out among people I get so scared I break out into a cold sweat and it's like I can't breathe," he goes on. "And one day last week when I was in the supermarket I left my groceries out after I'd paid for them because I couldn't even stay long enough to put them into the shopping bags," he says, and he gives a strained, high-pitched laugh, still looking me straight in the eye, and I'm growing more and more uneasy because I'm liking this less and less. It's good that he dares to be more open than he usually is, but still, it's not right to go dumping all of this on me out of the blue, we're not such close friends any more, after all. And anyway, he's a bit drunk himself now, it might be hard for us to look each other in the eye later if he's going to blurt out stuff like this. I pick up my whisky glass, take a sip and put it down again, then I look up at Per. I really don't feel like continuing this conversation, not now, I've got more than enough to worry about at the moment and I can't cope with acting as confessor for Per as well, I don't have the energy for it, but I can't give him the brush-off either. I know how much it costs Per to tell me what he's just told me. It's not the sort of thing a man from around here does just like that so I have to at least try to seem interested.

"Phew," I say.

Silence. Per just sits there looking straight at me. A moment, and then his cheeks start to flush.

"Yeah, phew is right," he says, then he grins and I feel a wave of mild panic wash over me: he thinks I don't want to know. He tells me something really serious and all I can say is "Phew"? Like I'm belittling his problems, as good as saying that I really don't want to hear about it, and now he's sitting there looking red-faced and embarrassed. He tries to disguise it with a grin, but I can see that he's embarrassed and he knows I can see it.

"Oh no, I didn't mean it like that," I say.

"Like what?" Per asks, still grinning.

"Well, I . . . ," I say, then I shut my eyes and shake my head. "I mean, have you tried to get help?" I ask, trying to pick up where we left off, trying to show him that I really am interested and that I do care, but it's too late, he's realized that I really don't feel like talking about this and that I'm only asking because I feel I should.

"Nope," he says cockily, reaching for his glass. "Aw, what the fuck—cheers!" he cries and he looks me straight in the face and grins, then he tips back his head, drains the glass in one gulp and slams it down on the table, still staring me in the face, flushed and grinning. There's a wild light in his eyes now, I can see the fire reflected in them, but this wild look can't just be put down to that, there's something else too, he looks almost crazy. It's only there for a second or two and then he pulls himself together, looks down at the table, stays like that for a moment, then raises his eyes to me again. He's still grinning, but his eyes seem calmer.

"Can I take another drop of your whisky?" he asks in a rather gruff voice, nodding at the bottle.

"Of course," I say and I pick up the bottle and pour whisky for both of us.

Then Helen comes tiptoeing back up over the rocks, shivering and bent double with her arms wrapped around herself.

"Brr, it's freezing out there," she says, planting herself in front of the fire. She's covered in goosebumps, shivering and chattering. "Ole, could you run up to the house and get me a towel?" she asks.

I don't answer straight away. I don't like the idea of leaving her alone here with Per with no clothes on. It's bad enough for her to strip off and go skinny-dipping in front of another man, but it would be even worse for her to be left here stark naked while I'm up at the house. I can't bring myself to say this straight out, but I look her in the eye, make it quite clear that I'm not happy about this.

"Well, could you?" she asks, acting all innocent, smiling at me as if butter wouldn't melt in her mouth.

"Oh, all right," I say, getting up from the bench. I hold her eye for a second longer, but she's still acting innocent and my stomach wrenches as I turn and start to walk up the path. It'll be good to get away from Per for a minute or two after what just happened—a little break, to give us a chance to forget what's been said and then we can talk about something else, but I don't like leaving Helen alone with him, not when she doesn't have a stitch on. I've never been a particularly jealous man, but there are limits and I don't trust her either, not when she's in this mood. I walk up the little hill, doing my best to walk as fast as I can without looking as if I'm hurrying, don't want to look like a jealous man who's terrified of what his girlfriend might get up to. I don't look back either, walk straight ahead at a normal pace until I'm out of sight and then I break into a run. I run all the way up to the house, up onto the terrace, through the living room and into the bathroom. I whip a bath towel off the shelf and dash out again. I bound back down the path until I'm almost at the top of the hill, then

I slow to a walk again and stroll down the slope, looking down at them: Helen huddled in front of the fire and Per still sitting where he was when I left. I don't quite know what I had imagined, but I feel relieved at any rate. I go over to her and hand her the towel.

"That was quick," she says. She knows full well that I ran half the way and she's making no secret of it. She looks at me and grins as she starts to dry her hair.

"Yep," is all I say, smiling back at her and playing it cool. I sit down on the bench, take a drink of my whisky and gaze out across the sparkling blue fjord. The water's like glass. On the other side, the island of Jøa lies bathed in the sort of warm, golden light that only the low evening sun can give. I put down my glass and look across at Helen. She's fiddling with the catch on her bra, tongue between her teeth.

"Per, could you help me with this?" she says. "My fingers are so cold I can't hook it up." She looks at Per and smiles and Per smiles back. I look at them and feel my stomach wrench again. I don't like this, it's not right, she should have asked me, not Per, but I try to look as if nothing's amiss.

"Well, I've actually got more experience of unhooking those things than hooking them up," Per says, "but I guess I can manage that as well." He eyes Helen and laughs that coarse laugh of his, and Helen laughs back, glancing me as she does so, hoping to see me looking upset now, that's what she wants, I know it is, but I won't give her the satisfaction. I look at them, force a little laugh as well, as if I'm chuckling at Per's joke, then I turn away, watch a couple of eagles circling over Tømmervikfjell, hardly using their wings, gliding around and around up there. I take another sip of my whisky, conscious that I'm getting angry, resentment starting to smolder inside me. I've had just about enough of her behavior, I'm getting sick of her walking all over me, but no fucking way am I going to give her the satisfaction of seeing me lose my head. I'm going to have to play it as cool as I can, let her carry on, she'll just have to take the consequences later, and this time I'm going to be firm, I'm not going to give in to tears or pleading. I've warned her before, but now I've had it, I'm not putting up with this any longer.

"You'll have some more, right?" I hear Helen say. She's dressed now and she's sat down next to Per. She leans across the table and grabs the whisky bottle.

"Yes, please," Per says.

I feel like saying that it's actually my whisky, not hers, but I bite my tongue. I gaze up at the two eagles and listen to the glug-glug of whisky being poured. After a moment or two I hear the sound of the bottle being set back down on the table. She might have asked if I wanted a top-up as well, but no. I turn and look at my glass: just as I thought, she didn't pour any for me either, only for Per. I turn away again, stare at the fire, feel myself growing angrier and angrier, but I try to look as if everything's fine. A couple the conversation they were having while I was up at the house fetching the towel. Per's talking about some apprentice who's apparently as thick as two short planks. He's not the brightest spark himself, Per. That's probably why he's brought up the subject of this apprentice, in an attempt to seem smarter than he actually is.

"I asked him to run down to the ironmongers and buy three kilos' worth of anvil clangs and he actually fuckin' fell for it," Per says, and he roars that coarse laugh of his again. And Helen gives him what he wants, she screams with laughter at this story, although she doesn't think it's funny, I know she doesn't, but she laughs anyway. I shoot a glance at them, feel like coming right out and saying that that story's as old as the hills, it's not something that ever happened to Per, but I don't, I just turn away and stare at the fire. I can't be bothered pretending I think it's funny, so instead I try to look as if I'm miles away. I might as well be, they're both pretty plastered and we've slipped further and further apart, so I'm not really with them any more. After a minute or so I turn to to look at them, they're sitting there gazing into each other's eyes, looking like they have some kind of understanding, and it stabs at my heart. It only lasts a second then their eyes unlock and they pick up their glasses. I don't say anything, but it stabs at my heart, tears at my gut and my resentment smolders more and more fiercely. I don't let it show, though. I won't let her see it, no fucking way am I going to give her the satisfaction of seeing that I'm jealous, because that's just what she wants, but there's no way I'm going to indulge her. Moments pass and then they start talking again. I should probably say something too, ought to take some part in the conversation, but I don't, I can't. The talk flows so easily between them, their words weaving together so naturally and it seems more and more difficult to say something that wouldn't be out of place, so I just sit here, slipping further and further away from them. I'm about to refill my glass, but I think better of it, I'm not in the mood to drink any more, I think it's time to bring this party to a close. I give it a moment or two then I stretch my arms above my head and yawn. I'm not tired, but I open my mouth wide and give a big, long yawn, as a hint to Per that it's about time to call it a night, that the party's over and it's time he went home.

"Aa-ah," I say, yawning and sighing.

"Tired?" Per asks.

"Hmm?" I say, acting as if my mind was elsewhere, acting a little woozy.

"Are you tired?"

"No, no," I say, but I rub my eye with my knuckle to make him think that I am. I wait a moment and then I turn and meet Helen's eye. She's onto me, I can tell, she knows what I'm up to. She flashes me a rather contemptuous little grin, then turns back to Per. She has a big smile on her face, acting even more bright and bubbly than she's been up till now, speaking even more animatedly, laughing even louder. Moments pass, then she suddenly edges even closer to Per, does it as if purely by accident, does it in a way that she can excuse later, if I confront her with it, by saying that she was just so caught up in the conversation. I feel my stomach turn at the sight, feel a silent scream slice through me, but I just sit here, trying to look as if there's nothing amiss, sit here acting as if I don't care, and I don't want to care. I wish I didn't feel what I'm feeling now, but I'm not made that way, my stomach turns and a moment passes and then Helen lays her hand on top of Per's, this too as if by accident, puts her hand on his as she leans forward, about to emphasize something she has said, and desperation grows and grows inside me. I just sit here yawning faintly, but it's tearing me apart.

"Gotta take a piss," Per says suddenly. A moment passes, but Helen doesn't remove her hand straight away, keeps it there a second longer than necessary before letting it slide slowly off his. "What goes in, must come out," Per says, with another laugh. He plants his hands on his thighs, gets up and walks off.

I look at Helen, give her a pained smile.

"Having fun?" I ask.

"Yes, as a matter of fact I am," she says. "Or is that not allowed?"

"No, of course not," I say.

"Great,"

Silence. She picks up her wine glass, drains it in one gulp, then she grabs the bottle and refills her glass.

"Don't you want any more?" she asks, not looking at me.

"No," I say.

"And why not?"

I shrug, give a smile that's a little feebler than I'd like.

"I thought it might be a good idea to have an early night if we're going to Sweden tomorrow," I blurt.

Her eyes bore into me.

"Ah, so we are going to Sweden now?" she says.

"Well, I thought you wanted to," I say, still with that feeble smile on my lips. "For Jørgen's sake, if nothing else," I add.

"Trying to make me feel guilty now, are you?" she asks.

"What?" I ask.

She looks me straight in the eye and grins.

"Christ. Using Jørgen to make me feel guilty," she says.

"Well, it was you who suggested we take a run over to Sweden, for Jørgen's sake," I say.

"Oh, ha ha," she cries.

"Keep your voice down," I say.

"Why should I?" she asks, her voice every bit as loud as before. She's drunk and spoiling for a fight and she's staring at me contemptuously.

I shut my eyes and clench my teeth for a second. I'm torn by indecision, don't want Per to hear this.

"Helen, please," I say under my breath.

I open my eyes and look at her. She holds my gaze for a second, then she sniffs and shakes her head.

"Okay, okay," she says airily. "Fine by me. I'm just a passenger, though, so I don't need to turn in yet. But just you go to bed, Ole, you want to be fresh and rested for the drive tomorrow," she says. "I'll stay up a while longer," she adds, looking at me and giving me that cold, hard smile of hers. She's goading me, she knows how much this hurts and it's on the tip of my tongue to ask her if she's enjoying this, but I don't, I just sit there doing my damnedest not to look as desperate as I'm feeling. One second, two, and then suddenly it's as if another person is looking out of her eyes, there's no longer any hint of anger or contempt in them. It's like a switch being turned on and off, now she's got that kittenish look about her again, she tilts her head to one side and flashes me a winning smile.

"My, but you were magnificent this evening," she says.

"Magnificent?" I murmur.

"Yes," she says, still giving me that winning smile.

"Well you certainly weren't," I retort.

"What's that supposed to mean?"

"What do you think?"

We sit like that, eye to eye for a second or two, then I look down at the table, run a hand over the top of my head and breathe a sigh. Then I look up at her beseechingly.

"Can't we go to bed soon, Helen. I'm getting kind of tired."

"I'm not," she says, and suddenly that hard smile is back on her face. She holds my eye, pauses, then: "And anyway, who is it who goes on at me about having a threesome every time we have sex?" she says. "Who is it who dreams about seeing me being screwed by another man?"

My stomach turns at her words and I feel a wave of despair wash over me, feel my face reddening.

"Helen, please," I murmur. "You're drunk. Can't we just go to bed?"

And then Per comes back. He strides across the wet, blue-black rocks, looking at us and smiling, and Helen smiles back at him. Then she turns to me again.

"What did you say?" she asked, pretending not to have heard me, she knows I won't ask again, not when Per can hear.

"Nothing," I say.

"Oh, right," she says, and she turns to Per as he sits down on the bench. "Ole's off to bed," she says in that butter-wouldn't-melt voice of hers, she knows how hard it'll be for me to go off to bed without her, but she doesn't let on. "But there's nothing to stop us staying up a bit longer is there?" she says.

"Not at all. We can't go to bed now, not when we're just getting into our stride," Per says, grinning and looking at me as he bends down and picks up a stick entangled in dry, brownish-black bladderwrack. "Hitting the sack already?" he asks, chucking the stick onto the fire.

I swallow.

"Yeah," I say, "it's been a long week and a long day and I'm knackered." I feel desperation tear at my gut as I say it. I don't want to go to bed without Helen, but I've said several times now that I'm off to bed and I can't bring myself to change my mind. And anyway, I'm not going to humiliate myself by sitting here watching her antics, I won't give her the satisfaction. I'm going to bed, she can do what she likes and take the consequences.

"Okay," Per says, he doesn't even try to talk me out of it, lets me go just like that. "Goodnight, then," he says.

"Goodnight," I say, letting out a yawn as I get up from the bench.

"Goodnight," Helen says, not even looking at me as she says it. I stand for a moment, stretching. No one says anything, the seaweed that Per threw on the fire pops and cracks and out on the skerry a gull cries, other than that all is quiet. I try to catch Helen's eye, but she's careful not to look my way. I don't say a word, just look at Per and give a rather feeble smile and he looks me in the eye and smirks back at me, the sort of smirk that says he know what's going on between Helen and me, he knows how I'm feeling right now and he does nothing to ease my pain, he does the exact opposite, he smirks, hinting at what he and Helen could get up to once I'm out of sight. I suppose he wants to pay me back for brushing him off earlier on. Either that or he misses having a woman of his own so much that he takes a sort of perverse delight in finding that other people's relationships aren't perfect—I'm sure that's it. I feel like saying something mean to him, something that'll hit him where it hurts most, maybe something about those panic attacks he was talking about, something that'll put a little dent in that tough guy image of his at any rate. I stand there looking at him for a second and then I just start to walk away, I don't say a word, I won't sink to their level.

Things gradually improved for the Albrigtsens. Most of the islanders condemned the attack on them and their home and those people who didn't openly express support and sympathy for Lasse and Lene tended to adopt a different and more pleasant tone when speaking of the "hippie family" after that incident. The headmaster of our school, Harald Hansen, even suggested throwing a big party for the Albrigtsens to show that the ordinary people of Otterøya did not want to be classed with Albert and the other yobs who had vandalized the townies' vegetable plot. This party didn't come to anything, it's true, partly because Lasse and Lene let it be known that they found the idea a bit tacky and over-the-top, and partly because its initiator and organizer, Harald Hansen, was forced to resign when he was struck by what could be called a personal tragedy. It came to light that he had faked his CV before his appointment as headmaster of Otterøya Primary and Lower Secondary School. Not only that, but in the course of the subsequent inquiry it came out that he had also falsified several of the main and most important sources cited in his university dissertation. Poor Mr. Hansen, he lost his wife, his job and his good name because of this and pretty much all of his life from then on was spent trying to make amends and prove to himself and

119

everyone else that he was, nonetheless, a decent and honorable person. Well, why else would he force himself to go on living here on the island, as my Dad always says, and why else would he invest all his time and energy in helping others?

But enough of that.

Another reason why people changed their opinion of the Albrigtsens, and possibly a more important one than their neighbors' desire to dissociate themselves from the attack and the vandalism, was that Lasse and Lene proved to be of much stronger stuff than the islanders could have imagined when the family first moved to Otterøya. As I've said, there were a lot of people on the island, my dad and Erik included, who had almost been looking forward to seeing Lasse and Lene struggle and eventually have to admit defeat. It wasn't that they were in any way spiteful, they simply wanted to be proved right in their belief that country life was far too tough and demanding for two fancy-pants Oslo types with romantic notions of living off the land. This in turn would make them feel better about themselves. Contrary to all expectations, however, Lasse and Lene proved to be every bit as enterprising, hard-working and tough as they needed to be in order to be accepted as "good people" by the locals. They were a bit disorganized, it's true, and they had way too many projects going on at one time, with the result that a lot of things were left half-done or unfinished, but they stuck at it and never gave up, not even when one particularly bad year was topped off by a gale that ripped off the new roof on the old farmhouse and smashed it to smithereens on the beach—and that despite the fact that they weren't insured, be-cause for some reason the Albrigtsens were against insurance.

That Lasse and Lene were always cheerful and smiling if you ran into them at the Co-op, that they had a sense of humor and could laugh at themselves, these qualities also had a lot to do with their gradual acceptance by the community. Take the day when you and I were over at Hauk's and Dad came to collect me. Lene was out on the lawn, emptying some bottles of home-made elderberry cordial that had gone moldy and was undrinkable and Lasse told Dad that she was making a libation to Mother Nature, asking her to grant them a bountiful harvest. Dad just stood there gawking. But when Lasse could no longer hold back his laughter and Dad realized that he'd been pulling his leg he roared with laughter himself and called Lasse a "rotten bastard"—a clear sign that Lasse had been welcomed into the fold and was almost considered his equal.

It wasn't long before you and Hauk and I were like the Three Musketeers, and as I say we spent a lot of time at the Albrigtsens' place back then. Although we were a bit scared of Grim, it's true. I don't know if he was ever diagnosed as being mentally disabled, but even though he was a big, lanky lout of sixteen he was happiest in the company of the Bruun boy, a young thug of just twelve years old, and your mother wasn't overstating it when she said he was "a bit simple." He couldn't concentrate on anything for long, his mind tended to wander and he had a hard time taking in the most basic, straightforward information. No matter how many times we tried to explain to him the punchline of some joke we had told, he would still come out with a comment or a question that showed he just hadn't got it. It was probably to compensate for the sense of inferiority this must have given him that he was so "physical," as Lene used to say. He was all right most of the time, but if for any reason he was reminded of how simple-minded he was he could turn really nasty.

Hauk was the same age as you and me, but very different in nature. He was tall and slightly built with long fair hair, blue eyes and clean-cut, almost feminine features—looks that made him infuriatingly popular with the girls. When he was thinking hard he always raised one eyebrow and this gave him a slightly hawkish appearance, which for some reason I felt fitted with his being as intelligent as he actually was. He soon showed himself to be the best in the class at math, I remember, and on his wall, next to a picture of the 1977 Liverpool team, hung a diploma certifying that he had won the Junior Chess Championship in Oslo in 1978—we were very impressed by that, you and I. This last, along with the fact that he was an exceptionally good football player, won him a lot of respect and made him popular with us and our friends, but even more importantly he was "such a nice boy," as your mom was always saying. He was the kind of kid who brought us grapes when we were sick or who could get upset and start to cry if he saw or heard about someone being unfairly treated or suffering some other misfortune.

But still there could be long spells of time when we had nothing to do with him at all. For one thing he never joined us in our favorite pastime: playing up at our camp. Even though building huts, climbing trees and running around in the forest were all things that Lasse and Lene encouraged him to do, they would not allow him to play with us up there because, as pacifists and members of the peace movement and CND, they felt that all games which involved fighting, violence or weapons could damage the fragile mind of a child.

A little of Hauk could go a long way, though. You used to get particularly sick of what you called his girly tantrums: his habit of sulking and moaning and resorting to tears whenever things didn't go his way, for example, or running telling tales to the grown-ups if somebody so much as laughed at him or slung some remark at him, and—not least—the way he sucked up to the teachers and was totally shameless when it came to boasting about his own achievements. All of this could make you and I so fed up with him that we would give him a wide berth. In fact that was why we eventually fell out with him completely. We were in your living room one day, playing some board game. He always got really mad and childishly determined to get his own back if we beat him at something he felt he was really good at, like nine men's morris or draughts or four in a row, especially if his parents could see that he was losing a game. His eyes would glisten with panic and desperation and if he didn't pretend to tip over the board by accident, scattering counters all over the floor and making it impossible to carry on with the game, he would either try to convince everybody that he had let us win or he would be overcome by a kind of pent-up rage that he couldn't control and that almost always led him to try to hurt us in some way.

The day we stopped being friends with him it was because of this last.

"Oh, by the way, is it true that Berit's been selling her body to Steinar?" he asked, looking at me and grinning spitefully.

I'm not sure he even knew what it meant to "sell one's body," but I'm pretty certain he didn't know what a terrible thing it was to say, because he was surprised, to put it mildly, by how angry Lasse and Lene were when they heard it. They both looked as if they wanted to leap out of their seats and tear the boy apart with their bare hands, but you and I knew of course that Hauk had only said what he said because he had heard his parents say it, and since our anger was therefore directed as much at them as it was at Hauk, there was no way they could act as referees, as they then tried to do. We got up and left and we never set foot in that house again.

Or maybe I'm wrong. Maybe we went back there lots of times after that and I've simply invented this rift between us because it fits with the rage we—but most of all you—felt when you realized that the Albrigtsens had thought of and spoken about your mother the way they obviously had, I don't know.

It's not for me to judge either Dad or your mom for having an affair and thus hurting Mom in a way that made life even harder for her than it already was. I don't know much about Berit, but I suppose that as a single woman she, like everyone else, must have dreamed of meeting the great love of her life. And even though he was married, Dad was also, to all intents and purposes, on his own, certainly after Mom was admitted to the psychiatric unit in Namsos.

Because of course she had to go into hospital. It wasn't safe to keep her at home, not for Mom herself or for Dad, who was just about dead on his feet by then. He had a sort of unspoken agreement with Mom's sister that she would take her now and again to give him a break, but that wasn't nearly enough because Mom was getting worse and worse. It had got to the point where quite frankly it was an absolute nightmare being in the house with her. It was terrible to see her lying in bed, limp and lifeless, smoking and crying for weeks on end, and it was just as terrible to watch her frantic attempts to pull herself together. But then she started to develop some rather more paranoid traits. She had been suspicious of Dad and me for a long while, accusing us of all sorts of ridiculous things, probably because she had no control over us when she was bedridden. She had no idea what we were doing, where we were or who we were with, and so she began to "get ideas," as Dad put it. But as time went on these ideas became positively morbid. We were used to hearing her say that we didn't love her, that Dad was running around with one woman or another and that I was only hoping that he would trade her in for somebody else so that I could have a new mother, but there came a point when she seemed to actually start believing these things herself. Her accusations were no longer simply an expression of the sadness, anger and self-loathing that her illness brought with it, they had been thought and voiced so many times that suddenly they seemed true to her. We could tell from the way she spoke to us, of course: there was a new weight to her accusations. But it wasn't until she started acting on her suspicions that we realized she was losing touch with reality. One day when we were having breakfast she got it into her head that we had injected poison into her boiled egg. She had spotted the tiny pinprick in the eggshell when she lifted the egg out of its cup, she said. What was that, if she might ask? Dad explained that we always made a little hole in the egg before boiling it so it was less likely to crack, but even though she couldn't argue with this she was far from convinced. Dad even offered to give her his egg instead, but she still wouldn't eat it. And she got worse. More and more often she would demand that we taste her food before she ate it, or she would suddenly decide to take my plate or Dad's and shove her own over to us. She was convinced that we had it in for her, and her efforts to keep tabs on us in order to catch us red-handed, as it were, became more and more extreme. She had been listening in on Dad's telephone conversations for some time, but one day we found a bag of cassettes in a cupboard and when Dad played them he discovered that she had hidden the cassette recorder under the telephone table and taped all our calls. It was a pathetically amateurish attempt at phonetapping, of course, but it was done in deadly earnest and when I think back on that day I find it strange that my dad let it go so far before having her hospitalized.

But eventually he'd had enough. The proverbial last straw came when she rigged up a sort of alarm system that was supposed to wake her up if Dad tried to sneak in and kill her while she was asleep. She had quite simply knotted one end of a length of string around the leg of the bed and the other to three pots that were tied together and balanced on the very edge of a chair. When Dad went into the bedroom to ask her about something the whole lot crashed to the floor with a terrible clatter. That did it. Dad said as little about this as he had about all the other things she had done, but he called the psychiatric unit in Namsos more or less immediately and the very next day he enticed Mom into the car. He was going into town to pick up some paint for the cottage living room, he said, and he would like her to come with him and help him to choose the color because he wasn't so good at that sort of thing. And surprisingly enough Mom fell for it. It wasn't until they turned onto the road to the hospital that she realized what was happening and it was all Dad could do to stop her from jumping out of the moving car. She freaked out completely, biting and punching and clawing, and Dad told me later that he'd had to pick her up bodily and carry her into the hospital. The worst of it was, though, that this only went to show that she'd been right in what Dad and I had always called her groundless accusations. She'd been claiming for ages that we wanted rid of her and clearer proof of this would have been hard to imagine.

I don't know when my dad and your mom started seeing one another. Dad seems to have had a reputation for being something of a charmer and a ladykiller in his younger days, so for all I know it could have happened long before Mom became ill, but at any rate it was while she was in the hospital that Berit started coming to see us much more often than she had ever done before. The excuse given to neighbors and everyone else was that with Mom in the hospital Dad needed help in the house and on the farm and that was true enough up to a point, but even though Berit did clean the house and cook and help out in the barn, the work was plainly not the main reason for her visits. The neighbors didn't latch on to this, not right away, but I did. As I say, I was only nine or ten at the time, which is probably why Dad and Berit made no great effort to hide their relationship from me. I suppose they thought I was too young to understand what was going on. But the mere fact that Berit stayed the night was enough for me to get the picture. Not that it was unusual for people to stay the night at our place, especially if the grown-ups had had a bit of a party, but Berit stayed even when not a drop of alcohol had been consumed and she stayed the night more and more often. Granted, she always slept on the sofa in the living room while Dad was in the bedroom upstairs, but it wasn't at all unusual for me to come down in the morning and find Dad's clothes lying scattered around the living room floor, or for Berit to have to run upstairs to fetch hers.

But however careless they might have been, they obviously didn't want me to know what was going on between them. If, for example, I accidentally walked in on them when they were kissing and cuddling Dad would make the most ridiculous excuses. Like the day when I caught them sitting at the kitchen table, holding hands: "Oh, yes," he said quickly, "I think your watch is running a bit fast." As if I was dumb enough to believe it was Berit's wristwatch he'd been so busy stroking. And then there was the time when my football training was canceled and I came home to sighs and groans and creaking bedsprings. I knew better than to walk in on them, of course. I was even considerate enough to blunder accidentally on purpose into the coat stand in the hall and knock it over, to warn them and give them the chance to finish and compose themselves before coming out and carrying on as if nothing had happened. And they did make some effort to act normal, but Dad was so embarrassed and flustered that he just couldn't. He tried to fob me off with a different explanation for the groaning and creaking, even though I knew very well what had been going on. "Hell, that wardrobe was heavier than I thought," he said as they came down the stairs. "I didn't realize it was solid oak. I worked up a helluva sweat there, so I did."

Later that night, after I'd gone to bed I heard them laughing and joking about this little incident. "Solid oak," your mother giggled. "I came up against something in that bedroom that felt like solid oak, but it was no wardrobe," she said. "And I worked up a sweat as well," she added and then they both howled with laughter.

Actually, that's what I remember best from that time, that she brought laughter and joy into our house again. Because Dad had been miserable for a long time. He'd been run off his feet, almost all of his time taken up with looking after Mom or working in the house and on the farm. And when he did have a little time to himself he usually spent it just sitting in an armchair staring into space. I still remember how much of an effort he made to look cheerful when I came home. He would paste on a strained smile and ask how I'd got on at school, but he could never concentrate on my reply, certainly not if it amounted to more than a few words. If it did he would usually interrupt me, with a gentle, but weary "Oh, really, is that right?" and then he would turn away, still smiling, and stare at the wall again.

But when your mother starting coming to the house, slowly but surely he became his old self again. She was so full of life, she talked all the time, laughed easily and often, and her good humor rubbed off on everybody around her. Dad started talking again, he became more enthusiastic and interested, he was happier and more carefree, and this man who had for so long been dour and dismal was suddenly transformed into a wit and a wisecracker, a role that he thoroughly enjoyed, I could tell. I remember, for example, the time when he fell off the ladder while painting the barn. This was after your mother had started bringing you with her when she came over during the day, so you were there too, in the yard with me, eating waffles, and Berit was sitting on the front step smoking a cigarette, tired out after cleaning the house.

"For heaven's sake, what have you done to yourself?" she suddenly exclaimed, and when we looked up we saw Dad coming limping across the yard, his eyes screwed up and his face all twisted in what was obviously pain.

"I fell off the ladder," he said, sinking down into one of the garden chairs with a groan.

"Oh, my God," Berit said, "you poor thing. Were you high up?"

"To start with, yeah," Dad said.

We had a good laugh at that.

Mom couldn't stand that side of him. It infuriated and annoyed her when he made quips like that, and this in turn annoyed Dad and brought a sneer to his lips and sarcastic edge to his voice as he remarked that being half-Nordlander she was probably incapable of laughing at anything that didn't include the word "horsedick" and the Trøndelag sense of humor was obviously too sophisticated for her.

Berit, on the other hand, laughed her head off when he came out with one of his wry comments and, no matter how hard Dad tried to act as though he couldn't see what was so funny, it was no good. He could stay perfectly deadpan for two or three seconds, but then his face would start to crack and eventually he would give up and burst out laughing too.

They were well-matched, so I wasn't the least bit surprised when Dad came to me one day and told me that you and Berit were going to move into the cottage. I don't know whether he was aware of it himself but not a day went by without him saying or doing something that testified to him and your mother wanting to live together. He became more and more keen to know what I thought of her. "Berit says you're such a good boy and so likeable," he might say, for instance, after Berit and I had spent some time together just the two of us. Or: "Berit was really impressed by what a big help you were with the firewood yesterday," he might say, even though Berit had shown up when we only had a little firewood left to stack, so she couldn't possibly know whether I had been a big help or not. I was just a little boy, but these reminders of how much Berit liked me were so frequent and could be so over-the-top that I realized his main aim was to assure me that I had nothing to fear if Berit moved in with him. Although I'm sure he would also have liked me to say as many nice things about Berit as he reported her saying about me. He also began to take an interest in how you and I were getting along together even though we'd been friends for years and Dad had never given any more thought to our friendship than he had to my friendship with Per, say, but now all of a sudden he kept wanting me to say things that would confirm what good friends we were, you and I. He dug and probed and asked leading questions designed to get me to sing your praises. He even started making special arrangements for you and me to meet and spend time together. "Would you and David like to go to the pictures this evening," he might ask. Or: "Why don't you and David bike down to the Co-op and buy yourselves an ice cream." It was as if he wanted everything I did or was planning to do to include you as well, and if it so happened that it didn't he would look surprised and wonder if there was something wrong. "So where was David?" he would ask if I'd been with Hauk and Per, just the three of us. "There's nothing wrong, is there? You haven't fallen out?"

One day when we were winding fuse wire around the spokes of our bike wheels I remember I tried to talk to you about what was going to happen. And to show you that I had nothing against Dad and Berit being together and them moving in with us I did more or less the same as Dad had done with me: I started talking about the four of us as if we were a family. "Maybe we should ask Dad and Berit if we can go fishing to-morrow?" and "D'you think Dad and Berit would let us watch *Centennial* tonight?"—that sort of thing. But you got so mad, I remember. Dad and Berit were still trying to make us believe that Berit was only working at the farm and that it was simply more practical for you and her to move into the cottage. But even though you must have known what was going on be-tween them you asked me what I was babbling on about. "Have you gone off your rocker as well now?" you said, a remark which obviously hurt me and upset me because it made me think of my mom. I didn't speak to you for a couple of days after that.

I'm not sure why it was easier for me to acknowledge what was happening than it was for you. Maybe it was because it's easier for a son to share his dad with someone than to share his mother with someone, I don't know. All I know is that I no longer felt I was betraying Mom when I accepted that Berit was a part of Dad's life. Because I had done to begin with. I had felt really guilty about Mom and even though I was a cautious child, almost too well behaved, I suppose I did sometimes take my distress and anger out on Dad and Berit. When she first came to live with us I was huffy and moody. I'd often make a point of mentioning Mom and asking whether we weren't going to go and visit her soon, as if to remind Dad of what he was giving up and probably also to pile some of the guilt I felt onto him. I remember I used to get out family photos from the time when he and Mom were still happy together and leave them lying around, where I knew he and Berit couldn't help but see them.

But after a while all this changed. Mom's absence probably made me realize how hard, not to say really awful, it had eventually been to have her living at home, and even though I wasn't an old guy like him I understood that Dad had to get on with his life. Besides which, I could see how fond he was of Berit, how happy he was when he was with her.

But once the two of you were settled in the cottage your aforementioned dislike of the new arrangement soon vanished. Although you did try for some time to maintain the impression that you weren't happy. Our drinking water tasted of iron, you said, and there were a lot more midges and mosquitoes here than at your own place because of all the birch trees and bushes that grew so close to the house, and the television reception was so rotten that you didn't even want to talk about it, it made you so mad.

But you only said these things because you felt you would be letting Erik and your childhood home down if you didn't protest against moving into the cottage, of that I'm sure. Because other than that, from the way you spoke and acted it was clear that you liked living with us. In fact you perked up a lot after you moved in. You'd always been moody and unpredictable, there were times when you seemed to withdraw into yourself and wouldn't talk to anybody, and there were times when those of us who were with you had to watch what we said or did because you could fly into a terrible rage over the slightest thing.

After you moved in with us, though, I saw little or no sign of this. I seem to remember you being more even-tempered, more relaxed. Which isn't to say that you were quieter in a physical sense, because you weren't. Quite the opposite, really: you were brighter and livelier than ever, firing on all cylinders from morning till night. But you seemed more easy in your mind, more secure somehow, less tense, less wary. You weren't so quick to take offense at things I said or did, nor did you have the same need to dominate me and boss me around. This may have had something to do with your having moved in to my home and feeling therefore a bit like a guest in the house, feeling that here at least you weren't in charge. In any case you certainly didn't seem to resent the fact that I was now on a more equal footing with you. You didn't kick against it, if I can put it like that.

I might be exaggerating this and representing the change in you as greater than it actually was, maybe because subconsciously I want to paint a rosy picture of our life on the farm, yes, I'm sure I do, but still: it's perfectly true that I remember you as being particularly cheerful and contented back then, maybe because you saw how happy your mother was. I don't know, but it's possible. I certainly felt very peaceful and secure when I saw how good Dad and Berit were together. I remember one day we were in the garden and a flock of little birds flew down and landed on the berry-laden currant bushes. The bushes were swarming with them, they seemed to come alive and Berit pointed to them, wide-eyed.

"Look!" she cried, "look at that!"

"Hmm?" Dad said, looking up from his newspaper.

"Look at all the birds!" Berit cried.

Dad turned around slowly and looked at the currant bushes.

"That's not all the birds," he said, totally deadpan, then he disappeared behind the newspaper again.

Silence for a couple of seconds.

And then all four of us burst out laughing.

Oh, I remember plenty of incidents like that from those days, incidents that testify to how happy Dad and Berit were together. And obviously this happiness somehow transmitted itself to you and me.

And of course the fact that Dad did his utmost to make you feel welcome must also have had something to do with your sunnier frame of mind. Not only was he better than ever at suggesting things for us to do together—us menfolk, as he said. And not only was he a bit more expansive and easygoing than usual, he also did all he possibly could to treat you and me exactly the same. We weren't living in the same house, I know, and the story still was that you and Berit were living in the cottage because it was more practical, what with her working at the farm. But the fact that we were actually becoming more like one big family was clear from the way he assigned us both much the same chores and accorded us much the same rights. We both had to muck out the barn and tramp silage and help out with all the other jobs on the farm, and we were both given pocket money and other forms of payment for this, always the same amount for each of us and always as often. Looking back on it, I almost find it a bit strange, admirable even, that he didn't make more difference between us than he did. He could, of course, have succumbed to the temptation to give me preferential treatment because I was his son, but he could also have gone so much out of his way to make you and hence Berit feel welcome that he ended up treating you better than me. But he did neither. This strategy even extended to him calling the two of us "my boys." In the Community Center Café in Namsos on a Saturday, for example, and other places where no one knew us he always referred to us as "my boys": "And coconut buns and fruit drink for my boys," he'd say. Or: "They're a bit boisterous, my boys, but if they're making a nuisance of themselves just let me know." That's how he went on. There was one time, I remember, when he took it so far that I actually felt a little bit jealous. We had gone to pick Dad up after he'd been on maneuvers with the Territorial Army and one of the other TA soldiers started talking about you and me as his two sons. Not only did Dad say nothing to correct him, but when the man pointed to you and said you were the spitting image of your father—the exact same eyes, he said—Dad actually said: "Aye, he struck lucky there, the boy!"

But I wasn't normally jealous of you, not at all. We got on extremely well and I thought it was brilliant that I always had someone to play with. You were the brother I had always wanted and it got so I could hardly do without you. If, for instance, I happened to get up very early in the morning I wasn't supposed to wake you, but I would either go out and start up the lawnmower or find something else to do that would make such a racket you'd wake you anyway and come on out. I simply couldn't wait, we had so much fun together: we made bombs that we let off behind the barn, shot at targets and hunted squirrels and crows with air rifles; we played pranks on Erik's brother Albert and on Johanna Mørck, the classic ones such as ringing their doorbell and running away and rubbing their windows with Styrofoam; we made bike trails through the forest, played football on the lawn and as I write this I'm looking at the old pouf in which I used to keep all the Legos that we still enjoyed playing with.

But what we liked best of all was to be up at the camp with the other Indians.

One day: warm and sunny, the occasional breeze sweeping through the forest and making lovely rustling sounds in the tall birch trees.

So, still perfect.

But suddenly a scream pierced the air.

"The Husvikings!"

It was Per. He was up on the hilltop, keeping watch, and he had spotted someone coming up the path from the housing development. It was the Husvikings. "They're coming!" he cried. "It's really them! The Husvikings are coming!"

Uproar in the camp. War cries and calls to arms and urgings to fight to the last man. "Charge!" you yelled, brandishing your spear above your head. And one of the little kids, the one that had picked crowberries and made warpaint from them, smeared three red stripes on each of his cheeks and muttered that it was now or never.

Ah, but there weren't as many Husvikings as we might have imagined, no horde, not nearly as many as there were bison on the prairie. In fact there were only a couple of them and what's more they came in peace.

"Can we play too?" one of them asked when you were standing right in front of them, fearless, arms folded. I don't think you took too kindly to them showing up like this and then refusing to be your enemy, but at least we had shown that we were prepared for the worst and not to be trifled with, so you decided to be magnanimous and show them mercy. Yes, of course, they could stay, you announced, after consulting Per and me, we three being ten years old and the elders of the tribe. There was plenty of room, they could park themselves over by the big rock covered in green moss. Go right ahead. The two Husvikings were very happy about this and they showed their gratitude by raving about what a brilliant place we had up here. "Aw, jeez, what fantastic shelters—especially yours, David," they said, keen to butter up our chief. And it was very wise of us to have a lookout post and stockades, they went on, because Grim had been saying that some day, if the mood took him, he might just come up and tear down our camp.

"Let him come," you said, seizing this golden opportunity to show what you were made of. And the rest of us were eager to do the same:

"He'll get a welcome he won't forget in a hurry," I said.

"He's got no idea what he's got coming to him," you said, looking as though you couldn't help but laugh at the thought.

"Oh yeah?" one of the Husvikings said, grinning at you expectantly. "So what does Grim have coming to him?"

But then your mind seemed to wander for a moment.

"Hmm?" the Husviking said, not to be put off.

You scowled at the little pest.

"You'll find out soon enough," you growled, not about to give anything away.

But this particular Husviking was a right little pain in the butt. "Grim could beat the shit out of everybody up here with one hand tied behind his back, so what were you thinking of doing? Were you going to set a trap for him?" he said. "Hmm? Was that the plan?"

That did it, your patience snapped. It was bad enough him going on and on at you like some fucking woman, but then he had the nerve to suggest that you couldn't run rings around anybody who came along. That was going too far. Beat the shit out of you with one hand tied behind his back, he had said. And in front of the girls, at that. In front of Karoline. You couldn't help but shake your head and laugh, it was so ridiculous, but I knew right away that you wouldn't be content with that. And sure enough, it wasn't long before you found a focus for your fury because it stood to reason of course that these Husvikings had been sent here to infiltrate our camp—you'd seen that straight away.

Huh?

Aw, it was no use playing the innocent. Why else had he been so keen to hear all about our plans and strategies, if you might ask?

But . . . ?

Ah, see, he had no answer to that.

The Husvikings protested their innocence, they swore they were innocent, but innocent or guilty, they had been found out once and for all, and the mood in the camp was heated now.

Scum!

Dirty dogs!

They'd pay for this, you told them and you gave orders for both Husvikings to be marched over to the totem pole and tied to it.

We had dreamed for ages of getting hold of an anthill and placing it right underneath the totem pole, but so far we'd had no luck with that, so the Husvikings could actually think themselves lucky, we informed them. Okay, so we did throw tomahawks and shoot arrows at them while they begged for mercy, but at least they were spared being eaten alive by ants.

They'd have had to be pretty hungry ants in that case, one of the Husvikings declared.

Two short grunts of laughter from the other Husviking.

Silence.

You looked at them.

What had we here? A couple of tough guys? Well, we'd see how cocky they were when we were finished with them, you said.

You dealt one of them a little slap on the back of the head, gave us the nod and we dragged the Husvikings over to the totem pole. Now they were going to get what was coming to them.

"I wouldn't want to be in your shoes," I said.

But the Husvikings still weren't scared enough for our taste.

They neither begged nor pleaded for mercy, and when it turned out that we had run out of rope and had nothing to tie them to the totem pole with, they actually looked at one another and laughed, calling us amateurs. They shouldn't have done that, because if you hadn't been furious before you certainly were now. Okay, so we could either make them run the gauntlet or scalp them, you declared, and when, after a careful head count, we came to the conclusion that there weren't enough of us to make them run the gauntlet, the time had come for a bit of scalping.

"Down in the dirt, where you belong," you snapped and you grabbed one of the Husvikings, hurled him to the ground and sat on his back. He was a year older than you, but even though he wriggled and squirmed and struggled to break free he didn't stand a chance. "Ole, gimme your sheath knife," you said. I promptly handed you the knife and, while Per and two of the little kids held back the other Husviking, you began to hack off your victim's hair. He howled and screamed, no longer taking it like a man, but you were blind with rage and beyond showing mercy. You said not a word, let the knife do the talking for you.

Silence.

"Look, he's got a bald spot," Per said after a while, looking at me wide-eyed and pointing to the Husviking.

"Yeah," I said. "He looks like that guy that drives the school bus."

Laughter from everybody all around.

But you weren't laughing, you grinned and let the knife do some more talking, then you stuck your hand in the air, holding up the Husviking's scalp for all to see.

Wild whoops from all the warriors.

Then it was the other Husviking's turn. He could no longer see the funny side of this either, but he could have saved himself all his tears and curses, because you were out for blood, hell-bent on revenge and soon you were waving another scalp in the air for the whole tribe to see.

Once more the forest rang with wild whoops. Then a hush fell again.

"Now get out of here," you told the two Husvikings. "And let that be a lesson to you."

And the two Husvikings slunk off home. Per and I and some of the little kids followed them down the hill a little way, leaping and dancing around them, and they had to put up with a fair bit of jeering and sneering for having lost their hair and grown middle-aged from one second to the next. Oh, how they sobbed and wept, those two. They were devastated.

But immediately afterwards, when we returned to the camp, it was my turn to feel devastated, because there was Karoline, gazing at you in awe and being so nice to you. Oh, my stomach knotted at the sight. She had never looked at me like that, never, not even when I worked myself half to death building a shelter for her.

"Had you any idea what you were doing when you got so mad earlier on?" she wanted to know.

"We-ell," you said, wagging your head.

She just didn't know what had got into you, she said, you were like a wild beast, she had almost been scared herself, seeing you like that.

Really? Oh but she didn't need to be, you said, you could never hurt her.

"No?"

"No, of course not, what do you take me for?"

Your eyes met and held for a second or two, then Karoline blinked and looked at the grass, just the way she should. She waited a moment, then she looked up at you again and smiled. Oh, how it hurt to see this. I had a good mind to break in with a question, any question, whatever came into my head, but I didn't. It was time I stopped kidding myself, there was nothing I could do and there never had been, I had no wild beast inside me, like you had, and a brave who has no wild beast inside him will find it hard to get a squaw to share his tepee.

And to a great extent this was, of course, what it was all about, I see that now. The camp was our training ground, where we learned to become real men, that's true, but it was also where we learned about becoming family men, about making a life for ourselves with a house and wife and children and all the other things that go along with this. We didn't know it then, of course, but the more I think about it, the more certain I am that that is how it was.

Otterøya, July 3rd, 2006. Paralyzed

My eyes flutter open, close and flutter open again, the bedroom window is wide open and outside the birds are singing. Suddenly I notice that Helen's not there. I lie for a moment and then a wave of panic washes over me, she's not in bed and she hasn't been here either, her duvet is untouched, as smooth and unrumpled as when I came to bed. I sit up, stare at her duvet, and my stomach churns, it knots. I sit like this, rigid and tense, then I lay my hand on my head, sit like this for another moment or two, waiting. Okay, that does it, I've turned a blind eye to a lot of things, I know it's not that easy being her and I've tried to be as patient as I can, but I'm not putting up with this, I refuse to be that much of a doormat. I swallow, shake my head, and feel this bitter resentment, this rancor, well up inside me. Moments pass and all of a sudden I smell bacon. I look at the clock on the bedside table, it's only a little after half-eight, so it can't be Jørgen who's frying bacon, he's never been up this early on a Saturday as far as I know, so it must be Helen. I swing my legs over the end of the bed, place my feet on the floor, get up and walk over to the door, stop and listen. Just as long as Per's not here, I can't cope with both of them right now, I simply can't. I stand quite still for a few seconds, but there's no sound of anyone talking, all I can hear are faint sounds of movement down in the kitchen, the occasional rattle of cutlery and the sound of a cupboard being opened then closed again, so she must be alone. I grab my jeans off the back of the chair, get a T-shirt out of the wardrobe and get dressed, then I walk out of the bedroom, down the stairs and along the hall. And there's Helen, pouring coffee into the coffee jug. Looks like she's just had a shower, she's in her dressing gown with her hair wrapped up in a white towel.

"Hi," she says, looking at me and smiling, standing there looking as if nothing has happened. She humiliated me in front of an old friend and now she's acting as if everything's hunky-dory.

"Hi," I say shortly. I don't smile back, don't even look at her, walk straight past her, pick up the newspaper from the kitchen table, walk through to the living room and sit down where I can see into the kitchen.

"Did you sleep well?" she asks, still acting as though nothing has happened, bustling about the kitchen as she's talking as if this was any ordinary morning. I wait a minute before answering, let her know that I'm mad, that I've every right to be mad, and she's well aware of that, I know she is.

"Yes," I say, flicking over a page of the newspaper, I wait another minute. "And you, did you sleep well?"

"Absolutely," she says, looking anywhere but at me and still talking as if everything was perfectly normal.

"Oh, and where exactly did you sleep?" I ask, with a little edge to my voice.

"On the sofa," she says with a little laugh. "I sat down

to eat the last of the pizza before I came to bed and I nodded off. I must have been a bit drunk."

"Yeah, you must have been," I said.

Silence.

My eyes are fixed on the newspaper, but I'm not taking in one word of what's on the page. Moments pass, then Helen starts to hum, like she's in such a good mood now. She knows it'll be harder for me to be mad and have it out with her if she's feeling cheerful. But she's not getting away with it, not this time. I've got a right to know what went on last night and this time I'm not backing down.

"So, did you sit for long?" I ask, with that edge to my voice, not taking my eyes off the paper.

"Not very long," she says. "A little while, I'm not sure what time it was," she adds and then she yawns, as if it'll sound more credible if she yawns while she's talking, sound more convincing, that's why she's doing it, I know it is. "There's only so many awful jokes you can take," she says and she gives another little laugh, like she's inviting me to put down Per too, wants to have a laugh at his expense, so I won't think she likes him as much as she appeared to do last night. That way it'll seem less likely that anything happened between them, that's what she's thinking, I know it is, but I'm not going to play her game, I could say a lot of things about Per, but I won't, I'm not dumb enough to fall for that. "Aw, he was all right, really," she goes on, toning it down a bit now—well, I mean she wasn't exactly unfriendly to Per last night and she knows it'll only defeat the purpose if she bitches about him too much, knows it will seem suspicious.

I don't say anything, just keep my eyes fixed on the newspaper and after a few moments I feel a great sense of weariness creep over me. My body feels as though it's wilting and I realize how sick and tired I am of this game, of carrying on the way we're doing now, it wears me out, it drains all the energy out of me and I can't take it any more. A moment more and then I lower the newspaper onto my lap and stare at her. I don't quite know why I do this, I just do it. There's total silence. Helen knows I'm staring at her, but she doesn't let on, she takes the pepper shaker down from the spice rack and sets it on the table, crosses to the stove and starts to turn the bacon, still trying to pretend that this is just a morning like any other. Then she suddenly turns and looks at me, just by-the-by like.

"What's the matter with you?" she asks, trying to look kind of surprised, acting like she doesn't know what's the matter with me. I don't reply, just sit there staring at her. "Ole?" she says, but I still don't reply. There's so much, I don't know where to start, so I just sit there staring at her, feeling somehow overwhelmed, powerless, feeling more and more drained and weary, I can't face fighting with her, can't bring myself to call her bluff, can't bear to hear her twisting what actually happened, distorting the truth, because that's what she'll do, I know, if I call her on this. She'll come up with all sorts of excuses and explanations and counter-accusations and I simply can't cope with being drawn into that maze right now.

"What's the matter, Ole?" she asks again, trying to sound slightly worried now, as if that'll convince me that she really doesn't know what's the matter. I look her straight in the eye, try to let her see that I know that she knows, but she looks genuinely worried, she puts on such a good act that it doesn't look like an act at all and I feel myself giving up.

"Nothing," I mutter, then I get up and walk out. I walk straight past her. I'm close to tears now and I won't give her the satisfaction of seeing me cry. I refuse to be the poor bastard who cries because his wife has been unfaithful to him, I won't let her think I need her that much. But she follows me, I can hear it, I hear her draw the pan off the burner, turn off the heat and come after me.

"Ole," she says. "What is it?" she asks, managing to sound both surprised and scared. She acts so well that she doesn't sound as if she's acting at all, but I know she is, I know it's an act. I walk down the hall, open the bathroom door and a strong smell of shit hits me in the face, she hasn't put the lid of Daniel's diaper bin back on properly. I step into the bathroom and close the door behind me, but the key's not in the keyhole so I can't lock it. I just stand there looking around for the key. I look on the floor just under the door, on Daniel's changing table and on the shelf next to the mirror—and there it is, lying next to a squashed tube of toothpaste with a squiggle of blue and white toothpaste trailing out of the top. I lean forward to pick it up, but I'm too late, she's already opening the door.

"Ole," she says again, looking at me in alarm. "Can't you at least tell me what's wrong?" she says. "I'm worried about you," she adds, and she sounds worried too, she both sounds and looks genuine. I don't say anything, don't know what to say. A moment passes and then she moves in close to me, strokes my cheek as she gazes at me with those worried eyes of hers, as if meaning to comfort and care for me now. First she crushes me and now she's acting like she's coming to my rescue. This is her way of controlling me, I don't know if she's aware of it herself, but I'm aware of it, it's a way of gaining control and power. I don't say anything, don't know what to say, I just stand here letting her stroke my cheek, letting her comfort me. I don't want to be rescued like this, but I just stand here, I shut my eyes and swallow, smell her scent, the scent of shampoo and cigarettes. After a moment I feel her other hand on my back, she draws me gently to her, my body is rigid, my arms hang by my sides and all of a sudden she kisses my throat. I feel her soft, moist lips on my skin, once and then again, she kisses me lightly all the way up my throat to my ear, blows gently in my ear, she's trying to turn me on now, she knows how horny I can be the morning after a night on the booze and now she wants us to have a make-up fuck, a quickie in the bathroom, and that'll be the end of that, I know her, and I know that that's what she's trying to do. Another moment passes, then I feel her hand on my crotch, she curls her fingers around my balls, squeezes gently and I feel myself growing hard, I don't want to get a hard-on, but I'm getting one anyway.

"Hmm, it's so big," she murmurs in my ear, saying what she thinks I want to hear. "I want it," she says, raising her free hand and pulling the towel off her head. Her damp brown hair flops down onto her shoulders and for a split second the scent of shampoo is slightly stronger. I say nothing, just swallow, but this is not on, I want to, but I won't, I know what she's up to and she knows I know and I refuse to go along with this charade, it's ridiculous, it's so blatant, too good to be true.

"No, Helen," I say, pushing her hand away from my crotch.

She doesn't say anything, she just stands there looking at me, a moment passes and then I sink down onto the shower stool behind me, place both hands on the top of my head, sit like that for a couple of seconds, then I lower my hands, bring my head up sharply and look straight at her.

"I'm sick of this, Helen, I'm sick of you trying to control me the way you do."

"Control you?"

"Yes," I say, "maybe that's not the right word, but . . . that's how it feels to me. You made a fool of me out there last night, you ignored me completely and flirted blatantly with Per to drive me wild with jealousy and then, once you've brought me down far enough, you come here acting like you want to comfort me, like you're coming to my rescue. I don't know if you realize it yourself, but to me it seems like you're trying to make me feel like I can't manage without you, to me . . . it seems like a crude way of gaining control over me," I say.

"In what way is it not easy being me?" she asks.

I don't say anything for a moment, this isn't exactly the question I'd been expecting and I sit there looking at her, a bit bewildered. I know, of course, that this is a deliberate move on her part, that she's trying to throw me off-balance by confusing me like this, she always does this and I'm going to have to watch what I say now and not get drawn into a trap, shouldn't forget why we're having this conversation.

"You're always talking about how it's not easy being me, why do you say that?" she goes on. Then she stops, looks me straight in the eye, and I hold her gaze for a second then look at the bathroom floor, there's a used cotton ball lying on one of the tiles. I reach out my foot and nudge it forward an inch, look up at her again.

"Oh come on, Helen," I sigh, "don't dodge the issue."

"I'm not dodging the issue," she says. "I'm simply trying to tell you there's no reason to feel sorry for me."

"I've never said I felt sorry for you," I say. I don't want to get caught up in this maze she's trying to lure me into, don't want to rise to the bait, but I do it anyway, it just happens.

"No, but you've always behaved as if you feel sorry for me," she says. She tightens the belt of her dressing gown, crosses her arms and stands there looking at me. "I don't need you to save me, Ole."

"Helen," I say and then I stop, run a hand over my head. "Stop trying to talk your way out of it, that's not what I said," I say. "Why can't you . . . ?"

"No," she snaps. "I'm not trying to talk my way out of it, I'm trying to tell you that it's you who's trying to control me and not the other way round. You like to see me as this poor, pathetic creature that you rescued from ruin, and you do everything you can to get me to see myself that way too, because that gives you a hold over me," she says. "You laugh at Knut and all those other guys who buy themselves some poor hard-up Russian woman, but you're no fucking better, you think you own me just because you own this house and pay all the bills and buy all the food. Deep down you see me as bought and paid for, so don't you fucking talk to me about power and control," she says. "All I am to you is another piece of equipment you've bought for the fucking family farm. You've only one aim in life, Ole, and that's to run this farm as well as you can and make sure that it stays in the family after you've done your bit. And in order to do this obviously you need a woman to have children by. That's why you brought me here."

"Helen," I say, gazing at the floor and putting my head in my hands. "How can you say such a thing, that . . . that's not how I see you at all, you have to believe me,"

I say, and I look up at her again, pause. "You're not just a piece of equipment to me . . . I love you," I say. "Truly," I add.

"I don't believe you," she says. "You may think it's me that you love, but it isn't, the person you love exists only in your head, Ole."

"Helen, please, don't say things like that," I say, and I realize that I'm close to tears, I swallow, clear my throat, trying not to cry. " I love you," I say again. "You've had to cope with so much shit in your life that you find it hard to believe anyone might simply want to make you happy. I realize that, I realize you need time, that you have to learn to trust me, but . . . we've been together for almost two years now, we have a child, you have to believe me when I say that I don't want anyone but you."

"Oh, would you listen to yourself, Ole," she says. "That's the sort of thing they say in those Wednesday-evening rom-coms on the TV," she says and she looks me straight in the face and shakes her head. "I've had to cope with so much shit that it's hard for me to believe you really love me, you say, but that's exactly what I'm talking about . . . you think that everything I think or say or do can be put down to all the shit I've had to deal with in my life. But you're wrong, I'm not the poor creature that you love, Ole. You don't have to feel sorry for me, and I don't need all the care and kindness and tolerance that you're constantly lavishing on me, quite the opposite really, it almost makes me want to throw up the way you're always trying to be so fucking nice, you're so goddamn tolerant that you end up not really caring at all, Ole, not just about me but about everybody. It doesn't matter what the fuck people say or do to you, you make excuses for them, and it . . . it drives people crazy, or at least it drives me crazy, it makes me feel like behaving even worse, it makes me feel like hurting you even more. Partly in order to punish you and partly in order to find out how far I can push you, to find out what sort of man you really are, to . . . I don't know, but . . . I feel as if I don't know you, in fact sometimes I almost have the feeling that you don't actually exist, you're so fucking self-effacing that I lose sight of you completely. You just go along with things, and you keep going along with things until it's like there isn't anybody there at all and Christ, that really fucking gets to me!"

"But why can't you just be nice back?" I ask. "I know it's probably pretty silly and naive of me to ask, but why can't you try to treat me the way I try to treat you?"

"Oh, for God's sake, man," Helen says flinging her hand in the air. She stands there open-mouthed, glaring at me. "Don't you understand what I'm trying to tell you? All this tolerance, all this kindness of yours, it's not worth the effort. And it's wrong to call it tolerance and kindness anyway, because underneath it's . . . it's nothing but sheer selfishness. I don't believe for one minute in your kindness and tolerance, Ole. I believe you're suppressing the dark side of yourself and I believe you only pretend to be nice and kind to prove that you're better than me and everybody else around you. You know something? I've never felt as dirty or ashamed or like such a bad person as I have since I moved in with you, and yet I've never been treated with more tolerance and kindness. Even when I was living with Tom Roger and he was beating the shit out of me I didn't despise myself as much as I do now, I'm telling you. It was easier to hang onto my self-respect when I was with him than it is now. Not only because he sometimes behaved like an animal and I seemed human by comparison, but also because it was easier to safeguard myself against his way of controlling me. When he beat me up we both knew that it would end with him crawling back to me on all fours, begging for mercy and forgiveness. And sometimes—not often, just now and again—I'd actually do or say something that I knew would goad him into battering me, because that was one sure way of getting him to go to pieces completely and that gave me at least a little of the control and the self-respect that I needed and that I normally had so fucking little of. It sounds totally sick, but that's actually how it was with us by the end. But with you, Ole, I get nowhere. No matter what the fuck I do, I'm still the poor pathetic creature that you want me to be, no matter what the fuck I say or do I always end up confirming the picture you've painted of me, no matter what the fuck I do you have power and control over me."

"But I don't see you as a poor pathetic creature, Helen," I say, and I can no longer stop myself from crying, my eyes fill up and the tears stream down my face. "Anything but," I say. "I'm actually afraid of you sometimes. I often balk at saying what I think or feel because I'm afraid of how you'll react, it's like I'm walking on eggshells sometimes. I do everything I can to keep you sweet and I . . . I don't know what to say, Helen, but I love you, and it hurts that you don't believe me, it hurts me to know that I haven't been able to make you see how much I care about you," I say, then I put my head in my hands and sit there staring at the floor again, crying softly. Moments pass, then I feel Helen's hand on the back of my head, she pulls me gently to her, presses my brow to her stomach and lightly ruffles the hair at the nape of my neck, it's ending just the way it's not supposed to end:

first she crushes me, then she comes to my rescue, soothing and comforting me. I don't want it to be like this, but it is, there's nothing I can do to prevent it. A moment, and then I run a hand over my face, wipe away the tears.

Then: "You ought to be ashamed of yourself." It's Mom, I whip around and there she is in the doorway, looking daggers at Helen.

"What the fuck are you doing here?" Helen asks.

"What am I doing here? Well, in case you've forgotten, you have a little boy," Mom says. "I looked after him while you were getting drunk last night and now I've brought him back, he's in his stroller outside. Oh, and his name's Daniel, by the way."

"You might fucking well call before you go barging into people's homes."

"Oh, so that you can torment people in peace, you mean?"

"Mom," I say, wiping away a few tears. I put my head on one side and eye her, "don't . . ."

"Oh, but I will, Ole," she says, cutting me off. "Because this has gone far enough. I can't stand by and watch any longer, she's destroying you. You can't see it yourself, but everybody who knows you can see it. The whole island knows—you're not well and it shows, you look tired and run down, Ole. I hate to say it, but you seem to have aged ten years in the two years you've been living with her, and now you're taking after her and drinking more than is good for you . . . you simply can't go on like this, she's destroying you."

"What are you talking about?" Helen asks. "What the fuck do you know about what goes on between Ole and me?"

"Ole is my son and unlike certain other people I could mention I can see only too well when there's something wrong with my own son," Mom says.

"Oh, he's your son all right," Helen says grinning fiercely. "That's your problem in a nutshell, you can't bear the thought that I've taken your son away from you. You're so fucking jealous it's just not true, you've been out to get me right from the start, criticizing every single thing I do."

"Everything I do?" Mom repeats. "And what do you do, exactly? Apart from lying on the sofa moaning about migraines and pains in your face and God knows what other ailments you've dreamed up since you came here."

"What the fuck do you know about what I do or don't do," Helen screams. "Hmm? Nothing! You know nothing and yet you barge straight into my house and start pulling me to pieces. It's like I'm always saying to Ole, there's never come anything out of your fucking mouth but sour comments and cigarette smoke," she screams. She's quivering with fury and her eyes have changed color; her eyes are like little black marbles in their sockets. "Maybe it's time you cut that umbilical cord and accepted that Ole's a grown man and quite capable of deciding for himself what's best for him," she says. "You may find this hard to believe, but he's managing perfectly well without you now," she says and then she pauses, stares at Mom with those fierce black eyes. "Do you think he'd be living with me if I was as bad as you say I am? Well, do you think so?"

"Oh, for heaven's sake, woman," Mom says, almost shouting herself now. She keeps her eyes locked on Helen's, glaring at her. She's every bit as fearless as Helen. "Ole is terrified of losing Daniel, don't you realize that?" she shouts. "Don't you realize that he only puts up with you for Daniel's sake? Ole's not stupid, Helen, and contrary to what you say he's not selfish either," she says. "It's almost impossible for a man to get custody of a child as long as the mother's alive, and Ole's terrified that the same thing's going to happen to Daniel as happened to Jørgen, don't you realize that? Ole knows you're not fit to look after that wee boy on your own, he's terrified of what sort of man you might take up with, and . . ."

"Ole," Helen cries. She eyes me furiously, raising her arm and pointing at Mom. "I won't put up with this, not in my own house. I'll thank you to talk to her, because she's gone too fucking far this time," she yells.

But I don't say a word, I just sit there with my head in my hands, staring at the bathroom tiles and feeling more and more bewildered.

"Ole, be a man, for fuck's sake," Helen yells.

But I just sit here, I can't be a man, I just sit here like a fucking wimp, sit there doing nothing while my girlfriend is being bawled out, unable to come to her defense, I ought to come to her defense. Although to some extent Mom's right, everything's not okay between Helen and me, we have our problems, but it's not Mom's job to sort them out, I shouldn't need my mother to sort things out between Helen and me, I shouldn't be the sort of wimp who has to go running to her the minute things get difficult, but that's what I am—if it's not Helen who's coming to my rescue it's Mom, no matter how I look at it, I'm behaving like a fucking wimp.

"Ole," Helen says again. "You can't let her talk to me like that."

"Maybe he agrees with me," Mom says. "Maybe that's

why he let's me talk to you like that. Did that ever occur to you?" she asks.

There's silence for a few moments and then Helen seems to slip away from me. She just stands there waiting for me to say something and the more time that passes without me saying anything, the more convinced she'll be that I agree with Mom. If I just go on sitting here saying nothing I'm as good as telling her it's over, I know I am, and desperation grows inside me. A moment passes and then I start to rub the sides of my head with the palms of my hands, rub and rub, harder and harder, hear the chafing of hair against my scalp. I keep this up for a few seconds and then I abruptly stop.

"No, that's not why I'm not saying anything," I burst out, and then I pause. "I'm not saying anything because I'm a fucking wimp, that's why," I say, suddenly raising my voice. I almost jump out of my skin at the sound of my own voice. "I'm a coward, I'll do anything to avoid conflict, I'm scared and insecure," I go on, my voice loud and angry, I scarcely knew I had that voice in me and it almost seems to give me some of the confidence I'm claiming not to have. "And it's you who's made me like this, Mom," I say, and I raise my eyes and look at her, pause, feel myself getting worked up. "Helen's right—you're too critical, you're always criticizing me and lecturing me," I say, "you've been doing it ever since I was a little boy," I go on, "picking on me for the slightest thing. If I'd been good enough to wash the dishes for you, I'd be told that I might at least have dried them while I was at it. If I brought you breakfast in bed, I'd always cut the bread too thick or put too much butter on it, and when I came home with something I'd made at school I'd be told that it was nice, but it would have been even nicer if I'd only done this or that. Even when things were good they were never good enough," I say. I look at her, don't quite know why I'm coming out with all this right now, I'm not sure where it's all coming from, it just comes out, and one word leads to another, and I'm getting more and more worked up, getting carried away. "And you were always telling me how scrawny and weak and namby-pamby I was," I go on, letting it all pour out of me. "You signed me up for the football team even though you knew I hated football and was terrified of the ball," I say. "You put way too much food on my plate and refused to let me leave the table until I'd eaten it all up, because I was skinny as a Biafra baby, you said. Even when we had visitors you'd say things like that, you were never happy with me the way I was, you bought me cars and tractors and excavators for my birthdays even though you knew I hated playing with them," I say and then I pause.

I shoot a glance at Helen. She's standing with her hands on her hips, glaring at Mom, crowing over her, everything about her saying that she agrees with me and that we're on the attack now. I turn and look Mom again, getting more and more worked up, she's close to tears now, I can tell.

"And you . . . you're still exactly the same," I continue, not backing down. "When I finally find myself a girlfriend, she's not good enough for you. You made it quite clear from day one that you didn't like Helen," I say. "And the farm . . . when you and Dad were running the farm it was barely ticking over. If I hadn't reorganized things it would all have been in somebody else's hands now," I say. "And yet all I get is complaints. The fact that I've sold off part of the land as plots for vacation cottages, that I've leased out some of the fields and gone in for fish farming—that too is all terrible, according to you. I've saved the family farm from going bankrupt and having to be sold, Mom, but you try to make me believe that I've done the exact opposite. Nothing I've done is right, the . . . the way you talk anyone would think I'd destroyed your life's work, yours and Dad's, and I'm sick of it," I say.

"Yeah," Helen says with a sharp intake of breath, as if to say she couldn't agree more with everything I'm saying. She's still standing there with her hands on her hips, standing there gloating. I turn and look at Mom again, see how much this hurts her, her eyes are glistening, she's struggling to hold back the tears. After a moment or two I feel the guilt welling up. I can't do this to her, it's not even true, although it wasn't all off the top of my head either, of course. I mean, when she was ill she might have been the way I've just described her; back then she probably was as full of reproach and accusations as I just said, especially right before she went into hospital, in fact she was probably a good deal worse. But before that she was a good mother and after that too she was a good mother. I can't go reducing my mom to nothing but the person she was when she was ill, that's not right of me, it's not right at all, but that's what I'm doing, maybe because I need to. Yes, maybe I'm taking advantage of this situation to have it out with the person she was when she was ill, maybe I'm taking this opportunity to give vent to all the anger and the hurt that's been pent up inside me and that must stem from that time; all the sludge and the slag that I've done my best to suppress and forget and that we've never spoken about; maybe I'm simply taking advantage of this situation to get it all out of my system, maybe that's why I'm lashing out at Mom like this; it's as likely an explanation as me siding with Helen because I'm scared of losing her and Daniel.

"I've never been the person you wanted me to be," I continue. "You say you love me, but it's not true, I've never been the son you would have liked," I say and then I pause because it suddenly strikes me that I'm saying exactly what Helen said to me only minutes ago. You don't really love me, that's what Helen just told me. It's not me you love, she told me, saying exactly the same thing to me as I'm saying to Mom now. Helen might almost be speaking through me. A moment, and then Mom starts to cry. She looks at the floor, takes off her glasses and wipes her eyes, but this won't do, I don't want this, I don't want to say what I'm saying, but I'm saying it anyway. I just have to get it out of my system, it spills out of me. "I've never been good enough for you, Mom, so I could never like myself either," I say. "You've made me the wimp I am. You destroyed my self-confidence, you've made me insecure and afraid of conflict and . . . and," I say, pause, and then: "That's your way of controlling me," I say, "you've always done your best to make me feel as small as possible, you've always done all you could to dominate and control me by making me think I'm useless, so useless that I'm totally dependent on you," I say, and yet again it strikes me that I'm saying much the same as Helen has just said to me. Just as she said I tried to control her by turning her into a poor pathetic creature, totally dependent on me, I'm telling Mom that she tries to control me by making me feel small and dependent on her. I'm simply repeating what Helen has just said, everything she accused me of I'm now transferring on to Mom, it's almost as if she's speaking through me, almost as if she's a ventriloquist and I'm her dummy, almost as if she has taken control of me.

"But there'll be no more of that, we're not going to put up with being pushed around any longer," Helen says.

I look at her. She's standing there with her hands on her hips eyeing Mom triumphantly. She's used me to break Mom and now she's crowing over her. I stare at her and I feel a wave of anger rise up in me. It takes a moment, but then Helen notices that I'm staring at her, she frowns slightly and gives me a puzzled look, probably wondering why I'm suddenly looking like her like that.

"You fucking ventriloquist," I burst out.

"What?"

I look straight at her and I see how confused she is, she has no idea what I'm talking about, which isn't so surprising, really, it sounds as though I'm talking nonsense, it sounds as though I'm losing my mind and now I'll have to explain what I mean. I stare at the floor and put my hand on the back of my neck, stand like this for a moment or two then look up at her again. I open my mouth, about to explain what I mean, but nothing comes out, I don't say a word, I can't say a word, there's so much, such an awful lot, where would I start? I'm not up to it, I don't have the energy to explain or discuss what I meant, not right now. I glance across at Mom, she looks every bit as confused as Helen, she's just as nonplussed by what I've said, stands there with her glasses in her hand, eyeing me gravely and Helen eyes me gravely and I feel desperation tearing at my guts, all the anger has drained out of me and I feel nothing but despair and bewilderment, I feel so powerless. I put my hands to my head and then all at once I start to cry again, I don't want to cry, but I can't help it, it simply happens and yet again I'm showing what a wimp I am. For once they see me lose my temper and then only seconds later I back down and dissolve into tears again. I gaze at the floor and then Mom comes into the bathroom and over to me.

"Come on, Ole," she says, her voice heavy with sympathy, then she puts her hand on my shoulder and draws me to her.

Silence.

"I know what you're up to, Helen," Mom says. "But it'll be a long, long while yet before the 'cripple' and I move into the care home," she adds, a note of sarcasm in her voice as she says the word "cripple."

Silence again.

"For fuck's sake," Helen mutters under her breath.

"From the day you moved in you've been out to get us, but we're not leaving here and you can't make us," Mom goes on. "Even if you did succeed in your divide-and-rule strategy, even if you did manage to turn Ole against us, you still wouldn't be able to kick us out. Because we've got a legal right to stay on the farm, we made sure of that when we signed the deeds over to Ole, so no matter what you do, we're staying put."

"Ah, so it's you who's been reading my diary," Helen says.

A jolt runs through me at her words. I feel my mouth drop open, I don't raise my eyes, just sit here open-mouthed, staring at the floor.

"For fuck's sake," Helen says again. "You're even sicker than I fucking thought . . . you . . . have you been sneaking into our bedroom when we weren't home . . . and reading my diary?" Her voice rises steadily as she speaks, she starts out softly and shrieks out the last word. "Ole," she shrieks. "Ole . . . wake up, for fuck's sake, this is downright sick," she shrieks. "Your mother's sick in the head, Ole."

I still don't raise my eyes. I shut my mouth, swallow and give my head a little shake, because if it wasn't Jørgen who read her diary then it must have been Mom. Is this really possible? It reminds me of how she used to carry on just before Dad had her admitted to hospital. Going into our bedroom and reading Helen's diary, it reminds me of the time when she tried to spy on Dad and keep tabs on him, and maybe Helen's right, maybe Mom is falling ill again. Last time she was convinced that Dad wanted rid of her, now she's convinced that Helen wants rid of her and in both cases she starts spying on and keeping tabs on the person concerned. And then there's all the work she's been doing, it occurs to me, the way she's been racing around like the Duracell bunny recently, as Helen says, that too reminds me of what she was like when she was ill, although she's always liked to work, it's true, but lately she's been going way over the score. There's no getting away from it, she's been far too hard on herself, exactly the way she was when she started to lose it last time. Back then, too, she tried to keep her illness at bay by taking refuge in work.

"You fucking psycho," Helen says.

"You never stop. You do everything you can to turn Ole against me," Mom says. "You even have the cheek to play on the fact that I once had a mental breakdown," she says, and she stops for a moment. Then: "Ole," she says, and she takes me by the shoulders, gives me a little shake. "Listen to me, this is important. I went into your bedroom to fetch Daniel's pacifier, you'd forgotten to bring it with him when I was going to mind him three days ago and he was crying and crying, so I had to go and get it. I didn't sneak in there to read Helen's diary," she says, "of course I didn't. But it was lying open on the bedside table and the pacifier was lying on top of it. I couldn't avoid reading a few words, and when I saw that it was about me and 'the cripple' as Helen calls him, I couldn't help reading a bit more. I shouldn't have done it, and I apologize, but . . . well, if nothing else it confirmed a lot of my suspicions and fears about the way Helen sees us," she says, stroking my shoulder. And still I sit here staring at the floor, growing more and more confused and feeling more and more desperate. I don't know who to believe, I don't know what to believe, I can't take this any longer. I feel my eyes filling up again, the tears start to pour down and my body is suddenly shaken by two shuddering sobs.

"Oh no, Ole, Ole pet," Mom sighs and she pulls me to her, tries to comfort me, but I don't want to be comforted, not by Mom and certainly not by her instead of Helen. I don't want to be this wimp who runs crying to his mommy the minute things get difficult, but she presses my head against her stomach, I try to resist, but she's determined, she clamps me to her and I feel how I seem to shrink and become a little boy again, this is exactly what I was saying to her a minute ago and I was right, she makes me feel small, she turns me into that little boy who's totally dependent on her and whom she can boss around. She's doing much the same as she did that time when she was ill, so maybe she is losing it again. The moments pass and I feel anger welling up in me again.

"Stop it," I say, brushing her hands away. I straighten up

and stare furiously at her. "You are sick," I shout. "You really *are*," I shout and yet again I hear Helen speaking through me. Helen has managed to convince me that Mom is sick in the head and now I'm shouting it at her. It's true what I said about Helen too: she is a ventriloquist and I'm her dummy, she actually does speak through me, she steers and controls me, and Mom steers and controls me, the one's as bad as the other, there's nothing to choose between them. And maybe that's why I'm with Helen, maybe I've found myself a mother substitute, maybe it's as ridiculously simple as that. I stare at the floor, put my hand to the back of my neck again. Desperation grows and grows inside me. I have to get away from here, I can't stay here any longer, a moment goes by and then I stand up and start to walk away. I hear Helen call after me, calling my name, but I just keep walking, walking quickly, down the hallway, across the front hall and out into the sun, take the steps two at a time and march off across the yard.

"Uh, hey," I hear someone say. I turn and there's Jørgen, hunched over a rucksack with a yellow sleeping bag strapped under the flap. "Got invited to this festival, so I can't start work on Monday after all," he says.

Silence.

I just stand there staring at him. He doesn't ask if it's okay by me that he won't be able to work, let alone ask if he can go to this festival, he simply tells me that he won't be showing up for work after all. We had a deal, but he doesn't give a damn about that, acts like there was no deal, like it doesn't exist, acts like I don't exist. I stand there staring at him for a moment or two and then something starts to rise up inside me, all the stuff that's been building up lately, all the frustration, all the vexation and fear, all the anger, it all comes together into one great tearing rage and I start to walk towards him. He straightens up and looks at me, seeming a little unsure now, he tries to keep his cool, but he can't, he stares at my face and the tough guy image seems to evaporate.

"Whoa, chill out, dude," he says.

I don't say a word, I walk straight up to him, clench my right fist and punch him smack in the face, punch him as hard as I can, feel the sharp edge of his cheekbone against my knuckles, he gives a little grunt and I see his head jerk to one side. He staggers back onto his right foot, struggling to stay upright, but he can't, he topples backwards, his rear end hitting the dirt a split second before his head strikes one of the stones edging the flowerbed, strikes it hard. And then he just lies there, perfectly still, just lies there, bleeding, and I don't take my eyes off him, I watch the blood spread slowly over the round stone in the flowerbed, his head is bleeding and he's not moving and I just stand here staring at him. After a moment he stirs, opens his eyes then closes them, opens them again, lifts his head off the stone and eases himself up onto his elbow.

"What the fuck?" he mumbles, looking dazed.

A moment passes and suddenly it feels as though a cold hand curls itself around the back of my neck, I feel my neck turn clammy with fear: what have I done, oh God, what have I done? I put my hands to my head, shut my eyes and stand like that, just stand there, feeling the fear well up in my throat, feeling sick with fear, because that's it, I've lost Daniel. Helen's going to leave and she'll take Daniel with her, I know she will, she's going to demand sole custody of Daniel and she'll get it too, nobody's going to consider me fit to take care of Daniel after this. I might even be denied visitation rights after this, oh God, what have I done.

Suddenly I hear someone say: "Ole." I open my eyes and see Helen. She comes out of the door, rests her hand on one of the porch posts and stands there looking at me. I don't say anything, I can't say anything, I just look at her, then she catches sight of Jørgen. He has sat up, he doesn't say anything, puts a hand to his head, then brings it down and looks at it, blood drips from his fingers and Helen's mouth drops open when she sees it, in a kind of silent scream. And then Mom comes out onto the porch as well and her eye immediately goes to Jørgen. There's total silence. And then Daniel starts to cry, I turn around and see his stroller, it's standing in the shade of the cottage, and Dad is out on the front step of the cottage, he's in his wheelchair, scratching the cat behind its ear and looking at me, his eyes wide and solemn, and he doesn't say a word. I stand quite still and Daniel is crying even louder now, dear little Daniel, poor little Daniel, I gaze at his stroller and swallow, once, then again, and then I start to cry as well, because I'm going to lose him now, they're going to take him away from me and there's nothing I can do, I'm totally paralyzed, every bit as paralyzed as Dad.

Otterøya, July 12th, 2006

We were on our way up to the camp one day: gray sky, the air hot and close and flies buzzing around us as we walked up the path. We were sweating and the flies liked our sweat so they kept landing on us and bothering us. Ah, but even though they were driving us crazy we paid them no mind, not at all, because we weren't townies, we were children of the forest and all the creatures of the forest were our brothers and sisters, including those goddamn flies. We trod quietly. Every now and again you would raise a hand, signaling for us to stop and we would stand still, alert and listening for a moment or two before carrying on. You first and me right behind you, we didn't sound like a herd of bison the way townies did when they lost their way in the wild. We didn't step on dry twigs and we didn't wag our tongues all the time in the way of women, we were silent and if we had something to say that absolutely could not wait we communicated instead with the aid of mysterious signs and gestures. The flick of the hand you had just given might, for example, have been the signal for us to pick blueberries for making warpaint. That at any rate was what you did. You hunkered down, crushed some berries in the palm of your hand and drew a purplish streak across each cheek.

Then all of a sudden a wild light came into your eyes, you put one index finger to your lips and pointed with the other. And yes, there was something, there actually was something lying in the bushes, half covered by moss and twigs. I saw it myself, this time it was for real. With one hand you reached out behind you and plucked an arrow from your quiver. then you placed the arrow to your bowstring and began to creep forwards. I gripped my spear a little tighter and followed you, slowly and lithely as a cat.

And then we saw it.

It wasn't the enemy, it was Karoline. We could tell by the pale-blue T-shirt. She'd had her name printed on it at one of the stalls at the Namsos Fair the year before. We crept up to her, slowly, half-crouching and still on the alert. She didn't move. By Manitu, she was dead. The yellow dogs had killed her. They didn't even let women and children go free. She was lying on her back with her arms by her sides, from the waist down she was covered with moss and twigs and her berry pail lay next to her. She must have been out picking berries when they jumped her. Damned cowards, they had taken the life of a defenseless squaw. Karoline could be a bit of a wildcat at times, it's true, she'd shown that on a number of occasions, but she hadn't had a chance here, they had shown no mercy, they had made short work of her and now here she lay with her eyes wide and staring and purplish fingermarks around her throat. Oh, they would pay dearly for this, this would not go unavenged. I stood quite still and just stared at her. Karoline had gone to the happy hunting grounds, I couldn't take it in. You knelt down beside her, you slipped off your quiver and placed it on the mossy ground along with your bow, then you pulled off your T-shirt and laid it over her face, exactly the way one was supposed to do.

This is the best and most correct way I can come up with to describe what happened. We found Karoline raped and murdered in the forest and we experienced and interpreted this event in the language of our Indian world. Maybe this was some sort of defense mechanism kicking in, maybe we found it hard to take in such a terrible thing or maybe we were trying to render this situation harmless and distance ourselves from it by sticking to words associated only with our play. Or maybe we were simply slow to adjust, maybe we were so absorbed in our game and our imaginary world that we weren't able to drop the Indian talk straight away. I don't know. What I do remember, though, is how weird it felt to stand there looking down on her and feeling more and more that something wasn't right. I mean, strictly speaking it all fitted so well, the language we thought in and that we immersed ourselves when we were up at the camp was tailor-made to describe events like this—well, not rape, of course, I don't think we even knew what that was, but assault and murder, attack and defense, most of what we got up to at the camp related to this sort of thing, but still, even though everything here seemed more right than it ever had, it became more and more clear to me that in fact nothing about this was right at all.

Obviously this was reality starting to intrude. This was no game, this was real. And this was where you and I differed. I don't of course know exactly what was going through your mind, but it seems to me now that you took our discovery of Karoline as proof that our imaginary world wasn't imaginary at all, that it was real. Or maybe that's going too far. Part of you knew all the time that what we got up to at the camp was only make-believe, just a game, I'm pretty sure of that, but you wanted so much for it not to be make-believe and you got so caught up in our games up there that you actually greeted the discovery of Karoline's body with a kind of delight and gratitude—not because you were in any way a bad person, far from it, but quite simply because the sight of Karoline's dead body made it even easier for you to pretend that our Indian world was real. The discovery of Karoline represented a concrete realization, so to speak, of your imaginary world. See, we did have an enemy, here was the proof. That must have been more or less what you were thinking, and I've never seen anyone look as intent and electrified as you did when you stood up and began to search for tracks.

"David," I said.

But you didn't hear me, you paced back and forth, eyes scanning the ground.

"David."

Then you stopped short. You stood perfectly still, staring at the ground for a moment or two, then you raised your eyes and looked down the path.

"Follow me," you said, and off you went. We ran for all we were worth, the forest like a green waterfall on either side of the path, and we didn't stop until we were down on the road, because there was Albert, talking to Eva's dad.

"Grim's killed Karoline," you screamed. "She's dead, she's lying up there, near our camp."

Looking back on it I can see that this was where you put the final touch to your work. The two little Husvikings had already identified Grim as our enemy and by picking up on this and blaming Grim for the actual killing of one of the little Indians from our camp, you managed to make our imaginary world merge with the grown-up world. Not consciously, of course. Most likely you were simply satisfying a need or an urge to follow a logical line of reasoning and a pattern you had detected, what do I know. But whatever the case, these words were to have serious consequences, because as more and more people flocked to the spot and began to question us, you didn't just stick to your story that it was Grim who had killed her, you even went so far as to say that we had seen him running away from the scene and that he had had "this really crazy look in his eyes."

If only I had stepped in at that point, if only I had had the courage to speak up and say that we hadn't seen Grim or anyone else up in the forest, then none of what actually happened would have happened. But I didn't speak up. I didn't dare and the more the lie was repeated the more difficult it became for me to do so, because then people would have wondered why I hadn't said something right away. That must have been my thinking, and before I knew it there I was, telling exactly the same story as you had just told. And due to the way the grown-ups reacted to what we told them I eventually began to believe our lies, because even before the police arrived the mood had become that of a lynch mob. I've never seen anything like it before or since. And this: to be ten or eleven years old and experience the hate and the lust for revenge displayed by our male role models in particular as they stood there telling each other what they ought to do to Grim, that they should go straight over there and cut off his balls before the fucking social workers showed up and started going on about what a shame it was for him, this left us convinced that Grim was capable of doing what we had accused him of doing, and of course it was only a short step from there to believing that he probably had done it—no matter what we actually had or hadn't seen.

The way I see it, it's in the macho culture on Otterøya that one will find the key explanations for why things went the way they did. Because we were living in a fantasy world that mirrored the macho society we had grown up in and we interpreted everything around us—including the horrible thing that happened to Karoline—according to the values and norms instilled in us by that macho society. At the end of the day that is what prompted you to accuse Grim. Our male role models had taught us that a real man was brave and strong and smart and proud and dynamic and I don't know what else, and if that was the image we wanted to project, both to each other and to girls, we desperately needed to have an enemy, we needed someone to fight, to defend ourselves against and ultimately beat, and since we had no such enemy we had to invent one. And so you invented Grim, or to be more precise, you reinvented the real Grim as a terrible foe and a serious threat to us and to our camp. The only trouble was that you found it rather hard to distinguish between make-believe and the truth, not only because you were a little boy with a lively imagination, but also because, as I've said, our fantasy world closely resembled and was to a great extent a reflection of the reality we normally inhabited. And it was this, as well as a particularly powerful need to reshape reality and present your own version of it and the fierce grudge you bore against the Albrigtsens for having insulted Berit, that caused you to persist in maintaining that we had seen Grim running away from the scene of the crime, even after the police arrived.

Actually it's quite frightening to think back on how easy it was to persuade people that it was Grim who had murdered Karoline, not just because the Husvikings had said that Grim had been planning to come up and wreck our camp, and not just because he was big enough to be capable of committing rape but at the same time a bit "simple" and incapable of understanding the consequences of his actions, but also because he was from Oslo and because it confirmed a lot of the preconceived notions held by the islanders about towns and town dwellers that he, of all people, should be identified as the killer. The goodwill that people had begun to show towards the

Albrigtsen family instantly evaporated at any rate and suddenly people were vying with each other as to who had been most skeptical of the family when they first moved to the island and who had been the first to realize that it would all end in disaster. "I knew the minute I saw them that they didn't fit in," as Dad said. "This was the most peaceful place in the world until those goddamned hippies came here," Berit said.

Fortunately Grim was cleared of all charges, he had been wandering around on his own when the murder was committed, so he had no real alibi, but as the trial progressed you and I began to seem less and less sure that he was the person we had seen. Neither of us would admit that we had made it all up, but the more the defending counsel questioned us, the less and less certain we became and it ended with us saying that we thought we had seen someone running off into the forest and that this person had looked like Grim. But although his acquittal was a victory for Grim and the rest of the Albrigtsen family, the damage had already been done. The killer was never caught and since Grim had no alibi, and since the islanders needed an actual person to blame, they persisted in believing that Grim had done it. "It's the legal system that's at fault," as Erik said. "The laws are made by a bunch of wishy-washy, bleeding-heart social workers who're more interested in protecting the criminal than the victim."

The worst of it was, though, that Lasse didn't believe his own son when he said he was innocent and this tore apart the whole Albrigtsen family. I don't know very much about what happened because they left Otterøya long before the trial was over, but word had it that Lene had left Lasse and taken the kids with her, which was sad enough in itself, of course, but what was even worse was that without Lasse, who had helped her to get out of the drug scene and stay out of it, Lene ended up using again and obviously this hurt Hauk and Grim as much if not more than it hurt her.

On you, me, Dad and Berit the trial had the opposite effect. When we came under pressure and the defending counsel began to sow serious doubt on what we had or had not seen, and when the newspapers reported everything he had said and everyone began to discuss it and form opinions, obviously Dad and Berit did their best to support and stand up for us and this common cause brought our "family" even closer together than before. Officially, you and Berit were still living in the cottage, but more and more often you slept at the big house with us, and one night when I got up to pee I heard Dad and Berit in the living room, talking about how as soon as the trial was over and things had settled down Dad would get a divorce and they could finally put an end to all the lies and all the secrecy. "I want to marry you, Berit," I remember him saying.

But that was never to be.

Only a couple of days before we were due to give evidence for the last time, Dad was run over by the tractor. He had knocked against the gear stick while he was trying to switch over a plug under the seat, the tractor jerked forward and he was thrown off and crushed under one of the wheels. If it hadn't been for the fact that it happened out on the moor, where the ground was soft and spongy, he would have been killed outright. Luckily he wasn't, but he was left paralyzed from the waist down and confined to a wheelchair forever and that changed everything, of course, for him and for all of us who were close to him.

Dad, the workaholic whose day usually started around five or five-thirty in the morning and who scarcely took time to swallow his lunch before he was back out there, hard at it again; who took pride in being a free and independent farmer and

would put off asking anyone for help for as long as possible—
suddenly he was stuck in a wheelchair unable to do anything
for himself. He had to have help with everything: to get dressed,
to go to the toilet, everything.

And then, in the midst of all this, something else happened
that no one, absolutely no one, could have expected. When Dad
woke up in the hospital after having been in an induced coma
for almost a week, it wasn't Berit who was sitting by his bedside, watching over him, it was Mom.

Looking back on it now it has occurred to me that it must be
my memory that has linked these two events to one another.
That Mom should suddenly have got better just around the
time when she heard that Dad had been in a serious accident
simply seems so unlikely that I find it hard to believe. It must
be my imagination playing tricks on me, because both events
were so crucial for me personally, ushering in as they did a new
phase, as it were, in my life. So it makes sense to think of them
as one big event, that's what I must have thought, or something along those lines.

But that really is what happened, and according to a psychologist I've spoken to it probably wasn't as much of a miracle as one
might think. It was surprising, yes, but he had seen something
similar happen several times before and there was a perfectly
good explanation for it. The fact that Dad had been paralyzed
and suddenly needed help just when I was involved in a long
and unpleasant court case, the fact that both he and I needed
her more than ever must quite simply have galvanized her
into dredging up reserves of strength that no one—neither we
nor the psychiatrists nor Mom herself—could have imagined
she possessed, and her illness suddenly left her just like that.
Well, not just like that perhaps, it has to be said that she had
been showing signs of improvement for some time before this

happened, and it should also be said that she did have a number of minor relapses in the years that followed.

I don't know whether Berit and Dad had any chance to speak to one another after the accident, all I know is that Mom as good as chased Berit out of the hospital when Dad was in a coma and that was the end of that. Whether it was the gossip and rumors alone that prompted you and your mother to leave the island completely and move to Namsos not long afterwards I can't say, but I did hear that your mother was given a hard time of it after the two of you left the farm, so I suppose it had something to do with it. She was a trollop, a single mother who'd tried to get her hands on our farm by getting into bed with my dad, people said. She'd taken advantage of Dad when he was feeling lonely and needed help on the farm, and then the brazen hussy cold-bloodedly upped and left more or less on the very day that he was injured and suddenly found himself in sore need of support.

And while Berit was treated with contempt and condemnation by large sections of the community Dad got off scot-free: partly because he had been at such a low ebb and was easy prey when Mom was ill, partly because the sympathy he got after his accident was so great that it absolved him, so to speak, of all previous sins, and partly because he was a man from a society that set great store by macho values.

But there was one person who never absolved Dad and that was Mom. I may be exaggerating slightly when I say this, but even though Mom never said one word about his infidelity and his betrayal of her, not a day went by when she didn't punish Dad and remind him of what he'd done to her. I don't know how else to explain the excessively selfless devotion she displayed. Not only did she nurse Dad and take care of me, and not only did she do all the housework, but even though Dad felt it would be best to sell the farm she insisted on holding onto it and running it herself, single-handed. Granted, I was a big help and granted she hired extra help during the busiest periods, but the amount of work she had to do herself to keep the place going was nonetheless so enormous that it was anything but healthy. But she felt she had to do it for Dad's sake and mine, as she always said if people asked. After all, the farm had been in my father's family for generations. And the way I see it, this—that she always made sure Dad knew she was standing by him even though he had let her down when she was at her lowest ebb— was her way of punishing him. The way she sacrificed herself and drove herself to unreasonable and unwarranted lengths not only made Dad feel even smaller and more pathetic than the accident had already made him feel, it also meant that he owed her a debt of gratitude he could never repay. In many ways he was even more trapped and powerless in his marriage to Mom, paralyzed in fact in more than one sense of the word.

When I look out of the window now, as I write this, I can see Dad sitting on the porch of the cottage eating his supper and Mom is out in the yard, getting ready to mow a lawn that really doesn't need mowing at all; it strikes me that she's never been entirely well, that her illness is still there inside her, working on her. At other times it occurs to me that her behavior is simply a sign of what it was like to be a woman in the sort of macho society that Otterøya was back then. Everyone needs to be in charge of themselves and their own life and when both a person's spouse and the society they are a part of try to hinder them in this, he or she may well seek other, more subtle, ways of gaining power. This may have had a lot to do with Mom's manner and her behavior, in fact one might even say there was a link between this and her illness, I don't know.

As I say, shortly afterwards you and Berit moved to Namsos.

You came back to Otterøya now and again to visit Erik and we saw each other then, of course, but since his death sometime in the late 1980s I've only seen you once and that was at the Namsos Fair in 2003. I remember I'd been to a D.D.E concert and I was pretty drunk. I was standing in the middle of the festival ground, fumbling with my mobile, trying to call for a taxi when you walked by. Our eyes met and you immediately looked the other way and made to walk on like you hadn't seen me, but as I say I was drunk so that didn't bother me.

"David," I shouted, way too loudly of course, so loudly that people turned to look at me and at you. You weren't happy about this, I could tell, but you tried to smile and put a good face on it as you strolled over to me, and once we'd exchanged the necessary pleasantries I asked if you'd like to go over to Uncle Oscar's Bar for a beer, and you actually said yes. And one beer was all we had—well, it was understandable really. Not only was I way too drunk to be able to carry on a decent conversation, I'd also just been given the brush-off by a woman I really liked and who I had thought liked me too, so I was in a pretty maudlin frame of mind and you got the brunt of it, there's no denying. I poured out all my sorrows to you, went on and on about much I loved this woman and about all the things I'd done to make her see that I was the only one for her. I had done everything right, or so I thought. I was always bright and cheerful when we met and genuinely interested in everything she said. I'd given her to understand that I was comfortably off and led a settled, steady life, and I behaved like a true gentleman, pulling out chairs, lighting her cigarettes, opening doors for her.

But she'd still given me the brush-off, I told you. While D.D.E. were playing "E6" at that. Could you believe that? And did you know how hurt I had been? While up on the stage Bjarne Brøndbo sang that beautiful love song, I had tried to take her hand for the first time and she had given me the brush-off. She had smiled wanly, pulled her hand away and said: "No, I don't think so, Ole." Had you any idea how much that had hurt? That's how I went on, I was drunk, maudlin and shamelessly self-centered and in your situation plenty of people would have made some excuse to get up and move to another table as soon as they saw where this was going. But you stayed put. You tried to console me by saying there were "plenty more fish in the sea" and by letting me know that you were single and childless yourself, but that didn't mean your life was empty and meaningless. What you had to do, you said, was to focus instead on all the things life had to offer, all the things we could do that guys with wives and children couldn't. "The freedom we have," as you said, "think of that." But I was inconsolable. "You may be free, but I'm not," I remember saying. "Because you have a choice, David, you could get a girl any time. So I can see why you might look at it that way, the single life, when you can opt out of it any time you choose," I said. "But look at me, I'm skinny and bald and my head's way too big for my body. When it comes to women I can't pick and choose the way you can, so I feel like I'm stuck with being single, I'm not free at all."

I could tell that it embarrassed you to hear me speaking so frankly, being so upfront, but that still didn't stop me. I talked and talked and talked until eventually—surprise, surprise— you'd had enough. You pretended to have spotted an old friend up at the bar and just like that you were gone, without me having learned much about how you were and what you were doing with your life. Or, at least, a few details had come out during our conversation. You were single and childless, as I said, and you were living in Trondheim where you had a job as a parking attendant of all things. I seem to remember that you said yes when I asked if it was true that you'd had a novel published under a pseudonym a year or two earlier. It embarrasses me now, David, as I sit here writing this, to think of all we had to talk about, all we had been through together, all the things I had wondered about and all the things you must have wondered about. Here was our chance to talk about all of that and I blew it with my sentimental, drunken ramblings. Oh, well, I hope this letter will repair at least some of the damage.

Tom Roger

Namsos, July 4th, 2006. Can't we just get shit-faced?

We're walking hand in hand down the street, me and
Mona. I finish my ice pop, lick both sides of the stick and
chuck it away. We walk past the hotel, past Aakervik the
fishmonger's. Christ, it's hot. I put my hand to the back
of my neck. It's running with sweat, and there's patches
of sweat on my vest as well, I see—fuck, I've hardly
walked any distance and it's soaked through already. I
slip my hand off my neck as we cross the road, pinch my
vest between thumb and forefinger, pull it out from my
chest to let some air in. It's so fucking hot I can feel the
asphalt burning the soles of my shoes. Look down. Look
up again. And then I see Mona's mother. I jump at the
sight of her. She's heading straight for us. Looking right at
us, smiling that oh-so-sweet smile of hers, sweet and ice-
cold. Ice-smile. Then Mona spots her. Her hand tightens
around mine and she stops dead. It's pure instinct. She

wants to steer clear of her mother, go another way. But it's too late. Their eyes have met, she can't escape. She takes off her shoe and holds it up. Tries to disguise the brief break in her stride by pretending she's got something in her shoe. Just for a second, then she slips her shoe back on and starts walking again. Tries to act casual, lifts her chin a bit, tries to smile as confidently as her mother. But she can't quite manage it. She's rattled. I can tell by her face. And it doesn't help that she's chewing gum. She can't look as cool as she'd like.

"Well, hello," Anne says.

She adjusts her bag on her shoulder as she says it. Look straight at Mona. Doesn't look at me. Making a point of not saying hello to me, like. Only saying hello to Mona. Bitch, she's fucking unbelievable.

"Hi," Mona says.

"Hi," I say as well.

Say hi to Anne even though she's made a big show of not saying hello to me. Say it loud and clear. Lift my sunglasses up onto my forehead, look her straight in the face and smile. I know she's used to pushing people around and doing what she likes with them, but that won't work with me. No fucking way does she get to treat me like I don't exist. But she still doesn't look at me.

"Out for a little stroll, are you?" Anne asks.

She's still talking as if Mona's on her own. As if I'm not fucking well here at all. It's so far out it's almost funny, so it is. I look straight at her. That fat, pasty pug-face of hers. Puffy, powder-caked face with the fan of fine smoker's wrinkles on her upper lip. She sticks her thumb under the strap of her shoulder bag, it's pressing against her tit, I notice. Her tit's bulging out on either side of the strap. She shifts the bag slightly, still not taking her eyes off Mona. I look at her and give a little grin. Can't help it. Just have to show her how ridiculous she is, how ridiculous it is her treating me like this. But she takes no notice of me.

"Yeah, we've been out to eat," Mona says, trying to make the point that I'm here as well. She looks at Anne and chews her gum. Trying to look blasé by chewing a bit harder on her gum. Chomping.

"Oh, really," Anne says. "Where?"

"Rondo's," Mona says.

"Oh," Anne says, "do they do proper meals there?"

She raises her eyebrows, acting surprised. As if to say Rondo's isn't good enough. Not fancy enough.

"I thought they only did fast food," she says.

"Yeah, well we happen to like fast food, you see," Mona says.

She blinks slowly and gives a kind of weary smile, to show her mother how fed up she is of this crap, this farce.

"Oh, no, I didn't mean it like that," Anne says.

And she gives a little laugh. Trying to make out that she didn't mean to criticize, but she can't resist criticizing and then when people get upset she always makes out that they've misunderstood or they're overreacting.

"And we're all allowed to eat junk now and again," she adds.

She adjusts her shoulder bag again, looks at Mona and gives her that cold, charming smile again. Acting like she doesn't know we eat fast food all the time. Talking like it would be so terrible if we hardly ever ate anything but junk food and Mona's supposed to feel guilty and embarrassed because it's actually true. She doesn't. What a bitch, she's so fucking sly, a total fucking psycho.

"And anyway, you're so skinny, you don't need to worry about putting on weight," she goes on, and she nods at Mona, still with that ice-cold smile on her face. "I think you might've got even thinner lately," she says.

Christ, what a bitch, she's un-fucking-believable. She knows Mona has this huge complex about being so thin, and yet she goes and says something like that. Reminding her of the one thing she hates most about herself.

"Yeah, maybe so, Mom," Mona says.

She shuts her eyes as she says this. Showing Anne she doesn't want to hear this. Trying to show her that she's sick of it. But she's hurt. I can tell by her face. She goes on chewing her gum, trying to look like she doesn't care, but she's hurt.

"Maybe you should see the doctor, get checked out?" Anne says. "Just to be on the safe side."

Mona raises her thin, penciled eyebrows and sighs. Doesn't say anything. And Anne lays her pudgy fingers lightly on her arm. A broad gold bracelet slips out of her shirt sleeve as she does so. She keeps smiling that oh-so-sweet smile of hers.

"Oh, dear, now I've offended you, I can tell," she says with a little laugh, and she pulls her hand away, gives it a little shake, sliding the bracelet back up inside her sleeve. She looks at Mona. "But I worry about you, you know. You're my daughter and I really want you to be happy."

"I am happy, Mom," Mona says. "I'm happier than I've been in a long time."

"Hmm," Anne says.

And that's all she says. Just stands there looking at Mona. As if to show her that she has her own thoughts on that score. Like Mona can't possibly be happy with me. Like she knows more about how Mona feels than Mona herself. Fucking unbelievable, what a bitch. What a fucking psycho.

I stare at her.

"Well, you seem to be thriving, anyway, Anne," I say.

I nod at her and sneer. I can't resist it. If she can talk about how thin Mona is, we should be able to talk about how fat she is, shouldn't we? That puffy pug-face of hers, cheeks sagging on either side of her face. Pale powdery cheeks dotted with little red freckles. I glance at Mona and grin, and Mona grins back. I turn to Anne again. Sneer. She doesn't say a word. Doesn't even look at me. Keeps her eyes fixed on Mona, smiling her ice-cold smile. She's raging, but trying to look unaffected.

"Oh, by the way, I met Olav and Vilde this morning," she says, not taking her eyes off Mona. "They were on their way up to the family park in Namsos Forest," she adds.

She flashes that cold, hard smile. Un-fucking-believable— the bitch. Trying to make Mona feel guilty by mentioning Vilde now. Just to remind her, like, of where she really ought to be. As if to say she shouldn't be here with me. She should be with her husband and her kid up at the family park in Namsos Forest. That's what she wants Mona to think when she says this, wants to make Mona feel guilty for leaving her husband and her kid.

"So, only me missing, then," Mona says.

She looks up at me and grins, she knows exactly what her mother's up to and she's grinning at how ridiculous she is. And I grin back.

"Well, you said it, not me," Anne says.

She looks Mona straight in the eye, still smiling that cold, hard smile. She's raging, but she's doing her best to look as if she's not that easily rattled. And Mona looks at her and chews her gum. Like they do in films sometimes. Trying to look cool by chewing gum. Trying to show Anne that she doesn't give a shit what she says, that she won't be manipulated.

"Oh, well," Anne says, looking at her watch, expensive gold watch on her pasty, pudgy, red-freckled wrist. "We've got people coming for dinner, so I'd better be getting home," she says. She glances up at Mona again. "But it would be so nice if you could come and see us soon," she says.

Again that "you" directed only at Mona. Not a word to me. She's constantly making the point that I'm not welcome. Fucking cunt.

"I think your dad would really appreciate it if you came over," she says, her voice suddenly serious now. She holds Mona's eye.

"Oh?" Mona says.

She's still trying to look like she couldn't give a shit, but it's not quite working. Now she's wondering what's up with her dad. I can tell by her face. The cocky, laid-back pose kind of falls away. A flicker of unease comes into her eyes. A flash of panic.

"Oh, but we can talk more about that when you come over," Anne says.

She lays her pudgy fingers on Mona's arm again. Blinks steadily. Opens her eyes and gazes solemnly at Mona. Gives it a second. Then slides her hand off Mona's arm.

"Well, bye for now," she says. "You know where we live," she adds.

And off she goes. Like she hasn't got time to stand here talking any longer. Bitch—she's so fucking sly. Letting us think she's in a hurry, when what she really wants is to leave Mona in the dark. I know that's what she's trying to do. She wants Mona to be left wondering what's wrong with her dad, that way she'll have to go back on her word. She wants to force Mona to come home—and on her own, without me. That bitch, she's so fucking sly. I bet there's not a blind thing the matter with Mona's dad. She just wants Mona to think there is.

"C'mon, Mona," I say.

I put my arm around her shoulders. Look down at her as we walk on. She's trying to act like it hasn't got to her. She knows full well that Anne's trying to manipulate her and she's doing her best to fight it, to just shrug it off, but she can't. I can tell by her face. She looks up at me and smiles, but it's a sad smile. She's worried about her dad. I can tell by her face. And maybe she thinks it's her fault he's not well. Maybe she thinks her dad's in a state because of her. That all the worry about her has told on his nerves, that he's depressed or something. What the fuck do I know, it's hard to say, but that's definitely what Anne wants her to think. I pull Mona a little bit closer. Curl my hand around her skinny upper arm. Just over the snake tattoo. We carry on down the street, past Karoliussen's bookshop. Cross the road and walk past Haagensen Photo. Walk along side by side, neither of us saying a word. And then Mona starts to cry. Cries softly, keeping her eyes on the sidewalk. After a moment I stop, hug her close. Put one hand behind her head, the other on her back and gently press her face into the hollow of my shoulder. Stand there stroking her back and watching a truck reverse into the car park at Bailiff's Manor, stroke and stroke as I watch the driver switching between checking in his mirror and leaning out of the open window.

"Maybe you should stop over there anyway, Mona," I say.

I fondle her hair. Fine, fair hair. Long hair. Tuck it behind her ear. Lightly finger the three little ear studs in her earlobe.

"No," she sniffs.

I bend my head, bury my nose in her hair, it smells earthy. I stay like that for a moment then start stroking her back again. Feel her knobby spine under my fingertips.

"Mona," I say, "I think it's fucking brilliant that you don't let her run your life any more, but . . . I need to know that you're doing it for your own sake and not for mine.

"I'm doing it for our sake, Tom Roger."

"Yeah, I know," I say. "I just mean that you shouldn't stop going to see them because you think I want you to. I wouldn't think you were any less loyal to me if you went to see them," I say.

I hear what I'm saying. I'm not really sure I mean it. At any rate there's a bit of me that likes the fact that Mona refuses to go and see them as long as they refuse to let her bring me with her.

"Oh, God," she says.

And then she starts to cry again. Buries her face in my shoulder.

"You're so good, Tom Roger."

"Don't say that," I say.

"But you are."

"Well, I care about you, anyway," I say.

"And I love you," she says.

She sniffs. Gives it a moment, then straightens up and

wipes away the tears. Stands with her mouth half-open, drying her eyes.

Then: "What the fuck are you gawking at," she says.

That loud, in-your-face voice of hers.

I turn around and see two men walking by. Two suntanned thirty-somethings with short, spiky hair; hair glossy with hair gel. I've seen them before, but I don't know them. I don't know their names, but they know who I am, I'll bet. They look shit-scared, at any rate. I eyeball them, flex my biceps a bit and curl my lip, showing both my muscles and my broken front tooth. I've always felt that that broken tooth makes me look dangerous, that I look like a man with a past when I bare that tooth. They eye me, just for a second, then quickly look the other way, like they're trying to let me see that they don't want to get involved, they don't want any trouble.

"What—have you never seen people before?" Mona snarls.

She's getting herself worked up. Trying to offload her anger at her mother onto them. She knows she doesn't have to worry when she's with me, so she doesn't think twice about venting her spleen on a couple of random passersby. And they speed up a bit, looking the other way as they hurry across the road and around the corner.

"Christ, they seemed to be in an awful hurry," Mona says.

She wipes away the last of her tears. Looks at me and grins.

"Must've had an urgent appointment somewhere," I say.

I grin back at her. Lay my hand on her shoulders again. My big hand. Hug her close as we walk on, cross Namdalsvegen and step onto the sidewalk on the other side.

"Can't we just get shit-faced?" she says.

It comes kind of out of the blue. But I try not to look surprised. Raise one eyebrow and give a little shrug.

"'Course we can," is all I say. We're bound to get a drink at Ma's and Grandad's, and we can just take it from there when we get home.

I look at her. The glow in her eyes, burning eyes. She looks so much in love when she looks at me with those eyes. And she is in love, of course. Not just with me, but with being the sort of couple that we are right now. The sort of couple we see sometimes in films. Free spirits, rebels. The kind that tend to do things on the spur of the moment and like to live more fiercely and intensely than most people do. I know how she likes to identify with all that. She fixes her eyes on mine. A moment, then she puts a hand on the back of my neck. Closes her eyes as she draws me to her. Wants to kiss me now. Wants us to kiss right here in the middle of the street with people walking by. Wants to show everybody how little we care. Like there's nobody in the world but us. And I do what she wants. Kiss her.

Namsos, July 6th, 2006

Dear David,

When I think back on the 80s, it sometimes strikes me that it's not my 80s I'm looking back on, but the image of the 80s that's presented on the internet and in films, on TV and radio and in the newspapers now, in 2006. When I sat down to write this letter, for example, what I thought about was Sky Channel and Pat Sharp on MTV. I thought about BALL sweatshirts and down jackets with leather patches on the shoulders, about Toto and Alphaville and Dire Straits and Frankie Goes to Hollywood. I thought about pastel colors and mullets and fountain ponytails and marathon dances in the gym at Namsos Lower Secondary. Even though none of this was any part of my life or Bendick's in the 80s I sat down at the computer and thought of all this and a lot else that I knew little or nothing about back then and that I wouldn't have known anything about today either if it weren't for the fact that I once went out with a woman who tried to deaden her fear of getting old by refusing to let go of the 80s and still dressed in much the same way and listened to much the same music at the age of thirty-five as she had when she was a teenager.

This fact, that I remember somebody else's 80s better than

my own, reminds me of the time when we celebrated the fifteenth anniversary of us finishing lower secondary. I hadn't been planning to go to this party and I don't think anyone else expected to see me there either, but the very fact that they didn't, well, that brought out the devil in me and after a few drinks to give me Dutch courage I took a taxi to the Namsos Athenæum where the party was being held. And before too long I was sitting next to you, sipping a red-colored welcome drink, smiling happily at speeches full of references to Lacoste shirts, Levi 501s and red leather ties worn to confirmations. And shortly after that I was dancing to "White Wedding," joining in the chorus of "Buffalo Soldier," and laughing my head off at a sketch performed by a bunch from the A class, all about Pac-Man, Donkey Kong and the old Commodore computers.

But the uneasy feeling that this wasn't my 80s grew stronger and stronger. As if my ma could afford to buy me Levi's or Lacoste shirts or gear from Busnel or Matinique when those brands were all the rage. Never mind video games or a computer or cable TV or one of those electronic games that you saw kids playing with in the playground. As if I ever listened to the Top Ten or got asked to parties where they played "Forever Young," "Wake Me Up Before You Go-Go" and other hits from those days. That wasn't my 80s. That was the 80s of all the well-off, clever, popular middle-class kids who came home to tables set for dinner every day and whose parents promised to pay for driving lessons if they stayed away from cigarettes. And yet there I was nodding and laughing and having fun, and this gradually began to make me feel that I was betraying the kid I had actually been in the 80s. Not only did I not object when our successful former classmates presented this garish version of the 80s, I actually almost fooled myself into believing that that had also been my 80s. I was in the process of erasing the boy I'd been back then.

And if you ask me, that's exactly what's happening now, all over Norway. The popular, well-off, clever teachers' pets that you and I went to school with are all grown up now, and just as Audun and Marianne took over the planning committee and turned that evening into a carefree, innocent, safe, candy-colored version of the 1980s, so all the pampered, successful thirty-somethings in the country have taken over all the influential posts and appointments. In TV program after TV program, radio program after radio program, newspaper article after newspaper article they talk about how they represent you, me and everyone else. And eventually we start to believe them. Eventually we start to believe that their version of both the past and the present applies to us as well.

And exactly the same thing happened to our parents' generation, you know. Think of being young in the late 60s and early 70s and you immediately picture grim-faced Marxist-Leninists demonstrating against the war in Vietnam or long-haired, hash-smoking hippies sitting in a park listening to Jimi Hendrix and saying, "Far out, man." Everybody does it. Even my ma, although she probably doesn't even know who Jimi Hendrix was. She doesn't picture her own 60s and 70s, she pictures the 60s and 70s of the kids who were popular and good at school and well off when she was young, the kids who were born with a silver spoon in their mouths and sailed through their childhoods without a scratch and went on to become student radicals and academics. For decade after decade they have occupied their positions of power and presented their versions of the 60s and 70s and that is what Ma pictures. Even though she grew up in the small northern town of Namsos and has probably never seen a hippie in her life, even though she never went on a protest march and the closest she ever got to further education was sleeping with an asshole of a substitute teacher we had at Namsos Lower Secondary in the early 80s.

So I promise you one thing: this letter's not just going to be a fucking rehash of the version of the 80s we were presented with at that class reunion. Now that I've sat myself down here to help you "find out who you are," as it said in the paper, there's no fucking way I'm going to be tricked into writing Audun's and Marianne's story. I'm going to write about me and you and Bendik. I'm going to write about my tinker family and your family of hick farmers—and that story, our story, begins on the day that you and your mother moved in with your stepfather, a real sleazeball if ever there was one, notorious in the town for using his position as the local vicar to take advantage of single women.

I don't remember exactly when this was, but it was long before they pulled down the old fence separating the detached bungalows of the middle class from the public housing where Bendik and I grew up, so it was before I turned fourteen, at any rate. I was about eleven maybe, maybe twelve, maybe thirteen, I can't say for sure, but it really doesn't matter that fucking much. In any case, one summer's day in the early 80s a blue and white moving van was parked outside the vicarage, and me and Bendik were hiding up on the mound of grass where your stepfather used to empty the wheelbarrow after he'd mowed the lawn. The plan was for us to dash out and grab some stuff from the van every time the movers carried something into the house. Guerrilla tactics, Bendik called it, obsessed as he was with soldiers and war. Dart out, dart back, quick as lightning, dashing back and forth until we ran out of room in the old bike trailer we had left on the path behind us. We used to do little raids like that now and again because my grandad had a scrapyard and a junk shop and he bought just about everything we brought him, no questions asked, so it was an easy way to make some money.

But when we looked down from the top of the mound of grass and saw that the men carrying in your belongings were Uncle Willy and Odd Kåre Hindmo we immediately ditched our plan, because there was always the chance that they would get the blame for pinching the stuff and we didn't want that, obviously. So instead we lay there spying on them. They were puffing and panting, their faces shiny and running with sweat. Uncle Willy had taken off his shirt and was working stripped to the waist. He had a tattoo of an anchor on his forearm and a hairy belly that bulged and strained over the waistband of his trousers and jiggled when he walked.

"Fuckin' hell!" he wheezed, taking off his gloves, picking up a bottle of beer that was sitting on the trash bin next to the wooden fence and knocking back the last of it in one big gulp. "Don't you think it's hot?" he asked, looking up at Odd Kåre in the body of the van. Odd Kåre didn't answer. He looked dead beat; big, dark, heart-shaped patches of sweat had formed on the front and back of his white T-shirt. He stopped what he was doing, took hold of the hem of his T-shirt, pulled it away from his body and flapped it, airing himself. "The sun's nearly down and it's still hot as hell," Uncle Willy gasped. Odd Kåre just turned around, grasped the arm of a sofa and dragged it right out to the front, then he tramped off to the back again. "It's nigh on unbearable," Uncle Willy mumbled, then he set the empty beer bottle down on a little table that was standing in the driveway. Odd Kåre lifted a rolled-up carpet off a pile of boxes. "Christ Almighty, you'd think it was the middle of the fuckin' day, it's that hot," Uncle Willy said.

"Yeah, yeah," Odd Kåre growled.

"Eh?"

Odd Kåre heaved the carpet onto the sofa, took a fresh bottle of beer from the crate and handed it to Uncle Willy.

"You don't have to make excuses," he said.

"Fuck's that supposed to mean?" Uncle Willy said, sounding mad now.

"Aw, gimme a break," Odd Kåre sighed. "Yesterday it was because you'd eaten salt herring. What'll it be tomorrow, I wonder."

"What the fuck are you insinuating?"

"Cut it out, I said! Open your bottle, drink up and then get on wi' your work. I'm knackered and I'd like to get this done and out of the way."

Uncle Willy eyed Odd Kåre for a second.

"Who the hell d'you think you are?" Uncle Willy shouted.

Odd Kåre sighed and shook his head.

"Eh?" Uncle Willy shouted again. "Who the fucking hell d'you think you are?"

"Aw, please. I don't feel like arguing with you. You can drink as much as you like just so long as you do your work."

"So long as I do my work?" Uncle Willy stared at Odd Kåre, his mouth hanging open. "So long as I do my work? Are you saying I don't do my work now? First you insinuate that I drink too much, then you tell me I'm not doing my work. You've hardly been working here a fucking year and now you're talking to me like I'm a damn fucking errand boy."

"Save it!" Odd Kåre snapped.

Uncle Willy gave a bark of angry laughter.

"You've got a fucking nerve!" he cried.

Odd Kåre put his hands on his hips, looked down at the floor of the van and shook his head.

"I never said you weren't doing—"

"I'll tell you one thing, you great turnip!" Uncle Will bawled, cutting him short. He slammed the unopened bottle of beer down on the table next to the empty one and took a step closer to the van. "I'll tell you one thing," he said again, pointing up at Odd Kåre. "I tell you, you and those stringy goddamn arms o' yours don't lift half as fuckin' much in a day as I do. Do you realize that? Eh?"

Odd Kåre took a deep breath, about to say something, but then he flapped his hand at Uncle Willy and sighed. Uncle Willy licked his lips, looking madder and madder.

"Not even half," he said.

"Yeah, yeah, that's right," Odd Kåre said. "I'm weak and bone idle."

"Yeah, you bet your fucking life you are."

"Hmm," Odd Kåre said, opening his eyes wide and smiling sarcastically at Uncle Willy. "But d'you think we could get back to work now?"

Uncle Willy just stood there gawking at Odd Kåre for a moment or two, then he snorted, picked up a box of ornaments and set off up to the house. Then he suddenly stopped, turned and came back to the van.

"Oh, by the way, how was that daughter of Arthur's?" he asked with a snide grin.

Odd Kåre looked a bit taken aback.

"Oh aye," Uncle Willy said, nodding triumphantly. "I saw you the pair of you."

Odd Kåre didn't say anything.

"For fuck's sake!" Uncle Willy crowed. "As if screwin' minors wasn't enough, now you're havin' it off wi' your own friend's daughter. It's like I said, you've got a fucking nerve."

Odd Kåre's face was like stone, his eyes bored into Uncle Willy's.

"Oh, dear, what's the matter?" Uncle Willy sneered. "Did you eat something that didn't agree with you?"

"You'd better watch yourself," Odd Kåre said coldly and softly.

"I should watch myself?" Uncle Willy said. He stared at Odd Kåre for a second, then he put down the box he was holding and jabbed his chest with his finger. "I'm to watch myself. Me? Well, I'll tell you this much, you're gonna be in bi-ig fuckin' trouble if Arthur gets to hear about it, because you'll wind up right back in the slammer. You do realize that, don't you?"

Odd Kåre kept his eyes fixed on Uncle Willy's, saying nothing.

"And you're telling me to watch myself," Uncle Willy said again.

"Aye," Odd Kåre said, then he paused. "Well, I don't know if you remember anything about Friday night, but would it ring any bells if I said that there's an Audi lying at the bottom of the fjord and that both the police and the insurance company are wrong if they think it was stolen?"

Silence for a few moments.

"A-ha . . . now who's worried?" Odd Kåre grinned, leaning forward slightly and staring at Uncle Willy. "It's like I say, you drink way too much and you'd better watch out. It's easy to give too much away when you're drunk, you know. There's plenty of folk have got their fingers burned that way!"

They glowered at each other for a couple of seconds, then Odd Kåre turned away and started dragging furniture towards the front. Uncle Willy picked up the unopened bottle, pulled a tin of *snus* from his back pocket and flicked the cap off the bottle with a little pop. White foam gushed out of the neck and a little beer ran down the sides of the bottle and over his big fist. "Fuck," he mumbled, slurping up most of the foam and shaking his hand, sending drops of beer flying.

Suddenly a voice called from the veranda: "Excuse me!"

It was your mother, Berit.

She was standing with her arms crossed, looking down at Uncle Willy with a faint smile on her face.

"I was wondering if you'd mind not drinking beer while you're working here. There's a child in the house, you see," she said and she raised her hand and pointed to an open window on the first floor. And there was a tall, skinny boy of my own age. He was standing perfectly still with his arms by his sides, gazing down solemnly at the drive.

That was you.

There was silence for a couple of seconds.

Uncle Willy took the bottle away from his lips and stood there holding it out stiffly in front of him. He shot a surprised look at Odd Kåre and Odd Kåre looked back at him in equal surprise. Then they both turned and looked up at your mother. No one said anything for a moment or two, then Odd Kåre and Uncle Willy looked at one another again. Odd gave a little snort of laughter, Uncle Willy sniggered and shook his head, then he put the bottle to his lips, tipped his head back and took a long swig on it while you and your mother looked on. "Aaahh," he sighed, then he set the bottle on the ground, drew the back of his hand across his mouth, sauntered over to the van and began to lift off some of the stuff that had collected at the front. Your mother stood and watched him for a moment or two then she just turned and went back inside.

"There's a child in the house, you see," Odd Kåre said, mimicking her and making a face.

Uncle Willy grinned. "Who the fuck does she think she is?" Odd Kåre went on. He pulled his T-shirt over his head and tossed it onto the grass. "Eh?" he said. "And who the hell does she think we are? Does she think we're gonna talk or act any different just because there's a goddamn vicar in the house?"

"People like her, they've never broken a sweat in their lives, I'm tellin' you," said Uncle Willy. "They've never lifted anythin' heavier than their wallets and however heavy they may be it's not quite the same thing. They don't understand that it's thirsty work lifting and carrying."

"Gimme half an hour wi her an I'd make her sweat," Odd Kåre grunted, clutching his balls.

Uncle Willy gave a dirty laugh.

"Aye, I bet that's just what she needs," Odd Kåre went on.

"Yeah, you could be right," Uncle Willy laughed.

"Fuck yeah! You think I don't know the type? Eh? Women married to shrimps like him—men that feel guilty every time they get a hard-on—you think I haven't met their type before? What they need is a right good fucking from a man with more to him than a fancy CV, only they're not allowed to admit it, to themselves or anybody else. They're programmed to say that what they want are soft, gentle men who're always giving them hugs, who say gosh instead of fuck and who think it's so important to talk things over. No wonder they become frustrated and mean, no wonder they become bitter and miserable, no wonder they start to hate anybody that bears any resemblance to a real man."

Uncle Willy stood there with his hands on his hips, shaking with laughter, rolls of fat jiggling.

"They're all the same, vicars' wives and other churchgoin' women. The same goes for them women's-libbers and feminists. They're all the same, there's nothin' they'd like better than a real man, but there's no way they can let themselves or anybody else have that, so they start to hate men and sex and all that. Homespun psychology, maybe, but it's true!"

Uncle Willy's laughter turned into a long coughing fit.

"Well," he said, as soon as he was finished coughing, "why don't you tell her what she's missin', man?" He cleared his throat and wiped away the tears of laughter.

"Yeah, maybe I should," Odd Kåre said. "I'm not much of a

knight in shining armor, but I suppose I could make an exception in her case and offer to come to her rescue."

Uncle Willy burst out laughing again.

"Actually, that's not such a bad idea," Odd Kåre said, turning his eyes upward, frowning and appearing to consider the matter. Uncle Willy laughed and shook his head. Odd Kåre eyed Uncle Willy, then he cupped his balls and squeezed, making them bulge between his fingers. "I've got a long load here inside my Levi's, you see, and now that I think about it, I wouldn't mind runnin' it through the vicar's wife's tunnel," he said.

Uncle Willy's roars of laughter lapsed into another hacking coughing fit.

"Hey!" Odd Kåre suddenly shouted. "Mrs. Forberg!"

"No, man . . . don't," Uncle Willy gasped. He looked at Odd Kåre and shook his head, but the wicked grin on his beefy face was quite clearly telling Odd Kåre to go right ahead.

"Mrs. Forberg!" he shouted again, eyes fixed on the open veranda door.

"Hey! For Christ's sake," Uncle Willy said, grinning. "Leave the woman alone, you! We're working here."

But Odd Kåre was not to be put off.

"Mrs. Forberg!" he shouted for the third time.

And then your mother appeared. She stood in the doorway studying Odd Kåre for a moment, then she came down the short flight of steps and onto the veranda.

"Yes," she said.

"I was just wondering if it was going to be a while before the vicar gets home?"

She waited a second before answering.

"Why d'you ask that?"

"Well . . ." Odd Kåre said with a shrug. "You know . . . a lot of men don't like their wives being left alone when there are workmen in the house, so we were just saying that maybe we should put our shirts back on till he comes home. For your sake, I mean. So there won't be any ructions in the boudoir later."

A hiccup of laughter escaped Uncle Willy, he put a hand to his mouth and kept his eyes fixed on the gravel, shaking with laughter.

"Yeah, well, we talk from experience, you see," Odd Kåre went on. "There's a lot of jealous husbands around. And we can kind of see why. I mean, there's plenty of women that sit at home alone feeling frustrated, and naturally, if you've got a workman or two in the house, well . . . things can happen." Odd Kåre held your mother's eye and smiled innocently.

"Just get on with your work, would you please?" your mother said.

"Right you are," Odd Kåre said brightly. "Actually, we were just thinking it might be time to bring in the bed."

At this Uncle Willy doubled up, slapped his knees and howled with laughter.

"If that's okay with you, that is," Odd Kåre said, looking up at your mother with that same innocent look in his eyes. She said nothing, simply stood for a moment looking at him, then she turned and went back into the house. You were still standing like a ghost at the dark window upstairs. Rigid and staring with your arms hanging by your sides. Me and Bendik lay where we were for a little while longer, then we slid down off the warm, smelly mound of grass.

Had Uncle Willy and Odd Kåre Hindmo known that your mother was Erik's daughter they would obviously never have behaved the way they did when you moved in, and had me and Bendik known we would never have carried on where Uncle Willy and Odd Kåre left off, but because we looked up to them and thought they were great, that, of course, is exactly what we did, right? We pestered the life out of you and your mother from day one and we went on pestering you until we found out that you were Erik's grandson.

So who was Erik? Yeah, he was your grandfather. But who was he to us?

Erik wasn't just a close friend of our family, he was also our grandad's "business partner," as they called it. He worked on some of the fishing boats and shrimp boats when they needed extra men and at the sawmill when they were short-handed, but all of that and the little bit he made from selling firewood and Christmas trees from the little copse your family had on Otterøya was just a cover, because what your family actually made its living from back then was the "distillery" that Erik had built in the barn and that he ran with his brother Albert and the rest of the hicks on Otterøya. He was careful as hell, and even though he'd been making illicit liquor ever since he stopped working for the highway department in the late 60s or early 70s not many people knew what he did. Everybody in my family knew, though, because Grandad was one of several middlemen Erik used to sell his liquor.

Once or twice a month Erik would roll up in a battered old army truck with a tarpaulin over the back or a white Hiace with a number plate so caked in dirt and muck that the number was unreadable. Once Grandad had opened the doors of the big, yellow-washed shed behind our house Erik would back the vehicle up until the rear end was inside the shed, and then all they had to do was unload the jerry cans and stack them behind a whole wall of old banana crates that were only there to screen the booze from prying eyes. None of the neighbors suspected a thing: everybody simply assumed that Grandad was taking delivery of more stuff for his junk shop, but me and Bendik (and later you too) usually kept a lookout anyway, just in case some busybody should come by, the plan being that if we stuck our fingers in our mouths and whistled loudly Erik and Grandad would haul some scrap out of the van that Erik always had with him just in case, then they would pull down the tarpaulin or slam the car door shut and say: "Right then, that's the lot for now."

Erik had been delivering moonshine to us for as long as I could remember and was a regular visitor at other times too so I'd got to know him pretty well, not just directly, but also through the countless and outrageously far-fetched stories he and Grandad were forever telling about themselves. He had a big, pear-shaped face with eyes set close up against his nose; he was well over six feet tall, so broad that your mother had to sew a panel into the backs of his jackets and shirts so they'd fit, and if you took his hand it was like sticking your fist into a boxing glove. "The only thing that man bows his head for is the top of the door," Grandma used to say and it was true, because just like Grandad he had a remarkably powerful need to be his own man and a fierce hatred of being ordered about, managed or controlled. As far as Grandad was concerned I think this had something to do with him being a tinker, because if there's one thing about a tinker it's that he likes to be his own master and to go where he wants when he wants. Erik was a bit like that too, because as the son of a fisherman and farmer on Otterøya who personally provided just about everything his family needed, he had been taught to take care of himself and not rely on anyone else. And any man who learns to live like that is obviously also going to learn to love freedom as much as he learns to hate everything and anybody that tries to limit that same freedom.

"We're soon gonna have to ask the fucking authorities for

permission to wipe our own asses," he used to say. "There's no way I'm asking leave to put out a coupla salmon nets, and no way I'm asking leave to bury asbestos panels on my own land. It's a flaming dictatorship, that's what it is.

"Aye, and when some poor bastard up at Lierne shoots a bear that's attacking his sheep, fuck me if he doesn't get a stiffer sentence than if he'd shot his fucking neighbor," Grandad says.

"Aye, and they call that progress," Erik says.

That's how they went on when they were sitting having a drink. It was always the same: at some point they would start to get hot under the collar about something they weren't allowed to do, or that they'd been criticized for doing, and they would get more and more steamed up until they were sitting there fizzing and fuming at the council and the government and politicians and rich people and everybody else that poked their noses into things that were none of their business and that they knew next to nothing about. This need to be one's own master, to be a free agent, was also, I think, one of the main reasons why they made and sold illicit liquor. The money was definitely the chief incentive, obviously, but producing and selling moonshine was the same as breaking the law and breaking the law was the same as refusing to do what the authorities and power-mad politicians told them to do, and since this in turn satisfied their great need to see themselves as free men I think they would have done what they did whether they made money from it nor not. It's a bit like me taking a trip across the Swedish border to buy drink and cigarettes. I don't save a lot of money on it, but by Christ it feels good to do the greedy, toll-mad, duty-happy Norwegian state out of a few kroner.

I once visited the farm where you and your mother and Erik lived and where he had his still. Like I said, Grandad had a scrapyard and a junk shop, and one autumn day when I had gone with him to pick up stuff from an estate sale out on Otterøya he decided to call in on Erik and Albert and the rest of the hicks for a drink. After driving for a good ten to fifteen miles, stopping every hundred yards to shoo sheep and cattle off the road, we turned onto a narrow dirt road so rutted and potholed that Grandad's false teeth broke with a loud crack as we bounced over the last bump.

"You'll have to do something about the suspension on that pickup of yours," Erik remarked, grinning, once Grandad and I had climbed out of the truck and Grandad was standing there in the muck, glumly inspecting the damage to his dentures. "Ain't that right, Albert?" he said, glancing at his brother.

"Aye, must be somethin' wrong wi' the suspension," Albert agreed, leering and baring a row of rotten stumps that glinted in the sun.

"The suspension?" Grandad growled. "The boy and I switched places I don't know how many fuckin' times just over that last few hundred yards."

"Yeah, yeah, now come away in and sample the last batch," Erik said, laughing as he laid his great bear paw on Grandad's skinny shoulders and pushed him up the ramp and into the barn where the still was kept.

I'd seen plenty of illicit stills before this, of course, because back then most of the fathers in our neighborhood had their own still gurgling away in the basement, ensuring them of their weekend tipple and a bit more besides, but the sight that met my eyes when I walked into the baking hot, yeasty-smelling barn was something else again, and that's putting it mildly. The must was stored in three green septic tanks, each of which had to have held 5,000 liters; the three gleaming condensers at the very back of the barn were enormous and could probably have distilled hundreds of liters of must at one time, and in front of a whole wall of ten-liter cans containing the finished product hung row upon row of charcoal filters. I've no idea how much liquor Erik and his team produced in an average year, but we're talking thousands of liters, certainly. Thinking about it now, though, what really puzzles me is: what on earth did they do with the money? The profits must have been huge, but going by their homes and their clothes and their habits, anybody would have thought they were dirt-poor, every one of them. The house where you and Erik and your mother lived was small, crooked and lopsided and according to Grandad it was so drafty that there didn't have to be any more than a fresh breeze outside to give you a center parting as you sat in their living room watching the evening news. And as if that weren't enough, they went on using the outside privy in the barn until well into the 70s. Erik normally wore old, washed-out flannel shirts with leather patches on the elbows and when he paid us a visit I used to charge my friends fifty øre for a peek at his massive shoes parked in the hall, so I clearly remember how worn the soles were on one side and so thin that he must have felt every pebble or bit of grit under his feet when he walked. The only thing that Erik quite evidently spent money on was motors: he was a member of the local Amcar club and sitting in the yard alongside the Hiace and the army truck that he used for delivering liquor were a 1957 Chevrolet Bel Air and a 1960 Oldsmobile F-88 convertible—cars that cost a fortune even back then.

But however shabbily dressed Erik was and however dilapidated the house where you lived might have been, it was nothing compared to the state of his brother Albert's place fifty yards farther up the hill. Albert lived all alone in a tumbledown wooden shack with the once red paint peeling off its walls and two broken windows that he could never be bothered to change, but patched up instead with black plastic and bits of cardboard boxes. He never washed and rarely changed his clothes, and Grandma said the inside of his shack was a sight to behold, because he stoked his stove with tree trunks he found lying around in the forest and saw no point in chopping them up when he could simply stick one end in the stove and keep stuffing the trunk further in as it burned down. This meant, though, that the stove door had to be kept open while the fire was on, so the walls were pitch-black with soot and a heavy, acrid stench hung in the air, the sort of smell you get in old, burned-out buildings. Not only that but he couldn't be bothered throwing garbage in the bin or taking it down to the shore and burning it. He simply lifted the trapdoor in the floor and dropped it all into the cellar, where it lay and reeked and brewed and stewed, and the unbearable stink of the midden seeped through the cracks in the floorboards and mingled with the stench of smoke and soot. Albert himself was totally unaffected by it, he was used to it, Grandma said, and anyway he didn't smell any better himself, because not only didn't he wash himself or his clothes, he didn't bother to brush the few teeth he had left in his mouth either, so you had to stand well back when you spoke to him—word had it that the fetid odor of stale fish and sour roll-ups could kill flies at ten yards.

"I wash the kitchen from top to bottom every time he's been to see us," Grandma used to say.

Grandad believed there was only one explanation for Erik's and Albert's pauper-like existence and that was greed. Albert survived mainly on fish he caught himself and food that he got for free from the staff at the Co-op because it was past its sell-by date and they were going to have to throw it out anyway. His evenings were usually spent tucked up inside the foul-smelling shack drinking moonshine and cold water in the glow of a twenty-watt bulb, and the farthest he was prepared to go in terms of extravagance and generosity was to invite his only grandchild to the new Chinese restaurant in Namsos, because she was anorexic so she was never hungry anyway. Erik probably wasn't quite as mean, Grandad said, but he nicked toilet paper and packets of salt and pepper from the Community Center Café on Saturdays and if stewed prunes were fifty øre cheaper at the ABC supermarket than at Thor's Cut-Price, then you could bet your boots he'd put the pack back on the shelf and amble on down to the ABC. So yes, he was fond of money, too.

But we had no idea, when you and your mother came to town, that you were closely related to our good friends Erik and Albert and that you had grown up in deepest, darkest hick country out on Otterøya. Since you had moved in with the vicar we just took it for granted that you were a simple country boy who went to church every Sunday and never swore, and as far as me and Bendik were concerned I think this was an even better reason to give you a really warm welcome than our admiration for Uncle Willy and Odd Kåre Hindmo and our desire to imitate them.

It was one thing that Grandad was a tinker and that the Church's persecution of tinkers in Norway had left him with a hatred of churches and churchmen that had rubbed off on me and everybody else in our family, but quite another, and much worse, that your stepfather was a disgusting slimeball who was always making passes at my ma and other single mothers in the neighborhood. Before he got together with your mother he was actually known all over Namsos for using his position as vicar as a way of getting to meet single women—as he probably had to do if he was ever to get lucky, because to be perfectly honest Arvid wasn't the most attractive of men. He had no eyebrows, and he suffered very badly from psoriasis so his face was often covered in red, running sores. He wore freshly ironed shirts that he buttoned right up to the neck and their backs were always covered in a white dusting of dandruff and dead skin. Not only that, but he was a creepy, snakelike character who reeked of scheming and ulterior motives and put everybody with any sense on their guard when they saw him slithering towards them. According to Grandad he always wore that smarmy vicar's smile no matter how angry or annoyed he might be feeling, and whether there was any reason for it or not he would shower people with compliments, flattering and soft-soaping the women in particular, as I know only too well because when he was after Ma he was always clapping his hands and going into ecstasies over things that other visitors scarcely noticed, far less remarked on. "Oh, Laila, what a beautiful tablecloth," he'd cry. "Did you embroider it yourself?" Or: "I must say, Laila, these are the best doughnuts I've ever tasted." He chattered like a woman and the only reason Ma didn't tell him to go fuck himself was, of course, that she and Grandad and Uncle Willy and Odd Kåre were planning to milk him for a few kroner—and that they did, very successfully. One day when the vicar from hell was sitting on our sofa, trying to come up with more fine words, Ma resorted to the good old ruse of ripping her blouse and screaming rape. Me and Bendik were helping Grandad to fix his ancient Corvette that evening and I had gone in to get some soldering wire to mend a hole in the exhaust when I heard her scream. The next second Uncle Willy and Odd Kåre burst into the room through two different doors. They pretended to be outraged, shouting and bawling that they were going to kill Arvid and send him to the bottom of Namsos Fjord, and then Grandad walked in and played the good guy, urging everybody to calm down and trying to prevent things from turning violent. They were prepared to let Arvid go, that was no problem. They could even be persuaded not to report the incident to the police, but Arvid would just have to make it up to them in some other way, Grandad said—the message obviously being that the vicar from hell had better get out his wallet or else. And that he did, terrified and confused as he was.

But by paying up to avoid being reported for an alleged rape Arvid was as good as admitting to having committed said rape, and since he was terrified that Berit would get to hear of it, and of how he'd been going around slavering over every unattached woman in Namsos, he wouldn't allow me to set foot inside your house after we became friends. He told you and Berit it was because I was a thieving rascal who would make off with the silver first chance I got. But if that really was the reason then how the fuck was Bendik allowed in? Because everybody knew he was an even bigger rogue than me. But more about that later because, like I said, it would be some time yet before we became friends.

Namsos, July 4th, 2006. Grandpa don't eat prawns

Sitting in the garden at Ma's and Grandpa's. Me and Mona, Grandpa and Ma. Smoking and drinking beer. Ice-cold beer can in my hand. Green beer can beaded with glittering drops of condensation. Straight out of Ma's cooler bag. I take a little sip and sit there gazing at the garden, running my eye over the long green grass, dandelions sticking up all over the place and Grandpa's old Chrysler parked alongside the shed. It's crazy, really, what a great car, and it's just sitting there rusting away. I should really do it up. Some day when the mood takes me I should maybe suggest that to Grandpa, it would cost a fair bit and it's a lot of work, but it would look fucking brilliant, I'm sure it would. Ah well, we'll see. I rest the beer can on my stomach, shut my eyes and lay my head back. Feel the sun warm on my face. Burning my forehead.

"You got to hand it to them, though, them coloreds," Grandpa says,

Carrying on with what he was saying. Talking about all the coloreds that have been coming to the town lately. I open my eyes and look at him. At his tanned, wrinkled face. Lean face. Shiny with sweat. He rearranges the hankie on his head, a white checked hankie that's supposed to protect his scalp from the sun.

"They've got respect for their old folk," he says.

"Yeah, that's true," I say.

"They don't leave their parents to rot in an old folks' home."

"Nope," I say.

Short pause.

"To think that's what this society's come to," he goes on.

"Hmm," I say.

"I'd never have had the conscience to pack my parents off to such a place when they were alive. They took care of me when I was young, and when they got old it went without fucking saying that I'd take care of them."

I nod. Take another sip of my beer.

"Aye, that's life for you," Grandpa says.

"Would you stop your goddamned bellyaching," Ma suddenly bursts out, narrowing her eyes and shaking her head. "I've got no plans to pack you off to the old folks' home just yet, so you can relax," she adds, running a hand through her blue-black hair. She sits back in her camping chair, shutting her eyes and looking exasperated, then she opens her eyes and snorts, shooting another glance at Grandpa.

It takes me a moment to catch on, but then I realize what she's talking about. Because that rant of Grandpa's was obviously aimed at Ma. He's scared he's going to wind up in the old folks' home and he's trying to tell her that he wants, and expects, her to carry on looking after him. That's why he's going on like this. He sits there gawking at Ma, trying to look baffled. His nearly toothless mouth hanging open. Like a little black hole in his lean face.

"What the fuck are you jabbering about," he says.

He stops. Turns to me, looks at Mona. Flings out a hand and gives us a look, as if to say, "Did you ever hear anything like it?" I look at him and give a little shrug. Look at Mona. She's feeling a bit uncomfortable. I can tell by her face. She avoids my eye, pretends to be interested in something under the table, like she's trying to flick off an insect or something. She doesn't like it when they fight.

"Aw, don't act like you don't know what I'm talking about," Ma says, waving her hand at Grandpa, and I see the flab on her upper arm wobble, bingo wings flapping from side to side.

Grandpa stares at her. The baffled look seems to fade from his face. He looks angry now, offended.

"And don't you sit there harping on about what you've got or haven't got the conscience for either," Ma goes on, looking straight at Grandpa. "You weren't the fuckin' one that wore yourself out tending to your own parents at the end, were you? Oh, no, because you left that job to my ma," she says. "You had the conscience to do that, all right."

Silence.

No sound except the low drone of a lawnmower a few yards away.

"Somebody had to work and bring in some money," Grandpa mutters.

I see Ma's mouth drop open as he says it. Then she turns to me, looks at me like she can't believe her ears. A look of astonishment. Then amusement. I eye her, just for a second, and then I burst out laughing. I can't help it. One thing Grandpa could never be accused of is hard work. I don't think he's ever had a proper job in his life, so he laid himself wide open there. It looks like he's realized that himself now. And he starts to chuckle too. Laughs his creaky laugh as he picks up his beer can, takes a swig.

Laughter for a few seconds.

Then Mona dares to raise her eyes again. She doesn't look uncomfortable anymore, not now that we're all laughing. She smiles and looks almost happy. Relieved.

"What are you laughing at?"

Mom looks at her, nods at Grandpa.

"Him. He wouldn't have dragged himself out of his fuckin' easy chair if the goddamned house'd been on fire," she says. "So it's a bit rich him making himself out to be this great old worker."

And we crack up again. Nice one, Ma, and we roar with laughter.

"I don't know—what I've got to fuckin' put up with," Grandpa sighs.

But he laughs as well. He likes these stories about himself and he chuckles as he lifts his beer again. He takes another swig then rests the can on his pot belly. I study him as I sit there: funny-looking body he has, when you think about it, with his stick-thin arms and legs and a stomach like a football.

Couple of seconds.

Then a voice shouts: "Excuse me."

The laughter kind of peters out. I look behind me and there's Ma's and Grandpa's neighbor. Over by the trash bins, looking at us.

"Can I have a word with you?" he says, nodding at Ma.

"Talk away," Ma says.

"If you could maybe come over here for a moment."

"I can hear you perfectly well from here," Ma says.

Silence for a second, then:

"You can't keep dumping so much in the bins that the lids won't shut," he says. He motions with his head towards the bins without taking his eyes off Mom.

"Yeah, I can, as you can fuckin' well see."

The neighbor looks at the grass. Shuts his eyes and sighs. Opens his eyes again.

"The crows are pecking holes in the bags," he says. "And they're dragging the trash into my garden."

"Ah, so they must know where it belongs, then," Ma says.

And then she turns to us, laughs that rough smoker's laugh of hers. A hoarse cackle. Sidelong glance turning her eyes into two black slits in her plump face. I look across at the neighbor and grin. And Grandpa's laughing creakily on the other side of the table. The neighbor doesn't say anything, he eyes us for a moment or two then he just shakes his head and walks away. As if to say there's no point in talking to us right now. As if to say how hopeless we are.

"Fuckin' clown," Ma says. Says it loud enough for the neighbour to hear. Sits and stares at him for a couple of seconds and then she turns to us. "Maybe he should have thought about it before he blocked our view with that eyesore of a garage of his," she says.

"Nine hundred thousand kroner that garage cost," Grandpa says. "Remote controlled door and Christ knows what all."

"Oh aye, nothin' but the best," Ma says. "But he got the babysitter pregnant, so life's not all roses over there either, I don't think."

She looks at me and grins. And I grin back. Look across at Mona as I raise my beer can to my lips and swallow the last drops. She tucks her fine, fair hair behind her ear and gives me a faint smile. Feeling uncomfortable again. She doesn't like it when there's fighting and arguing. Never has done. And anyway, she understands why the neighbor is pissed off about the bins. She feels obliged to take Ma's side, but she probably feels some sympathy for the guy. That's maybe why she's smiling that faint smile of hers. She's trying to grin and be like us, but she can't quite manage it.

I set the empty can on the table, flip open the lid of the cooler bag and take out another beer.

"Well, well, look who it is!" Ma cries suddenly.

I look up as I flip the lid closed again. It's Jørgen and Sara. Jørgen raises a hand in silent greeting. Sara eyes us, smiling a little uncertainly, she probably feels a bit daunted, seeing all Jørgen's family gathered together like this. She doesn't really look straight at us either. A bit shy.

"Are you still wearin' that hat?" Grandpa says. "It's thirty degrees out here."

Jørgen just grins, says nothing.

"Ach, that's just the style wi' the kids now," Ma says.

Grandpa shakes his head sadly. Tips his head back, takes a swig from his beer can and sets it back on his potbelly.

"What on earth have you done to yourself, Jørgen?" Mona asks suddenly.

And only now do I notice that he's got a shiner, one brow purple and swollen and the eye half-closed. It's a wonder he can see out of it at all.

"Fell off my skateboard," he says.

He plants his hands on the arms of the one free camping

chair and eases himself down into it, looks at us and smirks as he pulls his *snus* tin out of his jeans pocket, a smirk designed to let us know that he didn't take a tumble on his skateboard at all. He's just saying that, and now he wants us to ask how he really got his black eye. I look at him and grin.

"Yeah, right, and the band played believe it if you like," I say.

I say what he wants me to say. Give him the chance to tell us what's he's dying to tell us. Because I know something's happened that he's proud of. That much I get.

Jørgen grins, waggles his head as he slips a *snus* sachet under his lip.

"Well, come on, tell us," I say.

"There's not much to tell," Jørgen says, putting the lid on the *snus* tin and slipping it back into his pocket. "I just got into a bit of a discussion with a guy in a taxi line last night."

"And he won the discussion, I see," Ma says, nodding at Jørgen's black eye.

"Ahhh," Jørgen says, "Well, maybe you should see the other guy before you say that."

I give a little laugh. And Jørgen looks at me and smiles, tobacco sachet glistening at me. It's like I thought. He looks proud. Proud and happy. Ma gives a little laugh as well.

"Too right," she says.

She exhales through her nose as she leans over the camping table. Drops her cigarette butt into my empty beer can. I hear the quick hiss as the glowing tip hits the dregs at the bottom.

"But don't you go getting into any trouble, Jørgen," Grandpa says sternly. "No shenanigans."

I turn to him. And Ma turns to him. We both stare at him in amazement. He's a fine one to go playing the man of peace, and I don't think. There's damn fucking few that've been in as much trouble over the years as he has. He looks at me, then at Ma. And then he bursts out laughing. It was just a joke and he gives that dry, creaky laugh of his. Acting all holier-than-thou again, like he did a minute ago. He tricked us again, the old rogue. And me and Ma and Jørgen, we laugh as well. And Mona laughs. I don't think she has any idea what Grandpa was like in his younger days, but I think she realizes that we're laughing for much the same reason as when Grandpa was making himself out be to this great old worker, so she laughs along with us. She even gives her head a little shake, as if the idea of Grandpa playing the man of peace is just too ridiculous for words. It's a way of trying to seem like one of the family. I realize that. I look at her and smile. I like the fact that she's making an effort to be one of us, part of the family. It makes me happy.

"Jørgen, for fuck's sake," Ma suddenly cries. "What are you doing—taking the last free chair and letting your girlfriend stand!"

"Yeah, well . . . I was here first," Jørgen says, flinging out his arms, acting all innocent.

"Heh-heh," I laugh, tipping my head back. "A fine fuckin' gentleman you are."

I eye him for a second, then I turn to Sara. Smile and shake my head, looking like I despair of him and sympathize with her. I always do this, it's a way of showing her that I like her and approve of her, that I like her so much I'll side with her rather than with my own son, or something like that.

"Is he always like this?" I say.

"Yes, actually," she says softly, smiling.

"Oy!" Jørgen cries, looking up at her like he's offended.

"Aw, come on, Jørgen," Ma says. "Give the girl the chair and get yourself another one out of the shed. You'll never get anywhere if you treat the ladies like that, you know."

"Christ—nag, nag, nag," Jørgen sighs, grinning as he gets up.

Ma glances across at Sara, nods to her.

"Aha, *that* got him moving" she says. "As soon as he thinks he might not get into your pants. Christ all-fucking-mighty, typical man, eh?"

She lets out a hoarse cackle, looks at Sara. The girl doesn't say anything, just tries to give a little laugh but it doesn't quite work, comes out as a strained giggle. It embarrasses her a bit when Ma talks like this. I've noticed it before, and it shows now too. She's probably not used to grown-ups talking to her like this, she's only fifteen so it's maybe not so surprising, she's just a girl.

"Yeah, like father, like son," Mona says.

She looks at Ma and laughs. Shoots a cheeky glance at me then looks at Ma again. And Ma laughs back.

"Yeah, do most of their thinking with that other head, both of them," she says. "Isn't that right, Sara?"

Sara doesn't say anything. She smiles faintly, doesn't quite know where to look. Going a bit pink now, too. I look at her and smile. Maybe I should change the subject before Ma follows this up with more sex talk. She's sitting there squirming, poor thing.

"Want a beer, Sara?" I say, looking across at her as I bend down, flip up the lid of the cool bag and take out a can.

"No thanks," Sara says.

"You don't want a beer?" Ma says. "Christ, you've got yourself a sensible girl there, Jørgen," she goes on, turning to Jørgen as he comes back carrying another camping chair. He doesn't answer right away, he's tripped over some bit of trash that's lying hidden in the long grass. He stumbles forward a couple of steps but manages to stay on his feet, curses under his breath as he looks back to see what it was, then turns around again and carries on over to us.

"Yeah, well, I don't know if she's as sensible as all that," he says. He puts down the chair, looks at Sara and gives a sly grin. A grin that hints at something that Sara has done, a grin that's meant to let us know there's more to Sara than meets the eye, that she's not as innocent as she seems or as we might think. And Sara plays along. Smiling, giving him a kind of stern look, like she's warning him not to say any more.

"What? What're you looking at me like that for?" Jørgen cries, raising his eyebrows and acting flabbergasted as he sets the chair down. "I've never said a word about how you've been feeding the fish for three days in a row," he says, and then he claps a hand to his mouth and goggles his eyes, acting as if it just slipped out. "Oops," he says, laughing.

"Shut up, you," Sara says, making a show of being annoyed and giving Jørgen a dig with her elbow, but she likes him talking about her like this, I can tell. She's sitting there smiling. And the rest of us chuckle. It wasn't all that funny, but we chuckle anyway, because Jørgen and Sara are inviting us to. This is something they're doing to make Sara seem more like one of us, I realize that. They're trying to show us that Sara's a grown-up too, that she's not a kid; that that's not why she refused a beer when I offered her one, and it's not because, doctor's daughter that she is, she thinks we're too common for her to drink beer with either, it's purely because she's been drunk three days in a row.

"Yeah, well the fish need to eat too, you know," I say, and I look at Jørgen and smile. And he smiles back. Christ he's got so big lately, Jørgen. I don't quite know what it is about him, but he seems to have become so grown-up in such a short time. Maybe it's his voice, the fact that his voice has got deeper. Or his eyebrows maybe, they've got darker and thicker. His hair is as fair as it's always been, but his eyebrows are almost black now and that makes him look a bit more grown-up somehow.

"Talkin' of food," Ma says. "I'm fuckin' starving. I think we should start making dinner. Jørgen, can you get the barbecue going?" she says.

Jørgen nods, gets up and wanders back over to the shed. He stops at the spot where he almost fell last time, bends down and picks up a rusty length of pipe, some old gutter, it looks like. That's what he tripped over, he chucks it into the nettles over by the Chrysler.

"It's pork chops for dinner," Ma says, looking at Mona as she plants her hands on the arms of her chair and pushes herself to her feet. "We were really supposed to be having prawns, but Grandpa didn't want them."

"I don't eat prawns," Grandpa says, picking up his beer can and taking a swig.

"Oh, but they're so good," Mona says, smiling.

"Aye, but I miss the old woman that fuckin' much every time I smell them," he says.

"Oh?" Mona says.

She looks at him, doesn't get the joke.

But I laugh. And Ma laughs, she looks at Grandpa and laughs so hard her rolls of fat jiggle. Her eyes narrow when she laughs as heartily as this, turning into two black slits in her pudgy face. And Grandpa creaks contentedly, he likes being the funny man, Grandpa does, likes to be the one who makes everybody laugh.

"Oh, God," Mona says, she's just got the joke and now she cracks up as well.

The only one not laughing is Sara, she looks at us, smiling uncertainly. She has no idea what we're laughing at.

"Don't you get it?" Ma says, looking at Sara.

"No," Sara says, shaking her head, the corners of her mouth lifting slightly in a smile.

"D'you mean to tell me the twat of a doctor's daughter doesn't smell?" Ma says. She gives that hoarse smoker's laugh of hers, glances around at the rest of us while Grandpa creaks even louder than his camping chair and Mona has to put a hand over her mouth to save spraying beer all over the table. I look across at Sara, she's flushed and smiling, like she's in on the joke but she's not comfortable. And Mona just laughs more and more, laughing with her eyes squeezed shut. I can't really remember ever seeing her laugh like this before. Maybe she's just laughing at Ma's comment, or maybe it's also because she's not the one sitting there feeling uncomfortable. Maybe she's enjoying seeing Sara in the same position that she used to be in and maybe that makes her feel a bit more like part of the family, I don't know.

I turn to Ma.

"For Christ's sake, Ma," I sigh, but I shake my head and laugh as well, I can't help it.

"Aw, she knows I'm only fuckin' jokin', right?" Ma says.

"She's fifteen years old," I say.

"I know how old she is," Ma says.

"Yeah, but . . ."

"You think a fifteen-year-old can't take hearing something like that? How d'you think fifteen-year-olds talk when they're with other fifteen-year-olds, eh? They'd make me sound like a Sunday school teacher in comparison, I bet," she says.

She picks up her pack of cigarettes, pulls out a cigarette and sticks it in her mouth, shuts one eye as she lights it.

I look at her, feel like saying something about it maybe making Sara feel a bit uneasy to hear grown-ups like us using the sort of language she might use with her friends. A lot of kids do, it confuses them when we adults aren't as boring and responsible as they expect us to be. I should maybe say something like that, but I don't, I just shake my head helplessly and laugh.

"Right, now I need to get some food inside me," Ma says, tilting her head back and blowing a smoke ring. "Anybody want to give me a hand in the kitchen?"

Mona and Sara both get up right away. "Of course," Mona says. And off they go. Ma first, with her cigarette between her fingers, spare tire hanging over the strings of her bikini bottoms, wobbling heavily with every step she takes. Then Mona and Sara. Mona wearing the black T-shirt with the words "Stiff Nipples" on the front, Sara in a yellow wool hat and a pair of those hip-hop pants, both of them thin as stick insects. I sit for a moment just watching them, then I grab the cooler bag and stand up.

"I'll get some more beer," I say. "It is 2006, after all, so I guess we can let the women do all the work."

I grin at Grandpa and Grandpa grins back. Then I walk

off. Feel the long grass tickling my legs. Place a hand on the rail and go up the steps and into the hall, join the others in the kitchen.

"I can set the table while you're doing that," Sara says. She has her back to me, she has opened the kitchen cabinet and is taking out the plates.

"Nah, we'll use paper plates," Ma says, taking a puff on her cigarette and nodding at a bag of paper plates on the worktop. "Saves us having to wash dishes afterwards," she says.

Sara turns to look at her, still with her hands on the plates. She looks unsure, almost as if she's trying to work out whether Ma's being serious. It's probably considered a bit common to eat off paper plates where Sara comes from, they probably don't use paper plates, or certainly not when they've got company.

"Oh, but I can do the dishes," Sara says.

"But Sara, pet, we've got enough paper plates, haven't we?" Ma asks. Her cigarette dangles from her lip and she puffs smoke as she crosses to the counter, picks up the bag and holds it up. "Oh yeah, plenty," she says, tossing the bag to Sara and Sara has to drop her hands fast to catch it. She stands there holding the paper plates, looking like she's just been handed a bag of radioactive waste.

"Sara's worried about the environment you see, Grandma," Jørgen says, right behind me.

I turn and look at him, he's leaning against the doorjamb, grinning.

"That's why she wants to eat off proper plates," he adds.

"Aw, Christ, don't tell me you're one of them?" Ma says. "Well, in that case of course we'll eat off proper plates," she says, talking with her cigarette in her mouth. Her voice sounds funny when she does that and the cigarette bobs up and down.

"No, no," Sara begs.

"But of course we'll use proper plates."

"Oh no, please, not for my sake."

Ma opens the fridge door, takes out a pack of pork chops.

"Oh, I wouldn't dream of doing it for your sake," she says. "We'll do it for the environment, of course. It would be just too bad if the oceans were to rise just because the Williamsens insisted on eating off paper plates."

She slaps the pack of chops down onto the counter, turns to us and gives that rough, hoarse laugh of hers again and Sara smiles that slightly uncertain smile. She's finding it hard to get used to this sort of humor. Something tells her she's being made a fool of and laughed at, I can tell by her face. She looks almost hurt now, poor thing. Jørgen should say something, explain to her that there's no harm in it, but he doesn't, he just stands there grinning and Sara's still smiling that uncertain smile of hers, a stiff, strained smile, and Ma laughs, and Mona laughs, feeling more and more like part of the family the more awkward Sara feels, so it seems. She's screaming with laughter now, shaking her head at how funny Ma is.

I look at Sara and smile. I'm just about to say that she shouldn't mind us, this is just how we are, but I don't get that far.

"But you eat meat, right?" Ma says. She flicks her cigarette out of the open kitchen window and turns to Sara.

"C'mon Ma, just because you care about the environment doesn't mean you have to be a vegetarian," I say, glancing at Sara and giving a little laugh, as if to say: don't mind Ma, but then I see that Sara's blushing, she stands there red-faced and smiling and Jørgen grins back at me.

"You don't eat meat either?" Ma cries, jutting her head forward and staring at the girl.

"No," Sara says with a little titter.

"So what the hell am I going to give you to eat?"

"I can just have whatever you're having with the chops," Sara says. "That'll be fine, really."

"Well, in that case it'll be potato salad with ketchup," Ma retorts.

Mona and Jørgen laugh and Sara just stands there, red-faced and smiling.

"You could have a little bit, though, surely?" Ma says.

"No thanks," Sara says with a strained little laugh.

"Just a little chop?"

I see how Sara seems to shrink. She's still smiling, but she's feeling less and less happy, poor thing, I can tell just by looking at her.

"Ma, honestly, would you just leave it," I say. I'm smiling, but the look I give her says I'm serious. She looks at me, raises her eyebrows .

"Oh, for heaven's sake, a little bit of meat's not going to hurt the girl," she says.

"Yeah, but that's not what this is about, is it?" I say.

"Oh, isn't it? So what is it about?" she asks. "If it's the pig then it was dead last time I checked, so she doesn't need to worry about that anyway."

And then Mona laughs again. Ma turns to look at her and she laughs as well. It's like they're allies now, these two. A couple of seconds then Ma turns to Sara. She lays her fingers lightly on the girl's arm, looks at her and smiles.

"No, no, that's for you to decide, of course," she says.

She takes the plates out of the cabinet and hands them to Sara. "Here, you take these environmentally friendly plates and set the table, pet, and while you're doing that I'll see if there isn't a pack of birdseed left over from Grandpa's budgie."

And she glances at Mona and laughs again. And Mona laughs back. I look at Sara and smile, try to reassure her with a smile, but she doesn't look at me. She keeps her eyes forward as she walks across the kitchen, red-faced and smiling. Jørgen looks at her and grins, teasing her a little because she still hasn't figured out how to cope with his family. She's met us all a few times now, but she still seems just as unsure and Jørgen finds that funny, I can tell. He goes on grinning as he puts his arm around Sara's shoulder and walks her out to the garden.

"Ma," I say. "She's fifteen."

"Still?" Ma says.

More laughter from Mona.

"I'm just trying to say you need to go a bit easy on her. You scare her," I say.

"Okay, okay," Ma says, not even looking at me. She kind of waves me away with a flick of her hand.

I'm just about to say that she might do it for Jørgen's sake, at least, because if Sara doesn't feel welcome that affects him too. But I don't say anything. Ma's never going to understand why Sara shouldn't feel welcome anyway, so there's no point. I look at her for a second, smile helplessly and shake my head, then I open the fridge door and take out two six packs of beer, pop them in the cooler bag and step into the passage. As I come out into the hall I hear the whoosh-whoosh of Ma's asthma inhaler.

Namsos, July 7th, 2006

The first time I met you face to face was down on the beach at Gullholmstrand. Me and Bendik were there and so were Janne and her dog, a fat old Labrador with a gimpy hip. It was half-blind, this mutt, and would have been put down long ago if Janne hadn't loved him more than anything else in the whole world and if her parents hadn't been convinced that she'd be even more sad and lonely if she were to lose him. Janne wasn't someone we chose to be friends with or invited to hang out with us, but she sometimes tagged along with Bendik and me because she didn't have anybody else, and even though we weren't always as nice to her as we might have been, we kind of accepted her and she was happy about that and grateful.

When the grown-ups talked about Janne they said things like "She was at the back of the line when good looks were being handed out" and "She's a nice, well-behaved girl, but maybe a bit more backward than other kids her age," but they only talked like that because they all wanted to be seen as nice people, when in fact what they actually thought was what me and Bendik said straight out: that Janne was ugly and stupid.

Because Christ knows she was. She had the kind of big, heavy glasses that left sore spots behind her jug ears and on her pug nose. She had a length of white elastic attached to her glasses that was supposed to keep them in place, but it was so tight that it made her hair stick up at the back, making her look like a peewee or a crested grebe or whatever it's called, the bird I'm thinking of. She also had a double chin that wobbled when she walked and an ass so big it hung over the sides of the chair when she sat down. Her face was broad and flat and perfectly round with a big mouth that she never closed, not even when she ate, something that came in handy when you and me and Bendik wanted to upset the stuck-up, oh-so-prim-and-proper girls in our class, I remember. All we had to do was give Janne one of the bars of chocolate we'd pinched from the corner store and ask her to sit down beside them at break and eat it while they were having their packed lunches. That put them right off their food, I can tell you, and sent them running out of the classroom to throw up into the drinking fountain in the hallway. It was just as hilarious every time, or so we thought.

But enough of that.

Anyway, me and Bendik and Janne were down on the beach. I remember Bendik was cursing Janne because she had laughed when her dog climbed onto his foot and started humping it. They were both too taken up with this to notice you coming down the path with your swimming things in a Co-op shopping bag. You sat down on the sand just a few yards away from us.

"You should've been an abortion, so you should," Bendik said to Janne.

Janne opened her big mouth wide and hooted with laughter, her eyes flicking between Bendik and me.

"D'you even know what an abortion is?" I asked her.

"Yeah," Janne said. "I'm not a complete idiot, you know."

"Now, now, don't exaggerate," Bendik said.

"Huh?"

Me and Bendik looked at each other and grinned.

"Okay, Janne, so what's an abortion then?" I asked.

"It's one of them black guys, in Australia, right?" she said.

Me and Bendik doubled up, howling with laughter. I shot a glance at you while I was laughing, but you weren't laughing. You weren't even smiling, you looked very serious, grim almost, and you scowled at us as you stuck your hand into the Co-op bag and pulled out a beach towel.

"She's thinkin' of aborigine," Bendik gasped. "She's thinkin' of aborigine."

Janne said nothing. She was still sitting there smiling with her mouth wide open.

"Holy shit," Bendik sighed, grinning. He wiped away the tears of laughter and shook his head. "You're unreal, so you are. How many chromosomes do you actually have?"

"More than you anyway," Janne said.

And that set us off again.

But Janne was laughing as well. That was the great thing about her. She seldom seemed to know when she had made a fool of herself or was being made fun of, so she was usually pretty happy and contented when she was with us. But you still didn't laugh. You sat there looking all pursey-mouthed, probably trying to show how morally superior you were to us and how much sympathy you had for those less fortunate than yourself, what do I know. But I must have been thinking something like that as I sat there, because it was really starting to piss me off that you wouldn't laugh at something as funny as this.

"I don't think the vicar's brat finds us very funny," I said, nodding to where you were sitting. Bendik turned to look at you.

"Oh yeah?" Bendik said, not taking his eyes off you.

"Don't call me vicar's brat," you said without looking at us. You wrapped your towel around your waist, stuck one hand underneath and started to take off your shorts.

"Well, well, look at him," I said. I looked at Bendik and gave a laugh that said no way could he tell me what to do.

"Who the fuck do you think you are?" Bendik asked. "Do you think you can come here and order us about just 'cause you're the vicar's brat?"

You didn't say anything.

"Hey," Bendik said, a little louder. "Hey you, vicar's brat. We're talkin' to you!"

You still didn't say anything. You pulled your shorts down to your ankles, slipped them off, put them in the Co-op bag and took out a pair of swimming trunks. Me and Bendik were just about to get up and come over to you, but we stayed where we were for a moment longer because suddenly Janne's dog waddled up to you and started sniffing under your towel. You tried to push him away, but that wasn't so easy to do because you had to hang onto your towel with one hand to stop it falling down and revealing all your equipment. In any case, the old dog had caught a whiff of your balls so he wasn't to be put off that easily, if you know what I mean. Normally he was so arthritic and stiff that you could almost hear him creak when he walked but now, suddenly, he was as frisky as a ferret. He scampered about, darting here, there and everywhere so that for a while it looked like you were surrounded by black Labradors. Bendik and Janne and I just sat there slapping our thighs and roaring with laughter, but when you fell on your ass in the sand and the dog grabbed the chance to start humping your leg, Bendik and I leaped to our feet. Neither of us needed to say a word, we were both thinking exactly the same thing: that we should hold you down and let the dog finish what it had started. It was disgusting, I know, and I've apologized to you lots of times since then, but we did what we did, so I'm writing it down here. At any rate, Bendik held your arms and I

sat on your legs and then the dog could get on with what he
wanted to do.

"Look at 'im go, look how horny he is," Bendik yelled, laughing
and nodding again and again at the pointy, pink dog dick rubbing up against your leg.

"I think he fucking likes you," I cried, grinning at you.

"He thinks you're a real sweetie," Janne piped up. Neither of
us had known that she could be deliberately funny, but apparently she could and Bendik and I laughed so hard we nearly
wet ourselves, and that in turn made Janne happier and more
animated than I'd ever seen her before. She hung over you,
laughing and laughing with that great, gaping mouth of hers.
"Sweetie, sweetie!" she cried and she went on like that until
the panting dog finally came, sending spurts of grayish-yellow
spunk onto your knee and your calf. Then we let go of you and
ran off sniggering, all three of us.

It was pretty rotten what we did to you there, of course, and
I've no decent excuse for it. Except that that's just how we were
and our background was what it was. And since this was the
background that you eventually fell into and became a part of,
I think I should tell you a little more about it.

To take Bendik first:

He had holes in most of his teeth, a mop of red hair and a
tiny upturned nose covered in freckles. I've always felt that all
of this, together with his skin, which was a sickly bluish-white,
like skimmed milk, fitted really fucking well with the uncontrol-
lable rages and wild behavior that would lead, a decade later, to
robbery with violence, double murder and ten years in prison.
Honesty and common decency were airs and graces that he
had no time for, and whether he was faced with other kids or

adults he didn't know, he was always just as pushy, cheeky and totally fearless. He fought and lied and stole, not just when he felt he had to, but just as often because he thought it was exciting and fun. If he was spotted and caught he would put on a brilliant act, sobbing his heart out, begging and pleading to be let go and swearing by all that was holy that he'd never do it again. But as soon as his victim took pity on him and Bendik got beyond arm's reach he would scoff and sneer and fire the most hurtful insults at the person concerned, and before too long he'd be off on yet another raid.

But behind the bandit's mask there was another Bendik, and even though it sounds so stupid that I almost balk at writing it down, this Bendik was an insecure boy with hardly any fucking self-confidence, partly because of the mother he had. Ingun Pettersen was well up in years when she had Bendik and by the time you moved to Namsos she was a wrinkled, bent old woman with mournful, doggy eyes set slightly too close to-gether in a face that was yellowish-brown from way too much Petterøes No. 3 tobacco. We just called her "the Chimney" and if you kidded her and told her that she ought to shut her kitchen window because she could be fined thousands of kroner if the fire brigade was called out to a false alarm, she would squeeze her doggy eyes shut and croak that hoarse, hacking laugh of hers. That's a sight that's stuck in my memory because it was pretty fucking rare for Bendik's ma to laugh or be cheerful at all. She was obsessed with sickness and death and disasters of one sort and another. She seldom talked about anything else and when people got fed up and remarked on her gloomy view of things she always responded by saying that they weren't strong enough to cope with the harsh realities of life. But if there was anyone who wasn't equipped to cope with the harsh realities of life, it was her. Because the fact was that she suffered from anxiety and hardly ever left her apartment. She was fretful and frightened of just about everything and no matter what Bendik might do or was supposed to do or felt like doing she was always sure it would end in disaster. "Well, don't blame me when you're sitting there in a wheelchair, paralyzed from the waist down," she said when Bendik was a little boy and wanted to jump from the big ski-jump hill along with the rest of us kids. "You'll know what I'm talking about when you're looking at your fingers lying on the ground," she said, when wee Bendik wanted to take his sheath knife out with him to whittle something. She also made sure that Bendik knew the emergency number for police, ambulance and fire brigade by heart and as if that weren't enough he was never allowed to go anywhere without a card in his pocket on which she'd written his blood type—just in case he had an accident and needed to have a transfusion.

Obviously a lot of her fretfulness and anxiety and pessimism rubbed off on Bendik and, knowing as I do how much he hated that side of himself, it was hard not to see his rough, tough manner as a kind of compensation for this. Sometimes, for instance, if we robbed a place where there was a particularly big risk of getting caught, he would be running with sweat and white with fear, but the minute he realized he was afraid and, even worse, that he looked afraid, he would do a complete turnaround and be so intent on seeming brave that he could become reckless and take unnecessary risks. He was the same in other situations too. In discussions or disagreements he'd do anything rather than say what he thought, and if he was unfairly treated in any way he would simply swallow it, go all quiet and look almost sad. But this never lasted long, because suddenly it would seem to dawn on him that he was acting like the spineless wimp he hated to be and he'd instantly switch back to being the tough, aggressive lout whom even grown men were loath to cross.

Me, I grew up in an old yellow-washed, two-family house further down the same street as Bendik. Ma and I had the ground floor and Grandpa and Grandma lived on the first floor, but I spent almost more time upstairs than down, certainly during those spells when Ma was seeing the most hopeless of the men she took up with. As to my Da, he fell off a crane and was killed when I was only three years old, so I don't remember anything about him. According to Ma I didn't miss much, though, because he was an even bigger bum and drunkard than the guy she was with when you moved to Namsos and that's saying something, since he drank aftershave and ate shoe polish when he was hungover and couldn't get ahold of anything else to stop the shakes. I know it's not normal to call a man a bum when his son can hear it, but that was Ma for you, she couldn't be bothered hiding anything from me, or certainly none of the things she should have hidden. She made no effort to put away the dildo that lay on her bedside table, even though she knew I'd be in and out of her bedroom. She'd come crying to me to tell me the latest on her love life. And when she had her gabby, chain-smoking women friends around, the air in the living room would be blue with talk dirtier than I've heard in any of the construction-site camps I've ever lived in. I remember, for example, one of the first times you came home with me, because Heidi Olufsen was there, the woman I would lose my virginity to at an after-party a year later and who then took it upon herself to teach me what Grandpa used to call the fine art of rumpy-pumpy. Oh, my God, what a glorious time that was. Anyway. You and I had come into the living room to fetch something and Heidi and Ma started asking us about our gym teacher.

"Do you take showers with him?" Heidi asked.

You were surprised and a bit thrown at being asked such a question. You didn't say anything right away, but then you saw me grinning and that reassured you.

"Sometimes," you said.

"Lucky bastards," Ma said pertly. She and Heidi looked at one another and cackled suggestively. They both bent over the coffee table, knocked the ash of their cigarettes, then sat back on the sofa.

"So, has he got a big dick?" Heidi asked. She took a quick puff on her cigarette and grinned at you, blowing smoke out of the corner of her mouth. You didn't say anything. I think you were wondering whether this was some kind of a joke or whether they really did want to know.

"Does he, Tom Roger?" Heidi asked, turning to me.

"Not as big as mine," I said, grinning. "But yeah, it's big."

Ma and Heidi looked at each other and cackled again.

"Ooh, look at him!" Ma cried.

"Big-head," Heidi said.

"No, but seriously," Ma said, stubbing her cigarette out in the ashtray and holding her hands out in front of her, a bit like an angler describing the size of a fish he has caught. "This big?" she asked.

"Bigger," I said.

"This big, then?" Ma said, holding her hands farther apart.

"Bigger," I said.

"Oh, my God," Heidi gasped. "Go into the bathroom, somebody, and get me a cloth. This sofa's getting wet."

So, as you can see, in our house there was no clear line between the children's world and the adult world. Ma spoke and acted around me pretty much the same way as she did with her women friends, even though the people from Child Welfare had advised against it and tried to persuade her to shield me from that sort of thing. "I've got nothing to hide and there's no fucking way those bitches from the social work department are going to make me pretend I'm better than I am when I'm with my kid. I'd rather he learned to have respect for himself and be proud of who he is and where he comes from."

That, more or less, was what she said, and she usually made a point of adding that those social workers didn't really want to help. What they wanted was to see people like her struggle in vain to be like them, because that acted as a sort of reminder to them that they'd done well for themselves and were better than ordinary folk. Not to belabor the point, but if you ask me she was right in a lot of what she said. Specially when it comes to what kids are supposed to be shielded from, it seems to me that things have gone way over the score. These days you can't even say the word "nigger" without the authorities moving heaven and earth to whisk the kids off to safety. I'm telling you, I've seen it happen more than once at parents' meetings at nursery or school.

There was one thing about Ma though that really fascinated you, I remember—and I'm not thinking about her tits, which were always bulging out of a bra several sizes too small and which you used to gaze at longingly when she was sunbathing in the garden. No, I'm talking about her work as a medium and clairvoyant. I was used to it, of course, and I couldn't really see the fun in hiding in the wardrobe behind the red velvet curtain to spy on her when she held her consultations, but I did it for your sake and I can still remember how mesmerized you were by the sight of Ma sitting there solemn-faced and straight-backed with her eyes closed, letting the dead speak through her or seeing into someone's future. A future which, as it happens, was usually either very bright or very bleak and seldom anything in-between. "I can taste blood. Promise me you'll see a doctor as soon as you leave here," she told the plumber who lived further down the street. Or: "Oh, I feel a pressure in my pelvis, you're going to have many children, at least three," as she said to Jenny Lund.

Once in the mid-80s, after you'd been going on at her for ages, she finally gave in and agreed to help you find your father. I haven't mentioned this before, but not only did you grow up without a father, you didn't even know who he was, because for some reason Berit refused to talk about the guy. So it was no wonder you were so tense and serious-looking as you sat there in the deep, red-plush armchair, watching Ma light the obligatory incense stick, closing her eyes and preparing to search. There was a long silence, then she suddenly began to speak in the flat, monotonous voice she always used when she travelled out of her own body.

"I smell baking, cakes . . . I'm in a cake shop . . . or a café . . . the walls are pink . . . and I hear voices, many voices . . . but I don't understand what they're saying . . . they're speaking another language . . . I don't know what language it is, some East European . . . no, wait . . . wait . . . there's one voice that's . . . that's rising out of the babble of voices, a deep male voice . . ."

She fell silent for a moment or two and then something happened that was unlike anything I've ever seen before or since. And it seemed to come as as big a shock to Ma as it did to us because even though she couldn't speak any language but Norwegian she suddenly started speaking very fast in what we at first thought must be Russian or Polish but which turned out to be Slovakian. Or at least the only sentence we could remember afterwards was "Stalo sa prvého septembra" and this was apparently Slovakian for "It happened on the first of September." Don't ask me what happened on the first of September that was so special, or whether this meant that your father was living in what was then Czechoslovakia and is now Slovakia, but that's certainly what we thought when Ma was finished and you got up from the armchair, pale and dumbstruck by what you had just witnessed.

While Ma was a medium and fortune teller, Grandpa ran, as I've said, a scrapyard and junk shop, so the garden, the yard and the garage were all overflowing with every sort of old trash. The neighbors were really pissed off with us about this, especially all those middle-class bastards living in the big villas on the other side of the fence. They saw red every time Grandpa rolled up with a new load in his blue pickup, because junk in the garden was one of countless things that didn't fit with the chocolate-box style of life they were trying to build for themselves. Not only did they write to the housing board to complain, they also started a petition which stated that Grandpa was "polluting the local environment" and "putting the lives and health of children at risk by allowing them to play freely in unsafe surroundings strewn with dangerous objects." But Grandpa was a tinker and used to being hassled so that sort of thing cut no ice with him, and he usually got his own back anyway. Not long afterwards, when the guy who had started the petition put his house up for sale, Grandpa made a point of inviting Erik and all his other drinking cronies over for a thumping great *karsk* binge in the garden at the exact time when the house was being viewed. Not only that, but he got Erik to bring an old toilet up from the basement and dump it right where it would be the first thing prospective buyers would see from this guy's veranda. Oh, God Almighty how Grandpa crowed when he heard some time later that the house had sold for way under the asking price. Best of all, though, was the time when the guy who lived right next door to us wrote a letter to the *Namdal*

Workers' Weekly that everybody knew was aimed at Grandpa and all his junk. Grandpa smiled and was as sweet as sugar and grovelingly polite when he ran into the guy in the street one day, but that very same evening he summoned you and me and Bendik and Uncle Willy to the yard. We left the junk exactly where it was, but we moved the fence several yards farther over into our property so most of the mess now seemed to be in our neighbor's yard, making it look as if he, and not Grandpa, was the neighborhood scrappie. A brilliant act of revenge, if you ask me.

Being looked down on by those middle-class bastards was one thing, but it was quite another matter, and much worse, to be looked down on by many of our own. Oh yes, because that we fucking were. Ma believed it was because we weren't as well off as a lot of other working-class people and because we couldn't join in the so-called consumer boom of the 80s, but I don't really think that had so much to do with it—there were plenty of folks around us who couldn't afford to run out and buy all the things the admen said they should buy, but no one thought any less of them for that. The difference between them and us was that they spent their time and energy on mending and fixing up, painting over and touching up things that were old and battered to make them look decent. We, on the other hand, didn't really give a fuck about all that. In other words, we didn't give a fuck about the ideals, the expectations and tastes they had picked up from the middle classes and which the middle classes must have picked up from the upper classes. That's why they looked down on us. Or at least that's how I see it today. We weren't to be intimidated. This could be seen even more clearly in our attitude to work, I remember, because, as with Erik, nobody in my family could be bothered pretending that the whole point of life was to slog your guts out from the age of sixteen to sixty-six. And it wasn't that some members of the family hadn't tried that either. Under pressure from Grandma, Grandpa did take a job in the quality control department of the Van Severen sawmill, for example, but he only stuck it out for two or three months because, as he growled on the day when he had finally had enough, "No fucking way was I put here on this earth to sit on a chair for eight hours a day, looking at wooden planks."

And Ma was exactly the same. She had tried a lot of jobs before setting herself up as a fortune teller and medium, but on those occasions when she didn't quit off her own bat she was given the boot and if anybody suggested that she only had herself to blame, for being such a slacker and a sloppy worker, she told them in no uncertain terms that she wasn't going to break her fucking back for fifty kroner an hour. She used pretty much the same argument in court when she was convicted of embezzling money from the newsstand out at the Prairie, I remember, because when the prosecutor asked how much she had taken she replied: "Only as much as I felt I was entitled to."

But this sort of protest, if I can call it that, didn't mean that we were ashamed of being who we were, and when I think about it I don't actually believe that any of us felt as much shame as Grandpa, who was a full-blooded tinker. Norwegians have never had any time for tinkers, you see, because the sight of a free and footloose tinker reminds the Norwegian of how tied he is to the clock and his employer and all the things he owns that he feels he has to guard. To save being reminded of how unfree he is, the Norwegian has done his best to wipe out the tinker society and this he has done in ways that are as bad as anything the Nazis did during the war. Grandpa's mother was forcibly sterilized after giving birth to his little sister, his uncle was shot full of LSD then given a lobotomy at Gaustad Asylum in 1946, and as far as Grandpa himself was concerned there was hardly a town in Trøndelag that he hadn't been beaten up in and run out of. It goes without saying that if you're treated like this then you will, unconsciously, seek the reasons for this. You'll start to wonder what's wrong with you. Well, as the good book says, "seek and ye shall find," and before you know it you find you hate yourself.

And if you ask me it was this sense of shame and self-loathing that also led Grandpa to beat up Grandma every now and again. I'm not making excuses for him, but because Grandma wasn't a tinker herself I think he sometimes saw her as a sort of representative of society at large and of his persecutors. She was the one who tried to get Grandpa to work and earn money instead of sitting on the porch playing guitar or lying in the hammock behind the shed reading pulp westerns. She was the one who insisted that it was worthwhile clearing the snow, even though Grandpa was quite right when he said that it would eventually melt anyway. She was the one who got mad at him when he came home from the shop with expensive steaks for dinner instead of the makings of four economical meals that she had sent him to buy. And she was the one who worked from the minute she got up until she went to bed, thus making Grandpa look like an even bigger layabout than he actually was. No matter how discreet and soft-spoken Grandma was she was still a constant reminder to him of what a failure and a misfit he was, so she was the one who had to pay the price when his self-loathing became too much to bear and his lust for revenge too great.

And speaking of revenge.

That incident with the dog on the beach wasn't exactly the best way to make friends with someone, and that's putting it mildly. It was a rotten thing to do and you had every reason to want to pay us back. And pay us back you did. One day Janne's dog's mouth started to bleed. The next day his nose was bleeding too and on the third day when Janne went to take him for a walk he couldn't make it any farther than the lamppost on the other side of the street. He had peed on that lamppost practically every day of his life and he had no doubt been planning to do so again, but that wasn't to be. The poor mutt was so weak that he couldn't lift his back leg, so he had to pee straight down onto the ground like a bitch. And not only was his pee pink with blood, as soon as he had done his business he flopped onto his belly and lay there flat out with his tongue lolling, dead as a doornail.

What you had done was to stuff as much rat poison as you could into three lung sausages and then you had thrown these to the dog, one a day, when he was chained to his kennel. Bendik and I honestly hadn't expected you to do anything at all. We thought you were a spoiled, mollycoddled vicar's kid, a middle-class bastard who would be far too much of a wimp and a coward to take revenge, and who would try to disguise his lack of courage and spirit by going on about how it takes much more strength to turn the other cheek. But we couldn't have been more wrong, because you didn't stop at killing Janne's dog with rat poison. A few days later when I was walking home from school you jumped out at me from behind the phone box next to the Favør Cut-Price Store armed with a chain. The last thing I remember, before I came to on the sidewalk with terrible pains in my head, my cheek and my left ear, was the dull click as you wound the chain around your hand, preparing to strike. This could very quickly have developed into a vicious circle of tit for tat, but it didn't, because when I staggered home and Grandpa asked who had done this to me and I told him it was the new kid at the vicarage, he realized I was talking about Erik's grandson. So a little meeting was arranged in the permanently dust-laden back room of the junk shop. There Grandpa and Erik told us in no uncertain terms that we had to make peace on the spot. We glared at each other and weren't at all keen to shake hands, I remember, but we knew they meant what they said and that we had no option, because even though they didn't say it in so many words, it was easy to see that they were scared we'd become so blinded by rage and vindictiveness that we would end up dragging our families into it, and that would have had serious consequences for both parties, particularly if one of us was stupid enough to tip off the cops about certain breaches of the law committed by the other lot. Anyway, what I'm trying to say is that this more or less enforced reconciliation paved the way for what was to be a long and happy friendship between you, me and Bendik.

To be continued.

Namsos, July 4th, 2006. Acid rain

I feel the heat hit me as I come out onto the steps, burning my shoulders, scorching. As I walk down onto the grass I hear the sound of an electric guitar, somebody playing the intro to "Smoke on the Water." I turn and look up, notice that the window of the old Nilsen house is open, the teenager in the family must've started playing guitar. He looks just the type, long hair and headband and all that. I stroll across the garden, take two beers out of the cooler bag and tuck it under the table.

"Here you go," I say, setting a beer in front of Grandpa. "Where've Jørgen and Sara got to?"

He doesn't answer, just nods behind us as he opens the can. I look around and there they are. Jørgen's sitting on the hood of the Chrysler and Sara's standing next to it. Something's happened between them, I can tell. Jørgen looks pissed off. Sara must have said something about that little incident in the kitchen, she must have made some remark that's annoyed him, or something like that, it's hard to say. I pick up the paper bag of charcoal and tip the whole lot into the barbecue. A black cloud of soot swirls up and I turn my face away, put my hand to my mouth and cough, glance across at Jørgen and Sara as I chuck the empty bag

onto the grass. They look like they're done talking. Jørgen
plants his hands on the Chrysler hood and hops down into
the grass, making the car rock slightly. Sara looks at him
and gives a little smile, a kind of apologetic smile, but he
doesn't smile back, he's angry and distant, I can tell just by
looking at him. They wander over to us, side by side across
the garden. I pick up the bottle of lighter fluid, squirt the
fluid over the coals and put down the bottle, look at Jørgen
and Sara as I sit back down in my chair.

"Maybe we should pop over and see Kjersti before we go
home?" Sara says, smiling at Jørgen.

"Are you in that much of a hurry?"

Sara looks at him.

"No," she says with a little laugh, a laugh that's meant
to tell the rest of us she doesn't know why he's asking that.

Jørgen doesn't say anything for a moment. He picks up
the beer I put out for him a few minutes ago and sits down
on the chair.

"I think I'll stay here," Jørgen says. "But just you go on
over to what's-her-face's . . . Kjersti or whatever her name
is," he says.

"Whatever her name is?" Sara says with a little laugh.

"Hmm?" Jørgen says, eyeing her blankly.

"You know what her name is," Sara says. "You've met
her loads of times."

"Yeah, of course, it's Kjersti, isn't it?"

She raises her eyebrows, stares at him.

"Yes," she says, giving a surprised little laugh.

"Okay, so I was right then," Jørgen says, turning away
from her and taking a long swig of his beer.

I look at Jørgen. He shouldn't do this, he shouldn't push
her away from him like this just because he wants to be

loyal to us, shouldn't push Sara away just because she made some remark about Ma. I feel like telling him this, but I can't, not when there are other people here. I open my can of beer, look at them as I take a sip.

"But like I say, you go if you want to," he says, looking at Sara and nodding in the direction of the garden gate.

I put my head on one side and look at him, begging him with my eyes not to do this. He's saying things that he doesn't want to say and doesn't mean. He doesn't want Sara to go, I know he doesn't, not really. I keep my eyes fixed on him, but he doesn't notice, he's looking at Sara.

"Oh, but . . ." she says, "I wasn't meaning to go just yet," she says and her voice falters for a moment. "And I don't really want to go without you either."

"For Christ's sake, Sara, I think we can survive being away from each other for an hour or two," he says, grinning at her.

Two seconds.

"Oh, all right," she says, shrugging. "Well, if it's okay with you I'll pop over there a bit later then."

"If it's okay with me?" Jørgen says, grinning at her again. "Why wouldn't it be okay with me?"

Sara looks at him, smiling faintly and giving another quick shrug.

Silence. And then I catch Jørgen's eye. I give him an almost sorrowful look, trying to let him know how stupid he's being, that he shouldn't push Sara away the way he's doing now, he should swallow that goddamn pride of his and meet her halfway. Otherwise he'll regret it. I hold his eye for a moment and then he looks down. He gets the message, I can tell by his face. His anger seems to drain away, suddenly he looks more sad than angry.

"Could I have a beer after all?" Sara asks. She adjusts her yellow hat, pushing it a little further back from her forehead. She looks at me. And I look at her. She's trying to show Jørgen that she means to stay here with him now, that's why she's taking a beer after all, I realize that, this is her way of trying to patch things up with him.

"Course," I say, reaching under the table and getting out a can, look at her and smile as I hand it to her.

"Cheers then," Grandpa says, raising his can and looking round the table.

"Cheers," we all say together.

I keep my eye on Sara and Jørgen as I put my can to my lips. Their eyes meet, Sara smiles hesitantly, tentatively. And now he has to seize the chance to meet her halfway, he mustn't do anything stupid now. A second and then he smiles hesitantly back at her. I put my can down on the table, catch his eye as I get up from my chair, smile happily at him, approvingly, try to let him see that I think that was well done, it's good that they've made up.

I pick up Ma's lighter, walk across to the barbecue and light it. Stand for a moment watching the flames spreading over the black charcoal, sort of rippling from one briquette to the next, soundlessly. And then I hear Ma's and Mona's voices, hear them laughing, Ma's hoarse cackle and Mona's clear, high-pitched giggle. I turn around. They're coming across the grass, each carrying a tray. I go back to my chair and sit down, take my pack of cigarettes from the table, pull out a cig and light it.

"Have you got a diaper on?" Ma asks, looking at Grandpa as she sets the tray down on the camping table.

I stare at her. Okay, now she's gone too fucking far, she can't talk to Grandpa like that, not when there's people listening. She knows he doesn't like there to be any mention of him wearing diapers. It's embarrassing for him and it's probably even more embarrassing now, with Mona and Sara here. He's always been one for the ladies, Grandpa has. He may be an old man now, but it's still there, I know it is, he still likes to look good for the ladies. I look at him, see his smile stiffen. He stares at Ma, holds her eye.

"Yeah, because if you haven't, then you'd better go and put one on right this minute," Ma goes on. "You know it just runs right through you when you drink beer."

Silence.

Ma raises her eyebrows and gives him a look as if to say: what are you waiting for? But Grandpa doesn't get up. He picks up his beer can and takes a drink, trying to look like he doesn't care, but he does care and he's raging, I can tell, he's mortified. Everybody just sits there for a moment, then a grin spreads across Jørgen's face. He shoots a glance at Sara, but she isn't grinning, she finds this embarrassing, I can tell. She acts like she's reading the label on her beer can, like she hasn't heard any of this.

"Well, go on," Ma says, talking to Grandpa like he's a little kid. And I see how bad this makes him feel. He's trying to look like he doesn't care, but his face is stiff with rage. I look at Ma. This isn't on, she can't talk to him like this, not when other people can hear. She can't show him up like this. I put my head on one side and sigh, trying to tell her that she's got to stop, but she doesn't notice.

"Well," she says. "I've said it before and I'll say it again, if you pee in your pants one more time you can find somebody else to do your washing for you, because I'm not fucking doing it."

Grandpa tries to grin, but his eyes are narrow with fury.

And it doesn't help that Jørgen is sitting there with his arms crossed quietly sniggering. And fuck me if Mona doesn't start laughing as well. She looks at Jørgen, sees him laughing and she starts fucking laughing as well, laughing at how Grandpa's being humiliated, trying to act the way she thinks a true Williamsen would act. This is yet another attempt to be one of us, I realize that. Trying to be as rough and tough as we make ourselves out to be, I can tell. And now I feel resentment building up inside me, anger. I don't like Jørgen and Ma making fun of Grandpa, but I like it even less when Mona does it, she's got no fucking right to sit there, making fun of Grandpa in his own backyard, who the fuck does she think she is?

"Well, are you going to or not?" Ma asks, not letting up.

"What?" Grandpa says sharply, almost snarling.

Jørgen and Mona exchange glances again, snigger softly.

"Dear God, give me patience," Ma says, laying her head back and staring at the sky for a second or two, then she looks at Grandpa again. "Okay," she says, shaking her head. "Have it your way."

"Yeah—did you think I'd have it any other way?" Grandpa says.

Ma snorts.

"Well don't say I didn't warn you, " she says.

Silence for a second then Sara gets up.

"I have to go to the loo," she mumbles.

She looks at Jørgen, gives him a watery smile, walks off towards the house. She can't stand to be here any longer. No fucking wonder, we'd scare the shit out of anybody the way we go on. Sara doesn't fucking dare to sit with us.

I take a drag on my cigarette, exhale.

"Hey, c'mon, why don't we all try to be civil to one another?" I say.

Ma turns to me as she lifts a full bottle of summer aquavit off one of the trays, raises her eyebrows, stays like that for a couple of seconds.

"What the fuck've you actually got in that?" she asks, nodding at my cigarette. "Can I have some?"

Then she looks at the others and gives that throaty laugh of hers.

And Jørgen laughs. And Mona laughs. I was being serious, but they're all laughing, apart from Grandpa. And I feel resentment building up inside me. I feel my smile stiffening, it's like my mouth is tightening.

"Oh, you can laugh," I say, wait a second, then: "But why d'you think Sara suddenly had to go to the toilet?"

"Maybe because she had to take a shit," Ma says.

She opens the bottle of aquavit and turns to Jørgen, looks at him.

"Well, I mean she must have to take a shit now and again even if her father is a doctor?"

"I suppose so," Jørgen says.

And they laugh again.

I feel myself getting more and more annoyed. I keep that tight smile on my face, but the anger is building up inside me.

"Would you like a little aperitif before dinner, Pa?" Ma says, talking as if nothing had happened. She looks at Grandpa, holding the bottle over a tumbler on the table. Grandpa doesn't answer, he's feeling mortified and he can't act as though nothing's happened, can't even bring himself to look at Ma.

"Pa?" Ma says.

"Are you talking to me?" Grandpa asks, eyeing her peevishly.

"Well, you are my pa, aren't you?"

"How the fuck would I know," Grandpa says. "Your ma wasn't much different from you, so it could've been just about anybody."

"Now you tell me," Ma says. "After I've had to put up with you all these years."

And she cackles again.

And Jørgen grins and take a sip from his can. And Mona laughs, she screams with laughter. She seems to find this very entertaining. I look at her, at her cheerful, lively face. The spiteful comments are flying and she sits there laughing and acting as though this is all perfectly okay, as if it's quite normal for us take the piss out of each other like this. Not that we haven't always had a pretty blunt, rough way of talking to each other in our family, but it's not usually as bad as this. There's always been a lot of kidding and banter and bickering, but over the past few years a more caustic note has crept into the way we talk and behave, particularly where Ma's concerned. It's like there's this anger underneath all her laughing and joking these days. A rage that wasn't there before, I feel.

"I'd say it's debatable who's had to put up with who," Grandpa mutters.

"Oh, is that so?" Ma says. "Well, why don't you move into the old folks' home then? If you can't stand me cooking your meals and keeping house for you, you can just pack your bags and leave right now."

Grandpa doesn't answer. He sneers as he raises his can of beer to his lips, takes a drink.

Then Sara appears, still smiling that kind of watery smile.

"Do you want me to help you, is that it?" Ma says, still not letting it go. She stares at Grandpa. "Come on then, let's go up and get you packed."

She puts down the bottle of aquavit and takes a step towards the house, gives Grandpa a look that says: what are you waiting for?

"Aw, shut your gob," Grandpa snarls.

"What? I was only offering to help you pack," Ma says, looking at Grandpa and smirking.

Silence.

Sara doesn't know where to look, she's feeling more awkward than ever, I can tell. Her face is red. Jørgen and Mona look at one another and grin. They're behaving as if this is just a bit of harmless fun, they don't catch the bitter, vicious undertone, the rage. After a moment Mona looks at Sara and smiles. Just relax, she says, says it without words, blinks slyly as she says it, trying to let Sara know that this is perfectly normal, this is just how we are and there's no need to worry. But Sara is worried, worried and uncomfortable, I can tell. She looks at Mona and smiles that faint smile of hers, smiles quickly, then looks away again.

"Well, are you coming or not?" Ma says. She just won't let it go, she stares at Grandpa, smirking, tormenting him, mocking him.

And the anger grows inside me. I stare at her. And now I've got to tell her to let it fucking go. She can't go on like this, not when Sara's here anyway. Can't she see how uncomfortable the girl is, how awful she thinks this is? Well, obviously not, she just goes on and on, I feel fucking ashamed for her when she carries on like this, it's fucking embarrassing. I lean forward, drop my cigarette butt into the same can that Ma dropped hers into, sit a little further back in my seat and look up at Ma. I'm just about to say that I think it's embarrassing when she carries on the way she's doing. But I don't get the chance. All of a sudden something white comes flying through the air. Comes rocketing over. I only catch a glimpse of it before it lands on the grass with a loud splat, lands right at Ma's feet. Ma screams. What the fuck was that, what the fuck's going on? I crane my neck and look down at the grass. There's a half-full Co-op bag lying on her foot. A burst Co-op shopping bag, carrot peelings and glistening coffee grounds spilling out of a big hole. Ma stands there with her mouth hanging open and her arms out, confused, gobsmacked, staring at the shopping bag.

"What the fuck," Jørgen says, sitting up in his chair, eyes popping.

Then something else flies over, sailing over the fence in a graceful arc to land with a clunk on one of the almost overgrown slabs a little further off. It's a yogurt carton. It shatters on impact, splattering yogurt everywhere, lilac-colored yogurt splashing onto the long, green grass. I look around and there's Ma's and Grandpa's new neighbor. Over by his garden sprinkler. Bending down. Picking up something from the lawn. A carton with something orange inside it, orange peel or something. Trash at any rate. The birds have dragged trash into his garden and now he's chucking it back at Ma and Grandpa. And Ma turns to me, open-mouthed, stares at me and points at the house next door.

"He's chucking trash at us," she says. "We're having a barbecue here and he's fucking well chucking trash at us."

I don't say anything. I just sit there. And she doesn't take her eyes off me, gazes at me in amazement, she must be wondering what's keeping me, why I don't run right over there and sort him out, because that's what she expects, she expects me to jump over the fence and beat the shit out of the guy, I know that's what she expects, what they all expect, I can tell by their faces. Grandpa and Jørgen, Sara and Mona, their eyes flick back and forth between the neighbor and me, they don't understand why I don't do something. This is so unlike me, I've beaten folks up for a lot less than this, and I feel like doing that now too, I'm itching to do it. I ought to run right over to that guy and knock him flat. Fat, pasty-faced fifty-year-old with skinny office-worker fingers. I could put him in a coma with one punch, but I don't. I just sit there staring at Ma, smiling stiffly at her, punishing her by not helping her. Because that's what I'm doing by sitting here doing nothing, punishing her for behaving the way she did and for not listening when I asked her to be civil. It's no good talking to her, but maybe now she'll understand, maybe she'll understand what I was talking about now that she's getting her comeuppance. I stare at her as she realizes why I'm not getting up. I can tell by her eyes that it's beginning to dawn on her. A more sober look comes into her eyes. I take a kind of grim satisfaction in this. It's on the tip of my tongue to ask her if it might actually be an idea not to stuff so much in the bins, but I don't get that far because suddenly Jørgen jumps up. He puts a hand on Sara's shoulder, using it as purchase to propel him out of the chair even faster. Then he's off like a shot, heading for the guy next door. Across the yard and up to the fence. Puts one hand on the fence and vaults over it.

"Jørgen," I yell, getting up and going after him.

And then the neighbor looks up, looks straight at Jørgen. He drops the carton with the orange peel onto the lawn and puts out his hands as if to fend off Jørgen as he takes a flying leap at him—the sort of jump kick you see in karate films, right leg tucked up to his backside and left leg stretched straight out. He rams the neighbor with his left heel, smack in the stomach. And the man hits the ground. Ass first. He lies there for a second or two, flat on his back, then he pushes himself up onto his elbows, puts a hand to his stomach and winces, clearly in pain.

And Jørgen walks towards him.

"Jørgen," I yell, breaking into a run, because he mustn't do anything stupid now, he mustn't do anything he'll regret. I keep my eyes on him as I race over, he's standing over the guy, standing there looking down at him.

"Leave him alone," I yell, yelling as I run. Run flat out, jump the fence without touching it, land on the grass, lightly, run on.

"Don't you fucking mess with us, okay," Jørgen says.

And he turns away. He does as I say, he leaves the guy alone. Simply turns and walks over to me. Thank Christ. And I stop, lay my hand on his shoulder, look at him, panting slightly. I don't say a word, I glance across at the neighbor, he puts a hand on the grass and gets up, heaves himself up onto his feet, very slowly.

"Fucking hell," he mumbles, obviously in pain, narrowing his eyes. He looks at me, shaking his head. "You haven't heard the last of this," he says.

I slip my hand off Jørgen's shoulder, saunter over to the neighbor, look at him, flex my biceps, big bulging muscles.

"I think the best thing you can do is to forget all about this," I say, looking at him and smiling, flashing my broken front tooth at him. A quiet but menacing smile. "Otherwise you'll have me to deal with, and that you really don't want, believe me," I say.

He looks at me, says nothing, shakes his head, and then he snorts at me and walks away.

I turn and walk back. Ma has picked up the trash in our yard and now she comes waddling over to the fence, apparently meaning to toss the trash back into the neighbor's. I look at her, about to ask if she shouldn't throw it in the bin instead, so we won't have any more crap from the neighbor, but I don't. She feels like she has the upper hand now, so she wouldn't listen to me anyway. And in any case I don't want to be the one to stop her from taking revenge, I'll only look useless and spineless if I do, and I don't want that, not again. Not that anybody here seriously thinks I'm useless and spineless, but still. I don't like to seem that way, it goes against the grain. I keep my eye on Ma as I hop back over the fence. She swings the Co-op bag behind her back then hurls it hard as she can into the neighbor's garden. I watch the trash spilling out of the hole in the bag and scattering over his lawn, a shower of food scraps and empty cartons.

I head back towards the table, hear three short slaps as Ma dusts off her hands.

"Sorry, Gran," Jørgen says. He standing in the middle of the lawn, looking at Ma. He knows Ma appreciates what he just did, but he's apologizing anyway. "I know I went too far, but I was so fucking mad," he goes on.

"You've no need to apologize," Ma says. I look at her as I sit down on the camping chair. She waddles over to us.

"Far from it," she says. "You deserve a medal."

"A right fucking Bruce Lee, so you are," Grandpa says,

eyeing Jørgen and grinning. Suddenly he's all bright and cheery, no longer angry.

I look at Jørgen, see how proud of himself he is. He wags his head and tries to look like it was no big deal, but he's struggling not to smile and laugh, I can tell by his face, he's so proud, so pleased.

"Oh, my God, he was twice your size," Sara says, gazing open-mouthed at Jørgen as he sits down in his camping chair, showing him how impressed she is.

"Aw, he was fat and slow," Jørgen says, trying to play down his achievement now, like he's not one to boast. He knows we'll think even more of him for that.

"Yes, but still," Sara says.

"Cheers!" Ma says, "Here's to Jørgen." She's half filled all the tumblers with aquavit, now she grabs one and raises it.

And then everybody reaches out and grabs a glass. Everybody but me. Something in me resists it. I don't like this, don't like us congratulating Jørgen for kicking a guy in the stomach. I don't really know why I don't like it, I mean it's not as though I've trained him up to be a pacifist, anything but. I've always encouraged him to stand up for himself and not take shit from anyone. I've taught him that by word and deed, but still, I don't like it.

"Here's to Jørgen," they all say together.

And I pick up my glass too, join in anyway.

"Cheers," I say. I down half of the aquavit in one go, lower my glass and glance around the table. Suddenly there's nothing but happy, smiling faces. That's so fucking typical of us. Give us a common enemy and suddenly everything's hunky-dory. I sit back in my chair, curl my hand around the tumbler of aquavit, try to smile and look as happy as the others, but I can't. I'm angry, I don't want to be, but I am. I don't like this, that we're congratulating Jørgen for behaving the way he did, behaving exactly the way I've always done. It was like seeing myself there. And maybe that's what I don't like. The sight of myself as a hothead and a thug—maybe that's what I'm not happy about. Or maybe it's the exact opposite: the fact that I just sat there watching, sat there like an old fucking woman while the neighbor chucked trash at us, maybe that's what's pissing me off: the sight of myself as a spineless wimp, that I came over as being powerless, what the fuck do I know. I raise my glass to my lips, knock back the rest in one gulp and put the glass on the table.

"Thirsty?" Mona asks, looking at me and smiling.

I glance quickly at her, but don't smile back, don't answer her either, can't be bothered. I just pick up the aquavit bottle and refill my glass, sit back in my chair and run my eye over the overgrown garden. I know that Mona's sitting there looking at me now, that she's wondering what's wrong with me. But I don't turn to her. I'm angry. I feel like going home, I feel like saying that Mona and I ate at Rondo's earlier and that we won't stay for dinner after all. But I can't do that, I can't change my mind now. I said I was hungry and that I'd eat here with them. I put the glass to my lips and take a sip. I'll feel better once I've had a bit more to drink, I suppose. A little more aquavit, that's probably what's needed to chase away this bad mood.

Namsos, July 9th, 2006

So we became friends and from then on we were almost inseparable, in fact there were long spells when you spent more time with my family than with Berit and Arvid. If I'd been allowed to come home with you we would probably have spent some time there too, although when I think about it I'm not so sure about that, because you didn't get on too well with your mother and your stepfather, and that's putting it mildly. Arvid was a real slimeball and you couldn't stand him. Erik used to describe him as a "tolerant tyrant" and he couldn't have put it any fucking better. You see, Arvid was the sort of person who would always ask your advice and want to hear what you thought, even though he had already decided what he was going to do, and he would go right ahead and put his plans into action with a sanctimonious smile on his face no matter how much you objected. He never tired of discussing Christianity with you, for example, but even though you told him quite clearly that you didn't believe in God he refused to give you pocket money until you agreed to say grace before meals and clasp your hands and bow your head during prayers at the vicarage. And: "What would you like to do today, David?" he might ask, but there was no point in saying you'd like to go to the cinema or to the swimming pool, because he would already have arranged with members of the congregation to meet out at Framnes to grill sausages, play volleyball and rehearse with the children's choir he had set up.

But back then you were even more mad at your mother than you were at Arvid, if that was possible, because it was, after all, her who had decided to leave Erik and move in with the vicar from hell. And this, together with the fact that she never protested and never spoke up for you when Arvid treated you the way he did, made you feel that she had let you down, isn't that right? Although she meant well, I'm sure. Grandma said one of the reasons why Berit went to live with Arvid was so that you could get on and go up in the world. What this getting on and going up actually involved I'm not quite sure, but according to Grandma she certainly felt it was very fucking important to get you away from hick country before you really took root there and turned into a scruffy, wily mini version of Erik with no ambition except to hang around the barn, smoking roll-ups and making moonshine.

Your mother was ashamed of being a hick from Otterøya and she did everything she could, from the minute you moved to Namsos, to hide who she was and where she came from. She put away the home-made dresses and jeans so short she looked like she was expecting a flood and took to wearing what she personally thought were very smart outfits, all color-coordinated. She ironed out every trace of her Otterøyan dialect and put on a kind of phony posh Namsos accent. But what was worse, according to what Erik said when he was at our place, was that she wanted less and less to do with him as well. And if he absolutely had to pay you a visit he was requested please to park his vehicle where the neighbors couldn't see it, especially if he was in the camouflaged Jeep or one of the huge American cars, because they attracted so much damn attention. She took this denial of her own background so far that she wouldn't admit to any knowledge of things that had been a perfectly natural part of your everyday life on the island, or so Grandpa said. When the Norwegian Farmers' and Smallholders' Association arranged a "farmers' day" at the Namsos Fair one year, for example, she acted like a dumb townie female, asking one of the farmers whether the pigs were dangerous. And nothing would persuade her to taste fresh milk straight from the cow, a treat that she and you and Erik had once fought over, competing to see who could drink the most. Oh, no, that couldn't possibly be fit for human consumption.

Naturally she expected you to consider this new life of yours as big a change for the better as she did and she couldn't understand what you were so damned unhappy about. Didn't you have your own room? Didn't you have a stepfather who could help you with your homework and answer all the odd questions you were always asking? And weren't you living within walking distance of the town, and in a neighborhood where there were at least twenty or thirty kids of your own age? That's the sort of thing she would ask you and then she would sniff and toss her long, red hair, as if to say she thought you were spoiled and ungrateful and absolutely impossible to please.

But all her snobbishness only pushed you further and further away from her and the vicar, of course. Having grown up without a father you had become unusually attached to Erik, and this made it fucking hard for you to see your mother suddenly turning her back on him and the life you had led on the island. And since you identified so strongly with Erik and all he stood for I can see how you must have felt that Berit was turning her back on you as much as on him when she wanted nothing more to do with her former life. Not only did such a rejection fill you with even more shame and anger than you had already been feeling, it also made it even more important for you to show who you were and where you came from. And this you did, of course, by acting even more like Erik and distancing yourself even more from everything that the new Berit stood for, particularly anything to do with her new Christian faith and lifestyle, since this was where the conflict between the new and the old life was greatest.

And once you know that, it's not so hard to understand why you gravitated towards me and Bendik, since the sort of scrapes we got into must have been about as far from a Christian life-style as you could get.

Anyway. The anger you felt towards Berit and Arvid just grew and grew. Not only did you spend more and more time at our house, after a while you even stopped speaking to your mother and Arvid when you were at home. You simply chose not to say a word. They begged and pleaded with you to speak, but as you said to me if they weren't interested in what you said or thought then you were going to show them that you weren't interested in what they said or thought either, and no fucking way were you opening your mouth again until they realized that. And they could get as angry as they liked.

Bendik and I were really impressed by this and even though we didn't actually plan it I remember we used this same strategy with the teacher we had at that time. Her name was Frida Iversen, but she had an enormous backside, a bulging stomach and stubby little hands that flapped back and forth as she waddled along the corridor, so we just called her the Duck. Christ, how we hated that woman. Or at least, although we didn't understand it at the time it probably wasn't her we hated, but the school that we associated her with. Because not only did the school try to fill our heads with knowledge we knew we'd never have any use for, and not only were we tricked into believing that we were stupid and lazy for not learning what the teacher said we had to learn, but we were even denied the fucking chance to develop the talents that we did actually have. None of the things we knew or that we could do were considered to be worth anything. Take me, for example: by the eighth grade I could have taken apart and reassembled the engine of Duck's ancient Datsun (which was always mis-firing) in just about the same time it took her to get it started, and yet she talked and acted as if, of the two of us, I was the stupid one. Or take Bendik. He was so damn clever with his hands, but at school he was fobbed off with one woodwork period a week and then he had to sit there like a retard, fin-ishing off a breadboard that the woodwork teacher had even gone so far as to cut out for him, because of course he couldn't be allowed anywhere near the saw. I mean, that could be dan-gerous, right?

The point is that school was a nine-year-long insult. It was a nine-fucking-year-long humiliation of those of us who were more practically than academically inclined, and it was proba-bly this, more than anything, that we were protesting against one day when we suddenly decided to adopt your strategy and refused to speak to the Duck. I don't remember what it was she had asked us, but whatever it was we couldn't be bothered answering and holy shit was she mad.

"Bendik! Tom Roger!" she shouted, slamming her hand down on her desk so hard that the pile of exercise books jumped. "For the last time! I'm talking to you, and when I talk to you, you will be so good as to answer."

But me and Bendik, we didn't say a word. We had both re-sorted to your strategy quite spontaneously and quite inde-pendently of one another, but once we realized what we had started it became a game to ignore her for as long as possible.

"Please yourselves," the Duck said. She pointed to the door. "Headmaster's office, now! Quick march!"

But we didn't budge. We just sat there, looking indifferent. I chewed my gum and blinked lazily and Bendik let out a long yawn, not so much sitting as sprawled in his seat.

"Bendik and Tom Roger, did you hear what I said?"

There was silence for two or three seconds and then I turned slowly to you.

"Oh, by the way, I found out why your Puch stopped running when you were out on it yesterday," I said. "The spark plug had sooted up again. It was totally black."

"Oh, right," you said, nodding slowly and trying to look every bit as laid-back and worldly-wise as we were all trying to seem back then.

"Tom Roger," the Duck shouted, angry and shocked.

But I didn't take my eyes off you.

"I don't really think there's any point in changing the plug, though," I said. "We'll probably have to adjust the carburetor to get it running smoothly again."

You nodded slowly and pursed your lips, as if to say, "Hmm, interesting."

"Tom Roger!" the Duck shouted even louder.

"The fuel mix is too rich," I said.

After a couple of moments I heard the scrape of a chair being pushed back sharply. The Duck planted her hands on the desk and jumped up. She wound up her hips and did a quick little duckwalk out of the room. There was total silence for a few seconds and then the class erupted. Kids screamed with laughter as they mimicked the Duck's voice and described to each other how furious she had been, and how crazy Bendik and I were for daring to do something like that, because there was going to be a helluva row now, they were sure.

"Huh," Bendik said with a little shrug, to show how little he cared about that.

Not long afterwards the door opened again.

The babble of voices immediately died away. The headmaster had a round, almost constantly smiling face that made him look like the man in the moon and this, along with a squeaky voice that we never tired of imitating, meant that he didn't exactly command respect. But he wasn't smiling now. He positioned himself in front of the blackboard. He said nothing for a few moments, just stood there looking at the floor, drumming his fingertips together and looking as if he was thinking. Then suddenly he raised his eyes and glared at me.

"What exactly is going on here?" he said.

I gazed blankly out of the window. It had been raining, the wind was ruffling all the glittering puddles dotted around the playground and a white plastic bag drifted slowly across the football pitch where the sixth-graders hung out during break.

"Tom Roger," the headmaster said.

I turned my head slowly. He carried on drumming his fingers as he paced steadily up to where we sat.

"What is going on here?" he asked again.

I shut my eyes and shrugged, opened my eyes again.

"Bendik?" he said.

"Nothing special," Bendik said.

"Nothing special?" he said. "That's not what I heard. I heard you and Tom Roger are refusing to answer when you're spoken to."

"Maybe you should get your ears checked," Bendik said. He looked up at the headmaster and smiled. "Well, I mean, I just answered your question."

The headmaster stopped in his tracks and stood for a moment with his mouth open, then he narrowed his eyes and looked at Bendik as if he couldn't believe his ears.

"What did you say?" he asked.

Bendik turned slowly to me and nodded.

"Yeah, he definitely needs to get his ears checked," he said.

We looked at one another and grinned and just in front of us I could see you shaking with suppressed laughter. The headmaster walked right up to Bendik, placed both hands on his desk and looked him straight in the eye. His moon face was scarlet with rage and he was obviously trying hard not to lose his temper and say or do something he would live to regret.

"Bendik," he said. "I've told you before, but this time I really mean it. I'm losing patience with you and Tom Roger."

"What have I done now?" Bendik cried. "You asked me what was going on and I answered you. Nothing special, I said. It's hardly surprising that I'm starting to wonder whether you're a bit deaf if you didn't hear that?"

"You answered me, yes," the headmaster shouted sticking his face a fraction of an inch closer to Bendik's. "But you didn't answer Frida."

"Who?" Bendik said.

"Frida," the headmaster shouted.

"I don't know anybody called Frida," Bendik said.

"Right, that does it," the headmaster roared, slamming the desk with his hand. "Pack your bags and get off home, the pair of you. I'm going to phone your parents immediately and call them in for a meeting."

"Okay," Bendik said brightly, giving the headmaster a look that said this was good news and hardly what you'd call punishment. And then he turned to me. "Shall we go to your house?"

"Yeah, sure," I said.

So in other words we said stuff school.

Ma and Bendik's mother weren't exactly happy about this, but they didn't get too upset either. Sometimes Ma did say things like "You have to finish school so you won't end up like me," or: "These days you need an education to get a job," but only when the situation called for it, like when she and I went to parent–teacher meetings and she wanted to give the impression that it certainly wouldn't be her fault if I didn't finish lower secondary. Because in actual fact she thought that most of what we learned in school was as much of a waste of time as I did, and she simply couldn't understand how anybody would take up a student loan and spend years studying to get a job that paid them half what they would have earned if they'd got a job as a car mechanic straight after ninth grade.

You worked harder and did much better at school than Bendik and me for the simple reason that you liked that sort of work and it came easily to you. It wasn't as though skipping classes and saying stuff school posed some threat to the great ambitions your mother had for you and that you therefore felt obliged to grind and do well at school. Far from it. In actual fact you tried to convince both your mother and Arvid that you cared even less about school than you actually did. You refused to give them the satisfaction of seeing you do well in an area in which they really wanted you to do well, so you didn't tell them when you got good marks, you often said that you'd skipped school even when you hadn't and you made it crystal clear to them that you wouldn't dream of going on to upper secondary.

Mind you, you were exactly the same with Bendik and me, I remember, but for a very different reason—not because you wanted to distance yourself from us but because you wanted to show that you were just like us. It was almost as though you felt you were letting me and Bendik down when you understood more and did better than us in school. I often noticed that you tried to act as though you knew less and could do less than you actually could. I never saw you put up your hand in class, for example, even if you knew the answer to whatever the teacher had asked. And if the teacher asked you a direct question, you always said, "I've no idea, ask Brainy there," then you'd nod at Audun and grin.

But back then the fact that you were good at school and Bendik and I were not didn't matter much as far as our friendship was concerned. None of that mattered until we left lower secondary. At the time I'm talking about here, when we were in our early teens, the bonds between us were greater than our differences. If you didn't come home with me right after school you'd come knocking at the door sometime later in the afternoon. Then we'd go and pick up Bendik and cruise around on our mopeds till late in the evening. We weren't old enough to drive mopeds but hardly anyone cared about that sort of thing in those days, which was just as well, because riding our mopeds made us feel every bit as free as anybody wants to feel during adolescence. The thing is, you see, if you grow up in a city you can take the tram or the train or the bus into the center of town and lose yourself in the mass of streets and buildings and people, but for kids like us, growing up in a small town like Namsos, that just wasn't possible. For us to feel anything like that as teenagers a moped was the thing. A moped expanded our horizons and our possibilities, a moped meant freedom, escape and independence, and from that point of view it was also a symbol of how we wanted to see ourselves and how we wanted others to see us. Which was probably why we spent so much time and energy on washing them and working on them. Because Christ knows we did: hour after hour, evening after evening in the garage or the yard at our place, unscrewing this, tightening that; you working on a '72 Puch with custom handlebars and aluminum wheels, Bendik on a '73 Tempo Panther with flames painted on the petrol tank and me on a Corvette 380 from 1974.

Even in those days these were, in fact, real old-guy mopeds, but since we liked fixing up bikes and since you didn't just go taking apart a brand-new moped for no reason, they were just the thing for us. And anyway, it was so fucking satisfying to see the looks on the faces of trust-fund brats on gleaming new FZs when we opened up the throttle and zoomed past them on our old, battered scooters, because our bikes were of course wolves in sheep's clothing—and how. Take my Corvette, for instance: it had a fairing and windshield, a cowl and original panniers that brought tears to the eyes of every man over seventy when they saw it coming, right? But what people didn't know was that I had bored out the exhaust, put in a Comet cylinder and 17 mm Comet carburetor and mounted new drive mechanisms on the front and rear gear wheels. Together, all of this gave the moped a top speed of around seventy miles an hour on the flat (we had a car drive behind it to measure the speed) and that was more than enough to allow it to zoom past the trust-fund brats and get away from the cops if that should be necessary.

So in this way too our mopeds reflected the way we wanted to be, right? People thought they were just useless heaps of junk, but when the shit hit the fan, when it really counted, they could leave just about anybody standing.

The fact that I knew how to use a spanner and was a better mechanic than most came in pretty damn handy when our business really got going in the mid-80s. Like I said, before you came to town we were already doing the odd little job, but it didn't amount to much more than breaking into the occasional holiday cottage, stealing the little we could find in the way of valuables and selling them to Grandpa, who then sold them in his junk shop. But back then holiday cottages were a bit more plainly furnished than they are now, to put it mildly, so there was never much for us to lug back to Grandpa except fishing tackle, transistor radios and old propane gas stoves, and we weren't exactly going to make our fortunes out of that.

Then one day something happened that marked the start of a new phase in our life of crime.

It was the 16th of May, the night before Constitution Day, and as always we had gone down to the beach at Gullholmstrand in the evening. But unlike other years when we drank beer and pretended to be drunk or made a bit of money by running around collecting empty bottles for the deposit and gathering firewood for the older kids, this time we were among the teenagers sitting round the bonfire drinking home-brewed hooch. There were some girls there from Høknes Lower Secondary that we were keen to meet, as they were supposed to be easy and willing to go all the way, so we stuck as close to them as we could. We were shy and unsure of ourselves and like most kids of that age we tried to hide this by acting tough. Both you and I added less water to our liquor than we knew we should, our accents got thicker, we cursed and swore and were even louder and brasher than usual. If one of us made some crack aimed at the other, he was liable to get a hard but friendly clout on the back of the head, and every now and again we would get up and chase one another along the beach or wrestle each other to the ground, making terrible threats that nobody took seriously. Bendik was exactly the same, of course, but because he was so fucking shy, especially where girls were concerned, he had to go even further than us to make himself feel tough and sure of himself, and on this particular night, as so often before, things got a little bit out of control. The first to suffer was Janne. She had attached herself to us as usual and was sitting by the fire, trying to unhook the coffee pot from its stick so she could mix herself a *karsk*.

"Phew, it's so damn hot," she said. "I think I'm gonna melt."

"Yeah, well it'd do no harm for you to melt off some of that lard anyway," Bendik said. He pulled a tin of General *snus* out of the pocket of his denim jacket, opened it and slipped a sachet under his lip. "You're starting to look like a fucking weather balloon."

Everybody sniggered.

"Sorry?" Janne said. She obviously hadn't caught what he said because she was smiling cheerfully at Bendik.

"I said you're looking very nice this evening," Bendik said.

Janne stuck out her tongue and made a noise meant to sound like "blah," then she turned away and carried on struggling with the coffee pot. We looked at Bendik, you and me, and grinned, and there were sounds of giggling and snickering round the fire.

"Would you look at her," Bendik said, nodding at Janne, grinning and shaking his head. "She's so fucking ugly a harelip would look good on her."

Everybody burst out laughing at this, great big belly laughs. A few of the girls nudged the boys and asked them to stop it, but even they couldn't help giggling a bit.

Janne sat there staring into the fire. Her eyes were swimming and she had to swallow once or twice, but she managed to hold back the tears. Only once the laughter had died down did she turn to Bendik.

"I know how I look, Bendik," she said.

There was silence.

Janne never took her eyes off Bendik.

"I do the best I can to . . . I try to make myself look nice, I do," she said. "But it doesn't matter how much time I spend on it . . . I know I'll never look good. But it hurts to have you always reminding me of it."

Silence, broken only by the crackle of the fire.

Suddenly it didn't seem so funny any more. Even you and I were a bit taken aback by this brutally honest answer and a few of the girls whom Bendik had probably been hoping to impress by acting tough and clowning about looked even sadder than Janne herself. But Bendik being Bendik he couldn't leave it at that. Even though you put your head on one side and sent him a look that said enough was enough the snide grin stayed on his face.

"Yeah well, you can doll up a toad, but it'll still be a toad. And you're right, you're never gonna look particularly good," he said. "But you might not look quite such a fright if you didn't slap on so much make-up. When we went on that school trip to Langvassmoen it looked like you'd left your fucking face behind in your sleeping bag when you got out of it in the morning."

Nobody was laughing now.

"Cut it out, for Christ's sake," one of the girls said.

"Can't you see she's crying," another one asked.

"Aw, shut your face," Bendik retorted. He snorted and sneered as he took a sip of his *karsk*.

"How would you feel, Bendik, if the only people who liked you were your mom and dad," Janne sobbed.

"Yeah, yeah," Bendik muttered.

After a moment or two Janne put her hands up to her face.

"I'm gonna kill myself," she said. She must have been feeling very hurt, but it was obvious that she also thought it was nice to have the other girls sympathizing with her and was trying to gain still more sympathy by acting even more heartbroken than she actually was. And it worked, because two of the girls got up and went over to her, put their arms round her shoulders and tried to comfort her.

"I'll kill myself," Janne said again. "I will, I'll kill myself."

"Is that a promise?" Bendik asked.

"Oh, for fuck's sake," one of the girls said. She eyed Bendik furiously for a moment, then she turned to you and me. "Hey, is that beast your friend?" she asked, nodding towards Bendik.

Obviously we had to stand by Bendik so we laughed in her face.

"Yeah, of course," I said.

"Deep down he's a really nice guy, you know," you said. She shot us a look of disgust before turning away and going back to comforting Janne, who was now sobbing harder than ever, of course. Bendik sat there grinning so broadly that we could see his *snus* sachet glistening at us, but he knew he'd made a fool of himself, I could tell, because he had that wide-eyed, very focused look that he got when he was slipping into the darkness that he sometimes slipped into. And when he was in that mood you had to watch your step because there was no telling what he might do

"Cheers, Bendik," I said, raising my mug.

"Cheers," Bendik said, doing the same. But his mug was obviously empty because he immediately put it down and picked up the bottle of beer belonging to the guy sitting next to him, cool as you like.

"Oy, that's my bottle," the guy shouted.

"So?" Bendik said. He put the bottle to his lips, drained it and chucked it down onto the rocks where it promptly shattered. For a moment the other guy just sat there open-mouthed, staring at Bendik, but then he clenched his left fist and punched Bendik in the face, hitting him so hard that he toppled off the rock he was sitting on and fell straight into the fire. He didn't lie there for long, of course, he kind of rolled over it, but it was long enough to singe his hockey hair and his eyebrows and so on, and when he got to his feet he looked like something out of the loony bin, he was so mad. The guy who had punched him must have been some sort of athlete because he had taken off like a shot and was already way down the road. Bendik charged after him but before he had rounded the bend in the road leading up to the housing development the distance between them had doubled and he was left standing, gasping for breath. But he wasn't about to be put off, not Bendik. He was blind with rage and the need for revenge and although the place was swarming with people he marched down to the parking lot, climbed onto a Suzuki 250 that was sitting there, started it and rode off after his assailant. Bendik never did catch the guy. He had either run off into the forest or he was holed up somewhere on the housing development. In any case, what I started to say before I got lost in all those fucking detours was that this "borrowing" of a scooter marked the start of what I referred to earlier as a new phase in our life of crime. What happened was that Bendik did a few rounds of the two blocks up on the moor, then he gave up and drove back down to the beach, but to save being caught red-handed by the motorbike's owner he left it in a grove of trees and walked the last couple of hundred yards to where we were sitting, right? And there the bike stayed, and not just for one day or a couple of days. Two weeks later when you happened to be in the neighborhood, it was still fucking sitting there, so we seized the chance and drove it back to Grandpa's shed, right? Then we sprayed it black and sold it to a moron from Nærøy for eight thousand kroner. Eight thousand! That was a goddamn fortune in those days, so obviously we were tempted to do it again.

And that is exactly what we did.

In the evenings we would ride around Namsos and the surrounding area, looking for mopeds and small motorbikes that would be easy to steal, and a few nights later two of us would ride back out there on my moped and drive two bikes back to Grandpa's shed, where we'd make the stolen one unrecognizable by stripping it down, replacing parts, respraying it and doing it up a bit. As usual Grandpa never questioned what we were doing. Not at all, he was keen to make a little money out of it himself, and as well as charging us a small amount for the use of his shed he started hinting that maybe we should expand our activities a bit more and bring him in on it. Not that he ever said so in so many words, but he kept giving us little tips, all of which were meant to get us to see things his way while still leaving it up to us to suggest that we team up.

"Looking damn good," he remarked one day as he stood with a cigarette butt in the corner of his mouth, eyeing up a Zundapp we'd just gotten ready for selling. Smoke coiled up from his lean face and he narrowed his eyes as he hunkered down and ran a finger over the freshly sprayed gas tank.

"Is it yours?" he asked, looking up at you with a grin that said he knew exactly what we were up to.

You stood there with your thumbs hooked into the loops of your belt, looked at him and grinned back.

"Yeah," you said. "I just bought it, but I'm gonna sell it again.

Grandpa nodded and stood up, still grinning. "Damn good," he said again, blowing smoke out of his nostrils. "I could sell five like that in a day if I wanted to. No bother." He stuck his hands in his pockets and stood leaning back slightly, inspecting the moped.

"Yeah, well, not here in the shop, of course," he went on, and then he looked at me and raised his eyebrows . "But around and about. I've had my own junk shop for thirty years, you know. I've traveled all over the country, clearing out houses and the like and I've made a lot of contacts," he said.

We looked at one another, not saying anything.

He swung his leg over the moped and gripped the handlebars. "Right then, how much do you want for it, David?" he asked.

You slid your thumbs out of your belt loops, turned your palms up and gave a little shrug. "A thousand kroner, maybe," you said.

"Is that all?" Grandpa said, looking at you and nodding. "I'm sure I could get fifteen hundred for it if I spoke to the right people. As much as two thousand, maybe."

That's the way he went on and we were smart enough to take the hint, of course, so the next day we wandered over to his place and suggested the very deal he had been priming us to suggest and after scratching his chin and looking doubtful for a minute he pretended to let himself be talked into it. And then we really were in business. We rode around the Namdal area, stealing mopeds that we fixed up and resprayed, then Grandpa sold them on to various friends and friends of friends. I don't know how much money we made at that time, but it was a fair bit and if you think we frittered it all away you're wrong, because even though we did spend more on beer and cigarettes and stuff than we would normally have done, you, Bendik and I all saved up for driving lessons and our own cars. And it has to be said that Ma and Bendik's mother got their share too. I treated Ma to a new TV, for example, and since Bendik's ma didn't have a freezer, just one of those fridges with a little freezer compartment inside it, he bought her a brand-new chest freezer. And as if that weren't enough, he filled the freezer with venison and elk meat that he'd got cheap from Erik and Albert, who—in addition to hawking illicit liquor—ran a large-scale poaching operation.

Both my ma and Bendik's knew of course that there was something fiddly going on as Janne so aptly put it. But being poor but proud and flatly refusing great presents just because

they'd been stolen or bought with dirty money was a luxury
neither of them could afford, so not only did they accept our
gifts and not only were they only too fucking pleased to do so,
after a while they also began to treat us like grown men. So,
while Arvid and Berit still expected you to tidy your room once
a week and made you blow in their faces so they could smell
your breath when you came home late and Christ knows what
else, Bendik and I were suddenly promoted to being the heads
of our households, or not far off it at any rate. We came and
went exactly as we pleased, we never asked permission to do
anything. We began to have a say in things and make the sort
of decisions about domestic matters that the man of the house
usually makes, like when Bendik's ma came home one day and
found him paneling the living room walls. "That old wallpaper
was looking so sad, I thought I'd freshen the place up a bit," he
said. Or when Ma had been out to the mailbox one day and
came back in with two electricity bills. "It was so damn big I
called and asked them to split it in two," I told her.

But in the autumn of 1985 something happened that turned
me back into a little boy overnight, so to speak, and not only
that, it threatened to overturn our whole business. What happened was that Ma got herself a new man, and not just any
man either, let me tell you because while Ma may have sneered
at Berit for being ashamed of her poor hick roots and marrying
for money and prestige when you got right down to it she was
no better herself. You see, this guy she had hooked was a little,
bald thirty-five-year-old with short legs and a lot of Sunday
dinners sloshing about under his chin. Ma was only thirty-two
back then, she had big brown eyes, long raven-black hair and
looked like a Colombian fashion model, but she still felt had
made a real catch because fatso had his own plumbing firm
with branches in several towns in Norway so he was rolling in

money, drove a white Mercedes and talked, acted and dressed as if he owned the world.

It was actually quite incredible to see how my family behaved once Peder Raade, as he was called, came into our lives. Grandma raised her eyebrows and tried to look as if every word that dropped from his lips was pure gold and Grandpa bowed and scraped and couldn't have agreed more with whatever this guy Raade said. Mind you, that was Grandpa all over. Whenever he met anyone higher up the social ladder with money in the bank he would play up to them and go along with everything they said. The difference in this case was, though, that while he usually sneered at and made fun of those same people the minute they were out of sight, with this guy he would still be going on and on about how right Peder was about this or that long after Peder was gone. "Aye, I'm with Peder on that—Social Democrat or Communist, they're all the fucking same," said the man who had voted Labor all his days, and: "No, it's true what Peder says, it's a shame that plane tickets are so expensive in this country"— this from a man who was terrified of flying and would not set foot in an airplane, not even if you put a gun to his head.

But Ma herself was the worst of the lot. She was so desperate to fit in with Peder and become a part of his world. She ditched the big red plastic roses she usually wore in her hair and the bracelets and rings and all the other trinkets Uncle Willy had bought for her on his trips abroad. She suddenly lost the taste for moonshine. It had to be gin and tonic for her now, preferably Bombay Sapphire, or at the very least Golden Cock, and as if that weren't enough she started talking about "funds" instead of money. Funds! It was so ridiculous you couldn't help laughing and fuck knows I did. And I wasn't alone either, you did too, because when you saw how Ma was behaving it reminded you of your own mother.

But the worst of it was, as I say, that she started treating me like a kid again. "Have you done your homework, Tom Roger?" she asked me when she and Peder walked into the living room one day and found you and I sprawled on the sofa watching a video. And one night when I was on my way to bed she actually asked me if I'd taken my cod liver oil. As if she had ever cared whether I did my homework or not, and as if I had ever been in the habit of taking cod liver oil. It was ludicrous. I realized, of course, that she said these things because she was hoping that she and Peder would eventually have kids, so she wanted to sound like a good mother when he was around, but even so, the difference between the way she had treated me right up until she met Peder and the way she was treating me now was so huge it was comical.

Peder himself scarcely seemed to notice how hard my family struggled to behave the way they thought he would want them to behave and if he had noticed he would probably have told them to relax, because I think he found it exciting, exotic even, to be a part of our family. He thought it was really funny, for example, when Ma forgot about acting posh and slipped back into her old rough way of talking, and he never tired of saying how relaxed he felt when he was with us, we were so easy to be with, as he said, so straightforward and so honest.

But there were two things he didn't like.

For one thing he wanted Ma to stop working as a clairvoyant and medium, because although he didn't say it straight out he made it plain that by putting the sort of ad in the paper that she did, she was as good as making herself the laughingstock of the whole town. What Ma thought about this I don't know, but her regular ad stopped appearing in the paper soon afterwards and her consultations with clients, on the phone or at home, came to a sudden end.

The other thing that Peder wasn't too happy about was, of course, our business. At first we lied in his face and told him we got paid for repairing and doing up mopeds, but the guy was no fool and when he noticed that every bike was given a respray and fitted with new parts that were little more than decoration he soon figured out what we were up to, right? I don't know what he said to Ma, but one day when you and I were in the shed, fitting chopper handlebars on an old Honda 50 and listening to W.A.S.P.'s "Animal (Fuck Like a Beast)" on my old tape player, she came in and asked us what exactly we were doing. She stood there with her head on one side, eyeing us up and fiddling with the catch on one of the earrings Peder had bought for her on his last business trip. They were blue and round like grapes, I remember, but they had cost a fortune, so she had got into the habit of fiddling with them. It was a way of drawing attention to what she was wearing in her ears, or at least that's what I thought at the time and it's what I still think.

I felt anger begin to smolder inside me.

"As if you didn't know what we're doing here," I said. "As if you haven't known all along."

"What?"

I got up slowly, picked up a rag from the black synthetic leather seat and looked at her as I wiped some oil off my fingers.

"Don't play dumb," I said.

She stared stonily at me, just stood there for a moment.

"I can see I've been too trusting where you three were concerned. I've been too naive, so I have."

I let out an angry little laugh, reached out a hand and turned the music down a bit.

"That's quite a performance, do you expect us to believe it?"

She didn't say anything for a moment, didn't take her eyes off me, but I could tell that she knew we were onto her and there was no point in keeping up the act, because suddenly she dropped her sad, disappointed expression. She jutted her head forward another inch or so and growled at us.

"I don't give a flying fuck what you believe, but if I see you bringing so much as one more moped here I'll call the cops," she said, and then she turned on her heel and stalked off.

Ma's threat to call the cops if we didn't pull the plug on our business didn't really bother you or Bendik or me, but from then on Grandpa became so cautious it bordered on paranoia. Not that there was ever any mention of him pulling out, he was too fond of making easy money for that. But he would no longer allow us to fix up the bikes in his shed and every time we had to talk to him about something to do with the business he would turn up the sound on the tape player and spend a minute or two racing around like a fucking ferret to check that Ma wasn't eavesdropping on us. As far as I can remember, at that point neither Ma nor Peder knew that Grandpa was in on our scheme, but Grandpa was so dead set on making sure they wouldn't suspect him that that in itself eventually began to look suspicious. Not only was he always jumpy and on his guard, but in the hope of making it seem utterly unthinkable that he could be involved in our activities he actually started acting as though he was worried about us. "I'm sure that whatever they're up to it's no more than boyish pranks, Laila," I heard him tell Ma one day, "but I am a bit worried that it won't stop there." And: "I wonder if those boys aren't a bad influence on one another. Maybe we should try to split them up." That's how he went on, and it sounded so phony and so out of character that I was sure it was only a matter of time before Ma would rumble him.

But I was wrong, obviously.

I was still living on the ground floor of Grandpa's and

Grandma's house, but Ma had moved into Peder Raade's house up on the hill at Høknes and even though she still had a key and was always popping in to see us, obviously she couldn't keep tabs on you, me and Bendik like before. We'd got our freedom back, and we made good use of it I can tell you. Within just a few weeks we had expanded our activities to include stealing boat engines. It was an amazingly easy way to make money, we didn't know why we hadn't thought of it before. Today such engines cost about a thousand kroner per unit of horsepower. Obviously it wasn't as much as that back then, but still, if we stole one fifty horsepower engine and one thirty horsepower engine in a weekend, for example, it goes without saying that we made a bunch. What we did was we borrowed Erik's boat and took it out to one of the many vacation cottage sites scattered along the shores of Namsos fjord. We would hide in some bay or inlet for a little while, then we'd row quietly over to the marina or floating jetty or wherever the boats were tied up, untie the moorings of the boat with the biggest engine and tow it to some place where we wouldn't be disturbed. Then we'd get out the blowtorch and remove the engine from the hull. As soon as that was done we'd load the engine onto our boat and head for some out-of-the-way spot where Grandpa would be waiting with the pickup truck. And then, after we'd maneuvered the engine onto some Styrofoam sheets that we'd spread out on the bed of the truck, we'd pull a tarpaulin over it all and set off to pick up another engine from somewhere else entirely. Grandpa was very particular about this last part. We weren't ever to take more than one engine from the same marina or floating jetty, and if we were going to steal several engines on the same night, we had to take them from different spots, all far apart from one another. If we didn't, it would no longer look like a scattering of one-off thefts, but more like a large-scale, well-organized criminal operation.

"And what do you think would happen then, Bendik?" Grandpa asked once when Bendik was insisting that we should take two engines from the same vacation cottage site in Flatanger. "Well, I'll tell you. If the cops didn't start investigating the matter off their own bat they'd be forced to look into it once the press got wind of it, and they would, you bet your life they would. So it's important not to get too greedy. Because if we get too greedy, sooner or later we'll get caught, that's for sure."

Namsos, July 4th–5th, 2006. A cold worm in the belly

. . . really shouldn't have any more to drink, had way too much aquavit at Ma's and Grandpa's. But I reach for the vodka. Lukewarm vodka, neat. Knock it back and set the glass down on the coffee table. Put my hands behind my head and lie back on the sofa. Look at Mona and grin. At her slim, white body. Her tiny belly button, pierced belly button. I like that piercing, little ring in her belly button. And her pointy little breasts, lovely breasts. She bends down and sets her beer bottle on the floor, just next to the rat's cage, and there's a faint rustling from the cage as she does it. It's that fucking rat of hers moving around, never liked that fucking rat. I gaze at Mona and she gazes back at me, comes over and stands in front of me. Stands between my legs, perfectly still. And I sit perfectly still. Sit with my hands behind my head and my fingers laced together. Flex my biceps slightly. Big, bulging biceps. Send little ripples through my biceps. I know how much she likes a bit of muscle. Big muscles corded with veins. I know how hot it makes her. I look at her and grin, flash my broken front tooth at her. I know she likes that too, don't know why, but she does, says it makes me look more manly. My eyes travel down to her cunt and I swallow. Smooth, shaved cunt. Right in front of me. And then she puts her hands on my shoulders. Looks down at me as she does it. Her horny eyes, playful eyes and half-open mouth. I look at her and grin, place my hands on her hips, my big hands. Draw her a bit closer. Just keeping my eyes fixed on hers now, her eyes are glowing.

"Sit on me!" I tell her.

My voice low, husky. And she does as I say. Sits astride me, one knee on either side of my thighs. Grips my cock, big cock, grips it with her left hand and slides down onto it, slowly. I look down at her as she does it, watch her wet cunt sliding down onto my cock, swallowing more and more of my cock. Stiff cock. Been drinking all evening and all night, but my cock's hard as a rock. I'm so horny. And then she starts to ride me. Rides me nice and easy. Moving gently. Feels so fucking good. I cup my hands around her buttocks. Big hands, broad. Dig the tips of my fingers into her buttocks, lightly. Massage them, knead them. And she moans softly. Tips her head back and shuts her eyes. Runs her tongue over her lips. Moistening her red lips. It's so fucking good. And I'm seething with desire. I gaze at her breasts. Little pointy breasts with stiff nipples. Stiff nipples. Just like it says on her T-shirt. And I'm seething inside. I feel my mouth fall open, feel my lips drawing back and curling slightly. It crosses my mind that I must look even hornier when I do that, look savage, like a wild beast almost. I picture it, that look, and I squeeze her buttocks a bit harder. Picture the marks on her white buttocks, it usually leaves red fingermarks on her ass when I do that. It's so fucking good. Savage. Run my fingertips down to her crack. Part her buttocks and feel her slide even further down onto me. I thought

I was as far inside her as I could go, but now I slide even further in. Her cunt wrapping itself round my cock. Tight, warm cunt. And I let out a great groan. From way down deep in my belly. A kind of grunt. And Mona moans. A short, high-pitched moan. Keeps on riding me, riding gently, steadily. And I gaze at her hungrily. Gaze at her with glowing eyes. And she shuts her eyes. Sticks out her tongue and licks her lips. Red lips, glistening lips. I shut my eyes.

"Oh yeah," I gasp, my voice husky, gruff. "Yeah! Come on baby! Ride my pony!" I say, my words a little slurred. I've had too much to drink, I shouldn't have knocked it back the way I did before we came home, had way too much aquavit. Didn't stop me getting a hard-on, though, no problem there. But what now? Why's she stopping. She's stopped riding me. I open my eyes and look at her. Suddenly there's laughter in her face. She looks away, tries to hide it by glancing to the side, but she can't. Tries to start riding me again, but can't do that either. She just sits there laughing, laughing at what I said.

A second, and then I feel my face getting hot. I hadn't meant to say what I said, but I said it, it just slipped out and now she's sitting there laughing. I'm getting hotter and hotter, I'm going red, I know I'm going red. As if I should have more reason to be embarrassed than her. As if she's any better than me. Sitting there with her eyes shut, moaning heavily and showing me her tongue. Trying to look like a porn model. That's what she was doing. And yet there she is, sitting on top of me, smirking. She's no fucking better than me and yet she's making fun of me. I stare at her. Feel the desire drain out of me, my cock shrink, feel it contract and slip right out of her. And all of a sudden I'm lying here with a limp little cock, a pygmy prick. And she's sitting on top of me, laughing. Smirking. And then comes the rage. This enormous wave. It rises up inside me. I stare at her for a second, then I feel my lips widen in a thin smile. A cold smile. There's this wild rage inside me, but on the outside I'm cold and calm.

"Sorry, Tom Roger," she says, laughing as she says it. "Sorry," she gasps again. A second, and then she puts her hand over her mouth. Tries to stifle her laughter. Her shoulders are shaking. And the rage builds up inside me. Sitting there laughing at me. Making fun of me. And the rage surges up inside me. This wild rage. Overwhelming me. But I keep smiling. Smiling calmly as I clench my right fist. Give it a second and then I let fly. All of a sudden. Smack on the mouth. Feel my knuckles connecting with her front teeth. That feeling of front teeth giving slightly, wonderful feeling. Hard teeth bending back into the mouth. It only lasts for a fraction of a second and then she topples off me and lands on her back on the floor. Cold, sharp slap as the naked body hits the wooden floor. Another second, then I get up off the sofa. Unsteadily. I'm even drunker than I thought. I stagger a bit as I make my way over to the armchair. Lift my boxer shorts off the chair, red boxer shorts. Taking it nice and easy. I've got this wild rage inside me, but on the outside I'm cool and calm. I don't even look at Mona. Smile as I step into my boxer shorts. Bend down and pick my trousers off the floor, put them on, nice and easy. Look at her as I zip up my fly. Smile calmly, coolly. And Mona puts a hand to her mouth and cries softly. The blood seeps between her fingers, red blood on her slim white hand.

"You've got no reason to laugh, Mona," I say. I hear my

voice. Cool, almost soft voice. "I'm not the only one who gets ideas from those porn movies we watch," I say as I bend down and pick up my vest. "The way you lick your lips, you didn't come up with that yourself."

I pause. Pull on my vest, tight-fitting vest, hugging my body, big brawny body. I blink. I'm drunker than I thought. I blink lazily. Look at her and smile. See her frightened eyes, bird eyes. The faint flutter in her throat as she swallows.

"But I don't laugh at you for that," I go on, smiling.

"I'm sorry, Tom Roger," she stammers.

"That's okay. Now go and clean yourself up and we'll forget all about it," I say.

My speech is a bit slurred. I give it a couple of seconds. But she doesn't get up. Just sits there crying.

"Hey!" I say. I give it a second, but she doesn't react. "Hey!" I say again, a bit louder this time. Sharper. "Don't give me that pathetic look," I say. But she just sits there. Sits there looking miserable, hurt. Puts her hand to her mouth, wipes the blood off her chin. A second, and then the rage surges through me again, explodes.

"Stop that, for fuck's sake!" I roar.

I hear my harsh, grating voice. A voice that fills the whole room. I see Mona jump. She flinches, puts her hands over her ears. I stare at her with wild, bulging eyes. There's this enormous rage pressing against the backs of my eyes, pounding. I give it a second, then I shake my head. Suddenly I'm perfectly calm inside, it's like pressing a button, it just happens.

"I'm sorry, Mona," I say. I pick up the vodka bottle and fill my glass. Look at her as I raise my glass to my lips. I really shouldn't have any more. I'm more than drunk enough, but I knock it back anyway. Lukewarm vodka, neat. "I didn't mean to shout, but I can't take that pathetic look of yours," I say, setting my glass down on the table with a little clunk. Wipe my mouth with the back of my hand. Look at Mona and smile. "But we'll forget all about that now," I say. "Shall we?" I ask. I look at her, give it a moment. But she doesn't answer. "Hmm?" I say.

"Yes," she says softly.

"And talk normally!" I snap. "I can't take that pathetic tone of yours either. Okay, now we're both going to get a grip," I say. "Right?"

She looks at me and nods. Tries to smile. But it's not a genuine smile. It's a watery smile designed to make me feel sorry for her. And I gaze at the floor. I sigh and shake my head. Stand like that, looking exasperated for a moment or two, then I raise my eyes and look at her again. Wait a moment. Blink slowly.

There's total silence.

"Well do it, then!" I roar.

I suddenly switch and start roaring at her. I explode. It just happens. A harsh, grating roar that comes from way down deep in my belly. A beast that wants out of me, needs to get out.

"Don't, Tom Roger!" she whimpers.

And I twist my face into a sneer.

"Don't, Tom Roger," I say, mimicking her.

I hear my voice, all distorted, stupid sounding.

"Oh, please!" she whimpers.

"Oh, please!" I repeat, mimicking her again.

I walk right up to her. Stare at her. See the terror in her eyes. Bird eyes. She edges away. Pushing off with her heels and trying to get away. But I walk after her. My feet. Feet walking across the living room floor. Walking slowly.

Walking right up to her. I tense every muscle in my body as I bend over her. My big, bulging muscles. And my eyes bulge, grow big and round as eggs. Big, bulging eyes. The rage presses against the back of my eyes, pounds, my eyes feel like they're about to pop right out of my head and my face is all twisted. I feel the rage pulling my face out of shape. The beast is taking over.

"Would you stop that, please?" I roar.

But she doesn't stop, she just carries on. Sobbing, pleading, with her hands covering her face.

"Stop it, dammit!" I roar, roaring as loud as I can, and it feels like my throat is going to burst, crack, it's like my throat is too small for such a big voice, a voice that fills the whole room.

"Tom Roger," she sobs, whimpers.

Two seconds.

"Hey," I say, and suddenly my voice is perfectly normal again, my voice is almost gentle now, I don't know why, it just is, it just happens. "Hey, didn't you hear what I said?" I ask. "Hmm? Didn't you hear me? Don't I exist?" I say, a little louder this time. "Is that it?" I say. "I asked you to wipe that pathetic fucking look off your face! Could you do me that one favor, please?" I say. "Is that too much to ask?" I say. "Well? Is it?" I say, staring at her with my big, bulging, egg-like eyes.

But she just keeps going. She won't fucking stop. Just sits there sobbing, whimpering. Doing exactly the opposite of what I've asked her to do.

"Stop it, Tom Roger," she sobs.

"I'm to stop it?" I shout, seething. I straighten up sharply. Stare at her and grin furiously. Fling out my hand and try to look as if I can't believe my ears. "I'm to stop it? I ask you as nicely as I can to wipe that pathetic look off your face and talk normally, but instead you do the exact opposite and start howling," I say. I bend down to her again just as sharply. Bring my face right down to hers. "But I'm to stop it," I say. "It's not enough that you sneer and smirk at me when we're having sex, then you try to fucking antagonize me as well!"

"Oh, please, Tom Roger!" she whimpers. Peers at me through the gaps in her spread fingers, her eyes terrified.

"Talk properly!" I roar, roar so loud that I see her hair lifting in the blast. "If I hear one more whimper out of you I'll punch you right through the ceiling!" I roar. "Get it?" I roar.

She draws her legs up to her chest, hides her face behind her knees and covers her head with her hands. And I just stand there. Staring at her. But still she won't fucking stop. She's doing the exact opposite of what I asked her to do. Always the exact opposite. Sitting there whimpering. Crying. And it explodes inside me. This great surge of rage. It fills me. It breaks out of me. This beast. It bursts out, leaps forward. And I put my left hand to the back of her head, grab hold of her long hair, coil her hair around my left hand, grip it tight, hold her fast. Grin furiously through clenched teeth.

"Ow, that hurts, Tom Roger. Let go, it hurts . . . it hurts," she cries and I haul on her hair, bend her head back . . . "Tom Roger, Tom Roger," . . . hoist her up by her hair, drag her up onto her feet . . . "Tom Roger, please. Let me go, let go . . ." Fine, fair hair coiled tight around my fist. I bend her head back until her face is turned upwards, white face shining at me, and her throat, long and exposed, the faint flutter in her throat when she swallows. I bring my face right down to hers, stare into her big eyes, scared bird eyes. "Tom Roger, let go, ow, ow, that hurts . . ." Her breath on my face, the smell of beer . . .

"No, don't hit me, Tom Roger, please."

I take a step towards her and she backs away, putting her hands out in front of her as she backs away, but I just brush them aside, brush aside both her hands with my left hand, roughly, so roughly that she loses her balance and staggers to the side, she has to put out a hand to stop herself from falling, knocks the cactus over as she sticks out her hand. There's a dull thud as the pot hits the floor, the huge cactus slips out of the pot. Dirt spilling onto the floor, a mini landslide.

"But I never said that, I didn't," she says.

Her frightened voice. I look at her, sitting there on the floor with her legs drawn up underneath her. What the fuck is she talking about, what did she never say? I stare at her. I put my hand on the kitchen counter, I'm not too steady on my feet, have to hold onto the kitchen counter. The kitchen counter? Are we in the kitchen?

"And I don't know how you can accuse me of something like that anyway," she says.

Her distraught voice. But what have I accused her of? I must have accused her of something. I look at her, give it a second. Don't say anything. Just let her talk now. Let her go on talking for a bit and maybe I'll figure out what we're talking about. I prop myself up against the kitchen counter. We're in the kitchen and I'm propped up against the kitchen counter. And the fluorescent tube over the sink is about to go out again, that buzzing sound, it's making this kind of low hum and it's flickering. I pull one of the kitchen chairs over. I'm in the kitchen. My head's

spinning. I shut my eyes, open them again. And the fluorescent tube is on the blink.

"I saw it with my own eyes," I say.

Mumble something about having seen something. I look
at Mona. And Mona eyes me fearfully. Her mouth half
open. Big tearful eyes, she shakes her head.

"What did you see?" she asks, staring at me, waiting for
me to answer. But I don't answer, don't know what it was
I saw. I gaze at the floor and shake my head. Run my hand
through my hair. Heave a big sigh. Don't say anything.
I'm so fucking drunk. And tired. I shut my eyes and open
them again. And the fluorescent tube is on the blink, fluorescent tube flickering, light flashing on and off. Shut my
eyes, open my eyes, shut them again . . .

And my hands are under her armpits. Her body's limp,
but easy to lift. She's so thin and light, hardly an ounce of
fat on her. I haul her up onto her feet, draw her close. Stand
there holding her. Unsteady on my feet. Sway slightly, bump
into the fridge, sound of a fridge magnet hitting the floor
right after. I'm so fucking dizzy, unsteady.

"Sorry," I say. Shake her, gently. And she cries and cries.
Tears on my shoulder, my shoulder's getting wet. And
blood on my upper arm and my vest. "C'mon, let's go to
bed," I say.

. . . open my eyes and gaze up at the lamp on the bedroom
ceiling. Flies buzzing round the lamp. Buzz, buzz, buzz.
Then I hear the clatter of the mailbox lid. Is it that late?
Must be the middle of the day if the mail is here. I lie for
a moment. And suddenly the whole of the night before
flashes into my mind. It's like seeing the whole thing in a

huge painting. Me hitting her. Pulling her up by her hair. Roaring in her face. See the whole thing at once. I lie for a moment, then I flip over onto my side. And there's Mona. She's awake. Lying very still and crying. There's this cold sinking feeling in the pit of my stomach the moment I lay eyes on her. Her purple cheek. The swollen lip and the dried blood, almost black blood. I don't take my eyes off her. Swallow. And the sinking feeling in the pit of my stomach grows stronger and stronger. My fist. Right in her face. I see it so clearly and my stomach churns. Nausea stirring. Lying there like a cold worm in my belly, writhing.

Silence.

"I'm so sorry."

My voice low. Regret and confusion in my voice, sincere regret. I regret it with every bit of me, an aching, tearing feeling of regret. I look at her and wait. Swallow. Open my mouth again. I'm about to tell her I love her, but I stop myself. I love her so much, but it would sound like a lie to say that only hours after I've hit her. I hit her again, knocked her flat on her back and pulled her up by her hair, then roared in her face. How rotten can you be? How low can you get? I sicken myself. What sort of a fucking man beats his girlfriend to a goddamn pulp. How can he even call himself a man. It's so fucking cowardly. I hate myself for it.

But that's it, it's over. Even if she forgives me, it's over. It has to be. It's time I took responsibility. If she doesn't end it, I'll have to do it. It's the only right thing to do. Because if we stay together I'm not sure I can stop myself from hitting her again. I didn't think I'd ever hit her again, but I did, and it'll happen again. I can't go on kidding myself. Once I've had a drink I can't control myself. Or when I start on the hard stuff anyway. There's this beast that comes out in me when I hit the hard stuff. I can't stop it. Booze is bad news for me and if I really love her I have to end it. She deserves somebody better than me.

I shut my eyes. I lie there, checking to see whether I really mean this. Am I going to leave her, or is this just something I'm saying to make me feel a bit better about myself after what I've done. If I were able to take responsibility and leave her that would be a redeeming feature, and maybe it's just something I'm crediting myself with just to be able to live with myself at all. I don't know. I open my eyes again. Look up at the lamp on the ceiling, flies buzzing around the lamp, knocking against the plastic again and again. I put a hand up to my brow as I turn my face to Mona. Look at her. Her thin, penciled eyebrows, eyebrows she has spent time getting just right. And then the mark I've made just under her eye, the swollen, purplish-blue cheek and the cracked lips. Dear Mona. She loves me, she's always so sweet and loving and yet I go and do this to her. Hit her. I lie for a moment then I take a deep breath. Kind of gathering myself. Summoning up strength. Because this really isn't on. I have to take responsibility and leave her. It's the only right thing to do and I have to be strong enough to do it. Not just talk about it, actually do it. I look at her. I'm about to say that she deserves somebody better than me, and that it'd be better if I moved out, but I don't. I can't say that. Because that's what I've always said after incidents like this, and it's never been anything but rotten self-pity. Something I've said to get her to feel sorry for me and forgive me. She always feels sorry for me when I start to blame myself.

Always starts listing all my good points. But I'm not going to do that this time. I have to be strong, have to be better than that. Have to spare her my self-pity and all my excuses. Spare her my promises. My begging and pleading and my tears. I've just got to go. I've got to take responsibility and leave her now.

"If you leave the door unlocked, I can pick up my things tomorrow while you're at work," I say.

I hear what I'm saying. I feel the fear inside me as I say it. Feel the regret hit me. Because I need her. Can't do without her. I don't know what'll happen to me if I lose her. I'm going to be in deep shit. That's for sure. I'll go right off the rails. I lie for a second and there's silence in the room. I look at her. And she's just lying there crying. Tears rolling down her nose. She doesn't say anything. And the fear grows inside me. I find myself wishing she'd try to persuade me to stay. I should take responsibility and leave her now. I should get up and go without another word. I know I should. But I don't, I can't. I need her, so now she's got to talk me into staying, now she's got to tell me she loves me. But she doesn't. She just lies there crying. She also thinks it would better if I moved out and she's doing nothing to stop me. Well, I can't blame her. It's a wonder she's put up with me as long as she has. But that doesn't mean it doesn't hurt. I love her and it hurts so much to lose her. A second, and then I feel the tears come. Feel them welling up in my throat. I swallow. Clear my throat. Because I'm not going to cry. No fucking way. I'm not going to give her any reason to feel sorry for me, not this time. I've got to be above that. It's her one should feel sorry for, not me. I've always known it, but this time I've got to do what has to be done. I've got to get up and go now. I push back the duvet and swing my legs

out of bed. Stand up. And my head spins. I must still be a
bit drunk. I stagger as I walk over to the wardrobe. Open the
wardrobe door. I'll just get some clothes, take a shower and
then I'm out of here. Don't know where I'll go, but I have to
go. It's the only right thing to do, and for once I'm going to
do the right thing. It feels kind of good. It hurts to go, I love
Mona and I don't want to leave her, but it feels kind of good
to do the right thing. To know that I can, that I'm strong
enough. I sling my clothes over my arm and walk out. No
turning back now, just walk out of the bedroom and into
the shower.

"Tom Roger, wait."

Her tearful voice. Frightened voice. She's asking me to
wait. Maybe she wants to stop me from leaving after all. I
don't know, but it almost sounds like it. That frightened
voice. She's frightened that I'm going to leave. I can hear
it in her voice and it's so good to hear it. It reassures me a
little. Now I know I have the chance to change my mind.
I don't need to leave her if I don't want to and that helps a
lot, it's comforting.

"Tom Roger," she cries.

Don't stop now though. Keep walking. Have to prove
to her that it's not just talk this time. I understand the
seriousness of the situation and I want her to know that.
If I stay it'll only be because she wants me to stay and I
want her to know that. So I don't stop. Or look back. Just
carry on into the bathroom and shut the door. I'm about
to lock it, but I don't. Want to give her the chance to come
in if she wants. Slip off my boxer shorts and step into the
shower. Nudge some Bratz and Barbie dolls out of the way
with my foot—Vilde's been playing in the shower again.
I turn on the shower, shut my eyes and turn my face up,

feel the spray hitting my face. I could do with a beer soon, I can tell, I'm thirsty, my throat's dry and there's this tension inside me, a jangling that's soon going to turn into the shakes. Need some hair of the dog, need a beer. I pick up the shampoo bottle, squirt some yellow shampoo onto the palm of my hand, soap up my hair. Rinse it off. Open my eyes every now and again and glance at the door handle. Waiting for it to turn, but it doesn't turn. I feel a flicker of unease. Maybe she's going to let me leave after all. Maybe she's changed her mind. I finish showering. Turn off the water, grab the big bath towel that's hanging over the side of the cabinet and step out of the shower. Keep shooting glances at the door handle. But it doesn't turn. She's not coming. And the unease grows inside me. I give myself a brisk rub-down. Start to get dressed.

Then suddenly the door opens and there's Mona. She looks at me with glistening eyes, swallows.

"Tom Roger, don't go," she says.

And my heart lifts again. What a blessing, that she won't let me go, it feels so good, such a comfort. But I don't let it show. I can't let it show. Have to prove to her that I'm determined to go. Prove how much I love her. Love her so much that I'm even willing to leave her for her sake.

"Tom Roger," she says.

"It's no use, Mona," I say, pulling my T-shirt over my head. "You're such a good person, you deserve something better than a life with me," I say, saying exactly what I shouldn't say. Blaming myself so that she'll feel sorry for me and start to play down what I did. I don't mean to do it, but I'm doing it. It just happens.

"I love you so much, Tom Roger," she says. "I don't want anybody but you." Her voice is thick with tears.

"I love you too, Mona," I say. "But I don't deserve you."
Still saying what I shouldn't be saying. I can't help it. It
feels so good. That's she's trying to stop me from leaving,
begging me to stay, it's feels so good and I've primed her to
do it. "You're too good for me," I say, and now she's supposed to start talking about all my good points. I shouldn't
do it, but I do.

"Oh, but you do deserve me," she says. "You deserve a
lot more than you think," she says, saying exactly what
I've primed her to say. "And . . . I think that's your problem," she says, coming up to me, putting her arms around
me, the warmth inside me as she does this, this wonderful
feeling that spreads through me, warmth radiating from
her fingers. "You have such a low opinion of yourself,"
she says, "that's your problem, you . . . always have to
act so tough and sure of yourself . . . and in a lot ways you
are . . . but sometimes I get the idea that you're not as
sure of yourself as you make out. Because if you were you
wouldn't always be on your guard the way you are . . . and
you wouldn't get so mad the second you feel offended,"
she says. "I've often thought that . . . well, my friends
just shake their heads, they say I'm naive and stupid to
think like this, but I really believe that if you can see how
much I love you that might help you to feel a bit better
about yourself. And I believe that might help you feel sure
enough of yourself not to have to beat up me or anybody
else just to defend your honor . . . or whatever it is you're
trying to defend," she says, then she pauses. "I . . . ," she
says, then her voice falters. She bursts into tears again.
Leans her forehead against my chest and cries so hard her
whole body shakes. And I just stand here. Rigid, my arms
hanging by my sides. "I love you so much, Tom Roger,"

she wails, sobbing and rubbing her forehead against my chest. I hear the rasp of hair. Her bangs scraping against my T-shirt. "You're so much better than you think," she goes on. "My friends get quite mad at me when I say it, but there's so much good in you, you're kind and considerate . . . and you're fun to be with. I've never laughed so much as I have since I've been with you," she says.

She's saying exactly what I knew she would say. Talking about all of my good points. And she presses herself against me. Holds me tight. It's going the way it always goes. She's forgiving me. Comforting me. No matter how big a bastard I've been she won't give up on me. And I just stand here, accepting all her love. It feels so good. Almost like being healed. Like being renewed. I lift my hands, place them on her back. Hug her to me, her slight figure pressed against my burly body. Feel her warmth. It feels so good. It's almost like being renewed. The only problem is that I'm not renewed. It may feel like I'm being renewed, but I'm still exactly the same. Here I am doing exactly the same as I did after the last time I beat her up, acting like the repentant sinner, and here she is forgiving me, full of love. This is exactly how it always goes. Nothing changes. There's this pattern we're caught up in. A pattern that we're stuck in and can't break free of. That's the problem. We may kid ourselves into believing that this time things will be better, but they won't be any better. I shut my eyes. Swallow. And suddenly I feel all the happiness drain out of me.

"I need to take a shower as well," Mona says. "I stink of booze."

Telling me she stinks of booze. Saying nothing about all the blood. Wants us to put what happened behind us so she doesn't say anything about the dried, black blood that she'll have to wash off. This is exactly how it always goes. It's this pattern we're caught up in. I take my hands off her back. The happiness is gone. And suddenly I feel sad, angry almost.

"Why don't you rustle up some breakfast while I take a shower?" Mona says. She's never asked me to cook for her before, but she says it like it's the most natural thing in the world. It's a way of trying to make me feel better. She's making me out to be more kind and helpful than I actually am and that's supposed to make me feel more kind and helpful. She's doing exactly what she always does in situations like this. Trying to boost my ego. Trying to fool me into thinking that I'm better than I am. But I don't want to play this game any more. Can't be bothered fooling myself any longer. I know who I am and I'm sick of myself. And I'm sick of our gutter romance. That's how we like to see ourselves. Like one of those white trash couples you see in films sometimes. The kind who've taken their share of hard knocks, but who hang on in there as best they can. The kind who may hurt each other and be mean to one another sometimes, but who still love each other more than any other couple could. That sort of crap. I can't do that any more.

"What's the matter, Tom Roger?" she asks, tucking her fine, fair hair behind her ear and looking at me.

"Nothing's the matter," I say.

I try to smile, but I can't quite pull it off.

"Is your stomach hurting again?" she asks.

She eyes me tenderly. Wanting me to say yes. Wanting me to play that same old game of ours. Wanting me to pretend that my stomach hurts so we can focus on my aching stomach instead of what happened last night. This, too, a way of moving on.

"Nah," I say, shaking my head.

But she won't let it go. Playing that same old game.

"Oh, you," she sighs, shaking her head. "Both your legs could be cut off and you still wouldn't admit you were in pain," she says.

She's making me out to be a real tough nut and acting like she despairs of me. She knows I like that. I like being told that I'm a real man. Always have done. But not right now. I can't fool myself any longer. I just can't be bothered. I'm about to pick up my toothbrush, but I don't, I need to get out of the bathroom now, can't bear to stay here playing this game, so I'll just have to brush my teeth later.

"But I know you, Tom Roger," she goes on. "I can tell when you're in pain, and I'm telling you, you've got to make an appointment with the doctor as soon as possible," she says. "I'm worried about you."

"Yeah, okay," I say, can't be bothered saying anything else, can't be bothered explaining and laying it all out for her, just want to get out of here now, out of this pattern, out of this flat.

"Promise me now," Mona says, actually making herself sound a little cross now.

"Yeah, yeah," I say, shutting my eyes, nodding and opening them again. Then I put a hand to the bathroom door and push it open, see the steam swirling up in the draft.

"Will you make breakfast then?" she asks as she steps into the shower.

"Yep," I say.

I hear the shower door sliding shut as I walk out of the bathroom. Catch the sound of her turning on the shower before I close the door. She's going to wash off the blood now. I beat her to a bloody pulp and now she's going to wash it all away. In a little while she's going to come out of there washed clean and that will be that. And we'll be so nice and attentive to one another for a while. I'll get around to doing jobs I should have dealt with ages ago. Fix the tap in the bathroom or clear up all the junk we've got lying in the storage area downstairs. That sort of thing. I'll throw myself into these jobs and pretend it's just a coincidence that I'm doing them today of all days. I know that's what I'll end up doing. And Mona will be happy. Not happy enough to remind us of why I'm getting around to these jobs today of all days, but happy all the same. She'll praise me, tell me what a great job I'm doing. Be amazed that I can do the things I do. And then she'll do something she knows I'll like. Buy something nice for dinner. Maybe rent a good film. And we'll watch the film and then we'll have sex. And not just ordinary sex. Serious fucking. Real hard fucking. She'll moan even louder than usual. Maybe cry out while we're at it. And afterwards she'll tell me how good I am in bed. You're the best I've ever had, she'll say. I know that's what'll happen. That's what always happens. But we can't go on like this. We have to stop fooling ourselves. Have to get out of this. For once I'm going to fucking well take responsibility. I'm sick of being the way I am. I hate it. But now it's got to stop. Now I've got to get out of here. Got to go. Don't know where. I'll have to see. In any case I've got to go. And I can't face talking to her before I leave. Because it'll just go the way it always goes when I try to talk to her and explain. We'll just fall back into the same old pattern. I've got to get out of here before she comes out of the shower.

I go through to the kitchen. The fluorescent tube above the sink is on the blink, I notice. It's flickering and making this loud buzzing sound. I put out a hand and switch it off, open the fridge and take out a beer. Open the can with a little pop, tip my head back and drink. Knock it back. Cold beer running down my throat. I feel the beer washing away the tension in my body, feel everything in me gradually relaxing. Christ, I needed that beer.

All of a sudden there's a knock at the door. One knock, then another. Who the fuck can it be at this time? Shit. I'm not up to talking to anybody right now. I set the can of beer down on the kitchen table. Very gently. And just stand there. Stand perfectly still. Just have to wait till they go away. Don't want to see anybody right now, I'm not up to it. One second, two. And I just stand here. Perfectly still. Then suddenly the front door opens. I hear the little click. Must have forgotten to lock it when we got home last night and now somebody's opening it and walking straight in.

"Hello," a voice calls. Aw, shit. It's Anne. And my heart starts to thud. Her—of all people it had to be that cunt. I wait a second. Don't answer. She'll probably go away if there's no answer, so I don't say a word. I just tiptoe over to the tall kitchen cabinet and tuck myself in behind it. Hide behind the cabinet.

"Hello? Anybody home?" she calls.

But I don't answer.

Silence.

"She's not out is she?" she asks.

At first I don't know what she's talking about, but then I realize it's Mona's rat, she hates that fucking rat as much as I do and she wants to make sure she's in her cage.

Silence again. And then I hear Mona say: "Oh, that was good." And I feel myself go cold. Because she's coming. She's had her shower and now she's coming out of the bathroom. And I have to get out of here. There's going to be trouble and I can't face it. Not right now. I can't face going head to head with Anne right now, so I've got to go. I'll have to walk straight past the two of them and out the door. Cut and run before anything's said. Have to get out of the house before Anne realizes what's happened. But I don't. I just stand here clutching the cold beer can, staring down at the froth that's gathered in the shining groove on the top of the can. I can't move a muscle. Just stand here listening.

"I didn't think you were home . . ." Anne says.

And then she breaks off. Stops in the middle of the word. She must just have seen Mona's face, that's why she's stopped so abruptly. And my heart's thudding. Because now there's going to be trouble. There's going to one hell of a fight.

Total silence.

"Walked into a door again, did you?" Anne says. She sounds calmer than I thought she'd be. Her voice is sharp, but she's not freaking out. One second. And Mona doesn't say anything. And I don't say anything. I stand perfectly still, staring at the beer can. Stand here like a big sissy. Don't show myself. Can't bring myself to. Stay tucked in behind the cabinet, listening. "Or maybe you fell down the stairs?" Anne says.

"Cut it out," Mona says.

"No," Anne says, raising her voice." "No," she says again, raising it even more, almost shouting now. "I've had enough of this, dammit," she says.

"*You've* had enough?" Mona says, speaking almost as loudly as Anne now. I've never heard her raise her voice to her mother before, but she's doing it now. "Believe it or not, Mom, but not everything in this world is up to you," she says. "Would you please leave me alone. Would you please stop poking your nose in. You live your life and let me live mine."

"Oh, for God's sake, Mona, don't be stupid, you . . ."

"I'm not stupid," Mona yells.

She's fucking yelling at her mother now. What the fuck's going on. I've never heard her yell like this before.

"Don't you call me stupid," she yells. "I'm not stupid."

"I never said you were stupid, I'm just say . . ."

"But you always manage to make me feel stupid," Mona breaks in, livid. "You've always made me feel stupid. The very fact that you can come barging in to our flat and . . . and . . . take charge like this . . . it makes me feel stupid. As if I'm incapable of making my own decisions. As if you're a better judge of what's best for me than I am. It's . . . it's . . . oh, my God, you've no idea how things are between Tom Roger and me."

"I know he hits you," Anne retorts. "And that's more than enough for me."

"It's not that simple. Yes, we have our problems, but we . . . we love one another," Mona says.

Coming out with all that gutter romance stuff now. Presenting this picture of us that we always try to present after I've done something to her. Trying to turn us into the sort of couple we've seen so many times in films. A couple who hurt each other really badly sometimes, but still love each more than any other couple ever could. "I don't want anybody but Tom Roger," she goes on. "I love him and no matter how hard you try you'll never manage to split us up, Mom," she says, glorifying our gutter romance, still making us out to be like one of those couples we see in films. "And anyway, I think you should be careful what you say about how Tom Roger treats me," she says. "What about all the fancy women Dad's had over the years? How humiliating that must have been for you, eh . . . you think I don't remember all the fights you had when I was at home? You weeping and wailing and threatening to kill yourself and him always apologizing afterwards, always promising that it would never happen again . . . and then the kissing and making up . . . when the three of us had to pretend to be all sunshine and light again and make everyone, including ourselves, believe we were the perfect little family. All that—was it so much better?" she asks.

"Oh, for heaven's, Mona," Anne says. "There's no comparison. Look . . . listen to me. You're my daughter. I gave birth to you, I brought you up, and I can't bear to see you being treated like this . . . no matter what went on between your dad and me. And besides, you've got a little girl of your own. This isn't just about you and me. It's about Vilde as well. Surely you can see that. Has it ever occurred to you that you're Vilde's role model? Has it occurred to you that everything you accept from Tom Roger, everything he says and does to you, Vilde's liable to accept from the future men in her life?"

"Don't you go bringing Vilde into this," Mona cries.

"But it's not me that's bringing her into it," Anne says. "It's you that's doing that. I mean, you're the one who's living with a violent man."

"Vilde has never, ever witnessed any violence, Mom. And, however much it may annoy you, she and Tom Roger are the best of friends. I know you'd like to believe otherwise, but Tom Roger is actually great with kids. Just as great with them as Olav is. He would never say or do anything to me or anybody else when Vilde was around."

"Oh, for God's sake, Mona, how long do you think you can go on fooling that girl into believing that you walked into a door every time you have a black eye? Hmm? Don't you realize it's just a matter of time before Vilde figures out what's going on? And don't you realize the effect it could have on her in the long run? She's going to grow up believing that that's how men are. That it's perfectly normal for men to hit their women, and that that's just something we women have to accept. Don't you realize that?"

Silence for a second or two.

Then: "Do you know what I think, Mom," Mona says, and her voice has suddenly changed. She doesn't sound all that angry now, instead there's a kind of grim satisfaction in her voice. "I don't think this is about Vilde or me," she says. "The fact that you hate Tom Roger and the way you're always poking your nose into our affairs, I think that's actually all about you. All the things you've always dreamed of, I think you're trying to achieve through us . . . all the things you wish you'd done when you were feeling most put upon, you're trying to make those wishes come true through me."

"Oh, for heaven's sake, this is absolutely . . . I mean . . . Mona. Don't you see that you're trying to play down what Tom Roger does to you, you're trying to convince me and yourself that what you have to put up with is actually perfectly normal, don't you see that? You're trying to convince us both that there's no difference between what goes on between you and Tom Roger and what goes on between other couples. But there *is* a difference, Mona. There's a huge difference."

"Oh, really?"

"Yes really . . . excuse me, he *beats* you. He tries to control you by means of physical violence."

"Well, for one thing I don't think you've any room to talk about controlling people, Mom. I've never seen you use physical violence, but I have seen you use loads of other methods. And for another I actually happen to think it's less humiliating to be given the odd clip around the ear than to have Tom Roger screwing around the way Dad used to do.

"The odd clip around the ear," Anne snorts. "My God. Even the words you use make it sound so harmless, honestly . . . Mona, you . . . you're breaking my heart, you . . . you keep dodging the issue, you do everything you can to avoid talking about you and Tom Roger. Every time I try to talk about you and him you change the subject and start talking about me or somebody else," she says. "But if we could just concentrate on you and Tom Roger for a moment, please . . . Tom Roger controls you, you can't see it yourself, but he does . . . and not just by means of physical violence either, he controls you in other ways too . . . through the guilt he makes you feel when he hits you, for example. I can't tell you how insecure you've become, Mona. You seem to have lost all your self-confidence. You may not see it yourself, but everybody who knows you can see it. And they all know why. They all know he makes you feel ashamed and guilty," she says.

I raise my chin and look at the ceiling. Bitch, what the fuck is she saying? She's fucking well saying that I'm to blame for all the guilt Mona feels. Un-fucking-believable. I mean, obviously I feel bad about all the pain I've caused Mona, but for fuck's sake, if there's one person who's done more than anybody else to make her feel guilty and ashamed it's Anne.

But she still won't stop. "You've absolutely no reason to feel guilty, Mona, of course you haven't," she says. "But like so many other women in your situation you think it's you there's something wrong with and not the man who batters you. If he beats you up it must be because he has a reason to beat you up, right? There must be something about you that's not good enough, right? That's how you think. That's how all women in your situation think. You're being eaten up by guilt and shame, Mona. You feel guilty because he hits you and you feel guilty for letting him hit you . . . you've got to get out of this. Now! This minute!"

I just stand here listening to what she's saying. This is un-fucking-believable. She's trying to get herself off the hook. That's what she's doing. Trying to pin the blame on me for everything she's done. A second, and then I feel a surge of anger. Rage. Because if there's one thing I can't be blamed for it's making Mona feel guilty. Far from it. In fact I've done all I could to boost her self-confidence, I've done my best to rebuild everything that that fucking mother of hers has destroyed.

"Sounds like you know what you're talking about," Mona says with a faint sneer and that same note of grim satisfaction in her voice. "You're never going to tell me that's how you felt when Dad was screwing around? You're never going to tell me that back then you thought it was you there was something wrong with and not him? That he screwed around because you couldn't give him what he needed or something?"

"Mona, would you . . ."

"There, you see, that's just what I'm saying," Mona says with a scornful little laugh. "This is all about you, isn't it. Not me, not Tom Roger, it's about you and Dad."

"No, Mona. No. I just don't know what to do. I'm so worried about you. And I'm worried about Vilde and I . . . I don't know what to say, but if your dad and I have had our problems too . . . and if there's any similarity between the way things were for me and how they are for you now, then . . . anybody might think I could give you some advice, anybody might think you'd do well to listen to what I'm saying."

"I am listening to what you're saying."

"Yes, but not properly," Anne says. "He's destroying you, Mona. He's breaking you down. Just the way you talk to people now, that snide, smart-alecky tone you've adopted . . . this need you seem to have to drag people down into the dirt just so that you can feel better about yourself, all of this . . . it . . . it reeks of self-loathing. He's done this to you . . . he's made you more and more like himself. Do you realize that?"

Fucking cunt, she just won't let up, she's still blaming me for Mona's low self-esteem. Blaming me for what she's done. Well, that fucking does it. I'm not going to stand here and listen to this. I have to be man enough to take responsibility for my actions, but no fucking way am I going to take the blame for all the things that cunt has done to Mona. I take a big gulp of my beer, slam the can down on the table and walk up to the kitchen door. Stand in the doorway. Smiling. I'm raging inside, but I'm smiling. I look straight at Anne. See her eyes widen when she sees me, wide eyes in that pasty, powder-caked face, see how surprised she is. But then she collects herself. Twists her face into a sneer.

"What the hell? Have you been hiding in there?"

"Yeah," I say, staring straight at her, giving her a cold, hard smile. "I'm so ashamed of what I've done that I didn't dare to show my face right away," I say. Say it straight out, still smiling.

"Yes, well, you've every right to be ashamed," Anne says. "Christ, what a gutless little bastard you are," she snarls, raising one pale pig's trotter of an arm and pointing at me. I see the gold bracelet slip down to her wrist as she does it. "You are . . ."

"Stop it," Mona cries, breaking in.

"No," Anne shouts, spinning around and stamping her foot. There's a little thud as the sole of her shoe hits the floor, a muffled thud. She glares at Mona. "You're far too good for this loser, Mona," she shouts. "He doesn't deserve you and I don't mind telling him so."

She turns to me again, stares at me.

"I couldn't agree more," I say, still smiling. It pisses her off that I'm smiling. Because it makes me look like I mean exactly the opposite of what I'm saying. But I don't. I really do mean what I'm saying. But I'm smiling anyway, I can't help it. It's this anger inside me.

"Well, then do the right thing, damn you," Anne shouts, glaring at me. "Get out of my daughter's life."

"Mom," Mona cries, leaning towards her. I see her long, fine hair slide off her shoulder and fall forward, curtaining her furious face. "Would you fucking shut up, would you just leave us alone. It's not Tom Roger who needs to get out of my life. It's you," she yells. "It's you!"

"Mona," Anne says, her voice shaking, faltering for a moment. "If I could just get a word in here. You don't know what's best for you, so if I could just . . ."

"Would you stop saying that," Mona suddenly screams, thrusting her head forward as she screams. Her red face, her arms thrown back, rigid, a bit like a longjumper preparing for takeoff. "It's not true," she screams. Her eyes wide, the big vein in her throat, blue veins expanding when she screams. "I do know what's best for me, I'm not stupid," she screams, "I'm not stupid," she screams, screaming as loud as she can, a cold, shrill voice, a voice that breaks on the last word.

And I look at her, smiling.

"Take it easy, Mona," I say. "Anne's right, and we both know it. You're far too good for me."

I walk up to her, quietly, put my hand on her shoulder, her bony shoulder. And then I turn to Anne. Look her straight in the eye and smile. And she looks at me. That thoughtful look in her eyes. She's sizing me up. Trying to work out where she has me now. She's confused, thrown by what I've just said. And by my smile. I can tell by her face that she's confused, thrown. I get a bit of a kick out of that. I go on smiling at her, just for a second, then I look at Mona again.

"And don't you start going on again about how I'm plagued by self-loathing," I tell her. "And how I've got such a low opinion of myself that I can't believe you could actually love me, and that's why I say I don't deserve you. Because it's not true," I say. "It's perfectly true that I don't deserve you. You come from a respectable and unusually well-off family, and I come from a family of drunks, benefit scroungers and petty criminals, so I never could deserve you either."

Then I pause for a moment. Still smiling. I look at Anne, two thoughtful eyes in a pasty, powder-caked face. Look at Mona, she seems confused too now, thrown, two little bird eyes, fixed. She probably wasn't expecting this, she was probably expecting me to back her up, to tell Anne to butt out of our lives. I'm kind of surprised myself. I wasn't expecting to say all this either.

Silence. Broken only by the sound of the rat in its cage, a soft scrabbling.

"And you know something, Anne?" I go on, turning to her again. "That's exactly why Mona wants to be with me. Mona's not living with me because she loves me. She may think that's why, but it's not. She's living with me because that's the best way of rebelling against you," I say. I hear what I'm saying, feel more and more surprised to find myself saying this, I've never even seen it this way before. "Mona can't stand all your expectations of her and all the demands you make on her," I say. "I don't know how many times I've seen her crying her eyes out and complaining about how hard it is for her because you're never satisfied with her, with who she is or what she does. In your world, yours and her dad's, a person can never be clever enough or perfect enough. There are always new goals to set for yourself, always something else to aim for. You never get to a stage where you can relax and feel satisfied with yourself. And that's what Mona's trying to rebel against. She can't handle it and she doesn't want to be part of that rat race. She says so herself and I'm sure it's true, I mean it's surely no accident that she's had problems with bulimia," I say, mentioning her bulimia now, there's nothing Mona dreads more than the thought of people knowing that she's suffered from bulimia, but I say it anyway, look at Anne and smile. "There's no way Mona can ever live up to your ridiculous expectations of her, and to save herself from being swallowed up by feelings of inferiority and self-loathing she's trying to show that she doesn't give a damn about your expectations or your demands. She's trying to show that she wants nothing to do with your ambitions and your social climbing," I say. "And what better way to do that than by shacking up with a man fourteen years older than herself who has done absolutely nothing with his life. And has no ambition to do anything with it either," I add with a little laugh. "Nothing could get up your nose more than to see Mona take up with somebody like me," I say. "A drunken waster, on welfare, with rotten manners and a police record," I say. "But I've had it. Mona can rebel against you all she likes, but I refuse to be part of it any more."

I hear what I'm saying. I don't know where all this is coming from, I can't remember ever thinking anything like this before, but it's true what I'm saying, it's absolutely true. I turn to Mona, gaze at her. Her thin penciled eyebrows are arched slightly and she gazes back at me, shaking her head. She looks almost frightened.

"I feel used, Mona. Do you realize that?" I say, still smiling. I stare at her, she's looking more and more frightened, she opens her mouth and goes on shaking her head, stares at me with wide, frightened eyes, frightened bewildered eyes. "I feel used," I say again. "You're fourteen years younger than me and when you're as old as me you'll find it impossible to believe that you could ever have wanted to get mixed up with someone like me," I say. "When you finally manage to cut loose, more or less, from your mother's apronstrings and start to feel a little more sure of yourself, you'll do exactly what she says you should do. And not only that. You'll actually want to do it. You'll be glad to move away from Namsos, you'll go to college, meet some guy of your own age who's also gone to college and before you know it you'll be living in a house with paintings on the walls and a library with those huge Chesterfield sofas in it, just like the ones your mom and dad have," I say, talking a bit faster now, faster and louder. I stare at Mona. Something's breaking loose inside me, this great, heavy surge of rage, breaking loose. "You don't love me, Mona," I say. "You're just using me as a stepping-stone to get where you're going. Maybe that's why I hit you, what the fuck do I know. I'm not trying to excuse or belittle what I've done to you, and I am ashamed of myself, I truly am, but . . . to be used by a spoiled brat who was born with a silver spoon in her mouth and coddled and God knows what all, it's . . . it's so fucking degrading . . . and it makes me . . . so mad," I roar.

I let out this roar. A wild roar, a roar that comes from somewhere deep in my stomach. And Mona and Anne both flinch, take a step back. And this great heavy weight, this surge of rage, it sweeps through me like a landslide. And I stare at Mona. Feel my eyes widening. Feel like my eyes are about to pop out of their sockets. "The way you drag me into this play-acting of yours," I shout, my voice deeper than normal, rougher. "Because that's what it is," I say. "The fact that you choose to live with me and the way you're always trying to talk and act like you're in *Wild at Heart* or *True Romance* or one of those other films that we've always thought were so great. It's really all just an act that you put on for yourself and your parents," I say. "Well, not for me it isn't. You may be playing at being white trash, but I'm not. For me this is no act. It's real. I can't just go back to my nice posh life when I get fed up with the way I'm living now," I say. I stare at her. At her big, wide eyes. Frightened, sad, bewildered eyes.

"No," she says, says it without making a sound. Shuts her mouth and opens it again. "No," she says again, shaking her head as if she can't believe what she's hearing, doesn't want to believe it. "I love you, Tom Roger," she says, her voice thick with tears, broken-hearted.

I look at her, shake my head, and then I start to walk away.

"Tom Roger, don't go, please."

But I keep walking.

"Let him go, Mona," Anne says.

"Tom Roger," Mona says, crying my name.

But I grasp the doorhandle and open the door, walk out. Don't know where I'm going. Just know that I have to get away from here. I hear Mona roar as I step out into the backyard, her voice furious, she's so furious with her mother, screaming that she's going to kill her. "Get out of my life or I'll kill you," she screams. And I walk away.

Namsos, July 10th, 2006

In the autumn of '85 we stole so many mopeds, motorbikes and boat engines that Grandad was hard put to get rid of them all. He felt it was too risky to sell everything we brought him in the same district that it had been stolen in, so we either had to scale down our activities drastically or find ourselves another middleman because he didn't dare to go on the way we were going. We were getting too greedy.

But we didn't scale down. Anything but, in fact, because around this time Uncle Willy and Odd Kåre Hindmo started using the moving van to deliver liquor for Erik, and the motorbike club in the Oslo area that bought and resold his booze was only too happy to buy and resell the stuff we pinched, so we ended up stealing even more than before. Not only that but, when Bendik asked, the bikers confirmed that they also had the odd thing to sell and since it seemed a waste of time and money to drive all the way back to Namsos with an empty van, we started taking their contraband and stolen goods back north with us. Usually it was just cigarettes or a batch of quality wine and spirits that we sold to restaurants and bars on the way north, but sometimes we also carried watches, sunglasses, jewelry, perfume and other stuff, and whatever Uncle Willy and Odd Kåre didn't manage to shift Grandad took it upon himself to flog.

More often than not Uncle Willy and Odd Kåre asked you, me and Bendik to come with them on these trips. Not so much to help with loading and unloading the van, although obviously we did that too, but more because then we actually looked like a team of movers, sitting up there in the cab in our baseball caps and tatty T-shirts, with our work gloves in our laps. Besides which, it was a long trip and since one of the two adults always drove a couple of miles ahead of the van in a car so he could come back and warn us if there happened to be a police road-block or anything else a bit dodgy on the road, we were also there simply for the company.

How cool we felt, sitting there with the windows rolled down and our elbows resting on the sills, listening to Lynyrd Skynyrd, smoking, cursing and swearing. It's a bit embarrassing to think about it now, but I remember how we changed our way of talking and started using the sort of lingo we thought real crooks would use. We referred to the police as "the cops" or "the fuzz," money was "dosh" or "dough" or "bread" and once, when a dissatisfied business associate threatened Odd Kåre by saying he was going to call the police, Bendik was all for "liquidating the bastard."

"Why do you talk like something out of a Donald Duck comic," one of the bikers asked us once when we were lugging boxes of liquor into the storeroom behind their clubhouse. And when Uncle Willy and Odd Kåre both burst out laughing and we real-ized that they had been asking themselves that same question, well, I have to admit we felt pretty small and stupid. After that I seem to remember we toned it down a bit and went back to talking more or less normally. But the nickname they gave us stuck: from then on we were the Beagle Boys or the Beagle Gang, eventually shortened to the B Gang, and this, mark you, was long before the rise of that other notorious B Gang in the Oslo underworld.

You might think we would have dropped out of school completely by this time, but we hadn't. Far from it, in fact. The more we got up to, the greater the risk became, and the greater the risk, the more important it became to put up a good front and not be associated with any stupid shenanigans, Uncle Willy said, and so we actually started to behave ourselves. We were quiet in class and polite to the teacher and what's more we almost stopped skipping school completely. And while Bendik and I pulled ourselves together enough to get pass marks in all our subjects and even got the odd "G" for "Good" in our report cards, you grabbed the opportunity to show what a bright pupil and bookworm you really were. Suddenly you didn't need to hold back in order to seem like one of us. With Uncle Willy's warnings as an excuse you would sit down with your books at the oddest moments in the strangest places, and it wasn't always school books either, it could just as easily be books you'd bought or borrowed from the library, or that you'd taken from the vicar from hell's bookshelves. You never let us see your report card, though, that I remember. No fucking way. Probably because your marks were so much better than Bendik's and mine that you saw them as some sort of proof that you weren't one of us after all. Like you had to draw the line somewhere.

In any case ninth grade was one long success story for all three of us.

I remember the Duck came over to us one day when we were sitting outside on a bench and she was on playground duty. "You know," she said, "you three ought to be really proud of yourselves."

I doubt, though, that that's what she said when the cops called her in for an interview and she found out how we'd been spending our evenings and nights for the past two years. Because of course we did eventually get caught. One July evening in '86 the doorbell rang and no sooner had I opened the door then I was in handcuffs, looking on open-mouthed as two burly policemen pulled out drawers and looked in cupboards and turned everything in the apartment upside down. I acted innocent, pretended to be mystified and asked them what they were doing, but they wouldn't tell me a thing. Then, with nosy neighbors leaning over the fence, gawking and pointing, I was led out of the house and placed in the back seat of one of the two waiting police cars. The other car was for Grandad I realized, because just before we drove off I heard him whining and complaining and asking the cops if they thought this was any way to treat an old man.

I don't remember how long I sat in that cell, but I certainly had plenty of time to wonder how on earth they'd caught onto us. I just didn't get it. We'd been so damn careful. We'd even stopped using Grandad's shed to store our plunder. Instead we stashed everything we pinched in an old barn belonging to Uncle Willy that was just next to his cottage out at Gullholmstrand.

My first thought was that Janne must have ratted on us. Even though we'd seen less and less of her towards the end of lower secondary she did still know a fair bit about what we got up to and considering how we'd treated her over the years, it wouldn't have been so surprising if she'd decided to get back at us by going to the police and telling what she knew. The fact that by this time she had gotten herself a boyfriend also made me think it even more likely that she was the culprit, because it was easy to see that this guy had given her self-confidence and self-respect. I had bumped into her one day coming out of the corner store in the Prairie with him, carrying bottles of cola and a pile of videos and it was as much as she could do to say hello. Fucking unbelievable. Only months before she'd been just about begging to be allowed to tag along with us, but now that she was with her boyfriend—who was ten years older than her and every bit as fat—she felt so superior that she couldn't even be bothered to stop and talk to me. Because that's exactly what happened. I stopped and made it quite clear that I was all set for a bit of a chat, but even though both she and the boyfriend could see this, all she said was "Hi, Tom Roger," then she stuck her nose in the air and walked on.

So the thought that crossed my mind as I sat in that cell staring at a wall covered in swastikas and dicks and I love so-and-so and so-and-so was that this new confident and oh-so-fucking-high-and-mighty Janne had finally felt able to get angry at her tormentors and that this in turn had prompted her to call the cops and tell them what we were up to. That she was going out with a guy who was ten years older than her must have made her feel safe and thus brave enough to do it, or so I thought. Even though she had absolutely no reason to feel safe, of course, because if it turned out that she really had been the one to inform on us, we wouldn't just say "naughty, naughty" and leave it at that, that's for sure.

Another possibility was that one of the neighbors had got suspicious and called the cops. Like I said, we had stopped using Grandad's shed for fixing up the bikes and storing stuff, so they couldn't have seen us bringing in stolen goods, that I simply don't believe. But there was always the chance that somebody had begun to wonder how come Grandad could afford all the things he could obviously afford. Because no matter how many fucking times Uncle Willy and Odd Kåre Hindmo told him to be careful and not throw money about, he was—and still is—such a terrible dandy and if he saw something he liked—a gold chain or a watch, say, or something to wear—he just had to have it. He loved to strut around in his new made-to-measure suit and he could hardly take a walk down to the newsstand for cigarettes without lugging the huge mobile phone he'd bought along with him. "I was so poor when I was a boy," he used to say if anyone criticized his extravagant ways, "I've got a lot of catching up to do."

A third possibility was that Arvid and Berit had got wind of our activities. As far as I was concerned there was no way you would have said anything to them. You were a cold, hard bastard and an exceptionally good liar and you would never have admitted anything no matter how much pressure they put on you. On the other hand, though, they were worried sick about you at that time. For at least a year you'd done your very best to make them think you didn't give a shit about school and that you were in grave danger of failing one subject and another. In fact, just before the Christmas break in eighth grade you even went so far as to doctor your report card so it looked as if you'd gotten much worse marks than you actually had, and obviously this, together with the fact that you spent all your time, day and night, with Bendik and me, meant that they kept even closer tabs on you than ever, so who knows what they might have discovered with all their spying. You took precautions, of course. You knew that they searched your room every now and again, so you kept your money and anything else that might arouse suspicion at my house, and you knew they read your diary, so you invented a day-to-day routine that was a far cry from your actual life. But still, when they kept such a fucking close eye on you there was no telling what they might find out.

But the most likely explanation, as far as I could see, was that the informant had been Peder Raade: after what had happened at his birthday party that year he certainly had a clear motive, but he had also made certain remarks that seemed to point the finger at him and no one else. What had happened at his birthday party was that Ma had been entertaining some of his friends with routines from her time as a clairvoyant and medium. Not only did she read the tarot cards and tell the fortunes of those who wanted her to, she even spoke to the late grandfather of one party guest. Apparently Peder hadn't said a word while all this was going on, in fact he'd looked as though he was enjoying himself and when his guests remarked that he'd have no problem playing the stock market now that he had a fortune teller to consult he just chuckled. But once the last guest had gone he hit the roof. "What have I told you about that goddamn gypsy crap," he roared at Ma, and when she tried to excuse herself by saying that the others had encouraged her and that they had even seemed to think it was fun, he had asked her how stupid she could be. Didn't she realize they'd gone along with it just so they could make a fool of her and him? Didn't she realize that they'd been laughing at her all evening, he roared, and then he'd beaten the shit out of her. "She looked like her nose and her mouth had changed fucking places when she came home," as Uncle Willy said.

Naturally the stupid bastard regretted it afterwards, but even though he begged and pleaded with Ma to come back to him, and even though Ma later admitted that she had been tempted to return to a life where she never had to worry about money, there was no way that was ever going to happen. She had lived with wifebeaters twice in her life and if there was one thing she had promised herself it was that if ever a man lifted his hand to her again, just once, she'd be out of the door that very minute. But then, of course, Peder Raade felt insulted and humiliated. How dare a woman like Ma say no to a man like him, that's what he must have been thinking. So then he started phoning the fucking house and writing letters in which he made all sorts of threats: how he was going to destroy her and that crooked fucking family of hers and all that kind of thing, and that was why I was so sure it was him who had ratted on us.

When I got out of jail and was able to talk to you I found that you'd had exactly the same thought and had come to exactly the same conclusion, and when I shook my head and told you what had really happened your face fell, just as mine had done during my first interview when the cops told me that this was the first major drug bust they had made in Namsos.

Drug bust?

Talk about being taken for a ride.

Here Bendik and Odd Kåre Hindmo had been, going behind all our fucking backs and doing deals with those bikers, and when we thought we were carrying a little batch of cigarettes here or a box of watches and jewelry there, we'd actually been driving from Oslo to Trøndelag with a vanload of drugs. Once, twice or sometimes even three times a month for a whole year we'd done this. We'd been running the risk of several years in prison or various young offender institutions and we'd made nothing out of it.

Luckily, at the trial Bendik and Odd Kåre swore that no one but them knew about the drugs, so Grandad and Uncle Willy and I were only found guilty of theft and handling stolen goods. And if they hadn't found so much cash at our house we would probably have got off scot-free, because strictly speaking the cops didn't know shit about what we'd been doing. They had simply been following a tip-off about this fucking motorbike club being involved in drug trafficking and it was pure coincidence that Uncle Willy happened to have parked the moving van outside our house on the very day that the police made their move. At first I refused to say anything about how I had come by so much money, but when it dawned on me that the cops actually believed I had made it from running drugs and that I risked being sent to prison for however many years, I had no choice but to tell them about our little business.

But neither you, Erik or Albert had been dragged into it, which was always something. And you couldn't do enough for me, I remember, to repay me for keeping your name out of it. When we went down to the video store to rent some films you always insisted on paying; that same summer, when Grandad and I had to scrape and repaint the outside of the house, you came over every single morning to give us a hand, and if anybody did or said anything to me that wasn't exactly nice you would get way angrier than you needed to on my behalf.

But in actual fact our time together was over and we both knew it, and not just because you were starting upper secondary in the autumn and I was going to do mechanics at the Tech. During that last year it had also become more and more clear how different we actually were as people. We had both worn denim jackets with the badges of hard rock bands sewn on the back, W.A.S.P. on mine and AC/DC on yours. But while you were actually into the music and spent more and more time listening to it and reading about it, I didn't really care. I tended to get the song titles, the bands and the musicians all mixed up and I couldn't have cared less whether a record had been issued in one year or another or on which label. Hard rock was just a way for me to tell the world who I was and who I wanted to be, no more than that. The same went for a whole lot of other things. When it came to politics, for example, you, Bendik and I all claimed to be as left-wing as it was possible to be, but while you defended your opinions with long speeches about capitalism and the exploitation of the working class, Bendik and I confined ourselves to stating that we "hated the establishment," as we put it. What mattered to us was to be extreme, and to be honest we could just as easily have been at the opposite end of the political spectrum.

In the end the only thing we had in common was the business, and when that collapsed, we drifted quite naturally and painlessly apart. I suppose we could have carried on stealing bikes and so on and through that we might have managed to stay friends, but that was never an option: unlike Bendik, you and I weren't cut out to be crooks. All three of us had had much the same motive for doing what we did. We had all had a vague sense of having been hard done by and we tried to rid ourselves of the anger and shame and self-loathing that this filled us with by breaking the law. When we stole we weren't really doing it for the money and other stuff, or not to begin with anyway. What we were after was respect and self-respect. Breaking the law quite simply made us feel free and powerful and independent. We were our own men and we did as we pleased, just like Erik and Grandad did when they produced and sold illicit liquor.

But unlike Bendik neither you nor I were able to ignore the consequences of our actions. Neither of us was particularly scared of being caught or of the punishment that awaited us if that happened, that's not what I mean. In fact I seem to remember that we had a pretty romantic view of life behind bars, liked to picture ourselves as the sort of jailbirds you always saw in Hollywood movies—you know, the sort of tough guy who everybody respects and who's liable to punch or do a lot worse to anybody who so much as looks at him the wrong way or makes some snide comment. What I mean when I say that we couldn't ignore the consequences of our actions was that our consciences began to trouble us more and more. We tried to ease our guilt by making it a sort of a rule that we would only steal from people who could afford to live without whatever we took. But even though this made it easier for us to keep going it still wasn't easy. After all, just because a boat engine was expensive didn't necessarily mean that the owner was rich, right? I mean it could just as easily belong to a family that had scrimped and saved for years to be able to buy that particular engine. Or to some poor, hard-up fisherman come to that.

"So what," Bendik would say when we made such objections. "They can claim it back from the insurance. It's not the owner we're stealing from, it's the fucking insurance company, that's how you've got to look at it."

But we found it hard to look at it that way. We simply didn't have it in us, neither of us, and once I'd done my time that was it for me, from then on I was going straight. Okay, so I've swindled a bit on benefits and I've notched up a couple of convictions for assault since then, but I'm glad to say I've never been mixed up in anything more serious than that. While Bendik has been a professional criminal all his adult life, or so I've heard, I've supported myself and my family by working as a car mechanic, a bouncer, a laborer, a vaccuum salesman and God knows what else. In the mid-90s I even set up and ran my own bodybuilding gym in Namsos. So I've tried my hand at various things over the years.

As for you, well, you went on to upper secondary then spent several years at university, but when I met you at that class reunion you were working as a fucking receptionist in a hotel in Trondheim. I've heard a lot of weird things in my time, but for somebody to go to school for more than twenty years and then take a job as a fucking hotel receptionist, well, that takes the fucking cake, if you ask me, and I told you so, but you were hurt by that, I remember. You laughed and tried to make a joke of it by saying that you were a resting night porter, you could spend most of your working hours asleep, and this allowed you to make a gentle transition from student life to working life or something like that, but I could tell that you didn't like being seen as the sort of guy whom everybody had expected such great things of, but who had never fulfilled his promise. Because that is how you were regarded at that goddamn class reunion if I'm to be perfectly honest. Not only by me but by just about everybody else as well. That whole party was just one big competition to see who had been most successful and gone furthest in life. While the hits of the 80s flowed from the loudspeakers, people stood around in their glad rags, smiling and bragging about themselves for all they were worth, not in so many words of course, no, no, they did it as subtly and discreetly as possible, usually by steering the conversation around to a topic that would allow them to shine and stand out from the crowd. That fucking jerkoff Audun, for example, the biggest trust-fund brat of the lot, kept trying to bring up the subject of taxes and customs duty, not because he disapproved of the high rates of taxation in Norway or the extortionate duty tariffs, not at all. I know this for a fact, because at one point, when he started complaining about how the duty on alcohol meant that his favorite brand of cognac cost three times more in Norway than it did anywhere else and I said that in that case he ought to do as I did and vote for the Progress Party, I'll be fucked if he didn't turn around and start defending the Norwegian tax system. No, all this talk about taxes was just an excuse to allow Audun to work his way around, slowly but surely, to letting us all know that he had paid over a million kroner in income tax the year before, thus leading everybody to understand that this was a man who was earning three or four million kroner a year, right? That's why he went on the way he did. He just wanted to let us know how rich he was.

I'd known before I went, of course, that that's what it would be like. Which is why I really hadn't been planning to go, you know? I mean, it's not a whole lot of fun to be the kind of guy that everybody looks at and thinks, "Well, at least I've done better than him," because I know that's what people thought when they saw me. Oh yeah, and not only that, a few of the girls came up to me and said things that made me realize they hadn't expected to see a loser like me there at all. "How nice that you could come," they said, with the stress on that "you." Or: "Well, if it isn't Tom Roger," they said, looking at me like I'd just risen from the dead. Bendik and Janne and all the others who knew they didn't stand a chance in the great competition to see who was the most successful had had the sense to stay away and these girls simply couldn't understand why I hadn't done the same.

Those same people probably weren't quite as surprised to see you there. Well, after all you had spent half a lifetime at university and that in itself was more than enough to move you up from the division in which Bendik and Janne and I were still stuck, right? But, like I said, this meant that you were regarded as a young man who hadn't lived up to the great expectations people had had of him. And if anybody didn't feel sorry for you for that, well, when they heard that you weren't an academic of any kind but a hotel receptionist you could see them thinking that nothing had changed. You'd really fooled them for a while, stayed on at school, gone to university and forged ahead, but your past and your background had finally caught up with you and now you were back where you belonged in the social pecking order.

Your way of dealing with this was to act as though this fucking receptionist job was just something you were doing to make money. At first you said you'd applied for a post at the University of Science and Technology in Trondheim and fully expected to get it, but then, once you'd had a bit more to drink you started telling people that you meant to be writer and that you were actually working on a novel. But what a lot of people knew, and what you didn't know that they knew, was that you were mentally ill and unfit to work. I happen to know a little bit about this because I heard about it a while later from a guy who had been in the parallel class to ours at school. Although he didn't know all that much either. You'd spent some time in a mental hospital, he said, and you hadn't been able to finish your university course.

Well, anyway, the point is that we both began to feel more and more out of place. We had tried to have fun and fit in but we had gradually drifted farther and farther away from the other partygoers until eventually we couldn't take it any more. You'd asked the DJ to put on AC/DC's "Back in Black" because, amazing though it may seem, we had spotted it when we glanced over the side of the booth at his collection of CDs, but Brian Johnson didn't even get to scream his way through the fucking chorus once before those assholes who had once been the rich, preppy kids in class started shouting "oh, come on" and "turn down that racket" and when the aforementioned jerkoff-in-chief, Audun, took charge and ran up and asked the DJ to put on something else we just walked out.

Like I said at the start of this letter, that wasn't our 80s, that wasn't our party. It took a little while for us to realize this, but once we did we could hardly wait to get out of there. Or at least, before we left the building we made a point of locating the main fuse box, pulled out all the fuses and pocketed the two backup packs. And even though it may have been a pretty feeble protest, still it felt so good to hear Bonnie Tyler's gravelly voice die out right in the middle of "Total Eclipse of the Heart."

It was only a little before one in the morning. I asked you

whether you wouldn't like to come back to Ma's and Grandad's and carry on partying there. Ma had invited some of her women friends over and that lot really knew how to put it away, so if we were up for it we had hours of fun ahead of us. You'd like to, you said, but you were afraid you were kind of tired and would rather just go back to your hotel and get some sleep. A few days later somebody told me that they'd seen you sitting in a corner in Uncle Oscar's Bar later that night. You'd been drunk and drowsy, sitting there half-asleep with your chin on your chest, this guy told me, and there was a big dark patch around the crotch of your suit trousers so it looked like you'd either pissed yourself or spilled your beer. I was a bit disappointed, I remember, to learn that you'd chosen to round off the night like that rather than come back with me to Ma's, especially because I felt we had got on so well together at that fucking reunion, it had been quite like old times. But the reason we had got on so well was, of course, that we were both so pissed off with the rest of the people there. I wasn't stupid, I realized that. So I wasn't sad or anything, not exactly, that's not what I mean. We'd had our day, I knew that.

Ma really went downhill after the split with Peder Raade. It's not like she cared for the guy, that I don't believe, but he had given her a taste for the good life and it wasn't all that easy to have to move back into a scrapman's house after two years in a villa up on the hill at Høknes, if you know what I mean. And it didn't exactly help that Grandma never stopped reminding her that she had thrown away her one big chance in life.

"If you'd played your cards right, you wouldn't have had to worry about all that," she'd say when Ma was sighing over the mounting pile of bills or complaining about something that we needed but couldn't afford. Ma would lose her temper completely and snap at her that Peder Raade had just about beaten her to death, but that cut infuriatingly little ice with Grandma. She would simply turn away with a little smile on her face, muttering something about there being some things you just had to put up with if you wanted a worry-free life—and anyway, Peder must have had his reasons for hitting her and Ma would never make her believe any different.

Grandpa wasn't as bad as Grandma as far as this was concerned, but it was years before he stopped hinting to Ma that she ought to get in touch with Peder again. The fact was, you see, that once, when they were having a drink together, Raade had promised Grandpa a job as a manager in his plumbing firm and Grandpa had never got over this. To hear him talk you'd have thought that strutting about with a pen in his breast pocket, issuing orders and bossing people about was his big dream.

I don't know, but I think that all Grandma's and Grandpa's nagging and complaining made Ma feel obliged to find herself another Peder Raade. And I'm sure she would've liked that too, but if it hadn't been for them always going on at her I don't think she would have wound up in all the hopeless relationships she got into after that: one smarmy geezer in a suit after another, most of them married and promising to leave their wives soon—not that any of them ever did of course, they were just out to have a little fun and a bit of an adventure and as soon as they'd tired of the fun that Ma had to offer away they went. And every time this happened and she was left alone again Ma got a little bit older and a little more worn and haggard, which obviously reduced her chances of getting lucky next time around. Eventually she realized, of course, that her days as a femme fatale were over and from that moment on it was almost as if she made up her mind to let herself go as much as possible in as many ways as possible. Okay, maybe that's a slight exaggeration, but at any rate she did nothing to hide or to gloss over her decline. She ate so much that in less than a year she was as fat as a pig. She looked awful; she got sloppy, stopped bothering about her personal hygiene or her clothes. It was like she was trying to show everybody how little she cared that she had never become the grand, elegant businessman's wife she had once dreamed of being.

Your mother's efforts to rise above her hick existence and become the grand, elegant vicar's wife weren't that much more succesful than Ma's attempts at social climbing. True, she stayed married to Arvid till the day she died in 1987, but half the town knew that for the last few years it was a dead, empty marriage. Well, what could you expect? I mean, of course people can escape from their background and adapt to new surroundings and new people, the way your mother tried to do when she was living with the vicar from hell, but only to a certain extent. You can put a horse in a pigsty, but no matter how fucking long you leave it there it's never going to turn into a pig, if you know what I mean. According to Erik your mother realized this after only a short time in the town. Her marriage to Arvid had been one huge mistake and Berit was totally incapable of living the way he and all their churchgoing friends did. The problem was, though, that she was far too proud to admit it, or so Erik said. She had staked so much on this new life and she did everything she could to convince herself and everybody else that it was absolute bliss compared with the old one, so to suddenly go back on this, to have to admit that her new life wasn't all she had dreamed it would be and that she was actually living a lie, that was more than she could cope with. So she simply had to stick it out, and that's what she did until the day she dropped dead.

I'm not quite sure why I'm finishing this letter by talking about our mothers. Maybe it's because I'm writing this at home

in my old room and because Ma is always fucking there; because I can see her lying flat out on the chaise lounge right outside my window, and because every now and again I can hear
her gabbing on her mobile. That could be it. Or maybe it's just
a half-assed attempt to gather together all the loose threads
and finish off all the little stories I've started to tell you in this
letter. That too is possible. But mostly I think it's just that my
ma's and your mother's stories have something relevant to say
about us, you and me. Exactly what, I'm not sure, to be honest,
but it probably has something to do with that vague sense of
having been hard done by and looked down on; with feeling
ashamed of where you come from and who you are and trying
to do something about this. These were major forces and motivations in our mothers' lives and the lives of everybody who
came from the same background as us and maybe it's because
I'm afraid that these forces and motivations will lead us to
make the same mistakes as them that I'm finishing by writing
about them. What the fuck do I know.

Paula

Otterøy care home, July 4th, 2006. Talk of the devil

Dear, oh dear, the filth they print in the newspapers these days. I shake my head. I'm so sick of it, it's just about all they write about, filth. I don't know, I really don't, why can't they find something nice to write about for once? I turn to the next page, run my eye down it. Well, would you look at that—isn't that Harald Hansen? Aye, it's him right enough, what's he doing in the paper this time, I wonder—the Pensionist Party and Age Concern, is it? Oh aye, of course, calling for a new senior citizens' revolt, it says. Harald Hansen the pensioners' champion lashes out at politicians, it says, and there's Harald Hansen shaking his fist. Aye, well he's persistent is Harald, you've got to hand it to him. Although, I think maybe he rants and raves a bit too much on behalf of us old folk sometimes, the old dog forgets that it was once a pup. According to Harald it's beyond belief how awful young people today, it's outrageous how little respect they have for us old folk, how immoral they are and how much better things were in the old days. Mind you, he's right in a lot of what he says, there's no getting away from it.

I bend my head over the paper, screw up my eyes, trying to read what it says, but it's no use, I can hardly see to read now, the print's so small that I can't read much except the headlines. Oh, well, what can you do? He's coming here today, Harald is, to play the accordion for us, so I suppose I'll get to hear then what it says in the paper and what he thinks. Oh aye, no worries there, he's not usually one for keeping his opinions to himself, not Harald.

I close and fold the newspaper and glance around the dayroom. It's so quiet in here and almost deserted, Sylvia and I are the only ones here and she's asleep in the pink leather armchair and I just sit here and the moments go by, but it must be coffee time soon, surely, doesn't that clock say ten past five, yes, it most certainly does, so it must be coffee time soon, I mean we're supposed to have afternoon coffee at five o'clock. I turn and look at the door. Ah, yes! Yes, yes! There's that new assistant coming down the hall, I can see her through the new glass doors. This nice young fellow was here a while back to fit these lovely glass sliding doors, a skinny, red-headed Namsos fellow; a real character he was, and so funny, had relatives over in Skorstad, he said. And now the new assistant's coming into the dayroom, she's carrying a tray and on the tray are a cup of coffee and a plate with a slice of cake on it, what sort of cake is it today, I wonder, ah, almond tart again. It's a bit on the dry side the almond tart they have here, I feel. They usually buy it at the Co-op, I know. Well, I don't suppose they have time to bake it themselves, and anyway they might not know how, I doubt there's many folks do their own home baking these days. Ah well, it'll go down okay, I suppose, it usually does, oh aye, no worries there.

Now the new assistant's coming over to me. "Here you are, Paula," she says, bending down and setting the tray on the table in front of me, but what's that smell? Is that drink on her breath, well I never, it is drink. I look at her and she straightens up and stands there looking at me, and then she smiles. "Thank you," I say, and I smile back at her and I nod, and then she turns and goes over to Sylvia.

So it's true what Therese said, after all. She said she saw the new assistant sneaking a drink down by the lockers. She'd caught a glimpse of a bottle containing some clear liquid as she came around the corner, she said, but I wouldn't believe it, well, you like to think the best of folks, don't you, and anyway it doesn't do to take that Therese too seriously, she tends to look on the black side and always see the worst in people. But there you go, it was true after all. Oh my, that's just tragic, so it is, dear me, it's terrible the things that go on, such a lovely young girl too, and at work at that.

"Sylvia!" I hear the new assistant say. She's trying to wake Sylvia, she's got her hand on her shoulder, shaking her gently, but Sylvia's sleeping so soundly, she doesn't wake up. She sits there with her head back and her mouth open, sits there in the pink leather armchair looking like a hungry baby thrush with its beak open. "Oh well, we'll just let her sleep a while longer," the new assistant says, then she turns and looks at me and smiles, and I look at her and smile back.

"Well, he who sleeps does not sin," I say, and there's silence for a second.

"Hah, well in that case it's time you were in bed." I look around and see Therese making her way over, her blue-white claws clamped around the handles of her walker and her slippered feet shuffling across the polished floor. She stops next to me, puts out a hand and picks the newspaper off my table, she doesn't ask if I'm finished with it, I can hardly see to read and I'm not interested in hearing about all the filth they print in it, but all the same, I think she might ask if I'm finished with it, but no, she doesn't, she's not made that way, Therese, she simply picks up the paper and carries on. She's heading for the armchair on the other side of the room, shuffling straight towards it. "Aye, it's bedtime for you," she says. "If that's what it takes to be free from sin," she says. I glance at the assistant and smile, and the assistant smiles and raises her eyebrows, because there's no point getting upset about it, Therese is Therese, there's no one like her. Aye, she's a one-off is Therese.

"Can I get you some coffee, Therese?" the assistant asks.

"Get me coffee—*you*?" I hear Therese say scornfully and then she snorts. "God, your hands are shakier than mine," she mutters. I duck my head at her words and stare at my coffee cup, a white coffee cup with a light brown band running around the rim, and I pick up my cup, because the new assistant mustn't know that I heard this remark, it'll only be more embarrassing for her if she realizes that I caught it, so I'll just have to act like I didn't. I raise my cup to my mouth, pucker up my lips and blow, making little ripples on the glossy black surface.

"Oh, all right, get me a cup of coffee then," I hear Therese snap cheekily, as if she's doing the assistant a favor and not the other way around. Out of the corner of my eye I see her shuffling over to the armchair. When she gets to it she lets go of the blue walker, then she drops the newspaper onto the little table next to the chair, turns around, places her hands on the arms of the chair and lowers herself slowly and shakily into it. Therese's arms are as weak as mine, so they are, she's as frail as me, and now she's sitting there in that chair, gazing sidelong at the floor and gasping for breath.

"I soon won't be able to do anything," she says. "It's an effort just getting down into a chair so you can take it easy," she says. "It's all going to rack and ruin," she says. I put down my coffee cup and look at her. "No, it's no joke getting old," I say. "But we have to try and count what blessings we do still have," I say. "It makes it a bit easier to cope with the bad bits," I say, and I look at her and smile, but she still doesn't smile back, she just stares at me with those beady little eyes of hers. She has these black, beady little eyes set deep in her head and she's glowering at me, muttering something. I can't hear what she's saying, but I can read her lips, stupid fool, she's calling me a stupid fool, ah well, never mind, I've been called worse things.

I pick up my coffee again, it's steaming hot and I blow on it, glancing across at Therese as I do so. I see her pick up the paper and lay it in her lap. She licks her thumb, licks her index finger, then she turns the first page and starts to read. And the new assistant comes back in with her coffee, she's wearing white sandals with air holes in them and the soles stick to the floor and make a sort of soft squelching sound every time she lifts her feet.

"Here you are, Therese," the new assistant says, putting the tray down on the table. Then she straightens up and smiles so pleasantly. And Therese scowls at the things on the tray. "Hmm," Therese says, "well, you managed to keep some of it in the cup, I see," she says. Oh dear, oh dear, that Therese, now she's gone too far, now she's gone way over the score. I mean, really, what a way to behave, how can she be so rude and tactless. I fix my eyes on the table, set my coffee cup down on the saucer with a little chink and gaze at it, a white cup with a light brown band round the rim.

"What was that?" I hear the new assistant ask. "Oh, you heard me," I hear Therese say and out of the corner of my eye I see the new assistant looking at Therese, waiting for her to repeat what she just said, but Therese just leans greedily over her coffee, she can't be bothered repeating anything. And the new assistant turns and starts to walk away, and I raise my eyes and look at her, smile at her and shake my head despairingly—we can't have the new assistant thinking everybody in here is as grumpy as that one, they do such a wonderful job, the staff here, and I don't want them to think we're all as ungrateful as Therese. "Dear, oh dear," I chuckle, shaking my head, and the new assistant looks at me and smiles. "Yes, you can say that again," she says and she gives a little chuckle as well, then she walks past me and out of the dayroom.

Oh, well, we can't all be blessed with a good sense of humor, we're all different, all cast in different molds and we just have to accept that and take into account. And anyway, it can't be all that easy being Therese either, that's for sure. I mean, she's the only one in here who doesn't get any visitors. My own Odd Kåre's hardly beating a path to the door every day either, but he does pop in now and again, so he does. He hasn't been in to see me today, though. It's his day off so I thought he might, but something must've come up. Ah well, these things happen.

I take a sip from my cup, dip the dry almond tart in the coffee to moisten it, pop the tart in my mouth and take a little bite. I smack my lips and gaze through the glass doors and out into the entrance hall, and there's Sylvia's son coming in with his wife and daughters. I feel my spirits lift a little when I see them, they're so nice to speak to, both Sylvia's son and his wife, they're always cheerful and smiling, it fairly brightens things up having them here. They walk past and the two adults nod and smile at me and I smile back. "Good afternoon, Paula," they say. "Oh, good afternoon," I say, looking at them, and they turn and stroll over to Sylvia.

"Sylvia's asleep," I say.

"Oh, is she?" her son says, turning to me and smiling. "Don't tell me she slept through afternoon coffee. That's not like her," he says. "And with such great cake and all," he says, nodding at my plate. "Ah, it's not that great," I say softly, putting a hand up to the side of my mouth and whispering from behind it. "It's a bit dry," I whisper, then I give a quick shrug, purse my lips and giggle at my own daring and both he and his wife laugh and say, "Oh dear." "You should be in charge of the baking, Paula," Sylvia's son says. "They'd like that in here, I'll bet. Even Mom might put a little bit more meat on her bones then," he says. "Oh, no," I say. "My baking days are over," I say. "Ah, I wouldn't be too sure of that," he says, smiling again, then he gives a quick nod to Therese, but she just glares at him, she doesn't smile back.

I take another bite of my almond tart and put it back on my plate, then I glance across at Sylvia's son, see him put his hand on his mother's shoulder. "I'll go and get us some coffee," his wife says and he smiles and nods at her then he gives Sylvia a gentle shake. "Mom," he says. "Wakey-wakey." Just then somebody starts plonking the piano behind me. I look around and there are the two little girls, sitting on the piano stool. "My, aren't you clever, you two," I say to them and they turn and look at me, and they smile at me and say thank you, then they turn away and carry on playing. "Twinkle, Twinkle, Little Star," isn't that what they're playing? Yes, of course, that's what it is. I face front, look at their father again. He's still trying to wake Sylvia, still has his hand on her skinny shoulder, shaking her gently. "Such well-mannered children you have," I tell him and he looks across at me and smiles. "Do you think so?" he asks. "Ah, well they must've got something from me then," he says laughing, and I feel my spirits lift. "You know, I think they have," I say, laughing back at him.

Then he lays his hand on Sylvia's brow, runs it over her thin, gray hair. "Right, Mom, you've got to wake up now, it's coffee time," he says. And Sylvia wakes up. She doesn't open her eyes straight away, though, she sits for a moment opening and closing her mouth. It must be all dry after her sleeping so long with it hanging open, so she'll be trying to work up some saliva to moisten it. "Wakey-wakey, Mom," he says again, "it's coffee time," and now Sylvia opens her eyes and looks at her son. After a moment she seems to come to, then her face lights up in a big smile.

"Oh, it's yourself," she says. "Yes," he says. "The kids kept asking when we were going to see Grandma," he says. "So I thought we might as well drive up a little earlier than usual. We didn't mean to disturb your afternoon nap, though," he adds. "Oh, don't be silly," Sylvia says, and then she catches sight of her grandchildren. "Well, hello," Sylvia says. "Hello, Grandma," the girls say, smiling at her, and they slide off the piano stool and come over to her. "Oh, it's so good to see you," Sylvia says.

"That's two lovely granddaughters you've got there, Sylvia," I say, but Sylvia's so taken up with the two little girls that she doesn't even notice me. I turn to her son. "How old are they again?" I ask, and Sylvia's son looks at me and smiles. "Six and eight," he says. "Is that all?" I say. "But they're so good at the piano?" I say. "Good heavens," I say, and I look at the two little girls coming across the dayroom. "So are you going to be pianists when you grow up, do you think?" I ask, smiling at them. The younger one just walks straight past me and over to Sylvia, but the older girl looks at me and slows down a little. "I don't know," she says, almost coming to a complete halt and smiling politely at me. "Well, it's bound to be something to do with music anyway," I say. "Don't you think?" I ask. "I don't know," she says again. "No, of course not," I say. "You've got plenty of time to decide what you want to do," I say, and she nods, still smiling politely, looks at me for a moment then turns and runs over to Sylvia, and Sylvia stretches out an arm and wraps it around her.

"Ah, kids, aren't they wonderful," I say, smiling at Sylvia's son. And he turns to me and smiles back. "Oh, they are that," he says. "They're a lot of work, but you get so much in return," I say. "Oh yes, it's worth it all right," he says. "Yes, isn't it just," I say. "And the best children in the whole world, every single one of them," I say, laughing. "Yes, that's how it goes," he says, smiling back at me and then he turns to Sylvia.

"I have a son," I say. "Odd Kåre Hindmo. Do you know

him?" I ask, looking at him and smiling, and he looks at me again and smiles back. "I know who he is, yes, but I don't know him personally," he says. "One son," I say, "and three grandchildren." "Oh, right," he says. "Three lovely grandchildren," I say. "Yes, I'm sure they are," he says. "Oh yes, and the oldest one, she's doing so well at school," I say. "Oh, really?" he says. "Oh yes, she's getting such good marks, you know," I say. "Oh, that's great," he says. "Oh, yes," I say. "That girl could be anything she wants to be in life," I say. "Uh-huh," he says, still smiling, his voice a little higher than usual. "I don't know where she gets it from, but it's not from me, anyway," I say. "Ah, I'm not so sure about that," he says, raising his eyebrows and giving a little laugh, and I look at him and give a little laugh too. I'm just about to tell him a little bit more about my grandchildren, but I don't get the chance because just then his wife comes in with the new assistant right behind her, they're each carrying a tray and Sylvia smiles and says hello to her daughter-in-law and her daughter-in-law smiles back at her and says hello too and I look at them and smile.

"Just take the trays into my room," Sylvia says, nodding in that direction. "Oh?" says the daughter-in-law. "Yes," Sylvia says. "But won't it be a bit of a squeeze with all five of us in there?" her daughter-in-law asks. "Yes, but we'll get no peace here," Sylvia mutters with a sour glance at me. And her son and daughter-in-law turn to look at me and the new assistant looks at me too, suddenly they're all looking at me and everything goes very quiet, and after a moment I feel my cheeks start to burn—oh, no, I've done it again, oh, I have, haven't I, I've made a nuisance of myself. Sylvia's quite right, I wasn't giving them any peace, I was talking too much and making a nuisance of myself. I don't mean to, but I do. It's just that it's so nice when people come to visit and then I get carried away and start talking.

"Oh, I thought we were perfectly all right out here," Sylvia's son says, raising his eyebrows and shrugging. He realizes this is awkward for me, so he's pretending not to know what Sylvia's talking about. He's so nice and considerate, that man, and now he's trying to make this a little less embarrassing for me. "Oh, well," he says, "we'd better just do as we're told, I suppose." And he looks at me and gives a little laugh, and I look at him and give my faint smile.

I pick up my cup and take a little gulp of my coffee, glance across at Sylvia and her family as I put the cup down again. They're going to talk about this the minute they get to her room, I know they are and I can hardly blame them, I mean I didn't give them any peace, I tried to steal Sylvia's visitors and Sylvia has a perfect right to call me a nuisance and a pest and she will, I know she will, and once she's said that they'll start talking about how seldom they see Odd Kåre and the rest of my family up here. No wonder Paula's so desperate for company when she hardly ever has any visitors, I bet that's what they'll say. And that's not altogether untrue either, I don't have many visitors, almost as few as Therese, and maybe that's the main reason why I'm sitting here with my cheeks burning. If nobody comes to visit me it must be because I'm not worth visiting, and maybe that's the most embarrassing thing about all of this, the thought of being so worthless. I don't know.

Then suddenly I hear Sylvia say: "No, actually, let's just stay here. Then the kids have more room to run about." A moment later who should I see coming along the corridor but Odd Kåre. Well, well, if it isn't Odd Kåre, so he came after all, well I never, talk of the devil and he's sure to appear. Well, isn't that nice, oh, I'm so happy. I see now why Sylvia suddenly changed her mind and decided to stay here. She knows I won't be bothering them now that I've got a visitor of my own, that's why it doesn't matter so much whether they move into her room.

I look at Odd Kåre and smile. But who's that with him, who's that right behind him, is that Johnny? Well, I never, it is, oh my, isn't that nice, what a lovely surprise. I look at Odd Kåre and Johnny, and I smile at them, but oh, my heavens, Johnny's getting to look so like his dad, he's put on a bit of weight and his cheeks have got plumper since the last time I saw him, he's really starting to fill out now, seventeen and the spitting image of his father. Well, I never. And seventeen already, would you believe it, my, my, how time flies. It seems no time since he was born, but to think that I should have visitors after all, well, isn't that just lovely. And now they're coming into the dayroom.

"Hello," I say.

"Hello there," Odd Kåre says.

"Hello, hello," says Johnny.

Dear David,

My name is Harald Hansen. I am a retired headmaster and I have been asked to write this letter on behalf of Paula Hindmo, former assistant nurse, now retired and living at Otterøya residential care home. Everything that Paula tells me will be treated in the strictest confidence and all information will be deleted as soon as this letter has been sent to you. Paula has made me swear to this. The only exception to this being if anything illegal should come to light in the course of our conversations. In which case naturally I reserve the right to inform the police.

As former headmaster of Otterøya Primary and Lower-Secondary school I remember you myself, and since I also knew your mother and your grandfather some of my own memories may well find their way into this letter. It's also quite possible that I will ask some of the other care home residents to tell me what they know of you and your family. Otterøya is a small place, you see, where everybody knows everybody else, so I'm sure a good few of them will have something to contribute.

Essentially, though, this is Paula's letter.

Paula worked as an assistant nurse in the maternity ward at Namsos Hospital from 1955 to 1981 and one of the first things she said to me once we had settled ourselves in her room was that she and the midwife were the very first people to see you and that they were the very first people you saw. She seemed quite moved when she told me this. "Imagine that, Harald," she said, "that there could be such a first time. It's almost like imagining that there was once a very first spring on this earth."

You two would see one another many, many times after that because Paula and her family lived less than five minutes away from where you and your mother and your grandfather lived and during the years before you and Berit moved to town she and your mother were very close. Paula had always known your mother, but she was nearly seventeen years older than Berit so it's not surprising that they didn't become bosom friends until later, once your mother was a grown woman—in fact Paula thinks it must have been two or three years after you were born.

They first became friends through the sewing circle to which they both belonged. A bunch of the local women used to get together at Dagny Pedersen's house on one or two evenings every week: Dagny had her own weaving workshop in the basement and they could sit in peace down there catching up on the latest gossip while they sewed, embroidered, knitted or wove. To begin with, Paula says, it was Dagny who was closest to your mother. She was only seven years older than Berit and every bit as fond of going to parties and having fun as she was, and even though there weren't as many nights out in Årnes and Devika after Berit had you to look after they did still manage the occasional one, just the two of them, all done up and giggling with half-bottles of moonshine in their handbags.

But it didn't take many meetings of the sewing circle for Paula and Berit to discover that they were two of a kind. You see they both had a darkness inside them that neither Dagny nor any of the other women had, as Paula herself put it. Take

Dagny, for example. She had been the baby of her family, a little afterthought. Not only that, but she had been born into a pretty well-to-do home. All of this had endowed her with the confidence and the free-and-easy nature so typical of all privileged individuals. She knew no fear, she had been a sheltered, much-loved child so she was never afraid of being rejected, she took it for granted that people would like her and so she could allow herself to be totally frank about just about everything with just about everybody.

With Paula it was the exact opposite. While Dagny could reveal the most intimate details of her own life without a blush, Paula would almost always ask herself whether the others would be interested in what she had to say. And since very often the answer to this was no, she tended to be the quiet one of the group, the one who listened attentively to the other women's stories and confined herself to responding with a little comment or quiet laugh.

Let it be said right away that Berit was not like that. Quite the reverse, really. She was outgoing, pert-tongued, almost a little too outspoken at times, and to anyone who didn't know her all that well she seemed more like Dagny than like Paula. But unlike Dagny, in Berit's case this persona was more of a mask. Berit hid in the spotlight, Paula says, and it was when Berit realized that Paula had grasped this that the friendship between these two really began to grow. The bond between them wasn't formed through long heart-to-hearts or by the confiding of those secrets which, it would later transpire, they both harbored. No, all that came later. They felt a rapport before they had so much as said a word to each other, or at any rate before they had ever spoken one to one. There had been something about the way they looked at one another when they were sitting there in Dagny's weaving room, Paula says.

It was as if they saw themselves mirrored in each other's eyes. Berit might have been flighty and outgoing, but she had these dark eyes full of gravity and depth, eyes that said she knew something nobody else knew. What this "something" might be Paula had no idea as she sat there with her embroidery or her knitting, but that it was there at all, that your mother had it in her, was enough to tell Paula that this was someone to whom she could really talk, someone who would understand.

You always went along with Berit to those sewing-club evenings, and willingly at that. In fact you insisted on going with her, because this was long before sugar was considered a health hazard and there was always a good chance that one of the aunties—as you called the ladies of the sewing circle— would slip you a chocolate or two, if you just sat on their knee or gave them a hug in exchange. And you enjoyed impressing them with all the things you knew and could do, not so much because this earned you more chocolates, but because you loved their reaction, you positively beamed when they gazed at you wide-eyed and exclaimed that they didn't know how you did it. "Fancy that, only four and he can do a backward roll already. Oh, you'll have to be a gymnast, David, that's for sure." That's the sort of thing they said to you. But when you weren't watching they sniggered at you, their bodies shaking with laughter, because being fond of chocolate and sweeties has its price and your backside was so solid that you sometimes had difficulty lifting it over your head to roll over. Oh, Paula says, it could be quite hilarious, to see you lying on the floor heaving and straining,until you were red in the face.

You knew, of course, that you weren't any good at gymnastics, you knew very well that you weren't particularly good at drawing or reading or any of the other things that the aunties praised you to the skies for, you'd always known that. But for a long time you did believe that they thought you were, and when it began to dawn on you that they didn't something happened to you. When someone receives a lot of undeserved praise it's usually because he is regarded as a poor soul who needs a bit of a boost, and when you realized that the aunties didn't mean all the nice things they said to you, you began to think that they actually felt a little sorry for you and that in turn seemed to fill you with shame. The compliments and the praise and all the little rewards they showered you with were obviously well-meant, but as time went on they appeared to leave you with a feeling of being looked down on and underrated, to the point where you no longer seemed able to cope with being praised. It was as if you found it impossible to believe that such compliments could be sincerely meant, Paula says, and if she made the mistake of congratulating you on something you'd done you could get quite angry and upset.

But it wasn't just compliments you couldn't cope with. Suddenly you also started avoiding, nay, fleeing from events in which you played or rather, were supposed to play a central part. Like your birthdays, for example. No matter what Berit said you refused to celebrate your own birthday. All you wanted was for this day—a day that every other six- or seven- or eight-year-old looked forward to all year—to be treated as a perfectly ordinary day with fish pie for dinner, as Paula put it. To begin with your mother thought it was just something you were saying; that you were actually as keen to celebrate your special day as any other child would be, but that you were possibly worried that someone whom you really wanted to come to your party would turn down the invitation or that some of the guests might think your party wasn't good enough or something. But on the one occasion when she arranged a surprise party for you and you got back from Johanna Mørek's, where you'd been sent to borrow some butter, to find seven kids all dressed in their best waiting for you in a living room hung with balloons and streamers, she realized that you meant what you said. Because you simply turned on your heel in the doorway and left. Everyone was dispatched to look for you, but you had disappeared into the forest and you didn't come back until you were sure all of the party guests would have been sent home.

It was also around this time that you started having spells when you refused to speak to grown-ups, Paula says. You were as talkative as always when you were with other children, but the minute an adult appeared you clammed up completely. You wouldn't even answer questions requiring a simple yes or no. Berit found this very frustrating, she would lose her temper and tell you off, threatening to thrash you and take away various privileges. Or she would be sweet and gentle and try to coax you into talking. Either that or she would get upset and plead with you to answer when people spoke to you. But none of it did any good. You were bright and cheerful and behaved just as you always did, but not a sound passed your lips. This could go on for weeks and then, as suddenly as you had stopped, you would start speaking again. There seemed to be no particular reason for this. Or if there was then those around you had no idea what it was. It could happen any time and anywhere, it was as if you had got fed up with staying silent and simply decided to speak again. And you wanted no fuss made about this either. Naturally Berit was always happy when you broke one of your long silences. The first time it happened she made no secret of it. She praised you and told you how relieved she was, she even bought you presents. But you didn't like that. You got sullen and resentful and accepted her gifts only with the greatest reluctance. The child psychologist you spoke to some time later believed that you had reacted in this way because you saw

Berit's happiness as an indirect rejection of the boy you were when you wouldn't speak. You were probably suffering from selective mutism, he said. Selective mutism was an anxiety disorder. In other words it wasn't your fault and you certainly weren't doing it for the fun of it so Berit was going to have to be careful not to scold you when you were having one of your silent spells or praise you when you started talking again, he said. She had to let you see that she loved both the David who spoke and the David who didn't speak or else she could make things worse, because nothing could do more harm to a child than to be rejected by his own mother.

But what everyone was wondering, of course, was what could have caused this anxiety.

Initially the blame fell on your babysitter, Johanna Mørck. Before you started school Berit had a job as a home help in Namsos and during the day when she was at work you were either with your grandfather, Erik, or Johanna came over to look after you. It wasn't the ideal solution because Johanna Mørck was not exactly the most caring and nurturing of individuals. She was rather like Krösa-Maja in the films of Astrid Lindgren's Emil books, the old hunchbacked lady who loved a good gossip, preferably gossip relating to scandals and disasters. Not that Johanna was all doom and gloom, not at all. She was a lively character, always joking and laughing. But she loved to tell stories and she did so want her stories to make a real impression on people, and there's nothing better designed to make an impression on people than stories concerning matters of life and death—preferably quite literally. The only problem was that she didn't tailor her stories to suit her audience. She had no children of her own, just a whole pack of dogs and it never occurred to her that, as a child, you ought to have been spared the grisliest of her yarns. Take, for example, the time when your gums started to bleed. Only a little bit, but Johanna construed this as a sign that you were coughing up blood. "Aye," she said, "we could well be looking at tuberculosis here." She had lost her own little brother to TB when she was a girl and that had started in exactly the same way, she said, with him coughing up blood onto his handkerchief. This had been followed by a long and painful illness and confinement to a sanatorium far, far from home, and there he had ended his days, poor soul, alone and forsaken and only six years old, exactly the same age as you were then.

On another occasion she led you to believe that your mother was in great danger: Dagny was going to Trondheim to see her cousin and Berit was going with her just for the trip. Trondheim was quite a place, Johanna told you. She had lived and worked there one summer years before and once, when she was on her way home from the hotel where she was employed as a kitchen-maid she had witnessed an armed robbery in a newsstand. And if you absolutely had to know what it looked like when somebody got shot between the eyes then she was here to tell you that it looked a bit like a jar being shattered. The head just sort of split wide open and the insides ran out, she had seen it with her own eyes. But that was nothing in Trondheim she was wont to add when she told this story. She could tell a lot worse and she really hoped that Berit would be careful. In fact it would be best if she stayed indoors after nine o'clock at night and if she really had to go out then she should do what Johanna herself used to do when she was living there and carry a four-inch nail in her hand. It wouldn't be enough to overpower an attacker completely, but a hard jab with a four-inch nail would give him a shock and put him out of action long enough for her to take to her heels and run for her life.

It was even worse though when Johanna told you stories from

the Bible. Or rather, according to Paula, took biblical tales and then embroidered them, making them even scarier than they already were. To begin with I found it hard to imagine how the grimmest of the Old Testament stories could be rendered even more hair-raising but no, Paula says, it was simply a matter of telling them in such a way that the listener could identify more closely with them. Once, for example, when you had got salt in a cut and were crying because it smarted so much, Johanna seized the opportunity to tell you how much worse it was for sinners in hell. Because down there, the Devil would peel the skin off people, much as we would peel the skin off a sausage, and when their bodies were totally covered in open sores he would roll them in salt for a whole three weeks. And when she recounted extracts from the Book of Revelations she always set them on Otterøya. "D'you see Grønskard Fell there?" she would say. "Well, come Judgment Day, it'll crack down the middle and out of that crack will come a pillar of smoke, and out of that smoke will come grasshoppers as big as horses. They'll be wearing coats of mail, they'll have lion's teeth and where the horses' tails should be there'll be huge scorpion tails, and these they'll use to scourge all those who don't believe in God."

Had Johanna been a religious person, her behavior might have been understandable, but there is nothing to suggest that she was. Indeed to judge by her habits she was anything but. She smoked a pipe and drank moonshine like a man, she cursed and swore and lied when it suited her and, as if that wasn't enough, more than once she had been caught stealing from the homes of people she visited. On one occasion, for example, after Johanna had been in the house Paula discovered that the unopened pack of brown goat's cheese was gone; another time it was half a kilo of coffee that went missing, and on a third occasion some teaspoons that weren't in the drawer where they had been before Johanna arrived. She only ever took little things, nothing to make a fuss about really, but still, it didn't exactly testify to a Christian way of life.

Anyway: at first Paula and Berit convinced each other that Johanna Mørck's stories had scared the wits out of you and that this was the source of your anxiety. True, you had never mentioned anything at home about Johanna having frightened you, Paula says, but apparently you weren't the sort of boy who would have done that anyway, you weren't one for telling tales. But at the same time there had been days when you had been unusually thoughtful and withdrawn and your mother thought she had noticed that on such days you would often ask seemingly casual questions possibly designed to lead up to a conversation about things that frightened you. "Is that smoke up there?" you asked one morning when you saw mist drifting over Grønskard Fell. "Smoke? No, that's the sea mist rolling in, can't you see that?" your mother said. "Why on earth would there be smoke coming out of the mountainside?" "Haven't you read the Bible?" you asked, thus paving the way for a little chat during which your mother was eventually able to reassure you and tell you quite truthfully that the Bible said nothing at all about the Day of Judgment starting with smoke seeping out of a crack in Grønskard Fell. "You mustn't believe everything Johanna tells you," she said.

Berit had never worried too much before about Johanna's habit of making up stories and filling your head with her fanciful notions, she had neither approved or disapproved, Paula says. But the child psychologist's conclusion that you were suffering from an anxiety disorder made her think again and one of the first things Berit did was to take the matter up with Johanna. This was no easy task, since spinning yarns wasn't just one of Johanna's many foibles. Her tales were also her way of explaining and expressing herself and the world around her, and to criticize—no, not only criticize but condemn—her storytelling was tantamount to condemning her personally. So of course she was hurt. Berit asked her if she couldn't tell you stories about other things instead. About what life had been like in the old days, for example, what sort of food people had eaten, what sort of clothes they wore, the houses they lived in, the schools they went to and so on, ordinary, everyday things. It didn't all need to be about life and death, surely.

Johanna was amazed that anyone could think there was a connection between your bouts of silence and her stories, but she would certainly curb her tongue, she declared, if only to prove how very wrong your mother was, in fact she wouldn't open her mouth at all unless she was spoken to, Berit could be sure of that.

Whether she kept this promise or not, Paula didn't know, but you didn't get any better. Far from it. Your condition steadily worsened. Your bouts of silence grew longer and longer and where previously you had at least spoken normally when you were with other children—even during one of your silent spells—that too now stopped and instead you took to speaking a kind of "robot talk": "beep," you would say if one of the other kids asked you a question. And when things were particularly bad you even started acting like a robot, or so Paula says. You would walk in a jerky mechanical way and no matter what people said or did to you—even if they got really mad and yelled at you or said they wouldn't let you play unless you stopped acting like a robot—you would just stand there with a little smile on your face.

Johanna tossed her head and took this as proof, of course, that whatever was troubling you it certainly had nothing to do with her and her stories. But Berit did not agree and Paula backed her up. The fear that Johanna had been instilling in you repeatedly since you were a toddler must, they felt, have become ingrained in you. To begin with it was probably the case that when Johanna told you some scary story the fear of it would stay with you for a while afterwards, but at some point the fear had taken root in you and now you were afraid all the time without being able to say what it was you were afraid of. That had to be the explanation, they eventually concluded.

And when your psychologist didn't dismiss this theory out of hand, but instead said that yes, that was exactly what anxiety was—being afraid without knowing what one is afraid of— they were even more convinced, or so Paula says. And thus the smoldering resentment that Berit already felt towards Johanna turned to downright hate. If anything went wrong at home, if something went missing, for example, Johanna automatically got the blame: she had taken it, she must have. And if you did anything wrong, it didn't matter what, that too was Johanna's fault, you'd got it from her. That was how Berit thought, Paula says. And not only that: for a time she seemed to be obsessed with Johanna. If I understand Paula correctly, it was almost as if Johanna were a channel through which she could give vent to all the rancor and the rage that had built up inside her. They could be sitting in their garden chairs over by the redcurrant bushes, smoking and drinking coffee, and no matter what they were talking about something would always remind Berit of Johanna, something she could use as an excuse to start going on again about what a nasty piece of work she was.

Whether Berit actually believed all this talk herself or not, she was finding it harder and harder to defend the fact that she had allowed Johanna to look after you. If she did believe the charges she leveled against Johanna and didn't fire her she was a bad mother and if she didn't believe them and chose to let Johanna carry on she would still seem like a bad mother to everybody else on the island—if, that is, she didn't change her tune completely and admit to all and sundry that obviously she and Paula had merely been gossiping and dishing the dirt. But that probably wasn't an option. So there was nothing for it but to ask Johanna to find some other employment.

In any case, you were six by then and pretty self-sufficient, so being without a babysitter wasn't the disaster it would have been only a year earlier. And besides, you had your grandfather for company. Granted, he had his work on the farm to see to, but for one thing you were now big enough to help him with most of his chores, and for another he was never that far away if you needed him.

According to Paula, you and your grandpa were also very attached to one another. Since you had grown up without a father he had been both father and grandfather to you: a father in that he set limits and rules for you and a grandfather in that he always had time for you, he never told you to be quiet because he was reading the paper or watching the news and he was patient and able to put up with more pestering than any father. Not only that but he could be playful in the way that only grandparents can be with their grandchildren, Paula says.

But there was one snag:

Erik would not tolerate you showing any weakness. Boys would one day become men and so they had to be toughened up right from the start, because if they weren't they wouldn't be able to fulfil the obligations that a grown man had to fulfil in order to ensure the survival of himself, his family and society at large. There was much to be said for this way of thinking, of course. Everyone who knew you well could see that, Paula says. Erik would often ask you to do things that most people would consider too difficult, too strenuous or too dangerous for a child of your age. "Would you mind chopping the rest of that wood for me, David?" he might ask when you were just seven or eight years old, and possibly because he took it for granted, or at least acted as if he did, that you were capable of doing it he also made you believe that you were capable of doing it, thus equipping you to actually do it. In this way you had become very good at lots of things, so good in fact that you were the talk of the surrounding farms, I remember that myself.

But that you should be suffering from anxiety, that was hard for Erik to take because he didn't have much time for scaredy-cats. He had nothing against girls and women being frightened occasionally, of course, Paula says—far from it, because as everyone knows the more frightened a woman is, the tougher she makes a man look. But boys and men? No. And the idea that his own grandson in particular could be fearful and anxious and hence incapable of being the boy and man that he wanted him to be, which is to say a carbon copy of himself, that he found hard to swallow.

Erik's response to this whole business was to become even harder on you and expect even more of you, especially when you were going through one of your silent spells. He didn't give a damn about the advice the psychologist had given, nor did he pay much mind to Berit's opinions or her admonitions to do this or that. Partly because he did not understand the difference between anxiety and fear he insisted that the only way to cure you was to expose you to situations that required a certain amount of courage. For one thing this would get you used to dealing with challenges and situations that you perceived as dangerous, and for another you would gradually discover that these situations were not in fact dangerous at all. He duly proceeded to put this theory into practice. For example, Paula says that when the barn had to be painted he asked you to climb up to the top of a fifty-foot ladder. It didn't seem to occur to him that there actually was some danger attached to climbing fifty feet up a wobbly ladder and when you stopped halfway and refused to go any further, his face took on the look of somebody who's just drunk sour milk. "Aw, don't give me that," he said. "You're not a goddamn girl." And once you were safely down again he shook his head and told you to "go on inside along wi' the other women."

But you were suffering from selective mutism, not fear of heights, so obviously this strategy did not work. On the contrary. If I understand Paula correctly, Erik's reaction and the fact that the other kids in the neighborhood were avoiding you and excluding you more and more from their games actually seemed to exacerbate your condition. You responded by acting as if this was a fight between you on the one side and them on the other; a contest of sorts in which you had no intention of surrendering, quite the opposite: the more they rejected you the more silent and robotic you became.

And the worse you grew the more frustrated Berit became, and the more frustrated she became the more fiercely and bitterly she hated Johanna until—according to Paula—it had grown out of all proportion. She could hardly open her mouth without criticizing Johanna and she no longer cared who heard her either: acquaintances of Johanna's, friends, relatives, it made no difference, she was an endless fount of invective and derision and she didn't give a damn what those who heard her might think.

But one day when Paula and Berit were sitting in the yard sampling that year's currant wine, Berit suddenly broke down and said that it was all her fault. She was so moody and unpredictable and this confused you and made you feel anxious and unsure. This, she was certain, was the cause of your anxiety, not Johanna Mørck's stupid stories.

And according to Paula there may have been some truth in this, because your mother's mood did tend to fluctuate drastically. One day she could be bright and cheerful and outgoing, talking nonstop and clowning around, full of fun, and the next—or no, it didn't even have to be a day later, it might only be hours, or even minutes—you would suddenly notice something different about the way she moved, her actions would become somehow sharper and jerkier than usual. And something happened to her eyes, they grew darker and began to burn. At the same time she almost stopped speaking. Usually, according to what she told Paula one day when they were discussing this side of her character, she would find herself looking for reasons to get angry. Or rather, the anger was already there but she would look for things in the people around her on which to hang her anger, so to speak. She didn't mean to, but she did. She watched everything going on around her like a hawk and the minute someone said or did something that she could criticize or get worked up about, she would pounce. And if someone apologized or admitted that they had done or said something wrong, she didn't relent. Far from it, because the person concerned had thus acknowledged that she had reason to be angry and then she was liable to let fly at them in earnest. She could tear people to shreds, hurting and humiliating them in the worst possible way and knowing full well, even as she was doing it, that she was being totally unreasonable, or so she told Paula. She knew her response was out of all proportion to what her victim had said or done, but she couldn't stop herself, no matter who the poor object of her wrath might be, she just couldn't, not even if it was Paula, or Erik; not even, sadly, if it was you.

There seems little doubt that this would have made you feel frightened and insecure. To be four or five or six years old and never quite know how your mother will react to whatever you say or do, to know that you might be subjected to a storm of abuse just for taking too long to get dressed or forgetting to flush the toilet or spilling a little food at dinner. It can't be easy, that sort of thing could make anyone nervous and fearful. Unfortunately, however, women do have a woeful tendency to consider themselves more at fault than they actually are, or so Paula maintains. Indeed it sometimes seems as if women have an urge or a need to make atonement, not only for things that are their fault, but also for things of which they know full well they are blameless. In fact they may even be more eager to take the blame for and atone for the latter, as if a person convicted of a crime of which she is innocent were somehow a cut above the rest, and if you look at it that way there might well be a certain pleasure and satisfaction to be had from atoning and suffering even though one has done nothing wrong. It makes you feel like a better person.

I'm not entirely sure that I'm interpreting Paula correctly here. She talked a great deal about this, and at some length, and I didn't catch it all. At any rate, her main point seems to be that Berit shouldered more than her fair share of the blame for the problems you were having. Paula says that she talked a lot to Berit about this. Johanna Mørck had spent several hours a day with you so she must have had some effect on you, or so Paula tried to tell your mother. And there was always the possibility that you had quite simply been born this way, that it was in your genes, a matter of instincts and impulses within you for which no one, not Johanna or Berit nor anyone else, was to blame. Or that the cause lay somewhere else again, in something that neither Berit nor Paula knew anything about, that too was a possibility.

But it was no use. Berit persisted in believing that it was all her fault, she was a bad mother, she said, she wasn't good enough and she never would be. She had always told herself that her mood swings, the abrupt shifts in temper and sudden outbursts were simply the result of low blood sugar and that all she had to do was eat something and it would pass, but that wasn't it at all, she told Paula. And it wasn't that she was tired, as she also told herself sometimes, it wasn't because she had too much to do and wasn't getting enough sleep, nor because she had pressing problems or serious worries of one sort or another, not at all. Blaming such things was just a way of kidding oneself. No, this went much, much deeper, deeper than she was capable of seeing within herself.

As I touched on briefly at the beginning of this letter, this very aspect of your mother's character was one of the reasons that she and Paula were such close friends. Because even though it could be unpleasant to be in the same room as Berit when her mood darkened, it was this same darkness in her that had led Paula to suspect that here was a person who knew and understood more than the other women in the sewing circle. The gaping void your mother had inside her, that was what Paula saw in her eyes, and that was what made her feel comfortable with her, she says. What scared off other people and made them feel nervous and uncertain, made her feel comfortable because, since Berit had this gaping void inside her, Paula took it for granted that she would understand and be less critical of her own gaping void.

Otterøy care home, July 4th, 2006. Johnny's filled out

Odd Kåre and Johnny sit down across the table from me. Odd Kåre runs a hand through his hair as he sits down, it's rather greasy, I notice, it glistens slightly in the light from the ceiling lamp, I see, and he looks at me and smiles. "Well," he says, "how're things here then?" "Oh, you know," I say, dragging it out a little and wagging my head. "All right, I suppose." There's a second's pause and then Odd Kåre nods. He doesn't say anything, he just looks at me, and I look at him and smile, but he's not smiling now, his smile is gone, maybe he thinks I mean to complain when all I'll say is that things are all right instead of saying that everything's just grand, maybe he thinks I mean to complain, maybe he even thinks I'm getting at *him*, maybe that's it, maybe he thinks I'm trying to make him feel guilty for hardly ever coming to see me. But he mustn't think that, although I'm not saying I wouldn't like to see him and my grandchildren more often, but I'm so happy when they do come that I'm hardly going to waste what time we have together complaining, I'm hardly going to do that. If I did that they'd come to see me even less often than they do now, so no, he mustn't think I'm going to moan and complain.

"No, no, I can't complain," I say. "We couldn't be any better off than we are here," I say and I look at him and smile, and he looks at me and nods. "That's good to hear," he says, smiling again. He sits back in his chair, props one elbow on the back of the chair. "Well, have you polished your dancing shoes, Ma?" he asks, eyeing me mischievously and nodding. "I saw on the noticeboard in the corridor that there's an accordionist coming to play for you this evening," he says, and he looks at me and smiles, and I shake my head and give a little laugh. "Oh, no, Odd Kåre, I think my dancing days are over," I say. "Ah, that I don't believe," Odd Kåre says. "Once Harald Hansen picks up that accordion I bet your toes'll start tapping," he says. "Aye, well that's as may be," I say, "but even so, I doubt I'll be doing any dancing," I say. "Oh, and why not?" he says. "What, with this?" I say, patting my thigh. "It'd have to be a pretty slow waltz in that case," I say with a little laugh. "Ah, well there you are then," Odd Kåre says, nodding at me again. "First a slow waltz, then back to your room for a little party, eh?" he says, and he gives a little laugh and I shake my head and laugh at how silly he's being. "Eh?" he says. "You and your gentleman friend from the room next door—right?" he says. "My gentleman friend?" I say. "Yeah, you know, Odd Aunet," he says, and he looks at me and laughs and I look at him and shake my head. "Well, for one thing, he's not my gentleman friend, and for another I don't think there's much go in him either these days," I say. "No," Odd Kåre says, "I wouldn't be surprised if he had to stand on his head to get it up," he says, and then he roars with laughter, turning to glance around the dayroom as he laughs, checking to see whether the other people in here heard what he said, but everyone else is sitting quietly minding their own business, it doesn't look as if anyone heard, which is just as well if you ask me, that was a little too close to the bone for my taste.

I look at Odd Kåre and Odd Kåre looks at me and laughs, and I can't help but laugh as well, nobody else heard it so I laugh and shake my head at how silly he's being. After a moment I turn to Johnny. And I look at Johnny and shake my head at him too, shake my head at what an idiot his dad is, and Johnny looks at me and smiles back. Oh my, he looks so like his father so he does, with the lovely plump cheeks he's got now, seventeen and the spitting image of his father.

"It's so nice to see you, Johnny," I say. I stretch out my hand and give Johnny's knee a little pat, look at him and smile. "And how are you getting on?" I ask. "Great," he says, smiling back at me. "Well, you're looking very well, anyway," I say. "And you've got such lovely plump cheeks," I say. He just sits there for a second and then his face goes all funny, he looks so embarrassed, his cheeks turn slightly pink and he sort of looks away. What's he doing that for? Surely not because I said his cheeks were a bit plumper, I mean there's nothing wrong with that, he looks fitter and healthier now, he used to be so thin, he looked quite ill. I look at him and smile and it's on the tip of my tongue to say this to him but I don't, we're not to say any more about this, I realize.

I turn to look at Odd Kåre. But he's sitting there grinning and looking at Johnny, taunting Johnny with his eyes. And after a moment Johnny turns to Odd Kåre and glowers at him. "What's up with you?" Johnny asks. "What's up with me?" Odd Kåre says, eyeing Johnny scornfully and grinning. "Not a thing," he says. "Oh, so what're you grinning at?" Johnny asks. "What? Is there a law against smiling now?" Odd Kåre says. "Asshole," Johnny says and the next moment I hear the talk on the other side of the room die away. I shoot a glance at Sylvia and her family, they're all looking at Odd Kåre and Johnny. And Therese, she's looking at Odd Kåre and Johnny as well, and everything goes very quiet for a second and now I have to say something, I have to get Odd Kåre and Johnny to talk about something else, I can't have them arguing and falling out, not in here, not with people sitting here listening.

"Well, well—and how's school, Johnny?" I ask him with a wary smile, but he doesn't seem to hear me, he just sits there staring at the floor with a face like thunder, and I turn to Odd Kåre, but he's still grinning and eyeing Johnny. "Your gran's right, you know, you've fairly filled out since you stopped playing football," he says, and everything goes quiet and I see how angry Johnny is, angry and red in the face. "Why don't you just shut your gob?" Johnny says, raising his voice a little and I give a little start when he says it, I turn and look at the other people in the room, they're still staring at us, and I feel my face getting hot, I look at them and give a faint little smile, trying somehow to make light of this by smiling, but they don't smile back, just gaze stonily at me for a moment or two, then they turn away, exchanging meaningful glances. And my face is growing hotter and hotter. It's not nice, showing this side of ourselves, that this is what people see when Odd Kåre, Johnny and I finally get together, it's not pleasant, but I keep smiling, try to make light of it all by smiling.

It's so quiet you could hear a pin drop and I turn back to Odd Kåre and Johnny. Odd Kåre is glaring at Johnny and Johnny is staring at the table with a face like thunder.

"Behave yourself!" Odd Kåre hisses at Johnny. "I was only kidding," he says. "Surely you can take a fucking joke," he mutters, then he stops, gives a snort of annoyance and runs a hand through his greasy hair. Then he turns to me again, gives a little shake of his head and smiles apologetically at me, and I smile faintly back at him, then I look at the table, and after a moment or two the talk on the other side of the room starts up again.

And now Odd Kåre's talking about the house. The house needs doing up, he tells me. The bathroom is riddled with damp and will have to be completely renovated. "Pa didn't do a proper job last time he fixed it up," he says, and he looks at me and I look at him and this sounds a bit odd to me. Johan didn't do a proper job? Johan, who was so thorough and so particular about everything, no, I'm not sure I believe this, it's probably just something Odd Kåre's saying to get a dig in at his father, he never misses a chance to criticize him, so I take this with a pinch of salt.

"You should never tamper with a bathroom yourself," Odd Kåre goes on. "The bathroom's the trickiest room in the house and it ought to be left to the professionals," he says. "Oh, yes?" I say. "And we need to put in new windows upstairs, the old frames are absolutely rotten." "Is that so?" I say. "Yeah," he says. "They haven't been painted in God knows how long," he says. "The bathroom alone's going to cost about a hundred thousand kroner. And the windows could easily come to another forty or fifty thousand," he says, and he's about to go on, but he doesn't get the chance because just then the new assistant comes over to us.

"Can I get you some coffee?" the new assistant asks. Odd Kåre sits back in his chair and looks at her. "Get us coffee? Well, that's what I call service," he says. "Is this something new they've started?" and he gives that big, loud laugh of his, and the new assistant smiles awkwardly at him, smiling just to be polite, I can tell by her face, but Odd Kåre doesn't notice, he doesn't notice things like that, Odd Kåre doesn't. "Yeah, a cup of coffee would be great," he says and the new assistant nods. "Would you like milk or cream in your coffee?" she asks. "You don't have anything stronger to put in it, do you?" Odd Kåre asks and he gives another big, loud laugh, laughing with his mouth wide open. He props his elbow on the back of the chair and turns to the others in the dayroom, to check whether they caught that remark, I suppose, and the others in the dayroom did catch it, I can tell. They don't laugh back though and they don't smile either, they just sit there stony-faced. But Odd Kåre is still laughing his head off. He turns back to the new assistant and she gives another strained, awkward smile. "No, I'm afraid not," she says. "Damn—oh well, never mind," Odd Kåre says, and he laughs yet again and the new assistant gives that awkward smile of hers, then she turns and walks away and Odd Kåre follows her with his eyes, and I turn to Johnny and I look at him and smile. Poor Johnny, that must have been a bit embarrassing for him, getting all upset and losing his temper like that, and having people turning to stare at him, that must have been a bit embarrassing for him.

"So, how's school, Johnny?" I ask, smiling at him. "Aw," he says with a little shake of his head. And Odd Kåre suddenly turns to him. "Yeah," he says and there's a sharpness to his voice again and he grins sourly at Johnny. "Why don't you tell your gran how it's going at school?" he says. There's silence for a moment and then Johnny turns to Odd Kåre and snorts loudly at his father and I look at them, oh no, no please don't let them start arguing and falling out again, why can't they just get on?

"For God's sake," Johnny says, jerking his head at Odd Kåre. "As if you were any better. You dropped out of school and started working as well," he says. "Yeah, but back then there were jobs to be had for somebody who hadn't finished school," Odd Kåre says, his voice low but shaking with anger. "There are jobs to be had now too, there are plenty of vacancies I can apply for," Johnny says. "Yeah," Odd Kåre sneers. "Working at the checkout in some supermarket," he says. "So, what the fuck's wrong with that?" Johnny says, raising his voice a little again, and I shoot a glance at the others in the room. They're all staring at us again, and I feel the heat rising into my cheeks. "You're the one that's always complaining about the powers that be and singing the praises of what you call the common people?" Johnny says. "Yes, I am," Odd Kåre says. "It's just that you can't live on what you make working at a supermarket checkout." "Yeah, well I'm not planning on working there for ever," Johnny snarls. "Well, if you don't stay on at school and get an education you might have to," Odd Kåre says. "Oh, *Jesus Christ*, would you just shut up!" Johnny cries, looking daggers at Odd Kåre, and Odd Kåre sneers back at him and I'm getting hotter and hotter. Okay, now they have to stop this and be friends again, this isn't how I want people to see us when we're together, we have to show a better side of ourselves when we're finally together.

"Well, well," I say, because now I'll have to butt in, I'll have to bring the conversation around to something else, something more pleasant. I look at them and smile, but they don't even look at me, they're so angry at one another and they just go on arguing and arguing and Sylvia and her family are just sitting there staring at us, they look almost frightened, they exchange worried glances, I simply don't know where to look, this isn't nice, and here I was saying such good things about Odd Kåre and my grandchildren, boasting about them to Sylvia's son, so I was, telling him how proud I was of my family, so I was, and then they do this.

"Yeah, yeah," Odd Kåre says, sneering at Johnny. "Go right ahead and drop out of school, it's your funeral," he says. "That's right, it is," Johnny says. "So I don't know why you care, it's not up to you anyway," he says. "Oh, no?" Odd Kåre says, with a laugh meant to show how ridiculous this shot from Johnny is. "But I think you're forgetting one important point here," Odd Kåre says. "I'm the one who pays for your food, your clothes and the roof over your head." "Yeah, and that's exactly why I want to find a job as soon as I can," Johnny says. "So I can leave home. So I can move as far away from home as I possibly can." And Sylvia and her family are staring at us in horror and I'm getting hotter and hotter, so embarrassed that Sylvia and her family should see us like this, that this is the side of us we let people see when we're finally together, it's not nice, not nice at all. I can just imagine what they'll say about us afterwards. What a dreadful way to behave, Sylvia's family will say, never seen anything like it, they'll say, as if it wasn't bad enough that they hardly ever come to see her, when they finally do show up they behave like that, they'll say. And then Sylvia will get on her high horse and tell them what she's probably been dying to tell them all along, out she'll come with all those spiteful comments. Parents can't expect to be shown more love than they've given, she'll say, or something along

those lines. No wonder Odd Kåre hardly ever comes to
see her, she'll say, and no wonder he's turned out the way
he has, she'll say, molested by his father the way he was,
she'll say, molested by his father for years, ever since he
was a little boy, she'll say, that whole dirty business, it's
past, it's all in the past, but she'll drag it all up again, all
the stuff that Odd Kåre and I have spent so much time and
energy on putting behind us, she's going to drag it all up so
her son can compare himself to mine and tell himself what
a great upbringing he's had, oh yes, because that's what
Sylvia wants, of course, she wants to be seen as the good,
successful mother. Our family's a disaster and she's lapping
it up because it makes her look like such a great success.

I look at Sylvia, but she isn't looking at me, she's looking at Odd Kåre and Johnny. She and the rest of her family
are looking at Odd Kåre and Johnny, and Odd Kåre and
Johnny are still arguing and I just sit here smiling, trying
to make light of it all by smiling, but no one else is smiling, no one thinks this is anything to smile about. Sylvia's
son is looking at me with pity in his eyes and there's pity
in Sylvia's daughter-in-law's eyes too, and Odd Kåre and
Johnny just go on arguing and arguing, their voices low
and fierce.

"Now, now, you mustn't argue like that," I say, as
pleasantly as I can, still smiling, and Odd Kåre is about to
say something but before he can say it the new assistant
comes over to us again. She's carrying a tray with coffee
and almond tart on it and she sets the tray down on our
table. "Here you are," she says. "Thanks very much,"
I say. "Yeah, thanks," Odd Kåre says. He glances down
at the almond tart. "Gosh, you didn't go baking a cake
just for me, did you?" he says, and he looks at the new

assistant and laughs and the new assistant gives a strained smile but doesn't meet his eye, then she straightens up, looks down at me and gives me the kind of smile that Sylvia's son and daughter-in-law just gave me, a smile full of pity, and I smile back at her as naturally as ever I can, then I look at Odd Kåre and Odd Kåre looks at Johnny.

"You're supposed to say thank you when somebody gives you something?" Odd Kåre says, but Johnny doesn't say thank you, he just glares at Odd Kåre, who grunts and looks up at the new assistant. "Yeah, we live a bit farther out on the island, you see. North of manners," he says and he roars with laughter again. "Oh, right," the new assistant says, forcing another awkward smile, then she turns and looks at me again and gives me that pitying smile again and I feel a little surge of annoyance, because she needn't think she's any better than us—her, drinking during working hours, she needn't get all uppity and think she's got the right to look down on me or Odd Kåre or Johnny, because that's what she's doing when she looks at me like that, as if she feels sorry for me. That's what they're all doing actually, her and Sylvia's son and Sylvia's daughter-in-law, they feel sorry for me for having the son and the grandson that I have. As if my son and my grandson weren't worth loving, as if they didn't have their good sides too, as if we didn't have our good times together. We've had our ups and downs over the years, God knows we have, but who hasn't. I look at the new assistant and I'm feeling more and more annoyed, but I keep smiling.

"Did you see that Paula's bought herself a new dress?" the new assistant says suddenly, looking at Odd Kåre. "Isn't it lovely?" she asks. She pauses for a second, then she turns to me and smiles. "Oh yes, lovely," Odd Kåre says and he looks at me and my new dress. "That's right, Ma," he says. "You spend your money. I mean, you haven't exactly spoiled yourself in the past, so just you go right ahead," he says, and it feels good to hear him talking like this and I look at him and smile and Odd Kåre smiles back, then he looks up at the new assistant again.

"I keep telling her she ought to treat herself to a vacation in the sun," he says, nodding at me, and I look at him. I don't remember him ever saying anything about a vacation in the sun to me, but never mind, it doesn't matter. I look at Odd Kåre and smile. "Oh yes, that would do you good, I'm sure, Paula," the new assistant says. "D'you hear that, Ma, you should take yourself off to Gran Canaria, get a bit of heat on your bones," Odd Kåre says. "Spend your money while you can, enjoy life," he says. I look at him, and I hope that the other people in the room can also hear what he's saying now, I hope Sylvia and her family are hearing this, because if they are they'll see that there's more to Odd Kåre than they thought, and if they do that they'll also see that Sylvia's not the only one with children who care about her.

"I can book a ticket for you any time," Odd Kåre goes on. "Oh, the way you go on," I say, laughing and shaking my head. "Aye, that'll be right, an old body like me sunning herself on the beach," I laugh. "What a sight that would be," I say. It feels so good to be talking like this, I laugh and shake my head. "No, but you get these vacations designed specially for the elderly," Odd Kåre says. "It's all organized for you so you don't have to worry about a thing," he says. "Oh, get away with you, I've never heard such nonsense," I say, laughing and waggling my head. "No," I say, "my traveling days are done." "Your traveling days?"

Odd Kåre says. "You've never been outside Norway," he says. "That may be so," I say, "but at least I've seen my own country," I say. "Johan and I, we drove the length and breadth of Norway, so we did," I say. "And there's not many that can say that." "No, that's true," the new assistant says, nodding at me and smiling. "But still, I'm sure a couple of weeks in the sun would do you the world of good," Odd Kåre says. "You're retired, you've got plenty of money in the bank and you're withering away up here. You could be having the time of your life," he says. "Oh, don't be silly," I say. "Silly?" he says. "If you wanted you could be sitting on your balcony, soaking up the sun and gazing at the sea right now," he says. "With a glass of sherry in your hand," he adds. "Eh?" he says, nodding at me and smiling. "Who knows, you might even find some Spanish gentleman to dance with you," he says. "Oh, stop it, you silly thing." "Wouldn't that be something, Ma?" Odd Kåre says, and he looks up at the new assistant and laughs, and the new assistant smiles at him, and Odd Kåre looks at me again and I shake my head and laugh at how silly he's being, and it feels so good to be able to show this side of ourselves as well, so the other people here can see that we love each other too, it feels so good.

Otterøya, July 10th, 2006

This morning I took your newspaper advertisement over to the care home to speak to the residents about you. Otterøya isn't a big place, as you know, so just about everyone up there remembers you and Berit and Erik and they were bursting to talk about the old days now that they had the chance. You should have seen them: people who've been more dead than alive for years suddenly perked up and launched into descriptions of family histories and connections, of working life and everyday life, births and deaths, good times and bad, accidents and disasters, progress and optimism. You should see what you've started up here, David, you've breathed life into the old folk, something I've been trying to do ever since I retired. I go up to the residential care home almost every day to read the newspapers to those who can't manage it themselves. I've filled in pools and lotto coupons for them, I've read poetry and epigrams, told tall tales and funny anecdotes, organized bingo sessions and quizzes and occasionally I've taken along my accordion and got them up for some old-time dancing. But even though they've taken an interest in and enjoyed most of these activities it's nothing compared to what I witnessed this morning. At long last someone was interested in hearing the stories these old folk had to tell, not just listening out of politeness, but really listening to them, taking what they said seriously. Because presumably this was what had fired their enthusiasm: the thought that they were being taken seriously, being appreciated, being of use.

It was particularly interesting to listen to my former fellow teacher, Odd Aune. He is an old local historian and co-author of several books on the area and he treated me to a vivid and detailed account of how your great-great-great-grandfather on your mother's side brought the steam-powered saw to Namdal, thus enabling Namsos to grow into the largest and most important town in the Namdal region. Prior to that, all the timber in Namdal had been cut with a water-powered saw, he told me, and for a water-powered saw to work you had to have falls and rapids with a drop of at least twelve feet. This meant that all sawmills had to be built farther up the valley where the falls and rapids were. The timber was felled in the forest, transported to the water-powered sawmill, cut there and then floated down the River Namsen to Namsos for stacking and shipping.

But one day in the 1840s a ship docked at the mouth of the Namsen and on board this ship was your great-great-great-grandfather Oliver Dyrbakk, a young engineer, entrepreneur and businessman. With him on this ship he had a steam-powered saw and this, along with the abolition of the sawmill monopoly some years later, spelled the start of a new era in Namdal. Not only was the steam-powered saw far more efficient than its water-powered forerunner, it was not dependent on falls and rapids. The timber could be floated down the Namsen and cut at the river mouth where a large, ice-free shipping harbor had been built.

All this was to have great, not to say massive, consequences. As you probably know industrialization came only relatively slowly to Norway, but in the latter half of the nineteenth century, in timber production hubs such as Namsos, here in Namdal, there really was talk of an industrial revolution, of a fundamental transformation of society, economically, politically, socially and culturally. Within a very short space of time more than twenty sawmills sprang up in Namsos and the surrounding area, some small, some large, and all of them in need of workers. Many of these workers brought wives and children with them when they moved to the area and naturally these workers and their wives and children had to have food and clothing and medicines, so then came the general store and the chemist and the draper's shop. They had to bury their dead and christen their newborn, so a church was built and a vicar hired. They wanted their children to go to school, so a schoolhouse was built and a schoolteacher hired. They wanted help when they were sick, so a hospital was built and doctors and nurses hired. In due course they discovered that they also needed a newspaper. And a townhouse. And a public hall and so on and so forth. And in no time at all Namsos was unrecognizable. Within just a few years what had once been a handful of buildings clustered around a jetty had grown into a small town, a sawmill town. According to Odd Aune one can gain some impression of what happened here by looking at the censuses for this area. In the nineteenth century the county of North Trondheim was divided into three bailiwicks, he told me, and while the population of the Stjørdalen and Verdalen bailiwick remained static and the population of the Inderøen bailiwick fell during the latter half of the century, the population of Namdal rose by fifty-five percent. And this despite the fact that migration to America had been as great from Namdal as from the other two bailiwicks. Given that more or less the whole increase occurred in Namsos itself, then it is quite clear that we are talking here of a genuine industrial revolution.

And your great-great-great-grandfather played a central part in this revolution, David. Not only did he introduce the steam-powered saw to Namsos. His sawmill, Vigen Sawing & Planing Mill, was also the most successful in the keen competition that gradually developed between the local mills. As a qualified engineer he kept abreast of new developments in sawmill technology and since he had the capital to invest in new innovations he was always able to run his mill more efficiently and systematically than his competitors. He also had an excellent head for business. He bought up the quotas of the smaller mills as one by one they went bankrupt, and by cultivating various diplomatic contacts he also succeeded in securing contracts which, in practice, granted him sole rights to export sawn timber to England and the Netherlands, where there was a great shortage of forest and timber and a desperate need for wood. Of all the Namdal mills Vigen Sawing & Planing was also the one with the highest sales to the tree-poor areas of Nordland County and Svalbard.

It's no secret that all of this made Oliver Dyrbakk a rich man. Just how rich was brought home to me when Therese Skorstad disappeared into her room and came back with a Lions Club Calendar containing pictures of old Namsos which she handed around for everyone to see. In this calendar was a photograph of the house that your great-great-grandfather built for himself and his family on the leafy outskirts of the town at Bjørum. I have that photograph lying in front of me as I write and what I am looking at is nothing short of a mansion, not unlike the houses in that television series on Norwegian mansions. It is a black wooden house with arched windows, two balconies and an imposing flight of steps sweeping from the veranda down to a huge garden full of fruit trees and shrubs, with a fountain in the middle of the lawn. The grounds are surrounded by a wall of what looks like fieldstone and at the bottom of the gravel path is a black, cast-iron gate leading to a long avenue lined with oak trees that runs up to and round the side of the house, to what I assume must be the front entrance.

Vigen Sawing & Planing Mill has been in the hands of the Dyrbakk family ever since, and even though the fortunes of the sawmill business and the timber trade fluctuated during the rest of the nineteenth century and the first half of the twentieth, the family has always been extremely wealthy, and major shareholders and directors of the company have wielded a lot of influence in Namsos, both politically and financially.

But there was one specific chapter of the family history, an incident which occurred during the first half of the twentieth century, that got everyone talking at once when it came up in the conversation in the dayroom this morning. At some point your great-grandfather, Erik's father that is, severed all ties with the Dyrbakk family. He changed his surname and after a brief period during which he worked in the planing yard of the Namsen Timber Association he moved to Otterøya, where he supported his family by fishing and farming until his death in the late 1950s.

Then as now Otterøya was a small close-knit community so almost everyone, and certainly all of us in that dayroom I think, had heard about this rift—well, it had been the talk of the town at the time. But there were various theories as to the actual reason for it. Sylvia Skog had heard that your great-grandfather had got a housemaid pregnant and when his father tried to force him to marry the girl he quite simply walked out and never went back. Therese Skorstad on the other hand had been told that your great-grandfather had been his father's close confidant and colleague, as well as the natural heir to the business and his fortune, but that they had become estranged when your great-grandfather tried to save a lot of money by not insuring a small sawmill owned by the family. When this mill burned to the ground, your great-great-grandfather was so enraged by the loss and this breach of faith that he disowned his son.

But none of these theories is correct, Odd Aune says. According to him your great-grandfather broke with the family for political reasons. Even as a young boy your great-grandfather was troubled by the huge differences he saw between the lives of his own wealthy family and all the poor men working themselves half to death at the sawmill, so Odd says, and when he joined the company he was far more open to discussing things and cooperating with the workers and the trade union than your old-fashioned, deeply paternalistic and pretty uncompromising great-great-grandfather. While your great-grandfather supported the union's demand for a cost-of-living allowance after the outbreak of the First World War, your great-great-grandfather rejected it on the grounds of high war taxes and an uncertain timber market; while your great-grandfather defended the workers' right to free firewood from the sawmill, your great-great-grandfather stuck to his decision to deprive them of this right, and while your great-grandfather was prepared to give in to the demands for higher and higher wages, your great-great-grandfather would not yield. And so it went on. They held fundamentally different views on the relationship between employer and employee and this led to violent clashes that rendered relations between them more and more strained. The friction between them did not escape the notice of the workers and union men, who exploited it for all it was worth— which in turn made the relationship between father and son even more fraught.

Eventually something had to give. The son was every bit as

stubborn, proud and hard-headed as the father and neither of them was willing to make any concessions. Far from it, the more personal the feud became, the wider the gulf between them grew until the day when your great-grandfather simply upped and left the company. And not only that. Inspired by the Russian Revolution and a trade union movement that was becoming more and more radicalized, he announced that he was now a socialist, said so long and farewell to his old life and took a job as a sawmill worker with the Namsen Timber Association. But that wasn't such a good move, Odd says. Your great-grandfather was a tall, strapping young man so the work itself was no problem for him, but to the other workers he was still a Dyrbakk, and no matter how hard he tried to fit in he was never accepted. He was shunned and cold-shouldered and so after only a year or two he moved to Otterøya, where he built a little wooden house down on the shore.

And many, many years later you would grow up in that same house.

Odd Aune is a knowledgeable and, not least, an honest and reliable fellow, so I've no doubt that he's right and that most of what he says is true. But still, I can't help thinking that he and those who were most in agreement with him are as much intent on conveying a message that's important to them as they are to presenting an accurate account of past events. It seems to me that they are creating an image of your great-grandfather that will reflect their own ideal of a sober, thrifty character, content with little. Their admiration for and animated accounts of a man who lived a life of affluence and had everything but chose to forsake all this wealth to live instead much the same sort of life as themselves, the life of a fisherman and farmer on the island of Otterøya, are as much an attempt to invest their own lives with value and meaning as to tell the truth about your great-grandfather. And naturally they want you to learn from this, David, they want you to identify with the great-grandfather they speak of and embrace the values and the qualities which they say he possessed. Not, of course, that I think they do this consciously or that it's in any way planned. They do it instinctively, they present it this way because it feels good and right to present it this way, it satisfies a need in them, that's all.

Actually it was interesting to talk to Paula about this afterwards. Because she told me that this aspect of your family history meant a surprisingly great deal to your mother. Berit felt cheated, you see, Paula says. She felt that, in choosing to cut himself off from his family, her grandfather had deprived her of the chance of a happy, carefree life. She knew it was ridiculous to think like that, she even laughed and said she was just being silly, but still, that was what she thought. "I should really have been rich and successful," she used to tell Paula and then she would launch into a description of what this life of wealth and luxury would have been like. She had two different scenarios, and if I understand Paula rightly it depended on how she was feeling, mentally and physically, which one she would pick on any particular day. One version saw her happily married to a handsome, well-dressed gentleman, and during the day, when he was out attending to business, she had her hands full looking after three bonny, rosy-cheeked children, running the house and seeing to it that the housekeeper and the other staff did what they were supposed to do both inside and outside the family mansion. In the other, she painted a picture of a rather decadent, opulent existence in which she lounged around feeling bored in an interesting and charming fashion; a life laced with irony and sarcasm in which she stayed in her silk dressing gown till mid-afternoon, smoked cigarettes in a holder and sipped drinks while waiting for her secret lover.

But the most interesting thing about this is that Berit actually seems to have tried to win back the life that she believed her grandfather had cheated her of. The year after you were born, she took a job as a cleaner at the dairy in Namsos, but when she heard that Anton Dyrbakk the sawmill owner was looking for a maid of all work for the aforementioned mansion in Bjørum, she left the dairy and went to work for Dyrbakk instead, even though it was a more demanding and less well-paid job. Her reason for doing this was, of course, that this was the family and the house that she had once been cheated out of. In other words, applying for and getting the job as a maid with the Dyrbakks was the first step in a bigger plan to regain what she had lost.

And as I understand it from Paula, Berit was well aware that this was what she was trying to do. Speaking of it later, she would say that she had had a vague idea that she would start by impressing the Dyrbakks by being exceptionally conscientious and hard-working and in due course, either by accident or chance, it would come out that she was actually one of them and she would immediately be accepted as such. Yes, and not only accepted, Paula says, but as one would expect in such a classic, not to say almost archetypal, tale, your mother saw herself staying there with them and eventually marrying the son of the house, a good-looking young man who was studying economics and wore a suit every day.

And the first part of her dream did in fact come true. Berit showed herself to be an excellent maid of all work and she hadn't been at the house for more than a few weeks before the lady of the house happened to hear that she was related to her husband. The only problem was that Anton Dyrbakk wasn't particularly interested in this revelation. He asked her a few questions about herself, just to be polite, and that was that. Nothing more was said to Berit about them being related and she certainly noticed no change in their attitude towards her. Later, when she talked about it she would laugh and say that she had been hopelessly naive, but according to Paula she felt both angry and bitter towards the Dyrbakk family, not only because they had failed to fulfil her naive and totally unrealistic expectations of winning back what she believed—or no, not believed, but felt—was rightfully hers, but also because a year later they had given her the sack, and in the most humiliating fashion. You see, the lady of the house found out that Berit had you, David, and that you had been born out of wedlock, and since Mrs Dyrbakk refused to have a young woman of loose morals in the house she was kindly asked to leave that very day.

All of this suggests that your mother was a woman with ambitions of getting on in life, something which Paula can confirm today and which is also clear from this entry in Paula's diary.

Otterøya, July 13th, 1977
Bit of an upset tummy today. Sat out in the yard, smoking and drinking currant wine with Berit until three in the morning. We talked about what we always talk about. Getting away from here and starting afresh somewhere else. A new life in a new place. As far as I'm concerned this is just a stupid dream. I know that. It's only when I'm with Berit, a bit tipsy and encouraged by how seriously she takes all our talk that I find it possible to believe in our plans. And even then there's a part of me that knows this is just a nice little bit of escapism, a pipe dream. I won't see forty again and I'm never going to get away. There's no way that's ever going to happen and all the currant wine in the world won't fool me

into thinking otherwise. It's different for Berit. She's not even twenty-five yet and she feels like she has all her life in front of her. And she has no husband to stop her. She's free to do whatever she likes and even though she has David, she sees no reason why we two couldn't move to Namsos and open a clothing store, the way we spent all night discussing. Oh, God. If I know her she'll already be looking for premises. And I'd bet anything that before the day's over she'll have rung the bank to ask about the chances of getting a loan. She's so enthusiastic, so full of get-up-and-go that I often feel like an old woman when I'm with her. She believes she can do anything, everything's possible. And when she comes to see me, to show me the premises she's found or to tell me what the bank said, it'll go the way it always goes, I'll start looking for gentle ways to demolish our plans. I hate myself for it. I'm the biggest coward in the world.

According to Paula it was this ambition to better herself and get on in life that led Berit to take up with several of the men she did in fact take up with. I don't mean she let herself be bought in any way, far from it. But she always had an eye for a man with money, in principle at least. Such an attitude is not unusual among people from poor backgrounds, of course. Not at all, it's probably more the rule than the exception, but still there's something slightly indecent about making wealth and status the criteria for choosing a partner, it seems at odds with the romantic ideal that we subscribe to today so most people won't admit that they do it.

Not Berit, though, according to Paula. She never made any secret of the fact that she went to this party or that simply because she had heard that one of the biggest landowners on Otterøya would be there. She mimicked and made fun of the high-pitched voice and effeminate appearance of a young man of her own age on the other side of the island but when out of the blue he inherited his uncle's grocery store she somehow managed to overlook these faults and enter into a relationship with him that Paula described as hopeless and doomed to failure. "Well, I just like the idea of being able to buy whatever I want, don't you?" she said bluntly when one of her friends reminded her of what she had once said about this young man.

And she was equally frank and outspoken when she broke up with Steinar Olsen in the early 80s. Or to say "broke up with" is possibly not quite right since they had never really been together—not officially at least. Steinar was a married man, you see, and his affair with Berit was only possible because his wife was ill and confined to the psychiatric unit in Namsos. Nonetheless, according to Paula no one, not even the staff at the psychiatric unit, believed that Steinar's wife would ever get better, so both Steinar and Berit felt that they were home and dry. It was only a matter of time before Steinar could get a divorce and their relationship could become common knowledge—as if it weren't common knowledge already, Paula remarked.

But then Berit discovered that Steinar Olsen wasn't as well off as she had thought. He was apparently one of the farmers who had done best out of the agricultural restructuring carried out in the 70s. He had bought land and some of the machinery from a neighboring farm that had been forced to shut down, he had invested in a big new barn and done up both the farmhouse and the farm cottage. So everything seemed to be perfect. But one evening when Steinar was sitting with a pile of bills in front of him, doing his accounts he suddenly broke down in front of Berit and said he simply didn't know what to do. The farm wasn't paying any longer, he was unable to pay off all his loans and was on the brink of bankruptcy.

Obviously Berit didn't break it off with Steinar right then and there, Paula says. She wasn't that cold and cynical. Nonetheless it was because of his money troubles that she made up her mind to leave him. "No way am I ever going to marry a bankrupt," as she said straight out to her friends in the sewing circle, "I've got enough worries as it is."

As it happens it was Berit's affair with Steinar that caused the rift between her and Dagny. Although their friendship had been on the wane for some time before Berit and Steinar started seeing one another. Your mother's mood swings had become worse and worse during the latter half of the 70s and when they met at sewing circle evenings or other gatherings, Berit could be downright horrible to Dagny, there's no getting away from it. She could, as I say, be rude and nasty to anyone when she was in one of her black moods, but Dagny was particularly easy prey. The jibes aimed at her were worse, they were more frequent and came more readily.

This may well have had something to do with Dagny being such a cheery person and always so infuriatingly happy. Her cheerfulness contrasted sharply with the way Berit felt when she was in one of her black moods. Well, Dagny reminded your mother of all the things she wasn't, but would have liked to have been and this must have filled Berit with the urge to punish her. And obviously it didn't help matters that Dagny was as naive as she was. She had never really known hardship or pain and as a result she was capable of telling Berit in all seriousness that "You have to think positively" and "What doesn't kill you makes you stronger," and if there's one thing that can really antagonize someone like Berit it's that sort of talk, because even though it's well-meant, it sounds and feels as though the person saying it is belittling the problem and turning it into something that can be fixed with a pat on the back and a good night's sleep. But it can't, of course. Far from it.

Anyway it was Berit's affair with Steinar that put an end to this once close friendship. Because you see in 1980 Dagny's husband had been diagnosed as suffering from motor neuron disease. He died less than a year later after a dreadful decline during which he slowly but surely lost control of his muscles and his respiratory tract. According to Paula, this happened around the same time as Steinar's wife's condition really started to deteriorate, so the heartbreaking experience of having to watch one's spouse gradually waste away was something that Steinar and Dagny shared. They understood one another, and out of this understanding grew a more emotional attachment. Open and ingenuous as she was Dagny told her friends at the sewing circle all about this, Paula says. She told them what she and Steinar had said to one another, what they had done together and, not least, how much they were coming to care for each other.

Whether it was solely in order to punish Dagny that, well knowing all of this, the younger and far more enigmatic and exciting Berit then seduced Steinar, Paula is not sure, but she has no doubt that your mother did take a certain malicious pleasure in stealing Steinar from Dagny. You just had to look at her and listen to her to know that. Granted, Berit used to say that she shouldn't do the things she did and that she felt bad about Dagny, but then—after adding that, well, no one could control who they fell in love with—she would grin wickedly, making it clear to Paula that love for Steinar was not the main thing here.

But still, she didn't do it simply for the pleasure of getting back at Dagny. The drama and excitement of the situation were probably as great an incentive. As I said Berit was something of a dreamer, fond of picturing herself in the sort of worlds she saw in films and read about in her weekly magazines and romantic novels, and according to Paula she clearly relished playing the part of the secret mistress and femme fatale. For Dagny this was deadly serious, but to Berit it was just a game. She loved all the lying and the subterfuge it entailed; she loved to sit there with the rest of the sewing circle dropping hints that might give her away, and the time when she had had to hide in Steinar's bedroom while he was downstairs, explaining to Dagny why it wasn't the best time for her to call, marked a high point in this adventure that she never tired of describing to Paula.

But when Berit realized that Steinar's wife was unlikely ever to get better and that Steinar actually meant it when he said that he wanted to be with her, it became less of a game and more serious for her too. It was then that the social climber in Berit came into play. At a sewing circle evening that turned out to be anything but pleasant she informed Dagny and her other friends that she had fallen in love with a man whom she knew someone else present was also in love with. All the air seemed to be sucked out of the room the moment she said this, according to Paula. Everyone sat perfectly still, holding their breath, eyes fixed on the needlework in their laps, and it wasn't until Berit started going on about how nobody could control who they fell in love with and that she hoped they could all still be friends, no matter what happened, that Dagny got up and dashed out of the room in tears.

After that Berit was quite simply banned from the sewing circle and the other women would have nothing to do with her, so Paula says. Although it wasn't something they discussed, one sewing circle meeting after another was ostensibly canceled and they started getting together without inviting Berit. Pauls feels a bit bad talking about this, she says. Well, she was

Berit's best friend and she didn't like going behind her back, but she enjoyed the evenings with her other women friends so much that she couldn't bring herself to refuse. "But at least I did try to stand up for Berit when I was there and get them to see it from her side," she told me, as if trying to excuse herself. Not that it did any good. Berit was and remained persona non grata, and it's no secret that she was the subject of a lot of talk and much malicious gossip back then. She was pretty much a regular topic of conversation at sewing circle meetings, Paula says, to the point where they had what they called "the Berit story of the day."

Naturally the gossip spread to everyone else on Otterøya. And people lapped up what they heard, then revised it and added a little bit here and there depending on who they happened to be speaking to and what impression they wanted to make, until it got to the stage where your mother was, by all accounts, the most despicable creature on God's earth. And it has to be said that Johanna Mørck played no small part in all of this. Johanna bore a grudge against Berit for firing her from her job as babysitter, so now she made full use of her storytelling skills to blacken your mother's name. There was no end, it seemed, to what she had seen, heard and had to put up with while she was minding you, each thing worse than the one before, but worst of all, according to Johanna herself, was the story of your father's identity. Oh yes, she said, she had heard it from Berit herself so she knew it was true.

When she told this story she always started by piquing the curiosity of her audience. This I know because she also told it to me. "No, no, I can't say, I really can't," she muttered, closing her eyes, shaking her head and trying to look as if it were simply too painful for her to reveal what she knew. But then, when I started to press her, insisting that if she started then she had to finish, she made a show of giving in, as if to say that whatever came out now it would be as much on my head as on hers. She began by telling me how everyone knew that when it came to money and property your mother would trample over anybody to get what she wanted. And then—after keeping me in suspense with a long digression on how she was never paid for minding you, she got her meals and that was that—at long last she revealed what she claimed to know for a fact, but which Paula says is absolute garbage, namely, that your father was none other than Albert from up the hill, Erik's brother and Berit's own uncle. Berit had quite simply sold her body to her own uncle for two thousand kroner, Johanna said, and it had come as a shock to them both when she became pregnant with you. It was a dreadful thing, but it was true enough. Well, why else did I think it was so frightfully important for Berit to keep your father's identity a secret? Had it been anyone else she would certainly have told you, she said.

How many people actually believed this rumor I don't know, probably not many, because Johanna changed the story and made it a little bit more dramatic every time she told it, which didn't exactly do much for her credibility. But no matter how untrue it was, those were terrible times for Berit, and for you too of course. Not only did you get called a bastard, it was also suggested that your mutism was a result of inbreeding. "Ah, now it's all starting to make sense," people said. "Now I understand why that boy's a bit touched and thinks he's a robot."

Obviously the grown-ups on the island didn't say such things when you were within earshot, but everything that was said around the dinner and coffee tables of Otterøya was picked up by the children and teenagers and they weren't necessarily as considerate. One of the biggest sinners in this respect was Grim Albrigtsen, a half-grown lout who was always eager to repair his battered self-esteem by hurting and doing down other people. According to Paula, many's the time you came home in a terrible state because Grim had sneered at you and called you a freak or told you you were lucky you hadn't been born with one eye and twelve fingers or something like that. On one occasion he sneaked into the announcer's box at the football pitch on Otterøya and announced over the loudspeaker that David was asked to go immediately to the car park where "his father, Albert, is waiting for him." You ran home in tears and it was several days before your mother could persuade you to leave the house again.

Deep down you knew, of course, that Berit could not help what went on, or so Paula says, but since everything you had to put up with could be traced back to her, so to speak, she was the one who had to bear the main brunt of your tremendous and ever-growing anger. It was painful to watch, Paula said. To see and hear you snarling and roaring and saying the most awful things to your own mother, repeating the rumor put out by Johanna Mørck and accusing her of the same thing. Oh yes, because that's what you did. You knew it was only a rumor, a piece of malicious gossip, but you were so distraught and so furious that you did it anyway, you accused your mother of having slept with her own uncle; you lashed out at her, screaming at her to admit it. "Albert's my father," you yelled at her, "he is, I know he is." Perhaps you did this in the hope that your mother would break down and tell you who your real father was, thus putting an end to the awful way the two of you were treated. It's hard to say, but it was certainly painful to watch.

And it was worse for you, Paula says. Berit could put two and two together, she understood why you were reacting as you did, so she didn't let it get to her and she never blamed you. You, on the other hand, were wracked by guilt afterwards, Paula says. Indeed, the way she sees it, this feeling of guilt led you to enter into what was to be your longest bout of silence so far. You went for almost a whole month without saying a single word. According to Paula it was as if you did this because you were scared that you would lash out at your mother again. So the psychologist was right, she says, your mutism was a kind of anxiety disorder.

And then, as if things weren't bad enough already, Berit tried to kill herself. Whether it was all the rumors and muckraking and being ostracized by her women friends that drove her to it is hard to say, but it was probably a combination of a lot of things. Like her unpredictable moods, for example. She was never diagnosed as suffering from any particular condition, but her mood swings became worse and worse around that time, and there were those, including Paula, who began to wonder whether she might be manic depressive—that is, after all, an illness that has driven many individuals to commit suicide. And that she had left Steinar some time before the worst rumors began to circulate and had, therefore, one less person to help her through that dreadful time, obviously did not help matters.

Here is what Paula wrote in her diary about this incident:

Otterøya, January 11th, 1982
A week ago Berit tried to kill herself. Erik had given me a lift home from the Co-op. We were just driving into their yard when we caught sight of Berit out on the ice. As soon as we saw her we knew what she was doing and we both started to run. If she hadn't slipped and fallen as she tried to get away from us, she would have managed it too, because the ice just ahead of her was paper-thin. She came back with us without protest. She said not a word on the walk home,

she didn't cry either. The first thing she did when she got to the house was to go to the bathroom, brush her teeth and gargle with mouthwash. As if it was just any ordinary evening. Oddly enough, that was what really struck me about it, that she did exactly the same as she did every other night in the year. Somehow this seems like proof that she really meant to do it. It wasn't just a cry for help. If it had been, she would most probably have taken this opportunity to talk about what was troubling her, she would have wanted to be soothed and comforted, she would have wanted sympathy. But only someone who wants to go on living needs all that. A person who has made up their mind to die as soon as they have the chance doesn't need to waste time and energy on talking about what's troubling them. All the pain and the problems will soon be gone anyway, death will see to that, so the person who's about to die can just relax while they're waiting.

But Berit won't be allowed to die. I won't give up on her. I've been staying at her house for a week now and I'm not leaving until I'm sure it's safe to do so. I don't trust the psychologists. I know she's serious about it and I think it's crazy that they won't admit her to hospital. Luckily Erik agrees with me. We take it in turns to keep an eye on her. We never leave her alone and we've removed all the keys from the inside doors so she can't lock herself in any of the rooms. We've also hidden her sleeping pills. And the razor blades from the bathroom, of course. And the biggest, sharpest kitchen knives.

She's not happy about this, obviously. Sometimes she pretends to be sweeter and nicer and more docile. Probably so we'll think the danger is over and stop keeping an eye on her. Other times she tries to make us give up by being mean and nasty. Yesterday she laughed in my face and told me I was only trying to compensate for not being able to save my own family. That being here for her and David was my way of redeeming myself. It hurt to hear her say that, but I can take it. I won't give up on her. And I won't give up on David either. He must be feeling so bad right now. The worst of it is that she left a note, and it was him who found it. He refuses to talk about it, but he must have been terrified, poor little soul. And he's still terrified. He's trying to block it out. He does his best to talk and act as if nothing has changed, but it's no use. It's almost painful to watch him playing with his friends. He tries too hard, throwing himself into their games in a way that isn't normal. It's like he's trying to escape into the game, lose himself in make believe. And he's obviously even worse when there are no adults around. Yesterday Per's father came to the door. The boys had been playing Indians up in the forest and David and a couple of others had taken Per prisoner and tied him to a stake. They said they were going to torture him. The other boys had only said it for fun, but not David. It was all they could do to stop him lighting a fire around Per's feet, it could have gone terribly wrong.

As usual Erik is trying to make light of the whole thing. Boys will be boys, is all he says, but to me it seems quite clear that David is trying to escape from what has happened. And not only escape. This is a way of giving vent to all his feelings. All the distress and anger and resentment he feels over Berit's attempted suicide, he's trying to burn off in their games. I'm sure that's the the explanation.

But I won't give up. I have to make Berit see that David needs her and that she has to go on living, for his sake if nothing else. And then I have to convince David that she's not going to leave us. He must have seen her suicide attempt as a betrayal and yet another rejection, and if she were to try it again I think he might have some sort of breakdown. But if I can just make him feel that it's the thought of him that has kept Berit alive and helped her to get through this difficult time then I think he'll be all right, then he'll feel every bit as loved as a child ought to feel.

Otterøya care home, July 4th, 2006. A lump in the throat

"No, no, they can keep their vacation in the sun as far as I'm concerned," I say, shaking my head and laughing. "Well, you can always think about it, Paula," the new assistant says. She lays a hand on my shoulder and leans down to me. "Although there's no point in going off to Gran Canaria or wherever when it's so lovely and warm here, I'm with you on that," she says. "Now, now, that'll do," Odd Kåre says. "I thought you were on my side," he says, and he looks at the new assistant and shakes his head, gives her that sly grin of his, and the new assistant looks at him and smiles back at him, a perfectly normal smile this time, not awkward or forbearing, and I look at them both and smile, because it's good that we can joke about things like this, that we can talk like this and that people here can see this side of us as well. It's so good.

"Who the hell put my walker in that cabinet?" Therese barks all of a sudden. "Was it you?" she barks, staring at the new assistant and jerking her head in the direction of the glass cabinet. "Oh, Therese, no," the new assistant says, trying not to laugh. "That's just a reflection. Your walker's over there, just where you left it," she says, with a nod towards it. She struggles for a moment, but she can't hold back the laughter any longer. She turns away, claps her hand to her mouth and hurries out into the corridor, bent double and shaking with laughter. I put my hand over my mouth and laugh too, and Odd Kåre bursts out laughing as well, we all burst out laughing, oh, dear, did you ever hear anything so ridiculous, a walker in that little glass cabinet, as if that were possible, how would that walker ever have fit into that little cabinet.

"What you are sniggering about," Therese asks me. But I can't do anything but laugh, and Odd Kåre can't do anything but laugh, and I look at Odd Kåre and Odd Kåre looks at me and we both shake our heads and laugh, and it feels so good to sit here like this, laughing together. It's maybe not very fair to Therese, but I can't help it and anyway she doesn't seem too bothered by it, she's already picked up the paper, I see. She's sitting hunched over it, fumbling with a bag of mints.

"Oh, my," I say, still chuckling, and Odd Kåre's still chuckling too. "Oh aye, it takes all sorts," I say, picking up my coffee cup. I take a little sip of my coffee. "Yeah, you can say that again," Odd Kåre says. We look at one another and chuckle and I put down my cup. I sit for a moment or two and I'm just about to ask Odd Kåre when he starts his vacation, but I don't have the chance because Odd Kåre has turned to Johnny, he's staring at Johnny and suddenly he looks annoyed again. Johnny has taken out this thing for listening to music on, he's got wires hanging down on either side of his face, he's stuck these earphones in his ears and he's fiddling with something on his lap. The muffled blare of music comes from the earphones. Odd Kåre is glaring at Johnny, but Johnny doesn't notice, he has turned away and he's gazing out of the window. I look at the two of them. Oh, please don't let them start arguing again, please don't let them fall out again, not when we're having such a nice time.

But Odd Kåre's looking more and more annoyed. All at once he reaches out a hand, grabs hold of one of the wires, gives it a tug and yanks the earphones out of Johnny's ears. Johnny just about jumps out of his skin. "What the fuck?" he yells, and I flinch when he says this and Odd Kåre flinches as well. Everything goes very quiet in the dayroom, everybody turns to look at us, they stare at us in horror and I turn quickly to Odd Kåre. He really ought to just leave it at that now, he and Johnny ought to make friends now. But they don't.

"Hey, just you fucking behave yourself," Odd Kåre says in a low, angry hiss, nodding sharply at Johnny. And Johnny stares angrily at Odd Kåre and everybody else in the dayroom is staring at us in horror and I feel my face starting to burn again. "Yeah, but I got a shock, for Christ's sake," Johnny cries. "Once in a blue moon I manage to drag you along to see your gran and then you sit there listening to your fucking iPod," Odd Kåre hisses, and for a moment they sit there eye to eye, and everybody else in the room is staring at us in alarm, and there's dead silence. Oh, dear, I don't like this, this isn't nice, this is so embarrassing. I just have to hope that Odd Kåre and Johnny will stop this, that they'll stop fighting and make friends.

"Now, now, you two, don't go falling out," I say, smiling, and I look at them and swallow, and they stare at one another, just sit there for a second staring at one another and then they both look away. Johnny crosses his arms and curls his lip, then he turns and gazes out of the window again. And Odd Kåre runs his hand through his greasy hair, turns back to me and shakes his head. "Jesus Christ," he says, "talk about manners, eh?" And he looks at me, and I look at him and smile. After a moment or two the talk starts up again in Sylvia's corner. I lift my coffee cup and take a little sip, and Odd Kåre lifts his coffee cup and takes a little sip.

"Well, anyway, about the house," Odd Kåre says. "I just don't know how we're going to manage, I really don't," he says. "We can't take out any more loans than we already have. And Margareth and I are both working so much over-time already there's no more to be had that way, either," he says. He blows on his coffee and takes another sip. I sit for a moment looking at him. It can't be my money he's angling for here, surely. Surely that can't be why he's tell-ing me what a terrible state the house is in and how much it's going to cost to do it up? Surely he's not angling for another advance on what's coming to him once I'm gone? He wouldn't have the nerve, surely?

"I just don't know how we're going to manage," he says again. "No, it's a lot of money," I say. "I know, it's fucking terrible the way it all mounts up," he says and he shakes his head sadly. "And it's not like I can put it off, you know?" he says. "I mean if I put it off and let it get even more run-down it'll cost even more to fix it up," and he shakes his head sadly again, gazing at the table. Then he looks straight at me and there's silence for a moment, then another moment. He's hoping I'll offer to help, that's what he's waiting for, I know it is. As if it wasn't enough that he got the house and the land for nothing, as if it wasn't enough that I gave him a hundred thousand kroner that he then went and threw away on a motorbike, now he wants me to pay for fixing the place up as well. That's probably why he's here, that's probably the only reason. He hardly ever comes to see me, and then when he does come it's to beg for money. He didn't come to see me, he can't even be bothered pretending he's glad to see me, neither him nor Johnny even bothers to try, they act like I'm not even here, sitting there arguing and arguing.

"I just hope we won't have to sell the place," Odd Kåre goes on. He's not about to give up, he's doing all he can to get his hands on my money. "It'd be too bad if the house had to go to somebody outside the family," he says, trying to make me feel guilty. He assumes it's important to me that the house stays in the family and he's hoping that this will persuade me to pay for the renovations. "Well, you know how it is," he says. "I mean, it's my childhood home," he says, not giving up, still trying to make me feel guilty, he'll do anything to get his hands on my money. Oh, it's all been planned and calculated from beginning to end. All that talk of a vacation in the sun, I suppose that was part of the plan too, his way of trying to seem less greedy and grasping than he actually is. "You spend your money, Ma," he said. "You haven't exactly spoiled yourself," he said, and I felt so happy when he said that, I thought he wanted to show me that he loved me, but he only said it so he'd seem less greedy when he started pestering me for money.

I look at him, smile at him, He's only after my money, he doesn't care about me at all, he embarrasses me in front of everybody in the dayroom, he acts like I'm not even here, he argues with Johnny, he's so brash and rude and I don't like him. I really want to like him, but I don't, I can't make myself like him, that's why I got so annoyed at the new assistant and at Sylvia and her family a little while ago. I'm not stupid, I know that much. I couldn't bring myself to get angry at Odd Kåre so I tried to take it out on them instead. I couldn't bring myself to admit that I don't like my own son, so I tried to fool myself into believing that everybody else in here is as bad as him. But that's not true of course. They're not as bad as Odd Kåre. Sylvia's son is so nice to his mother, he loves his mother and he cares about her. And Sylvia is so nice to her son, she loves him and she cares about him. But I don't care about Odd Kåre, maybe I've never cared about him, maybe it's true what people said about me, maybe I've never loved Odd Kåre, well, I mean what sort of a mother would do what I did, what sort of a mother would shut her eyes to such things? I pretended not to know, I wasn't strong enough to do what I should have done and I let Johan carry on with his dirty business. I was always careful not to walk in unexpectedly when he was alone with Odd Kåre. I was always careful to give him fair warning, give him time to finish whatever he was doing. I'd be deliberately clumsy and drop things on the floor before opening the door of the room they were in. I'd pretend to have a bit of a cold and cough loudly so Johan would know where I was, and if I'd been out somewhere I always shouted hello from the hall when I came home. If I hadn't seen it with my own eyes it hadn't happened. I suppose that was my thinking. And what sort of a mother would think like that, what sort of a mother would fail their own child like that?

I look at Odd Kåre, and there's a lump in my throat. Dear Odd Kåre, all the things he's had to suffer, all he's had to put up with. I tried to make up for that by being nice to him, I was so nice and kind and loving toward him, almost too nice and kind, I spoiled him so I did. As if that could make up for what Johan did, nothing can make up for something like that, can it? What we did to Odd Kåre, that was the biggest failure of all. And any minute now Sylvia's going to tell her son and her daughter-in-law all about it, I know she is. What sort of a mother would fail her own son like that, that's what she'll say. "It's no wonder we don't see much of that Odd Kåre here," she'll say, "and it's certainly no wonder he's turned out the way he has," she'll say. "You can hardly expect him to care about his mother when his mother never cared about him," she'll say, I know she will, she's going to revel in our misfortune, use our misfortune to make herself seem like such a good mother, and I'm crying inside, I need to get out of here, I don't want to be here any longer, and yet I go on sitting here.

"You know the money you were going to leave me in your will? You wouldn't consider giving me an advance on that, would you?" Odd Kåre asks suddenly. He asks me straight out and he looks straight at me, and I look at him for a moment and suddenly his cheeks turn pink and he twists his mouth into a grin, he knows what he's doing and he's trying to cover up his embarrasment by grinning, he's embarrassed but he's not giving up, he keeps going. He thinks he can ask anything of me, nothing can make up for what I did to him and he thinks he can ask for whatever he wants. "It would be a helluva help to us," he says. "I mean, it's now we need it," he says. "Not in ten or fifteen years' time." And he looks straight at me, and I look at him and smile this smile of mine. I'm crying and crying inside, but I just sit here smiling, what else can I do?

"Oh," I say. "Well, I'm sure something can be arranged," I say. I don't want to say it, I don't like being pushed like this. If I'm going to give something to someone, I want to give it out of love and I want the person I give it to to know that I'm giving it out of love. But this isn't love, this is nothing but a trade-off, and I don't want to say yes, but I can't stop myself, I've never been able to resist. I've always given Odd Kåre whatever he asked for, whatever he pointed at he got, and all the terrible things he did I forgave him. As if that could make up for what I did to him. Nothing can make up for something like that. I look at him, and I'm crying inside, crying and crying. "Great," Odd Kåre says. "Thanks a lot," he says. "We really appreciate it," he says, looking at me and nodding, and I smile at him, but inside I'm crying and I want to get out of here, I want to get away from all of this, but instead I just sit here, I don't go anywhere.

Otterøya, July 11th, 2006

The game's up, David. I know you haven't lost your memory. I
know you remember most of what we have spent time and
energy on recounting and writing down and then sending to
the email address you gave in your advertisement. You see I was
speaking to my grandson on the phone yesterday evening and
when I told him what I was doing at the moment he said he
was afraid we'd been conned. My grandson is part of an artists'
group in Trondheim and apparently there has been some discussion within the group as to whether your latest book project
is morally defensible or not. I didn't even know that you were
a published author, but it turns out that you are and according
to what my grandson has heard your alleged memory loss is
part of a new, autobiographical book project you're working
on. Apparently writing autobiographies is all the rage at the
moment and word has it that you're trying to put a new twist
on the traditional personal history by looking at your own life
through the eyes of others. He wasn't really sure about this, he
said, but you definitely hadn't lost your memory, because he had
run into you on the street the day before and there had been
nothing then to indicate any such thing. You had recognized
him right away and stopped for a chat as you usually did when
the two of you met.

Obviously I should have realized that there was something suspicious about all this. Obviously I've been stupid and naive. And now that I know what's been going on I can see how incredible and how unlikely it would have been for someone to lose their memory and then put an ad in the newspaper to find out who they are. There can only be one explanation for why I didn't immediately grasp the incredibility and unlikelihood of this situation, and that is that I find it even more incredible and unlikely that anyone could be capable of doing such a thing to their fellow human beings. It's one thing to be so ineffably self-centered as to take it for granted that I and other people have nothing better to do than to spend their evenings writing about you. Individualism, egotism and self-promotion—these are, after all, the very hallmarks of your generation, so to some extent I can understand it. You are as much a product of your time as most people are, I suppose. But that you can exploit other people's concern for a fellow human being as you have done, exploit their compassion and encourage them to expose themselves and others, exploit the good in them to provide you with character sketches and descriptions of all and sundry, and put it all into a book; that you could do something like that speaks of a cynicism beyond my comprehension. How do you think Paula will feel when she learns that you are planning to make public all the private, sensitive and intimate details she has been willing to share with you? Do you realize how hard and how painful it was for her simply to lend her diaries to me? True, she stapled together pages that she absolutely did not want anyone else to read, but still, she did not do it gladly, I can assure you. And then to have to see it made public. Published, in a book, and not to serve the purpose she has always believed it was meant to serve. There she was, thinking that she was helping a man in need, only to find that she has been used, sponged on, spat upon. Oh yes, you have spat upon her kindness and goodwill, that's what you've done. It's disgraceful. The idea, its execution, this whole project of yours is disgraceful and my greatest regret is that I have sent you each part of her story as I wrote it down. If only I had decided to wait until we were completely finished then you wouldn't have heard a word from us. Then Paula could have rested easier. Granted, she would have had to live with the fact that she had confided in me, but at least she wouldn't have had to suffer what you are clearly dead set on subjecting her to. Tell me, have you completely forgotten what it was like to grow up in a community as small as that on Otterøya? Have you any idea what all this will cost Paula and probably a lot of the other people who have sent you information that was meant for you and you alone? Have you any idea how disastrous it can be for a person to have everyone made privy to their innermost and most private thoughts? To have everyone learn what they really think and feel about people close to them or whom they see every day? Friendships can be ruined by such things, relationships shattered and marriages broken, relatives become estranged, whole lives destroyed, don't you realize that? Don't you realize what a responsibility you are taking upon yourself if you go ahead with this? Are you really willing to do this simply in order to publish a book about yourself?

I don't know if what you are doing is illegal. Probably not. These days anything goes, it seems. But it is most definitely immoral and all I can do now is to appeal to the little in the way of conscience that you may have and beg you not to complete this utterly narcissistic project of yours and not to use the information we have sent you. If, on the other hand, you decide to continue, I will of course contact the press and television stations and inform them of the suffering you are inflicting on other people. You may well be too cold and cynical to care about that, but by contacting the media I can at least prevent more people from making the same mistake as us.

I hope to hear from you as soon as you have read this. Now I have to drive up to the care home to inform Paula and all the others of my discovery. This is not something I am looking forward to.

Otterøy care home, July 4th, 2006. Into battle

I look at Odd Kåre. I want to get out of here, I can't stay here any longer, but I just sit here. "What's wrong, Ma?" Odd Kåre asks. "Nothing," I say, smiling at him. "It's just that you've gone a bit funny," Odd Kåre says. "Oh, I've always been a bit funny," I say and I try to give a little laugh, and I hear how sad my laugh sounds, it's a bitter, painful laugh, a laugh that falls aching from my lips, but Odd Kåre doesn't catch the note of pain, he's not made that way, Odd Kåre, he's not sensitive enough to catch that sort of thing. "Oh, Christ, you're right there," he says, laughing back at me, a loud, happy laugh, he's happy because he's managed to scrounge my money off me, he's delighted that he's managed to talk me into giving him an advance on the money he's got coming to him.

I look at him, and I don't like him, I do so want to like him, but I can't. What sort of a mother am I when I can't bring myself to like my son? I suppose it was true what people said about me back then, I don't suppose I've ever really loved Odd Kåre, or at least not the way other mothers love their children, well, what sort of a mother would do what I did? I shut my eyes and let Johan carry on with his dirty business, for years he was left to carry on with his dirty business, for years I failed Odd Kåre. I thought I could make up for it by being nice and kind. All the terrible things Odd Kåre got up to I let him get away with and everything he pointed to I let him have, as if it did any good, all it did was make matters worse, that's why he's turned out the way he has, that's what turned him into the sort of person who can come here and scrounge money off me. He doesn't care about me at all, he's only interested in my money, and I've only got myself to thank for that. I've got the son I deserve, it's my own fault that I've got a son I can't like, I do so want to like him, but I can't, he's so hard to like, he's greedy and brash and rude and I'm crying inside, crying and crying, and I want to get out of here, I want to get away, but I don't go anywhere, I just sit here, and Odd Kåre and Johnny are looking at me and it's very quiet, and now I have to say something, I don't know what to say, but I have to say something, and I look at Johnny and give him a faint smile.

"So, how's school, Johnny?" I ask. It just slips out. I'm asking exactly the same thing as I asked him only minutes ago, asking the very question that started that awful argument. They sat there arguing for a good few minutes all because Johnny has dropped out of school, and yet here I am asking him how he's getting on at school.

Johnny gazes at me in surprise and Odd Kåre gazes at me in surprise, they exchange a quick glance and then they turn to me again and I look at them and smile. I'm just about to apologize, I'm just about to sigh and say, "Oh no, of course, I just asked you that," but I don't. I don't know why not, but I just sit there looking at them, still smiling, and they just sit and look at me, and Odd Kåre's brow furrows slightly.

"Ma, we just told you—Johnny's dropped out of school," he says, sounding a bit taken aback and frowning at me, and I look at him and swallow, still smiling. "Oh, yes," is all I say, then I pause for a moment. "That's right, so you did," I say with a sad little laugh, a laugh that's somehow meant to make light of the whole thing, laugh as if I'm trying to hide how forgetful I am. I don't know why I do this, I just do. "It's so nice that you could come too, Johnny," I say. "I haven't seen you in ages," I say. "And you look so like your dad now. With a beard, and such lovely plump cheeks," I say. "So nice and chubby," I say, and I give a little start as the words leave my mouth, and Odd Kåre and Johnny seem to to start as well, because yet again I'm saying exactly what I said only minutes ago, yet again I'm repeating something that started an argument between them. They stare at me, then they turn and look at one another, and now they're wondering whether I've gone dotty. I can tell by their faces that they think I have. After a moment they turn to me again and I look at Johnny, still smiling, and this time he doesn't look angry with me for saying that he's fairly filled out. He just sits there looking a little confused, and this time Odd Kåre doesn't try to make fun of Johnny for having filled out, no, he just sits there frowning at me.

There's silence for a moment or two. But why am I doing this? Why am I turning into a dotty old woman before their eyes? Is it because I want attention? Is it because I want them to look at me and feel sorry for me? Or could it be because I'd like to start again? Is that why I'm asking the same questions that I asked before they started arguing and falling out? Am I trying to go back to a point before they started arguing, so we can start again and make this the sort of visit I would like it to be? I don't know, I really don't, but I look at Johnny and I keep going. "You're looking fitter and healthier than you used to," I tell Johnny. "You used to be so thin," I say, saying exactly what I had been meaning to say before they started arguing. It's like I've jumped back a few minutes and started again. I've rubbed out their arguing and fighting and they're just sitting there staring at me in confusion. They think I'm going dotty and I just let them think that and I look at them and smile.

Then out of the blue I say: "Can you forgive me, Odd Kåre?" It just slips out and I give a start as it slips out, because suddenly I've started talking about this thing that we never talk about, and there's silence for a moment and I look at Odd Kåre and my heart starts to beat a little harder and my pulse starts to race a little faster. "Huh?" Odd Kåre says. "Can you forgive me?" I say again, and I look at him, still smiling, and Odd Kåre looks at me, but he's not smiling, because now he realizes what I'm talking about, I can tell by his face that he does, his face goes dead, it turns white, it stiffens, and Johnny looks at Odd Kåre and frowns.

"What's the matter?" Johnny says, but Odd Kåre doesn't look at Johnny, he doesn't take his eyes off me, because now I've opened a door that neither of us has ever dared open before, I've plucked up my courage and said what I should have said long ago. Maybe that's why I suddenly started acting dotty, maybe it was because I needed someone to say what I'd never been able to say myself. Maybe that's why I turned myself into a dotty old woman, maybe I needed that dotty old woman to ask forgiveness for me. I don't know, I really don't, but here I am, asking Odd Kåre for forgiveness.

For a moment everything is very quiet, then the little

girls start playing the piano again. They've sat down at the piano and now they're playing "Twinkle, Twinkle, Little Star" again. And I look at Odd Kåre and smile. Now Odd Kåre has to walk through the open door with me, he has to step into that room that we've never entered before. He has to do this, for his own sake and for mine he has to. This has been eating away at me all these years and I would so like to find peace of mind before I die, that's all I want. I look at Odd Kåre and smile and the girls play "Twinkle, Twinkle, Little Star" and now Odd Kåre has to walk with me through the open door, but he won't, he won't come with me.

"What are you talking about?" Odd Kåre asks with what's meant to be an astonished laugh, but what comes out isn't an astonished laugh, it's an angry laugh, there's so much anger in that laugh. "Huh?" he says, looking at me, and there's anger in his eyes too. He's trying not to let it show, but it's no use. "Please, Odd Kåre," I say, still with that smile on my face, and I feel my smile sagging, feel the corners of my mouth drooping, and the girls play "Twinkle, Twinkle, Little Star" and I look at Odd Kåre. And now he has to go along with me on this, he has to come with me, but he doesn't, he won't.

"Aw, stop your nonsense," Odd Kåre snaps, narrowing his eyes and screwing up his face, then he opens his eyes again. He looks straight at me and there's blind fury in his eyes. He stares at me for a moment then he looks at the table, just for a split second, then he looks up again and turns, scans the dayroom, like he's searching for something or someone in the dayroom. "Thought I might get a refill of coffee," he says and then he pauses, trying to pull himself together, I suppose that's what he's doing.

After a moment he turns to me again. He seems to have pulled himself together a bit, he doesn't look angry any more. "Can we just help ourselves, do you think?" he asks. "Oh, I don't see why not," I say, and I look at him and smile, but the corners of my mouth are drooping more and more and my smile is getting fainter and fainter, and I'm crying and crying inside, and the moments go by, but I really don't want to be here any longer, I want to get out of here, I want to get away. "Oh, never mind, we'll just wait till the assistant comes back," Odd Kåre says. "She can't be too far away." "No, she can't be," I say. "But I need to go to the toilet," I say. "So I can pop my head into the staffroom on the way and say to her." I look at Odd Kåre and Johnny and smile, and my smile is faint and sad and the girls are playing "Twinkle, Twinkle, Little Star" and another moment goes by and then I place my hands on the arms of the chair and try to get up.

"Hang on. Let me help you," Odd Kåre says, jumping up. He slips one hand under my armpit and the other under my forearm and eases me up out of the chair. "Thank you, that's kind of you," I say, looking at him and smiling and Odd Kåre sits down again and I start to walk away. I shuffle stiffly across the room, look at Sylvia and her family and smile, look at Therese and smile. "Hey, isn't that the boy that used to live across the bay from you?" Therese asks, scowling at me and pointing at a picture in the paper, but I don't feel like stopping now, I don't feel like talking to Therese about some boy right now. I pretend not to realize it's me she's talking to and just walk on past her. I walk out of the dayroom and along the corridor, I walk past the staffroom and the toilet, I'm just walking away. It's hard to believe it, but I am. I walk down to the entrance hall and across to the door, and I see that the door is wide open, I see that the sun is shining. But who's that coming in? Well I never, it's Harald Hansen with his accordion slung over his shoulders, well, well, what do you know, fancy him showing up right now. But I don't feel like talking to anybody right now, I'd like a little time to myself right now. Oh, well, it's a good thing he's only arriving now and not ten minutes ago really, it's a good thing he didn't arrive while Odd Kåre and Johnny were going at it hammer and tongs, oh yes, because if he had it would have been even more unpleasant than it was, I'm sure. Harald's not exactly the sort to hold his tongue when he gets his dander up, he'd have read the riot act, I'll bet. He can get awful steamed up on behalf of us old folks.

He looks at me and smiles, and I look at him and smile back. "Well, well," I say, "if it isn't the pensioners' champion." And Harald looks at me and laughs. "Yes, I've got to inspect the troops before we go into battle, you know," he says. "And a right sorry sight that'll be, Harald," I say. "Oh no, don't say that," he says. "Well, they're all pretty worn and battered, already, your troops, so I sincerely hope you've got some more in reserve," I say and I let out a little laugh. And Harald laughs too, he puts out a hand and pats me gently on the shoulder. "Don't you worry, I always have," he laughs. "Right then, talk to you later, Paula," he says. "Right you are," I say.

And Harald walks on. I wait until he has disappeared down the corridor, then I walk on as well. I walk out into the sunshine. I'm in just my slippers, but I walk across the parking lot and out onto the road and I walk down the road. The gray, sun-baked asphalt burns the soles of my feet, what on earth am I doing? Am I really doing this, just walking away? Well, Odd Kåre and Johnny are really going to think I've gone dotty now. "She did a bunk while we were visiting her," they'll say. "Said she was going to the toilet and off she went," they'll say. "Walked out in just her slippers," they'll say. I feel my spirits lift a little at this thought, the sadness seems to gradually drain out of me, because it feels so right somehow, me turning into a dotty old woman while they're here. It feels both right and good, I don't quite know why, but it does. And I walk on, I walk down the hill. There's a warm breeze sweeping in from the right, a warm breeze that carries with it the lovely, fresh scent of sea and shore, and I walk on, I walk up the hill to the church, I walk and walk. People must be wondering where I've got to by now, they may even be looking for me, they may be searching the care home for me. It's too bad really that they have to go looking for me, they've enough to do as it is, the staff there, without having to spend time and energy looking for me as well. But I walk on, I don't know where I'm going, I'm not going anywhere in particular, I'm just walking, and up the hill on the right is the church, and I walk into the churchyard. It's like pushing a boat out from shore, I think to myself, me just walking aimlessly like this, me turning myself into a dotty old woman, it's like pushing a boat out from the shore and letting yourself drift with the current. And it feels right to do this. I don't know why, but it feels right and good.

Otterøya, July 13th, 2006

I never thought I would be writing to you again, but for reasons which I will explain in due course Paula succeeded in persuading me to finish what we have started. She was both sad and hurt when I told her that your memory loss was a complete hoax, but when I returned to her room after going off to tell the other residents what you had done, something had dawned on her, as she put it, and she now wanted us to finish writing this memoir anyway. In fact, not only did she say she wanted us to finish it, she insisted that we do so. If I refused she would ask someone else to help her, she said, and if she couldn't find someone else then she would do it herself, bad eyesight or no bad eyesight. It didn't matter that you had deceived us and that you hadn't lost your memory after all, because in all likelihood this had nothing to do with you writing a book about yourself, it had nothing to do with art and literature, she was sure, or not just that anyway.

When I asked her to be more specific she promptly proceeded to tell me about the time when Berit and Arvid were together and you and she moved into his house in Namsos—in the summer of 1982 this was. Arvid was a vicar in Namsos at the time and folks simply couldn't believe that someone as ungodly as Berit could have married and moved in with him of all people.

That she and Arvid were about as different as chalk and cheese didn't make it any easier to understand. They lived and walked at different speeds, as Paula says. Berit was impetuous, dynamic and purposeful. She talked fast, she was quick and restless in her movements and as I've said she had this capricious temperament: her mood could swing from bright to black in the blink of an eye.

Arvid on the other hand was so stolid, so sedate in nature that Paula says it made her skin crawl just to be near him. It took him forever to do anything, he was fussy and pernickety and when telling a story he could never get to the point, but would simply ramble on with that dopey smile on his face. And sometimes when he walked, or even if he just shifted slightly, it looked as though he was moving in slow-motion. "That man gives me the creeps," as Paula wrote in her diary on the twelfth of May 1982.

And yet, despite their differences, they were together. Or possibly precisely because of them, as many of the women in Paula's and Berit's sewing circle remarked. Dagny, for example, believed that Berit had picked Arvid because she had such a low boredom threshold and because everything about him, his manner and the life he led, was so very different from Berit's own personality and lifestyle that to her it seemed new and exciting. Spontaneous and impulsive as she was, she therefore did exactly as his grandfather had once done: she cut all ties with her family and started a new life in a new place.

But most people believed that Berit had hooked up with Arvid because she saw marrying a vicar as a step up in the world. Being a man of the cloth didn't have quite the prestige that it had once had, it's true, but the local vicar still enjoyed a great deal of respect, much more than today and possibly even more among the farmers and fishermen on the island of Otterøya than in Namsos, where the vicar had to compete for respect and prestige with businessmen, politicians, doctors and all sorts of other individuals, including celebrities, as Paula says. Plus Arvid had "money in the bank" and that made him a much more interesting prospect than he would otherwise have been. "He spoils me rotten, and I love it," your mother used to say to Paula.

Arvid, for his part, was intent on saving Berit from "that hole" as he once called the house on Otterøya. It was this—being allowed to play the prince who saves the princess from the dungeon—that caused him to throw himself into their relationship as wholeheartedly as he did, so Paula says, not without a trace of contempt. He rolled his eyes and shook his head at the tires, spare parts and hulks of cars scattered around the yard at Erik's place. He was sure that the walls of the house were permeated with the smell of boiled fish and he asked—in all innocence, seemingly, and with the best will in the world—if they ever ate anything but fish. The bathroom was riddled with damp and needed to be totally stripped and redone before they all succumbed to the effects of mold and mildew, he declared. The aspens up on the hillside would have to be felled before they were blown down in a storm and flattened the house while they were sleeping. The living room was so drafty that he caught cold if he spent any length of time in it. And he thought it was quite ridiculous that Berit had to cut the grass with an old-fashioned, mechanical lawnmower whenever Erik was away. He couldn't bear to see her sweating and straining like that, he said, and he insisted on taking over the job of cutting the grass. But according to Paula he only ever did it the one time, because he got such an ache in the small of his back from the way he had to stoop to push the lawnmower that Berit had to take over again.

He made everything out to be worse than it actually was and

of course he believed it was all Erik's fault. If I understand Paula rightly, Erik was the troll in the fairytale that Arvid liked to think he was living in. Not only was he a lazy so-and-so who never reinsulated the house or renovated the bathroom or cleared up the yard, and not only was he too mean to buy a motor mower or a snow-blower or any other labor-saving equipment, the fact that he liked a drink and maybe a bit of a party at the weekend made him an alcoholic and unfit to look after his family. The fact that he was honest and straightforward and spoke his mind branded him as rude, crude and vulgar; and that he read your comic books, or the western ones at any rate, made him stupid and childish. Even when Erik made an effort to make Arvid feel welcome he couldn't win. "I hope you don't mind pork chops," Erik said one time when Arvid came to dinner, thereby giving Arvid his cue to say that the pork chops were delicious. But he didn't. "Oh, pork chops are all right," was all he said, even though he must have known that pork chops were only ever a weekend treat in your house.

Obviously he behaved like this because he wanted to make his rescue of you seem as great a deed as possible. The blacker he painted Erik and your living conditions the more of a hero he would seem. And if I understand Paula correctly much the same thinking lay behind his virtual glorification of Berit's mother. Not that Arvid had known her, of course—she had died back in the 60s when she got caught up in the tire chains of a passing bus and dragged under it on her way home from the blueberry woods—but according to Paula he milked Berit's stories about her for all they were worth. He pumped and grilled her for information and everything Berit told him about her mother made her seem wonderful in his eyes: according to him she was practically a saint, another Mother Teresa, just because she'd been in the habit of giving eggs and milk to a neighboring family that had trouble making ends meet, "She must have been an extraordinarily good person," he said. And when Berit informed him that most of the neighbors had done what they could to help this family, providing them with food and clothing from time to time, he didn't even want to hear about it. All he said was, "I'm sure she was wonderful," and nothing would change his mind, probably because he wanted to provide Berit with a mother whom he considered worth resembling and emulating. This—if I understand Paula rightly—was not only a cunning way of controlling and manipulating Berit, but also a ploy designed to make his rescue of her seem even more impressive. The more beautiful the princess, the more splendid the deed, as it were.

As you may have noticed and may also have found surprising, Paula is remarkably interested in the relationship between Berit and Arvid. This fascination is also evident from one of her diary entries from that time:

Otterøya, May 29th, 1982
Berit and Arvid are getting married. All the blood seemed to drain from my head when she told me. I couldn't even pretend to be happy for her although she tried to make me say I was. She sat there with her head covered in electric rollers, smiling and trying to look radiantly happy, but I didn't feel like humoring her. I turned away and cried. I'm older and more experienced than her and I just know this will end in disaster, this is just another way of punishing herself, a way of making amends and winning the forgiveness and solace that she has so desperately been looking for. It's awful, painful even, to watch. She's already started dressing the way the women at the Salem Church do. She insists that David prays and sings before meals and yesterday she couldn't come and

meet me because she was going to church. She tries to act as though none of this is any big deal. As if it's pure coincidence that she has suddenly started wearing the old gold cross her grandmother left her, and as if it was pure coincidence that she has all but stopped wearing make-up. It's so obviously not a coincidence, and that in itself says a lot. The way she tries to convince me that it means nothing, that it is just co-incidence, that's simply her way of trying to ease the sadness she knows I'm feeling right now; her way of telling me that just because she's starting a new life that doesn't mean to say that we're going to lose one another. But we will lose each other. Not only because she'll be getting married soon and leaving here for good, but also because she's already starting to cancel herself out, she's already starting to disappear. This is just another way of taking one's own life. Soon the Berit I know will no longer exist, soon she'll be a fanatical Christian, I know she will, she has the temperament, the self-sacrificing nature and the strength necessary to reinvent herself; and, not least, she has an insatiable need for the solace and for-giveness that religion can offer. Because that is what drives her. Contrary to what many people think, she's not marrying Arvid out of love for him, and she's not becoming a Christian to please him. It's the other way around: it's religion she's looking for, it's God she's looking for. Arvid is merely a guide in all of this, a guide to lead her into the Christian church.

So you see, Paula has a quite different explanation for why Berit married Arvid. According to what she writes in her diary Berit did it because she wanted to make amends and because she sought forgiveness and solace in religion. But it is only when she starts to write about why Berit sought forgiveness and solace that I begin to understand why Paula was so intrigued by this marriage and why she is so terribly keen for us to finish this letter. Because it appears that all of this has to do with you and your advertisement in the newspaper, David. You see, Paula maintains that Berit was driven to join the Church by exactly the same urge that drove you to place a notice in the newspaper and pretend that you had lost your memory. Or rather, she maintains that both these acts can be traced back to one particular incident.

Let me explain:

According to Paula, your advertisement is not part of an artistic project, or not primarily at any rate. First and foremost it is an attempt to find your real father, she says. You placed that advertisement in the paper hoping that your father would recognize you from your picture and get in touch with you. It seems pretty obvious and self-evident now, as I write this, but even though I knew that Berit had always refused to reveal who your father was, I have to admit that this thought had never even crossed my mind before Paula mentioned it. Let me just say, though, that as soon as she said it I began to take a more clement view of you and your actions. All of a sudden you were no longer a cold-hearted cynic, you were a man who longed to find your own father, your own roots, your own history. I can understand how you would be willing to go to extremes to achieve your goal, which is why I agreed to finish this letter.

But enough of that.

From a very early age you had, of course, wondered who your father was. You had asked Berit about him every now and again, but she had always palmed you off with some story or other, for the first years of your life at least. Your father was an Apache chief, she would tell you on one occasion; on another he might be a pirate and on yet another an astronaut, living on the moon. If you didn't see through these lies yourself then naturally you realized that that's what they were once you started talking to other children. But that was the whole point, of course, because Berit didn't want you to grow up with the wrong idea of your father, she just wanted a little break from all your questions. As you got older though you were no longer content with such absurd answers. Your questioning of her became much more earnest and insistent. Sometimes you would act like a little adult, appealing to her common sense and telling her that you felt you had a right to know. Other times you would cry and beg. Or you would take a more cunning approach and bring up the subject when other people were present—presumably to show Berit that you would give her no peace until she told you. This last plan of attack could give rise to some painful scenes, however, so Paula says. Although I don't remember this incident myself, she says that during one Christmas assembly at the school, in 1979 or 1980, one of the teachers had read from and spoken about St. Luke's Gospel. And when he got to the part about the virgin birth you turned to Berit and asked if that was how you had been born. Everyone there had burst out laughing, of course, but not Berit. She had flown into a rage and to the shock of teachers, parents and the other children she had given your face a resounding slap.

It was clear to everyone, including Berit that you desperately needed to know. But still your mother refused to tell you. Not even when it was pointed out to her that your anxiety disorder might be linked to you not knowing who your father was, did she show any sign of changing her mind. So why not? What was so terrible about your father that his identity could on no account be revealed to you?

When I asked Paula about this she really surprised me: it's all her fault, she says. The day after you were born, she made a fatal mistake, a mistake which has certainly been made before by midwives and other hospital staff, although so seldom that most people associate it solely with American soap operas. What happened, quite simply, was that Paula got you and another baby mixed up. So you were put into Berit's arms and your real mother was given Berit's son. Naturally one has to ask how this could have been at all possible—that was certainly the first thing I asked. Surely the hospital had all sorts of safety procedures in place to prevent this sort of thing from ever happening? Oh yes, of course they had, Paula says, but due to a combination of chance and bad luck it did nonetheless happen. For one thing both births had been fairly unusual. Berit's son was delivered by emergency cesarean so she had been anesthetized and was therefore unconscious during the birth, and when you were born your mother was hit by a sudden fit of postnatal depression so bad that she would not even look at you to begin with. This meant that the next day neither woman was able to identify her own child—well, they had never laid eyes on them before. And for another, six babies had been born that night, an unusually large number for such a small hospital, and amid all the fuss and commotion Paula had forgotten to provide you and Berit's baby with the obligatory wristbands giving the infant's sex, blood type and mother's name. And as if that weren't enough, after helping to deliver so many babies Paula was exhausted. When she wheeled you and the other baby along to the postnatal ward the next morning she was dazed with tiredness and somewhat distracted—not only because of the two difficult births, but also because she was going through a tough time in her personal life and her mind was often elsewhere. And so, in an unfortunate momentary lapse of concentration, she managed to switch you and Berit's baby.

But now comes the part that I simply cannot understand:

As part of the aforementioned safety procedures, attached

to your cribs were labels giving exactly the same information as should have been given on your wristbands. No sooner had Paula handed over the two babies than she noticed that she had mixed up you and the other baby boy. So she realized that she had made a mistake. She saw it. With her own eyes. And she was just about to tell the mothers this, she says, when it occurred her that she couldn't remember putting wristbands on the two of you, and when she checked and discovered that she had indeed made this fatal error she held her tongue. "I was already putting out my hands to take David back, but then Berit looked at me and smiled and I let her think that I was just stretching a bit because I was tired," Paula says.

For a long while afterwards Paula tried to convince herself that she had done this because she was afraid she'd lose her job. You see the personal problems I mentioned had led her to make a number of mistakes before mixing you up with that other infant. In fact some of her colleagues had even hinted that her mind was never really on the job and that this inattentiveness had been partly to blame for complications during one birth in which a baby suffered brain damage due to lack of oxygen. This wasn't true, of course, Paula says. Nevertheless, a close eye was being kept on her and she wasn't trusted as she ought to have been, so from that point of view she had every reason to fear for her job. But this wasn't why she didn't tell your mothers that they had been given the wrong children. Nor was it because she was too embarrassed to admit her mistake. "The fact is that I wanted to do it," she told me. "Something inside me wanted to switch those babies."

And that is what I simply don't understand. How Paula could have wanted to do it. That this nice, kind and always warm and friendly woman should have wanted to mix up two new-born infants, giving the children the wrong mothers and the mothers the wrong children, this is beyond my comprehension and, to be honest, David, I'm not altogether sure whether you should trust her, not on this point.

But she insists that it's true, she takes full responsibility for what happened. To the question as to why she would do such a thing, all she says is that she doesn't really know. She only knows that she couldn't stop herself. As soon as she realized that no one would be any the wiser, something inside her drove her to do it. It was a terrible thing to do, she freely admits, a wicked thing. But she is also careful to point out that it was not planned, not in any way. A combination of accident and bad luck made it possible and for some reason she felt she had to fulfil this opportunity that had suddenly presented itself.

Later, although how much later she doesn't know—possibly a day, possibly a week, possibly a month—the enormity of what she had done began to dawn on her, but by then there was no way she could have owned up to it. She wanted to get in touch with Berit and your real mother, she told me, she was wracked with guilt and several times she tried to pluck up the courage to do so, but she couldn't. And the longer she left it the more difficult it became, of course. She lived very close to you and Berit, of course, so she could see how well the two of you were getting on, how attached you had become to one another. Was she to destroy all that by telling the truth? Now, after such a long time? What consequences would that have— for you, for Berit and for Paula? What good could ever come of it? She knew nothing about the other family, but you and Berit were doing just fine as you were, you loved one another and the very thought of splitting you up was a crime, Paula says. So was it only to ease her own guilty conscience that she even considered telling the truth? Or was she driven by some sense of duty, some inner conviction that blood is thicker than water and that a child ought to be with its own natural parents no matter what? Every day for a little over two years Paula wrestled all alone with these questions, but contrary to what I would have thought she did not become more and more troubled and burdened by the thought of what she had done. Not at all, she says. Instead it had become more like a habit to think about it. And not only that, but since this was something known only to her it was also something that she found herself reflecting on when, for whatever reason, she wanted to be by herself. The knowledge of what had happened was something that belonged to her and her alone, she tells me, or rather—that was how she saw it, as a kind of room in which she could take refuge when things became too much for her, a room where no one could get at her.

But in spite of all this she did eventually tell Berit the whole story. Or no, not in spite of but possibly because of this, is what I think she was trying to say. Because the more she thought about, it the less and less disastrous her action seemed, and obviously this made it easier for her to explain what had happened. Moreover, she and Berit had already become friends and begun to confide in one another. Indeed it was partly because she had the urge to own up to what she had done that she had continually sought Berit's company at the sewing circle evenings at Dagny's house. At the time she couldn't have said whether she did this deliberately, but now, looking back on it, she says, it's clear to her that she gravitated towards Berit because she was anxious to know whether it would be at all possible to tell her what had happened, whether Berit would be able to cope with this information. And, as I wrote at the start of this letter, Paula had discovered that Berit had a kind of darkness inside her, a gaping void, and because of this Paula felt sure that Berit would also be able to understand the darkness in other people, and possibly even the darkness inside her, Paula.

But still, she hadn't planned to say anything. It was a spur-of-the-moment thing, she says. They were on their way home one evening from a sewing circle meeting at Dagny's and suddenly she just blurted out the truth to Berit. Or at least, not the whole truth, because she missed out the part about having stopped herself from correcting her mistake while there was still time. That was one thing she was never able to admit to Berit, not even after they had become the bosom friends that Paula claims they eventually became.

But if habit and the passage of time had distanced Paula from the seriousness of what she had done, it was brought back to her full force when she saw how Berit reacted to her confession. Because, of course, she went into a state of shock. Her own natural color seemed to drain from her face and while Paula was overcome by the remorse and dread that she had until then more or less suppressed and sobbed and wept her way through all the details, Berit said not a word to what she was being told. Not then, nor in the days and weeks that followed. Later she told Paula that she had tried to block it out. Or, at least, not block it out, she had tried to convince herself that it wasn't true. She tried to tell herself that Paula must be mistaken. Either that or she was mad and incapable of differentiating between fantasy and reality. Or maybe she was a psychopath, intent on controling her in some way. Maybe she had made the whole thing up just so she could threaten to make it public if Berit didn't do what she wanted—it was, after all, a secret that could have appalling consequences for you and Berit should it become known.

And so, by clinging to the shred of uncertainty attached to Paula's revelation Berit managed to survive the first weeks and months. After a while she almost managed to convince herself that it was all a pack of lies, and so she did something that she would later come to regret often: she got in touch with a doctor she had become friends with while doing her nursing training in Namsos and got him to do a test—merely to confirm once and for all that you really were her son, she told herself. As an almost fully qualified nurse she took the blood samples herself, and when she went up to the hospital to deliver them to her doctor friend she told him it was a woman friend of hers who wanted to have this test carried out, she was just doing her a favor.

And you already know the result of that test, David. It was the exact opposite of what Berit had hoped for and believed.

It's hard to imagine how hard it must have been for Berit after that, how it must have eaten away at her. By which I mean the sorrow over the realization that she had never known her own son and probably never would, the feeling of loss and the yearning for him, to never know how he was—all of this must have been nigh on unbearable. And according to Paula it was. Berit spent her whole life feeling that she had failed her own son. Not a day went by when she didn't torture herself with the thought that he needed her and that she ought to be there for him. She would probably have done this anyway, but it didn't help that she remembered with horror how your real mother had treated the child she had believed to be her own, but who was in fact Berit's son. Not only had she screwed up her face and been reluctant to take the child Paula laid in her arms, and not only had she sat there with a cold and indifferent, not to say sulky, look on her face for the short time that she could be bothered to hold him, but when your real father came to see you both she had jerked her head in the direction of the little cart with the baby's crib on it and almost spat at him: "There, you see, that's what comes of you never being able to control yourself."

Berit never got over it. Even though Paula kept trying to re-assure her by saying that your real mother's behavior must have been a result of the aforementioned postnatal depression, Berit could never shake off the idea that her real son had been brought up by a ghastly, tyrannical mother.

And this of course only made the feeling of having failed her own son even worse than it would otherwise have been. History repeats itself, as Berit used to say of this. By not going to see the other family and demanding to have her son returned to her, she was doing exactly the same to him as she felt her grand-father had done to Erik and hence also to her, Paula says. She deprived him of the chance of a good life. And what is more, the constant feeling of guilt, the deep sorrow and longing and, not least, the uncertainty and the attendant fear, this welter of painful emotions—this was what found outlet in the seething rages by which, as Paula mentioned earlier, Berit was some-times overcome. Oh, yes, Paula declared, those fits of rage to which you were subjected were quite clearly connected to this. After all, it was you who had taken the place of her real son. Berit didn't want to think like this, of course, she knew it was totally unreasonable, but part of her did so anyway, and it was this part that caused her to treat you the way she sometimes did. As a little boy you were completely mystified by these violent and always equally sudden outbursts, the screaming and the tongue-lashings that could be triggered by the smallest thing you had said or done, Paula says, but she hopes that what she is telling you here, through me, will help you to understand them a little better. At any rate, her treatment of you only served to make Berit feel even more guilty and bad about herself. She felt that she had not only failed her own natural son, she had also failed you.

Knowing all this obviously makes it easier to understand

why Berit's mood swings became more and more frequent and more and more extreme, why she tried to take her own life and, not least, why she eventually sought solace and forgiveness in religion. Although it wasn't just solace and forgiveness she was looking for, Paula says, regarding this last point. It almost looked as though she had also chosen this new life as another form of penance. To start with she probably was seeking solace and forgiveness from God, but that she chose to marry Arvid, a man who was as different from her as he could possibly be and whom Paula is convinced she did not love, and that she not only accepted but also followed this man's old-fashioned and un-necessarily strict Christian way of life—this, according to Paula, smacked of self-torture. And not only self-torture. In speaking of this she actually reiterates what she wrote in her diary many, many years ago: marrying Arvid the clergyman was another way of taking her own life, she says. The countless thou-shalts and shalt-nots that were part and parcel of her marriage and her new life as a Christian caused the old Berit to disappear. The old Berit felt she didn't deserve to go on living, and being such an uncommonly strong and determined character she succeeded in erasing herself completely.

Having said all of this, there is one thing, however, that Paula cannot emphasize strongly enough, and that is how much Berit loved you. Because, while she may have missed and yearned for her real child and while she may have been almost drowning in guilt and self-loathing because she was not a part of his life, this did not mean that she loved you any less. You may think that when you read all this—when you read, for example, that Berit took her grief and frustration out on you for taking the other baby's place—but actually it was the other way around. The fact that Berit missed her real son as much as she did simply shows how much she loved you. There was only one reason why she did not try to trace the other family and tell them what had happened and this was, of course, that she was afraid they would want you back. You were her whole life, David, and she couldn't bear the thought of losing you, so instead she had to live with the pain of not having her own natural son.

And clearly it was this same fear that led her to react as she did when the question of your father's identity came up. Not only did this remind her of all the guilt and anguish, but if she were to answer this question honestly and truthfully, you and everyone else would know that she was not your real mother— and then she might lose you.

But there is one thing that I find odd, not to say almost incomprehensible, and that is that Berit and Paula should have been such close friends as Paula claims. I mean, Paula had after all made a mistake which had caused you and Berit great and irreparable hurt, and even though Berit never did discover that switching you and the other baby had to some extent been a deliberate act, still, somehow it would have seemed more natural for her to hate Paula than to accept her friendship.

When I ask Paula about this she gets annoyed and quite indignant. It's true that Berit had given her a wide berth for some time after she learned what had happened, Paula says. But eventually the need to talk to someone who knew had been too strong for her and this, together with the fact that she thought Paula had got the babies mixed up by mistake and was ridden with guilt over what she had done, helped her to overcome her anger and become her friend. Indeed as time went on that incident in the postnatal ward became more of a bond between them than a bone of contention, or so Paula maintains. They knew something that no one else knew and that no one else could ever know, and this formed the basis for a mutual sense of loyalty that was stronger than anyone could imagine, she says. They acted as each other's confessor, you might say. Paula confided things to Berit that she has never confided to anyone else before or since, and Berit was equally frank and open with Paula.

It sounds logical enough as far as it goes, and yet I can't help thinking that Paula is exaggerating and glamorizing their friendship a little. And possibly more than a little. For one thing it seems unlikely to me that anyone could find it in themselves to make a close friend and confidante of a person who had, after all, done them such great and irreparable harm, and for another I'm beginning to wonder why Paula gets so hot under the collar just because I ask how she and Berit could have been as close as she says. To be quite honest, the way she idealizes their friendship makes me think that Paula has something to hide and that she's afraid that I and then you will discover what it is.

I'm not sure, but sometimes it occurs to me that she describes their relationship as she would like it to have been, not only when talking to me about it, but also in her diaries. She hasn't allowed me to read everything in them, you see, far from it, but in those entries I have read, she keeps mentioning how close they were, how much they meant to one another and what wonderful times they had together. She lays it on so thick that I find it hard to swallow. I'm not sure why she does this; maybe it's easier to live with the knowledge that she switched you and that other baby if she idealizes her relationship with your mother. This is pure speculation, of course, but perhaps her diary entries and this letter are both ways of forgiving herself. I mean, if Berit of all people could forgive her—yes and not only forgive her but go so far as to become what Paula calls her soulmate—then surely anyone could forgive her, even Paula herself, and maybe even you, David. Maybe this letter is her way of asking you for forgiveness too.

Anyway, when I ask Paula why she has chosen to break the promise she once made to Berit and tell you all this now, she doesn't say a word about forgiveness. I feel pretty certain that this mattered a lot to her, but she says it was the news that you were only pretending to have lost your memory that made her change her mind. It made her realize how terribly important it was for you to learn your true origins, she says. And besides, she was starting to worry about what might happen if you were not told that it wasn't only your father you should be looking for but your mother as well. You might disregard letters that you shouldn't disregard and you might not disregard letters that you should disregard, and she couldn't live with that.

And finally, the question that must occupy you more than any other: who were your mother and father? Paula doesn't remember their surname, she says. All she knows is that they were living in Namsos when you were born and that your mother suffered from postnatal depression for a while afterwards. But it should be quite possible for you to trace the family yourself. As far as I can gather your parents' names will be in the files at Namsos Hospital and, if for any reason they have gone missing from the files, well, there are only five possible alternatives and with your date of birth as reference all of these families ought to be easy to track down and to contact. In any case, Paula and I wish you good luck.

CARL FRODE TILLER is the author of five novels—the last three forming the *Encircling* trilogy—and four plays; all of them are written in the distinctive language of Nynorsk ("new Norwegian"). One of the most acclaimed Scandinavian authors of his generation, Tiller has received multiple prizes, including the EU Prize for Literature and the Nordic Critics Prize, and *The Encircling Trilogy* has been twice nominated for the Nordic Council's prize.

Tiller was born in 1970 in Namsos, Norway. He now lives in Trondheim with his wife and three daughters. He was, until recently, a member of the rock band Kong Ler.

BARBARA J. HAVELAND is a leading translator of Norwegian and Danish. Her recent published works include *The Cold Song* by Linn Ullmann and new translations of Ibsen's *The Master Builder* and *Little Eyolf*. She lives in Copenhagen.

The text of *Encircling 2* is set in Trump Mediaeval and SansSemiLight to a design by Henry Iles. Composition by Sort Of Books. Manufactured by Friesens on acid-free, 100 percent postconsumer wastepaper.